OAK RIDGE PUBLIC LIBRARY
Civic Center
Oak Ridge, TN 37830

WITHDRAWN

EXPOSURE

Also by Susan Andersen in Large Print:

All Shook Up
Getting Lucky
Obsessed
On Thin Ice
Shadow Dance

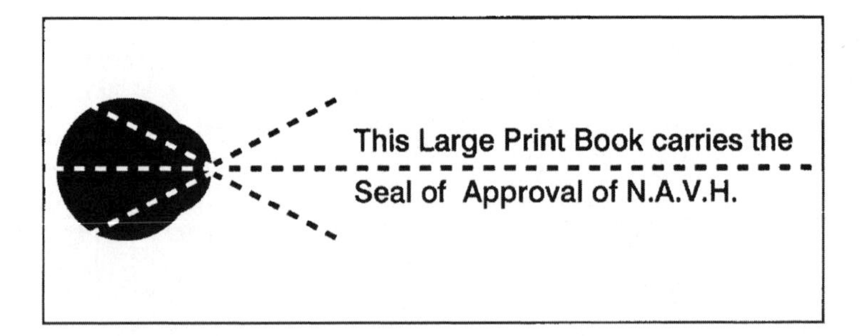

Exposure

Susan Andersen

Thorndike Press • Waterville, Maine

OAK RIDGE PUBLIC LIBRARY
Civic Center
Oak Ridge, TN 37830

Copyright © 1996 by Susan Andersen

All rights reserved.

Published in 2005 by arrangement with Zebra Books, an imprint of Kensington Publishing Corp.

Thorndike Press® Large Print Romance.

The tree indicium is a trademark of Thorndike Press.

The text of this Large Print edition is unabridged.
Other aspects of the book may vary from the original edition.

Set in 16 pt. Plantin by Al Chase.

Printed in the United States on permanent paper.

Library of Congress Cataloging-in-Publication Data

Andersen, Susan, 1950–
Exposure / by Susan Andersen.
p. cm. — (Thorndike Press large print romance)
ISBN 0-7862-7456-5 (lg. print : hc : alk. paper)
1. Runaway wives — Fiction. 2. Mothers and daughters — Fiction. 3. Washington (State) — Fiction. 4. Fishing villages — Fiction. 5. Sheriffs — Fiction. 6. Large type books. I. Title. II. Thorndike Press large print romance series.
PS3551.N34555E97 2005
813′.54—dc22 2004030141

LPF
Andersen

7/2005 010574838 $30.00
Oak Ridge Public Library
Oak Ridge, TN 37830

This one is for friends both old and new
Dedicated, with affection, to

Kathie Tagart
Who knew me before I was born

Jen Heaton and Teresa DesJardien
For conversations after midnight

Kimberly Deloach
Who has the most toys

Teresa Salgado,
For strokes, books, and photographs

and

Expert Readers Lara, Andrea, and Char
Who took the time to hand sell
when nobody knew my name

National Association for Visually Handicapped
serving the partially seeing

As the Founder/CEO of NAVH, the only national health agency solely devoted to those who, although not totally blind, have an eye disease which could lead to serious visual impairment, I am pleased to recognize Thorndike Press* as one of the leading publishers in the large print field.

Founded in 1954 in San Francisco to prepare large print textbooks for partially seeing children, NAVH became the pioneer and standard setting agency in the preparation of large type.

Today, those publishers who meet our standards carry the prestigious "Seal of Approval" indicating high quality large print. We are delighted that Thorndike Press is one of the publishers whose titles meet these standards. We are also pleased to recognize the significant contribution Thorndike Press is making in this important and growing field.

Lorraine H. Marchi, L.H.D.
Founder/CEO
NAVH

* Thorndike Press encompasses the following imprints: Thorndike, Wheeler, Walker and Large Print Press.

Prologue

"Mr. Woodard?" The intercom on the desk was the best that money could buy, its tonal quality clear as a mountain brook. Grant Woodard glanced up at the sound of his secretary's voice. "There's a Mrs. Muldoon here to see you, sir. She doesn't have an appointment —"

"That's all right, Rosa. Send her in." Grant took his finger off the intercom button and sat back in his chair, tugging lightly at his lapels to adjust the hang of his suit jacket. When the door opened and his secretary ushered in a plump, middle-aged woman, he rose to his feet. "Margo," he said genially, coming around the desk to greet her. "How nice to see you. Please, have a seat."

Margo Muldoon settled herself and refused the secretary's offer of coffee. She knew Grant Woodard's cordiality was a surface thing, primarily for show; and sitting with her knees pressed tightly together and her hands clasped anxiously over the voluminous handbag in her lap, she strove to contain her nervousness until the young woman had finally left the room, softly closing the door behind her. Then, leaning forward, she promptly got to her reason for being there. "Miss Emma is gone, sir."

"What do you mean, she's gone?" Grant snapped erect, all pretense of good humor eradicated from his expression. "I pay you good money to keep an eye on her, Muldoon."

"I know you do, sir, but I thought she was with you. She left me a note on Friday morning, saying she would be."

"Exactly what did this note say?"

"That she and Miss Gracie were spending Memorial Day weekend in the country with you. It didn't occur to me to question it until she failed to arrive back home this morning. And *then* I merely thought you must have returned late last night and she and the baby had spent the night in your guest room." She wrung her hands. "But when I called, your housekeeper told me neither Miss Emma nor Miss Gracie had been around for over a week, and the last time Miss Emma *had* been by to visit, she'd waited over an hour for you in the library before she finally had to give up and go home without seeing you."

Grant felt a chill crawl down his spine. Emma had spent an hour in the library waiting for him? Why the hell hadn't he heard of this occurrence before now? *Goddam incompetent help — I pay them top wages, and still I can't count on them not to screw up the simplest duties.* "Did you bring me this week's tape?"

"Yes, sir, Mr. Woodard." Margo Muldoon opened her purse, and when she didn't produce the article as quickly as Grant deemed suitable, he peremptorily snapped his fingers at her to hurry along the process. That merely added to her nervousness and she fumbled in her bag trying to extract the video tape. Finally, she got a grip on it and handed it across the desk. Grant immediately dismissed her with a curt nod and a shooing flip of his hand.

The moment the door had closed behind her, he stabbed the intercom button. "Rosa, something has come up. Clear my calendar for the afternoon." He'd started to lift his finger off the button when he was struck by another thought. "Oh, and locate Hackett. Tell him to meet me at the house."

"Right away, Mr. Woodard."

Twenty minutes later he walked into the library of his home. Crossing the room he went straight to the locked mahogany cabinet that held his library of tapes and retrieved the key from behind the decorative molding that ran along the top edge. He unlocked the cabinet's glass doors.

Everything seemed to be in order and Grant smiled, feeling foolish for his momentary lack of faith. Of course Emma hadn't gone through his archives; what possible reason would she have to do so? He poured himself a drink, put the newest tape he'd received from Mrs. Muldoon into the VCR, and sat down with the remote control. He smiled as he watched the scenes unfurl.

Suddenly, his smile congealed. Backing up the tape, he froze it and sat staring at the stack of tapes on the bed next to the suitcase Emma was packing.

Cold anger churning in the pit of his stomach, he crossed over to the cabinet once again. Grabbing a box at random, he ripped it open. The tape was there. He grabbed another and opened it. There. Yet another.

This one was empty.

Tossing aside the box, he went into a frenzy, grabbing box after box, slamming the full cassettes back on the shelf in roughly the same place from which he'd taken them and tossing aside the empties. When he was through, he had six neatly dated, empty tape boxes strewn around the room.

"That *bitch!*"

There was a rap at the door. Ramming his fingers through his steel gray hair, Grant looked at the mess he'd made and then shrugged. That was what hired help was for. Crossing the room, he yanked the door open.

"Hiya, boss." Hackett strolled into the room. "Rosa said you wanted to see me?"

"Sit down." Grant went over to the wall safe and positioned himself to block the other man's view as he worked the combination. From the safe's depths he extracted a stack of bills bound together by a narrow paper wrapper. Using his thumb to riffle them like a deck of cards, he watched for a moment as the denominations flashed past in a blur before returning to the desk where he slapped the packet down in front of Hackett and took his seat behind the huge mahogany expanse.

"Emma has taken off and she's got some property of mine with her." His eyes were frigid as a winter pond and harder than carbide steel as they bored into Hackett's. "That's for expenses," he said, indicating the money. Then he looked up again and met his employee's eyes, freezing Hackett to his seat with the intensity of his gaze. "I want her found," he said and there wasn't a speck of equivocation in his tone. "*Yesterday,* Hackett, if not sooner."

One

Emma swore softly. Wonderful. She couldn't have found a lousier place for the car to begin acting up if she'd tried. She'd just driven off the Washington State ferry ten minutes ago, and following a mix-up at the terminal, she'd disembarked on an island instead of the mainland destination one stop farther on. She didn't know if this small island even boasted a real *town,* let alone a garage with a certified mechanic. The engine noise grew louder and Emma feared they wouldn't make it over the next rise.

"McDonald's?" Gracie requested hopefully from the car seat next to her. She appeared oblivious to the horrendous racket the car was making.

"I don't imagine they have a McDonald's here, angel pie," Emma replied. She reached over and stroked a gentle finger down her daughter's cheek, giving her a soft smile. "I'll find us some place to eat, though." Or so she fervently hoped.

What she found was a picturesque town called Port Flannery, built on two levels around a harbor and attractive even in the gray light cast by a low ceiling of clouds that looked ready to open up and dump their contents at any moment. The tide was low and down on the bay was a boathouse and dock, a gas station, general store, several specialty shops, and a tavern. Up above was a town square, around which was built a town hall and the rest of the business section, including, thank goodness, Bill's Garage. Emma coasted the Chevrolet to a halt in front of the garage doors.

"So you say she's been runnin' rough, huh?" a man in greasy overalls with Bill embroidered above the chest pocket asked her a few moments later. He wiped his hands on an oily rag and then leaned over the engine once again.

"Running very rough," Emma confirmed. "And the engine's making a lot of noise. I think there's —"

"Now, don't you worry your pretty little head about it," he interrupted in a condescending tone that made the short hairs on the back of Emma's neck stand on end. She opened her mouth to cut him off at the knees but Gracie chose that moment to start squirming in her arms.

"Hungwy, Maman," she insisted querulously and drummed her feet against Emma's thigh.

Bill raised his eyes as far as Emma's breasts. "There's a café across the square," he informed them helpfully. "You go get your little girl something to eat and I'll have a better idea what's wrong with your car by the time you get back."

Emma gritted her teeth. She was tempted to impart a few home truths guaranteed to make Bill's ears ring, but Gracie was wriggling and demanding to be let down, and her own stomach was growling, so, swallowing a sigh, she let it pass. She set Gracie on her feet and took her hand. Moments later they were crossing the grassy square and climbing the porch steps of a large clapboard establishment. Red neon script above the navy-checked café curtains in the front window spelled out Ruby's Café.

By the time they walked out again, Emma was feeling a hundred percent better. Amazing, she marveled, what a hot meal could do for a woman. But it wasn't merely that; in addition to filling up on food that tasted like honest-to-goodness home cooking, she and Gracie now had a place to stay. Ruby's was a boarding house as well as a café, with big, spacious rooms to let upstairs. Emma had rented one overlooking the square.

The shortest lease Ruby was willing to

accept for one of her rooms was a nonnegotiable week — cash in advance — but that was all right with Emma. She was tired of being on the run and she was sick to death of living out of suitcases. It would be a luxury to be able to unpack and stay put for a few days. Sooner or later she had to stop somewhere anyhow, didn't she? Not to mention that with breakfast and dinner included in the rent, this was definitely cheaper than paying by the day at a motel, even cut-rate motels. So what the heck — why not here? It was an excellent, well-thought-out decision.

And one that, not five minutes later, she had cause to regret.

Sandy, the dispatcher, stuck her head into the sheriff's office. "Elvis, you better get on over to Bill's Garage," she said. "Some off-islander with an old car is over there raising Cain, and she's drawin' a crowd."

Elvis swore under his breath and headed for the door. Damn that Bill; he'd warned him before about his habit of padding the bill.

Sandy hadn't exaggerated; there was a small crowd bunched up in the doorway that separated the office from the garage bay. Most moved aside without speaking to him when Elvis appeared, but his friend Sam was there and he turned and gave him a grin. "Almost hate to see you break it up, Donnelly," he said. "This woman's good. Worth the admission at twice the price."

The car was the first thing Elvis noticed and he nearly choked. *Jesus, Sandy,* he thought, *an old car?* It was a classic '57 Chevy in mint condition, and Elvis would have happily ignored the argument raging over by the pit in favor of going over the thing from stem to stern with a fine-tooth comb . . . except by then he'd seen the woman, and both she and her argument were impossible to ignore.

His first impression was of a big blonde with a voice like molasses and a body built to stop traffic. Looking more closely, he realized she wasn't actually a true blonde. Her hair was more caramel colored, kind of a warm goldy-brown, but it had dozens of flaxen streaks that gave it the blond appearance. Elvis' massive shoulders twitched. Hell, close enough. If it walked like a blonde and talked like a blonde . . .

And the body was still built to stop traffic. She had a little girl riding her Levi's-clad hip, and he didn't think he was the only man in that garage who couldn't quite tear his eyes away from the chubby little dimpled hand that moved up and down the T-shirt covered, centerfold thrust of her mother's breast. "Itsy, bitsy *spi*doo," the child sang beneath her mother's harangue, little fingers pressing into the fullness. "Went *up* the water *spout*."

Jesus.

". . . lowlife, cheatin' *thief*," the woman was saying when he tore his attention back to the business at hand, and even in the midst of reaming Bill out, he noticed, her voice evoked images of sultry, magnolia scented, Southern nights. "Where'd you get your license, *cher* — from a Cracker Jack box?"

"Listen, you bitch," Bill snarled back with his usual inimitable charm, and Elvis' eyebrows snapped together.

He stepped forward. "What's goin' on, here?"

Emma's head swung around and she found herself gaping speechlessly for an instant. Standing in the doorway, a small island of space separating him from the rest of the gawkers, stood one of the largest men she'd ever seen in her life. He must have been six feet, six inches tall and probably weighed somewhere in the neighborhood of two hundred thirty pounds, all of it solid, khaki- and Levi's-covered muscle. But it wasn't simply his size that caused her to stare. It was the sternness of his expression. It was the fact that his left arm ended in an artificial limb with a metal clip-style hook where his hand should have been, and that a wicked raised scar zigzagged across his left cheek like an inch-and-a-half-long lightning bolt, pointing to his full lower lip where it ended at the outside corner.

She grew aware of Gracie growing quiet against her. The child's head lowered to nestle against Emma's breast and her thumb crept into her mouth. Emma glanced down and saw her daughter staring wide-eyed at the unsmiling man across the room, big brown eyes fastened on the angry red scar on his face. "Owie," she whispered around her thumb. It shook Emma from her reverie and she smiled slightly, pressing a kiss against her daughter's soft curls.

"I'll tell you what's goin' on," she said firmly and crossed the garage to stand directly in front of the gigantic man. Her head tilted back so she might look directly in his startling blue eyes. "I'm pretty sure I had a piece of carbon break loose and start hittin' the top of the piston," she said. "So I came in here to get it flushed out. But did this idiot —" She gestured expressively at Bill Gertz. "— squirt a bit of water in the cylinders or give it a bit of combustion cleaner to eat it up? Oh no, *cher.*" Her brown eyes flashed fire, and Elvis found himself taking a step closer. "No, he decides a rod bearing has come loose. A rod bearing! He can't show me this loose rod bearing, you understand, but I'm not supposed to worry my *pretty little head about it!*" She all but spat those last words out. "But, *no.* I mustn't do that. We're only talkin' about *hundreds* of dollars difference in the damn bill."

"Where did you learn so much about cars, miss?" Elvis inquired curiously, for it was clear that Bill had made a major miscalculation with this one. She knew exactly what she was talking about.

She met his eyes dead on. "From my brother, *cher.* Big Eddy Robescheaux ran the slickest chop shop in all of N'Awlins, maybe in all of Lou'siana. He and I — well, we were all the other had for years and years. I grew up in that shop. I could hardly help but pick up some pointers."

"Chop shops are illegal, Miss Robescheaux."

"Sands," she corrected him. "Robescheaux was my maiden name."

Elvis, aware of a fierce disappointment, gave himself a sharp mental shake. As if a babe like this one would ever give an ugly sonofabitch like him a second glance anyway.

"And I know they're illegal, *cher,*" she continued softly, a sadness creeping into her eyes. "They closed Big Eddy down, and he died in prison just before he was slated to be released." She sucked on her full bottom lip for a moment, then slowly let it slide through her teeth. That period of time surrounding Eddy's incarceration and death tied together with the beginning of her association with Grant Woodard . . . but that was another story and not something this man needed to know.

"I'm sorry, Mrs. Sands."

"Oh, call me Emma, *cher.* And you are . . . ?"

"Sheriff Donnelly."

"Hey, do the two of you friggin' well *mind?*" Bill interrupted in disgust. "What is this, the Sunday fuckin' social? Don't be taken in by a sweet pair of tits, Elvis."

"Elvis?" Emma questioned, blinking up at him. Gracie yawned around her thumb and started finger-walking her free hand up and down her mother's breast again. "Itsy, bitsy *spi*doo . . ."

Elvis shrugged his massive shoulders uncomfortably. "My mother's a big fan of the King," he explained. Then, his expression hardening, he turned to Bill. "I'll tell you what, Bill, why don't you leave the lady's anatomy out of it and just flush out her cylinders like she wants."

"The hell you say! It's a friggin' rod bearing, I'm tellin' ya!"

"Then you have nothing to worry about, do you? Of course, if the problem clears up the way Mrs. Sands here seems to think it will, she'll have to make a decision about pressing charges against you for fraud. If you prove correct, however, I'm sure she'll give you a nice, big, public apology."

"Oh, on my knees, *cher,*" Emma assured the enraged mechanic.

"Yeah? Well, while you're down there why don't you suck my big red di—"

Never in her life had Emma seen a man so large move so fast. Before the mechanic could complete his indecent suggestion, Elvis Donnelly was across the space separating them and his hook had flashed out to open and then close around the button placket at the collar of the man's greasy striped overalls. It lifted, bringing Bill up onto his toes.

"This isn't the first complaint I've had about the way you run this business," Donnelly said in a low, intense voice, bending his head to bring his face close to the mechanic's. "But it damn well better be the last, Gertz, or I'm going to shut your operation down so fast it'll make your head spin. Now, I'll thank you to keep a civil tongue in your head until your business is concluded. Get your mind out of the gutter and your butt in gear." Straightening, he allowed the hook to open up, releasing the fabric, and permitting Bill to settle back onto his heels.

Straightening his collar, Gertz stretched his neck first to the left and then to the right. "Well, big surprise that you'd take the side of a whore, Donnelly," he spat out, but took a hasty step backward at the look in the sheriff's blue eyes.

"*Excuse* me?" Insulted right down to her fingertips, Emma stepped without thought in front of the big law officer. It never occurred to her to let him handle the slur to her name; she was accustomed to fighting her own battles. Drawing up to her full height of five feet, nine and three-quarter inches, Emma faced the mechanic squarely.

"How would you like to find your scraggly little rear end in a court of law defendin' against a slander suit?" she demanded in a low but combative voice. Her brown eyes, boring into his, burned with outrage. "I've been in this town less than two hours and y'all don't know me from Adam, sir, so where do you get off castin' aspersions on my virtue?" Taking a deep breath, Emma felt her shoulders brush against the sheriff's chest, and she was curiously tempted for about two seconds to lean back and let it support her weight.

How ridiculous. She stood taller, blowing out an impatient little breath. "Legally, you're already treadin' a thin line here with my car," she informed Gertz coolly and then warned the belligerent mechanic, "I'd take heed if I were you, Mistah Bill Who-ever-the-devil-you-are, because I'm tellin' you right now as clearly as I possibly can. If I hear one more obscenity uttered in front of my baby, we won't be talkin' a nickel-dime-let's-settle-out-of-court lawsuit. I'll go out and hire myself the biggest legal gun this side of the Mississippi Rivah and y'all can bank on the fact that we won't rest until this sorry little garage is mine!" She gave her surroundings a disparaging glance, then met the mechanic's eyes levelly once again. "The place is obviously in need of somebody who knows how to run it right."

That's when she ran out of steam. *Yeah, sure, Em,* she thought with derision. *Big Talk.* As if she'd dare do anything that would draw attention to her and Gracie's whereabouts. But she neither blinked nor looked away from Bill Gertz's stare. She'd learned to bluff at a tender age and no crooked little backwater mechanic was going to jerk Emma Robescheaux Sands around. *Or* call her slanderous names in front of her child.

"*Maman?*" Gracie tugged on her mother's hair to get her attention. When Emma looked down, her daughter asked uncertainly, "We go bye-bye now?"

"Soon, angel pie." Emma dipped her head to kiss the child's chubby neck. Rubbing her hand gently through Gracie's curls, she raised cold and level eyes to meet the mechanic's gaze once again. "So, what's it gonna be, Mistah Gertz?"

Believing every word she'd said, he looked around, wishing to hell he'd never started this whole sorry mess. But who the hell woulda expected a woman — especially a woman who looked like this one — to know so much about cars? Conning unattached females had always worked just fine for him in the past.

Gauging the mood of the crowd, he could see there would be no help for him there. Most of those gathered might have little use for Elvis Donnelly socially, but they did respect him professionally. And Bill could see it had been a tactical error on his part to make crude remarks to a young woman who held a dimpled little angel in her arms. Shit. There was no help for it.

"I'll flush your damn cylinders," he muttered ungraciously. What the hell; he'd bluff his way out of this, then the woman would probably hit the highway and he'd never have to see her again. By this time next week no one would even remember he'd tried to cheat her. Except maybe Elvis Donnelly.

And who the hell cared about him?

Emma was wrung out by the time her car was once again in her possession and she'd driven it around the square to the small parking lot behind Ruby's boarding house. After spearing the mechanic with a contemptuous gaze one final time and garnering that unsmiling nod in exchange for the thank you she'd given the big sheriff for his assistance, she would have loved nothing better than to clear out of town. Unfortunately, she couldn't afford to do that.

She'd cleaned out her savings account when she'd left St. Louis and it had consisted of exactly one thousand, four hundred, thirty-six dollars and seventeen cents. She'd maxed out her Visa and Mastercharge by taking cash advances of four thousand dollars each on the cards

Grant had insisted on paying for her. That gave her a grand total of nine thousand, four hundred and thirty-six dollars and seventeen cents. It seemed like a lot of money to someone who hadn't had to pay her own bills in years. But when she considered it was all that stood between Gracie and the streets, and as an annual income went was right about poverty level, the cushion it provided became pretty thin. She had already used five hundred, ninety-seven dollars and change getting this far, and she sure as heck couldn't afford to throw away a week's room and board in a fit of pique.

Like it or not, she was stuck in unfriendly little Port Flannery for the next seven days.

Two

The town perhaps wasn't as unfriendly as she'd first believed. That night in the café, Ruby herself came over to deliver Emma's and Gracie's dinners. Sliding the fruit-garnished plate of macaroni and cheese in front of Gracie, she looked across the table at Emma. "I heard about your run-in with Bill this afternoon," she said, and Emma regarded her warily, unable to tell from the other woman's expression or tone what her opinion of the afternoon's debacle might be.

"I imagine it's the talk of the town," she replied noncommittally.

"Oh, that it is. Kind of gives you an idea of the entertainment potential in a town this size, doesn't it?" Ruby deftly slid Emma's bowl of soup and plate of salad in front of her. Then she stood back and regarded her. "There's been many a time I was positive he was cheating me, too, but what I know about cars you could print on the head of a pin in big, block letters, so I've never had the nerve to call him on it." Smoothing the pink cotton of her uniform over her sleek hips, she gave Emma an amused smile.

"Honey, it did this old girl's heart a world of good to hear a woman caused him to back down." Pushing a stray tendril of hennaed hair back into her coiffure with the eraser end of her order pencil, she regarded Emma quietly for an instant. "You really know as much about cars as folks are saying you do?" she finally asked.

"I know quite a bit," Emma admitted with a shrug. "I was probably the biggest tomboy in all of N'Awlins when I was a kid. My motto was 'Anything a boy can do, I can do better.' " She gave the other woman a wryly self-deprecatory smile and shrugged again. "For a lot of years it was just my big brother and me, and *chère*, from the time I was nine until I was fourteen years old I spent about every wakin' hour in his shop."

"Would you be interested in giving my car a tune-up?"

Emma's mouth dropped open, and she quickly snapped it shut. "Please," she said, waving a hand at the chair opposite her, "won't you sit down a moment? I'm getting a crick in my neck looking up at you."

Ruby grinned and pulled out the chair. Sitting down, she commanded, "Eat your soup before it gets cold." When Emma obediently picked up her spoon and began eating, Ruby leaned back in her chair.

"Bonnie!" she called out in the general direction of the counter. "Bring me over a cup of coffee, will ya, doll?"

"Sure thing, Ruby," the waitress called back, and Ruby straightened, turning her attention to the little girl seated on her left in order to allow the child's mother a few moments to finish her soup. "So, your name is Gracie, right?"

Gracie looked up. There was melted cheese ringing her mouth, but she was oblivious as she gave the red-headed woman a big, warm smile. "Wight! I'm fwee." Dropping her fork on her plate, she then bent in her little finger and held it down with her thumb, presenting the three remaining fingers in a crooked display for the woman to count.

"Three years old," Ruby marveled. "That's a big girl."

"*Big* girl," Gracie agreed. Always thrilled to entertain, and seeing this as an ideal time to show off some of her tricks, she splatted her hands in the casserole on her plate and grinned at her new friend as she chanted loudly in time to her movements, "*Pat*ty cake, *pat*ty cake, *bake*oos *man!*"

"Grace Melina!" Spoon clattering to the tabletop, Emma reached across the table to grasp her daughter's wrists. She pulled the little hands away from the plate and admonished her sternly, "Big girls do *not* play in their food, *chérie;* you know that." Deftly, she dipped her napkin in her water glass and wiped the child's sticky fingers free of macaroni and cheese. "You use your fork now or you can just kiss your dessert good-bye." Looking up at Ruby, she grimaced with rueful apology. "I'm sorry about that. Sometimes her manners leave a little somethin' to be desired."

"Don't worry about it; I've got two kids of my own. They're both in their teens now, but kids are kids. I know how it goes." She accepted her cup of coffee from the waitress with a smile and then sat back. After taking a sip, she put down the cup and, nodding toward Gracie, said, "She's a friendly little thing, isn't she?"

"Too friendly at times," Emma agreed. "Gracie subscribes to the Will Rogers school of friendship, don'tcha, angel? She's never met a man — or a woman, for that matter — she doesn't like. It scares me to death sometimes, because no matter how many times I've lectured her about not talking to strangers, I'm not one hundred percent certain she won't go waltzing off with the first one to present her with a persuasive enough story."

"Gwacie'd say *no,*" Gracie insisted, digging tracks through her macaroni with her fork tines.

"I know you would, angel pie," Emma retorted, but she raised a skeptical eyebrow at Ruby and changed the subject. "About your car," she said.

"I'm not asking you to do anything fancy," Ruby interrupted. "It's due for its oil change and — you know — that other stuff that usually goes along with a tune-up." She waved her hand in vague illustration, and Emma gave her a lopsided smile.

"Points and plugs, oil change, battery check, and a new filter?" From the way Ruby spoke Emma assumed she did not have a late model car that was electronically regulated.

"Yeah." Ruby smiled. "That stuff. How much would you charge me to do that?"

"I don't know. Is there a car parts store around here?"

"Mackey's, the general store down on the quay, has a parts department."

"In that case" — Emma quoted a price — "plus whatever the parts come to. For all I know island prices could be twice what they'd charge on the mainland," she warned. "So before you make up your mind maybe you'd better let me look into it. I'll drop by the store first thing tomorrow. Once we know more you can tell me if it sounds reasonable to you."

"Sure," Ruby agreed and then shrugged. "But I imagine it'll be fine. Bill usually charges three times that."

In a tone sweeter than sorghum and melodious as a soft, Southern breeze, Emma stated her opinion of Bill and his practices, and Ruby laughed. Emma then proceeded to garner all the pertinent details on the make, model, and year of Ruby's car before the older woman excused herself and pushed back from the table. As Gracie finished her dinner and ate her dessert, her mother hugged to her breast the potential she'd just been given to supplement her cache of traveler's checks. She felt like dancing by the time she let Gracie and herself into their newly rented room.

She didn't dare apply for a regular job; the moment her social security number went onto a paycheck, one of Grant's minions or a private detective was sure to be hot on her trail. It was a threat whose validity she didn't doubt for an instant.

And the good Lord knew the actualization of it was something she must avoid.

But tuning up Ruby's car . . . Oh Gawd, it was so perfect. No W2 to lead Grant to her *and* the opportunity to replace a little bit of what she'd already spent. Emma picked up Gracie and whirled her around, hugging her close and laughing.

The action sent Gracie a little out of control. She twirled in circles the moment Emma set her on her feet, spinning and laughing loudly. Grimacing over the tactical error she'd made in allowing her daughter to get so worked up, Emma went to collect the child's pajamas, not noticing when Gracie opened the door to their room.

Gracie danced out into the hallway; then twirled back in, slapping her feet against the hardwood floor as hard as she could, staring down at her little sneakers with their orange and yellow hand-painted fish. The door behind her didn't quite close.

Elvis, climbing the stairs, saw the little girl twirl like a top out into the hall, cheeks blazing and blond curls flying, and then stomp like a Charlie Chaplin wannabe back into the room. He hesitated at the top of the stairs before making his way quietly down the hallway.

He was surprised to see them still in town. Once Emma Sands and her little moppet had collected their great car in the wake of the brouhaha at Bill's that afternoon, he hadn't expected to see them again. The last thing he'd anticipated was coming home to hear the little girl screeching like a banshee just three doors down from his own room.

Hesitating at the side of the door, he looked into their room. Emma Sands was straightening from a crouch in front of the chest of drawers. She pressed a long-fingered hand into the small of her back and arched, stretching that long spine out. "That's enough, Gracie," she commanded quietly in the soft, accented contralto he remembered from that afternoon. "You're actin' like a monkey girl."

Elvis eyed that body, listened to that luscious Southern drawl, and wondered where in hell the husband was. He was amazed at how curious he was to know her story. Usually he didn't give a rip.

The hand that had been blown off by a car bomb commenced to itch like crazy, and he rubbed his forearm, where it attached to the prosthesis, gently against the seam of his Levi's. It was a conditioned reflex, an attempt to alleviate the genuine torment of a phantom limb. With an automatic eye for detail he simultaneously perused the room, taking a comprehensive inventory of the contents.

She wasn't simply on vacation; that was his first conclusion. Not with that small television set and VCR she'd set up on the dresser. People didn't drag shit like that along with them for a week in the country. Then, his massive shoulders twitched in a shrug. So, big deal, what the hell. Maybe she was moving.

But he had a cop's instinct that didn't think so.

Gracie was bobbing in place, scratching herself, and making monkey noises that were growing progressively louder. Finally, Emma tossed aside the pajamas she was holding and snatched her daughter to her. She wrapped both arms around Gracie's chubby little body, pinning the child's arms to her sides.

"That is enough, *s'il vous plaît,*" she said sternly, but then kissed her daughter's scarlet cheek and flopped down onto the bed on her back, holding the little girl to her chest. Gracie wriggled her arms free and wrapped them around her mother's neck. Rubbing her cheek against Emma's full breasts, she brought down one hand to slide her thumb into her mouth.

"There are other people up here," Emma continued admonishing her in a soft voice, smoothing tangled curls away from her daughter's flushed cheeks. "And, angel pie, somehow I doubt very much that they appreciate hearing you yell and scream while they're tryin' to watch TV or read their books."

"Gwacie's Monkey Girl."

"*Oui,* I know. And because I also know you're tired and because I'm the one who got you so wound up in the first place, I'm trying to make allowances. But no more noises, or *Maman's* gonna quit talkin' and take action. And Gracie honey, I don't think you wanna find out what that action's goin' to be."

Gracie yawned. " 'Kay," she said around her thumb.

"You want to take a bath tonight, sugar? There's a big ol' tub down the hall, and we've still got some of that bubble bath left that y'all like so much."

"Wanna call Gwandpapa."

Emma stiffened, but then immediately forced herself to relax. "Um, Grandpapa's out of town," she said with strained casualness. "I'm afraid we can't get ahold of him 'til he gets back. Want to read a book?"

Elvis abruptly straightened. He'd been admiring the way Emma handled her daughter, but the cop in him shifted to red alert at her words. He recognized a lie when he heard one and wondered what she was hiding. Then he frowned. What the hell, she hadn't broken any laws in his town. His curiosity about this woman was a radical departure from his usual attitude, and he wasn't sure he liked it.

He was nevertheless curious.

Unfortunately, the uncharacteristic interest she sparked in him also made him careless. He moved too abruptly and it drew her attention.

Emma, having discerned motion from the corner of her eye, whipped her head around in its direction. Her door was open a crack and a huge shadow out in the hallway absorbed the light in the space to the side of the doorway. Heart knocking up against her rib cage, arms tightening protectively around her child, she scooted back on the bed, struggling to sit up.

Elvis saw the alarm on her face and stepped in front of the opening, pushing it a little wider with his hand and bringing himself into the light. "Good evening, Mrs. Sands," he greeted her soberly.

"Sheriff Donnelly," she retorted stiffly. She hesitated then demanded, "Did you open my door?"

"No, ma'am. It was open when I came down the hall." He could hardly say her daughter had done it without admitting he'd been standing out here in the hallway watching them like some lowlife Peeping Tom. But his eyes dropped to study her baby's face.

The little girl nestled her cheek into her mother's breast and solemnly returned his look for several seconds. Then her lips pursed and she sucked hard on her thumb. Her index finger curled around her button of a nose.

Emma tucked her chin into her neck to look down also. "Gracie?" she questioned.

Gracie slowly raised guilty eyes to meet her mother's.

"Did *you* open the door?"

Gracie took several comforting pulls on her thumb and then let her lips go slack. "Uh huh."

"And did you leave the room?"

Gracie opened her mouth to deny it, figuring she'd already had more than her fair share of trouble that day and sure didn't need any more. But the Big Bird-large man with the owie on his face was watching her and she knew he could read her mind like Santa Claus. "Uh huh."

"Grace Melina Sands," Emma said with stern displeasure, "what have I told you about opening hotel-room doors or running out of them without me?"

"Woon't no caws or twucks, Mommy."

Big tears rose in her eyes, and her bottom lip started to tremble. She dug her head harder into her mother's breast.

Elvis watched in horror. Jesus. He hadn't meant to get the kid in trouble. "This is a real safe place, Mrs. Sands," he hastened to assure Emma, his gaze bouncing from the child's miserable expression to Emma's face. A fat tear rolled down the baby's face as he shifted uncomfortably. Oh, God. He couldn't stand this. "She'd never come to any harm out in the hall — hell, no one here would *dream* of hurting her."

Gracie blinked at him in wonder, her tears instantly drying up. She might be too young to articulate the concept, but she recognized being defended when she heard it.

Emma considered him also. Privately, she was rather amused by the panic one little girl's tears could cause in such a huge, stern man. Clearly this guy was not a father. "Do you live here, Sheriff?"

"Yes, ma'am. Across the hall and down a couple in G." It was convenient to work and saved him the hassle of having to cook for himself or keep up a house and yard.

Emma decided to let them both off the hook. "Well, I suppose the situation here *is* a little different from some of the motels we've stayed at," she allowed. "And since we're going to be staying for at least a week . . ." She looked down at Gracie again. "We'll discuss the new rules in the morning, Miss Sands."

Sitting up straighter, she rolled her daughter off her torso and onto the mattress next to her. "I think we might as well put off your bath until then, too. It's been a long day. Meanwhile, why don't you go pick out your bedtime story. It's time to get you into your jammies."

Gracie scrambled off the bed and trotted over to the stack of books on the wide sill of the window that overlooked the town square. Out in the hallway Elvis shifted to his other foot. "Well, uh, I'll just close this and be on my way," he said. He started to do that, then hesitated for an instant, giving Emma an intent, unsmiling stare. "Good night, Mrs. Sands."

"Good night, Sheriff."

The door closed softly.

Gracie was back in moments, leaving a messy pile of discarded books on the floor beneath the window sill. Her gaze went expectantly to the doorway, and she stopped in her tracks when she saw the closed portal. She turned disappointed eyes on her mother. "Where'd man go, *Maman?*"

"Sheriff Donnelly went to his own room,

angel. Come on over here. Let's get your jammies on."

Gracie obediently climbed up onto the bed, and Emma began removing her clothes. "But doesn't he wanna wead Pokey Puppy?"

"I don't think he knows too much about reading to little girls," Emma said as she set aside Gracie's shoes and socks and unhooked her OshKosh overall straps, then peeled the bib down. She whipped the little ruffled-neck T-shirt over Gracie's head. "You have to go potty, sweetie?"

"Uh huh."

Emma had to wrestle the temptation to take over as she watched her daughter pull the Barney pajamas up her sturdy little body. For she did it slowly. Soooo slowly. "Okay, then," she said, rubbing her itchy palms against the seat of her pants. "Whataya say we collect your toothbrush and toothpaste and do this all in one trip."

As usual, since the day almost two weeks ago when she'd grabbed Gracie and run, Emma managed to hold it together as long as her daughter was awake to command all her attention. It was in the quiet hours when Gracie slept that she invariably fell apart.

She stood at the second-story window,

arms wrapped around herself as she stared down at the dimly lighted square. Like most small towns, Port Flannery seemed to roll up its sidewalks shortly after nightfall. Oh, she imagined the tavern she'd seen down on the harbor was probably still doing a booming business, but up here it was quiet and still. The only sign of movement down on the shadowy grass common was a mongrel dog sniffing around the gazebo. As she watched he lifted his leg and anointed a patch of flowers that fronted the latticework. Emma pulled the shade and turned away from the window.

She was trying so hard to ignore the stack of videos in the bag on the shelf in the closet that it was self-defeating. The videos drew her, just as they'd done that day in Grant's library while she'd waited for him to arrive home. The day they had turned her entire life inside out.

She hadn't set out to invade his privacy that day. Ah, *Dieu,* Emma thought, trying to control a little bubble of hysteria, *his* privacy. Exhaling a bitter little breath, she hugged herself against a pervasive chill. There was an irony for you.

The fact remained, however, that she had merely been killing time that afternoon, not looking to pry into areas she had no business intruding upon. She'd seen Grant retrieve and replace the key to the cabinet a dozen times; but she had always assumed the tapes were records of business transactions and had respected the fact that they were kept behind lock and key for a purpose. That afternoon she had simply been passing the time by reading the dates on the video box spines. March 14, 1982 had naturally drawn her attention.

That was the day she had met the man who would become the closest thing she'd ever known to a father. The day she'd tried to steal Grant Woodard's Silver Cloud Rolls-Royce.

She wasn't supposed to have been involved. Big Eddy let her hang around the shop pestering him, the other mechanic, and the two auto-body men, but he was adamant about keeping her on the sidelines when it came to actually stealing the cars they chopped. He always said he might be nothing but a car thief, but he was damned if she was going to become one as well.

Eddy was funny that way. He made her go to school, made her brush her teeth morning and night, didn't let the other men in the shop talk too dirty around her. He taught her to drive a car before she was twelve, showed her how to break down an engine, pound out dents, and paint an automobile. But he kept her apart from the real meat and potatoes of the operation. He wouldn't let her do any of the fun stuff at all.

So she decided to heist this one on her own.

They'd seen the car often on the fringes of the Garden District, and because her brother and the men who worked with him raved about it every time they saw it, Emma just naturally assumed it would be a car they'd chose to steal. She wanted to beat them to the punch, to present it to them as a fait accompli, an acquisition she could point to as proof positive that she could handle this aspect of the job as well as any *guy* could.

Carefully obeying all speed limits, she was driving it back to Big Eddy's shop when a large black sedan forced her to the side of the road. She hadn't been in the car five minutes.

Before she had time to react, two very large men with thick necks and flat, cold eyes climbed out of the sedan and crossed over to rip open the driver's door. One of them stood to one side, his back to the car, his eyes scanning the area while the other leaned into the automobile. He stared at her without expression for a moment, then reached in and removed the keys from the ignition. "Get outta the car, sister."

They bundled her into the sedan and drove without speaking for several miles, eventually parking in the underground garage of a modern downtown office building. The two men then escorted her to an elevator and rode with her in silence to the seventeenth floor. After a delay in the reception area that lasted only the time it took to mutter a few low-voiced words into a telephone on the mahogany desk, she was ushered into an inner sanctum. When the door closed behind her, her guards remained on the other side of it.

Emma twitched her shoulders and straightened her clothing, swiping at streaky blond bangs with the back of her hand as she looked around the plush office and then out the floor-to-ceiling windows across the room to the spectacular view beyond. Huh. She wasn't scared.

Her heart slammed up against the wall of her chest when the high-backed forest green leather chair suddenly swiveled around to face her. A middle-aged man, distinguished and rich looking, regarded her soberly. Emma knuckled her hair away from her eyes again, raised her chin, and stared back at him.

"So," he finally said conversationally, "*this* is what a car thief looks like."

Considering how badly she'd wanted to do *everything* the men in Eddy's shop did, the depth of her hatred for the appellation surprised Emma. But she sucked on her lower lip to disguise its sudden trembling and swaggered around the room, picking up and discarding objets d'art that even she could tell were priceless. Turning one over in her hands, she examined it with the same lack of awe she'd display for a dime-store figurine before finally placing it back on the shelf where she'd found it. She glanced over her shoulder at the man across the room. "I prefer to call it auto liberation."

"Call it what you like, child," he said mildly. "It still carries five to ten in the penitentiary."

She had to squeeze hard to prevent her bladder from emptying itself where she stood. But she hadn't played poker with Big Eddy and his cronies for the past couple of years for nothing. She turned to face her adversary fully. "Get serious, *cher,*" she managed to scoff with credible scorn. "I'm fourteen years old, and that makes me a minor. Juvie's don't go to the pen, least not unless they murder someone."

"I see." The man picked up his desk phone and turned it around to face her. Tapping the receiver with expensively manicured fingertips, he suggested coolly, "In that case I suggest you place a call to your lawyer."

"Huh?"

"A big-time professional auto liberator such as yourself surely has a high-dollar mouthpiece on retainer. Don't you?"

She didn't reply. She simply stared at him with her brave belligerent eyes and trembling lower lip, and he heaved a sigh. "Call your parents," he suggested in a resigned voice.

She shuffled her feet and rolled her shoulders. "Don't have any," she muttered sulkily.

"Do you have a guardian?"

Emma picked up the phone and punched out the numbers to Eddy's garage.

An hour later a white-faced Eddy was hustling her out of Grant Woodard's office. His grip had her up on her toes and trotting alongside him in order to prevent her arm from being wrenched from its shoulder socket. When the elevator doors slid open Eddy hurled her inside with such force she cannoned into the mirrored back wall.

"Hey," she exclaimed indignantly, grabbing at the handrail to keep her balance. Rubbing her bruised arm, she turned to face her brother.

"A Rolls-Royce," he snarled. He was across the elevator in a flash, looming over her. As the doors swooshed closed he was already bending down to thrust his face aggressively close to hers. "Against everything I've ever wished for you, Emma Terese Robescheaux, you went out and thugged a car. And not just a regular, easily turned around Camaro or Jeep, oh no." He swore with creative fluency in Cajun French. "No, you gotta heist yourself a Silver Cloud, Rolls-fuckin'-Royce!"

"Well y'all always raved on about it so," she yelled back at him, but she was savagely interrupted when he grabbed her shoulders and shook her hard once. And then again. Soon her head was flopping.

"Hell, yeah, I raved on," he agreed between tightly clenched teeth. "It's probably one of the best-made automobiles in the world. But just how the *hell* did you think we'd get *rid* of it? *Mon Dieu!*" he growled impatiently. "That's not even the point. I've told you and I've *told* you, Emma: you're *bettah* than a common car thief. By God, I oughtta turn you over my knee and blistah your butt!" Instead he jerked her into his arms and held her so tightly she could barely breath. "Jesus, Em."

The pounding of his heart beneath her ear gave Emma the courage to admit, "I was scared, Eddy. I was so scared." His arms tightened even more. "I'm sorry he yelled at you," she whispered. "That wasn't fair."

Mr. Woodard had been so low-key with her that it had caught her by surprise to hear him light into Eddy the moment her brother had arrived. He'd dressed him down for a solid forty-five minutes before he'd finally let both of them go.

To her surprise, however, Eddy pulled back and looked down into her face. "No," he disagreed. "I deserved everything he said. And we got off light, sugah. That man could have made a whole lotta trouble for the two of us."

Watching her fourteen-year-old self now on the VCR, seeing the vulnerability and the fear so obvious behind the bravado and knowing that her entire *life* had been violated by hidden cameras, Emma had to wonder just how much trouble Grant actually had made for them.

It made her go cold, because even now, knowing what she did, suspecting other things, she still couldn't begin to estimate the damage he might have wrought. She thought she knew the worst.

But, ah, *bon Dieu,* what if she didn't?

Three

Gracie leaned heavily against Emma's calves for the third time in ten minutes. She emitted a heartfelt sigh. "Do sumpin' now, *Maman?*"

Emma just barely managed to suppress a sigh of her own. Replacing the spark plug she had removed with a fresh one, she lifted her upper body out from under the hood of Ruby's car and looked down at her bored daughter. "Soon, angel pie," she promised. "*Maman's* got to finish tuning up Miss Ruby's car first."

"Issa dumb caw," Gracie muttered under her breath. Emma gritted her teeth and disconnected the rest of the old spark plugs. She hadn't considered this aspect of the situation when she'd been so busy patting herself on the back last night for scoring a paying job.

"Hello," said a tentative feminine voice and Emma raised her head. Gracie's weight lifted from her legs.

Trying to locate the source of the voice, Emma's gaze skimmed the neatly kept back wall of the boarding house. No one stood at the back door or emerged out of the shadowy stairwell that led down to the basement entrance. Her gaze moved on to the little she could see of the narrow path that hugged the side of the building. It connected the small back parking lot, where she was currently working on Ruby's car, to the main walk at the front of the establishment. As she watched, a pretty brown-haired woman of approximately her own age stepped out of the shadows and walked toward her. She hesitated by the Dumpster, smiling uncertainly at Emma.

"I hope I'm not intruding," she said softly.

"No, of course not," Emma replied politely, although she was beginning to wonder if this was going to be one of those jobs destined for constant interruption. Then she shook off the tension. When it came right down to it, it wasn't as if she were racing to beat the clock. She straightened out from under the hood again.

"Oh, good." The woman's voice lost its tentative quality and she walked over to Emma. She stopped, feet together, posture erect, and thrust out her hand. "Clare Mackey."

Emma regarded her with interest. Showing the other woman her own surgically gloved hand, she didn't offer it.

"Sorry, I'm filthy," she said, then inquired, "as in the general store Mackeys?"

"Yes, 'fraid so."

"It's a very nice shop," Emma said sincerely. "I bought all this stuff there this morning." She indicated the sack of car parts next to the front tire and the empty boxes littering the lot at her feet. Then Gracie's squirming, and the way she was all but dancing in place awaiting an introduction, made her recollect her manners. "Oh, I'm sorry *chère,*" she said. "I'm Emma Sands, and this is my daughter Gracie. Gracie, say hello to Mrs. Mackey."

Gracie needed no second urging. "Hi!" she said, staring up at the newcomer with delight. "I'm fwee."

Clare Mackey squatted down to place their faces on a more equitable level. "Hello, Gracie," she replied solemnly. "I'm Clare Mackey. What a very pretty jacket you have on."

Gracie glanced down to admire her windbreaker for a second before raising her eyes back up to her new acquaintance. "Pwetty," she agreed. "It's lellow."

"Yes, I can see that. Yellow's a very good color on you."

Gracie preened and Emma gave Clare a wry grin. "Where were you this morning when I was fighting with her about putting it on? Y'all's June here is much cooler than we're accustomed to, but June is June as far as Gracie's concerned, and she thought she should be wearin' next to nothin'."

"It's summoo time, *Maman,*" Gracie insisted, picking up her end of this morning's argument. Then she let it drop. The windbreaker debate was old news; she had more important things on her mind. "My fishies are lellow, too," she told Clare, picking up a foot and thrusting it toward her new acquaintance. She teetered in place. "Some of 'em are. The west of 'em are owange."

Clare studied the hand-painted fish on the tiny sneaker. "Um hmm," she finally murmured with judicious admiration. "*Most* attractive." She looked up at Emma. "Listen, I couldn't help but overhear your conversation a few minutes ago, and I wondered if perhaps you'd allow me to entertain your daughter while you finish tuning up Ruby's car."

Emma could see it was a sincerely tendered offer, lacking dark or perverse undertones, but her immediate reaction was to snatch Gracie out of the woman's reach. The reason she and her daughter were on the run was all too predominant in her consciousness every waking hour of the day to allow her the luxury of taking anyone strictly at face value. "Oh, that's very generous of you, Mrs. Mackey," she replied uncomfortably, "but I don't think . . ."

"I meant right here in the parking lot where you could still keep your eye on her," Clare hurried to explain. "Of course you wouldn't allow her to go traipsing off with a virtual stranger. But I'd be happy to keep her occupied while you work on Ruby's car. And I'd very much enjoy spending a little time getting to know her."

"Well, in that case . . . thank you." *And don't* you *feel like ten kinds of a fool, chérie.* The smile Emma drummed up was a weak one. "That would be very helpful."

By contrast Clare's smile was unforced and dazzling. "It's settled then. And, please, won't you call me Clare?"

For the first time since the other woman had appeared at the corner of the boarding house Emma gave her a natural smile, the infectious wide and friendly grin that her daughter had inherited. "Thank you, Clare," she reiterated, this time more comfortably. "And I'm Emma."

The tune-up went much more smoothly after that. Emma listened to Clare and Gracie as she worked on Ruby's car and occasionally she even came up for air long enough to add a comment of her own. She was nearly done, pouring in the first quart of new oil, when Elvis Donnelly sauntered around the side of the building.

For a man so big, he moved like a cat. His walk was fluid, silent; padding across the parking lot, he came to a halt in front of Clare and Gracie. He gazed down at them. "Hey, Clare," he said neutrally.

She peered up at him and shaded her eyes with a hand. "Hey, Elvis."

He tipped his chin to indicate Gracie. "See you've got yourself a brand new friend." Then he turned to Emma and nodded. "Mrs. Sands."

"Hello, Sheriff Donnelly," she said cheerfully, wondering if the man ever smiled. "I really do wish you would call me Emma, *cher.* Mrs. Sands is so formal." Setting the empty oil can on the tarmac at her feet, she stooped to puncture a full one with the pouring spout. Looking up at him, she added for no good reason that she could think of, "Besides, I don't think of myself as a Mrs. Charlie — um, that was Mr. Sands — died before Gracie was even born." Then she shrugged uncomfortably, wondering why she'd felt compelled to tell him that. "At any rate, it's a title I didn't have much time to get accustomed to."

Elvis' stomach clenched and he took an involuntary step in her direction before he caught himself. *Don't be a fool, man; she's just giving you a little general information. Look at her, for Christ's sake. Then go home and take a good look in the mirror.*

A little hand tugged at the knee of his Levi's. "Shewiff? How come you don't say hi to me?"

He looked down at the little girl with the loopy blond curls staring up at him with big brown eyes and felt something melt in his chest. "Hiya kid," he said softly.

"Hi," she said brightly. "My name is Gwacie, and I'm fwee years owd, you know. One, two, fwee." She ticked out her fingers for him to count, and after he'd nodded and said, "Uh huh," uncomfortably, she held out her arms to him. "Up," she demanded.

He looked in panic first to her mother and then to Clare, but both women simply returned his look with interested speculation, as if wondering how he'd handle the situation. He turned back to Gracie. "I'm, uh, on duty now," he told her.

And discovered that excuse cut no ice. *"Up!"*

He stooped down and picked her up, carefully scooping his prosthesis under her little butt and placing his hand on her back to keep her steady as he rose to his feet.

She looked down at the hook that stuck out next to her hip. "Where's yoah hand, Shewiff?"

"I lost it in an explosion."

"Oh." Experimentally, she poked at the hook with her little fingers and he snapped it opened and closed. Gracie snatched back her hand with a screech, then cautiously reached out to poke at the foreign apparatus once again. Again he snapped the hook open and closed, and jerking her fingers out of harm's way she giggled. She looked up at him. "You funny man," she said on a deep chuckle.

Elvis could honestly say that wouldn't be the first characteristic most people would come up with to describe him. Tucking his chin into his neck he watched her closely as she occupied herself checking out the bits and pieces pinned to his khaki shirt. She bobbed her torso up and down on her perch as her dimpled fingers explored the grooves on his gleaming badge and then moved on to slip under the epauletlike loops of material on his shoulders. She pulled a pen out of his breast pocket, turned it end for end in examination, and then restored it to the pocket upside down. She moved on to slowly trace a tiny fingernail along the engraving on his name tag.

"Do you know how to read?" Elvis asked her. What with programs like Sesame Street and stuff, he figured kids these days probably learned that kind of thing pretty young.

"Uh huh." She skipped her finger along his title, which was etched white into the brown plastic pin, softly punching first Sheriff, then E., then Donnelly. "It say Mc . . . Donald's . . . to*day!*"

A corner of Elvis' mouth tipped up in a crooked smile, exposing several white teeth, and Emma stared. She'd been slowly pouring the new oil into the crankcase and watching him with her daughter, fascinated by the gingerly way he held her and the way his ruined face softened when he looked at her. It occurred to her for the first time that the sheriff had probably been quite a handsome man at one time. Actually, he still was; the livid scar just had a tendency to snag one's attention first. But if one took the time to look beyond that . . . Well. Seeing that one-sided smile now, spare as it was, made muscles deep in her belly clench and release.

Then she sucked in her breath and held it, for her daughter's attention had locked onto the angry red scar on the sheriff's face.

Gracie pressed her shins against Elvis hard stomach and bobbed on his arm a couple more times as she considered it. He continued to hold her as carefully as ever, but he'd gone very still and once again his face was coolly expressionless.

Finally, Gracie raised a soft little hand to carefully pat the raised scar tissue from zig to zag. "You get owie in a 'splosion, too?"

"Yeah."

She peered with concern up into Elvis' electric blue eyes. "Does it hoot?"

"Not so much any more." And the pain hadn't been the worst of it anyhow. What had really set his teeth on edge was the thick, numb feeling he'd experienced from eye socket to chin before the severed nerves had finally knit back together again. That, and the way people stared at it.

Placing her little hands on the broad ridge of his khaki-covered shoulders Gracie pressed her shins more firmly into hard abdominal muscle and raised her rump up off his arm. Leaning forward, she gave his cheek, where the scar bisected it, an enthusiastic if slightly damp kiss. She plopped back onto her perch and smiled happily up into Elvis' face. "All bettew," she said. Then she blew a raspberry on his throat just under the angle of his jaw and wriggling, commanded peremptorily, "Down now."

As he set her gently back onto her feet, for the first time in a pretty lonely life Elvis Donnelly thought he just might be in love.

He was trash — or so it was commonly agreed. *That Donnelly kid's got bad blood.* Elvis had lost count of how many times he'd heard *that* opinion expressed in one way or another when he was growing up. Enough times for him to try his damnedest to give the rumors some teeth the first seventeen years of his life. Hell, if this little one stop-signal town wanted disreputable, he'd give them disreputable like they'd *never* seen.

Which, given his mother's occupation, took a bit of doing. Elvis didn't know who his father was, but his mom . . . ? Well, Nadine Donnelly was Port Flannery's most notorious round-heeled working girl. Wasn't a citizen around didn't know about her — and God knew he had to go the extra distance to create more scandal than *she'd* already provided.

It was from her that he'd gotten his coloring — his thick black hair, his brilliant blue eyes. She was also the bestower of a name he'd been forced to defend with his fists from the time he was about eight years old until he'd finally gained his full growth

— and *then* it wasn't as if people had suddenly stopped snickering over it. They'd simply began exerting a little care to do their sniggering behind his back instead of to his face, because everybody knew that Elvis Donnelly would be more than happy to throw the first punch.

The matter of his paternity was a subject of much interest and even more speculation to the islanders. Theories ran rampant. As in any small town, the denizens of Port Flannery loved their gossip, and the sheer range of possibilities in this instance was deliciously lacking in limits. There was only one fly in the ointment; unfortunately it was a beaut. Elvis Donnelly was big, very big, and he'd showed every evidence early on of his ultimate height and muscularity. Who the hell could he have inherited these from?

His size did nothing to spare him from hearing the conjectures — in the general store, at Ruby's Café, even on the streets in the wake of people's passings. *Wasn't no one around these parts could come close to matching that boy for size,* they said, few even bothering to whisper, *and his mama's only average-tall. So who the hell can his daddy be?* It was a conundrum that seemed to occupy entire blocks of more than one person's free time.

Like many a sparsely populated, self-sufficient society, Flannery Island was class conscious and hierarchical, so Elvis didn't have many friends growing up. And those he did have were on the same lower stratum of the socioeconomic chain as he and by popular acclaim were considered trash also.

Except for Sam Mackey.

It was an odd pairing: the rebellious, bound-for-hell son of a prostitute and the Midas-golden only son of one of Port Flannery's most respectable families. But the two boys met on the first day of kindergarten, hit it off, and as far as they were concerned, that was that. It didn't matter what the adults thought about it. They'd been inseparable ever after.

It was to Sam that Elvis inevitably went when he found himself locked out of his own house because his mother was "entertaining." Enraged, hurting, he'd climb the tree in the Mackeys' back yard and let himself into Sam's room. The welcome he found there was the only outlet he could count on for the myriad emotions that roiled inside him. Dangerous as a pressure cooker with no safety valve, sometimes Elvis simply holed up for the night, brooding and planning trouble. Sam smuggled him food, talked to him, allowed him to let off steam, and tried to discourage the most reckless of his plans. When Elvis' pain drove him out looking for trouble anyway, Sam generally went along to exert what damage control he could.

And so it was the night Sheriff John Bragston changed the direction Elvis' life was taking.

"C'mon, Elvis; let's go back to my place," Sam suggested, shoving his hands into his jacket's pockets. He could see his every breath form an icy, vaporous cloud in front of his face, and stamped his feet in place to keep the circulation going. "This is crazy, man," he grumbled. "I'm freezing my ass off here." He was sixteen years old. Granted there weren't many things to do on the island on a Friday night. But there were at least half a dozen warmer things than watching his friend impatiently chuck aside half the stuff in the jumble that comprised the Donnelly tool shed. Losing patience, he finally growled, "What the hell you lookin' for, anyway?"

"This." Elvis straightened up, hefting a sledgehammer into view.

Sam's heart sank. "Oh, shit, Elvis, what're you gonna do with that?"

"Destroy the fucker's car."

"Nooo." But he could see he was wasting his breath. There was blind determination on Elvis' face and Sam swore roundly. "Dammit, man, trust me on this one," he urged. "This is not a good idea. You *don't* wanna do this." Ramming his fingers through his blond hair, he followed Elvis out of the tool shed and around the corner of the Donnelly house to where Lee Overmyer had parked his distinctive orange station wagon out of sight of anyone driving past on Emery Road.

Sam grabbed Elvis by the arm and said with quiet earnestness, "Bragston's gonna throw your ass in jail for this, E. Don't do it."

Elvis' blue eyes burned like gas flames as he stared down at his friend. "He's got a nice wife and three kids, Sam, and he's in there screwing my mother," he said furiously. "You can bet that tonight he's tellin' her, 'Baby, you're the greatest.' " Lips stiff, he added flatly, "Tomorrow he'll guffaw with his buddies and call her a whore." Which was what she was — he *knew* that's what she was. But still . . . "It's either this or kneecap the son of a bitch," he said honestly.

"Shit." Sam expelled the breath he'd sucked in deep. He let go of his friend's arm.

"Destroy the fucker's car," he said in resignation.

Elvis swung the hammer at the headlights, feeling a rush of savage gratification as, one after the other, they exploded in a hail of noise and shattered glass. He could hear the sudden scramble of feet hitting the floor and raised voices inside his house, but he knew that without backup Overmyer wouldn't come out to confront him. He had six inches and forty pounds on the older man easily, not to mention that he'd relish the opportunity to really mix it up.

Systematically, Elvis' hammer took out all of the glass in the vehicle; then he started in on the back fender.

Sheriff Bragston must have been in the neighborhood when the dispatcher forwarded Overmyer's complaint, because in record time lights from the department's car were sweeping the yard as it pulled off the country road into the drive. Gravel crunched beneath its tires and glowing red lights swirled from its roof, illuminating then retreating from the dingy white clapboard siding of Elvis' house.

Breathing heavily, Elvis dropped his arm to his side and turned to look at Sam who was sitting in the shadows on a tree stump a short distance away. The only distinct feature he could make out was his friend's cigarette glowing red as Sam drew on it. "You'd better take off," he advised him. They both heard the front screen door bang against the side of the house as Lee Overmyer rushed out to greet the sheriff.

Sam flicked the butt into the yard. "Forget it," he said. "I'm stayin' right here."

"No, Sam. You're gonna get into trouble, too, and you didn't do anything to deserve it."

"Big deal; so what else is new? You'll tell him I wasn't involved just like you always do, and eventually he'll let me go." Sam shrugged and gazed up at Elvis. "Like he always does." He crossed his arms over his chest and leaned into the weak pool of illumination that was thrown out by the bulb over the garage door. Tucking his hands into his armpits and slapping his elbows against his side, he hunched his neck into his flipped-up collar. "Jesus, it's cold out here."

"I mean it, Sam; take off," Elvis insisted urgently. "Bragston's been pretty good about you always being there when someone calls in a complaint about me. But I think some of the folks in my neck of the woods have been givin' him some grief lately about always lettin' the rich kid go while bustin' my penniless ass, and if the day ever comes when he gets tired of hearing it, he could make some serious trouble for you. Do us both a favor and get out of here. Please?"

Because Sam could see it was important to Elvis, he climbed to his feet. "Yeah, all right; I'm goin'. I'll see you tomorrow, though, huh?"

"Yeah."

"If you're not in jail, that is." Sam gave him a cocky smile. "Well, hey, if you are, I suppose I can always bake you a cake."

Elvis looked at the mess he'd made of Overmyer's car. Part of him was real pleased with the havoc he'd wrought. But there was another part that was ashamed, and he almost felt like crying. Deliberately he looked away, doggedly turning his attention back to his friend. "Good idea," he said with forced cockiness. "Be sure to include the file."

"You got it, babe." Sam hesitated a moment, then sauntered off into the woods behind the house, melting into the darkness just as Nadine Donnelly's customer and the sheriff rounded the corner.

Propping his hip against the front fender of the car, Elvis leaned over to place the sledgehammer, head down, on the ground, its handle against the car bumper. Then he straightened and clasped his arms defensively across his chest as he watched the two men advance.

"There he is," Overmyer snarled. His jaw dropped open when he saw the damage to his car, and he turned the air blue with his obscenities. "Arrest him," he ultimately demanded, shaking with rage. "I want the little bastard thrown in jail."

John Bragston eyed the "little" bastard. Mammoth within the play of moonlight and shadows that fell across his face and torso, Elvis stared back at him without expression, but there was no disguising the turmoil in his neon blue eyes. And as it always did, that suppressed emotion tugged at something in Bragston.

How the hell would *he* feel, he wondered, not for the first time, if it were his mother locking him out of the house while she serviced some self-important, pompous son of a bitch? It was difficult for boys that age to even acknowledge the possibility that their mothers might be sexual beings, never mind having the knowledge that yours was the town hooker thrust in your face night after night.

On the other hand, Elvis had destroyed

some property here tonight and his acting out couldn't be allowed to escalate this way.

Damn it to hell. What a mess.

He turned to Overmyer. "Well, I can arrest him, all right," he agreed easily. He pulled his handcuffs from his belt and approached Elvis, who without argument stuck his hands out. Starting to put them on, the sheriff paused to look back at Overmyer. " 'Course, you might want to consider what Margaret's going to say," he advised. "She might have a few choice questions for you once she hears where your car was parked when Donnelly here took the hammer to it." He snapped the cuffs over Elvis' wrists. Then turning back to Overmyer, he said amiably, "But, hey, I'm sure you'll think of somethin' plausible to tell her."

Overmyer had snapped upright and was regarding him in alarm. "You can't tell Margaret where the car was parked!" he protested.

"I don't aim to," Bragston retorted calmly. "But use your head, Lee. Pressing charges means going down to the station and filling out a report. There are people at the station, and just so you understand this right up front, when it comes to my reports I give special consideration to no man. It either gets filled out entirely or it doesn't get filled out at all."

He could almost see the wheels turning in the other man's head. *Hell, I can get away with it,* Overmyer was thinking. Then, *Shit, no, I'll never get away with it.*

"Give it careful consideration," Bragston advised, "because you're going to be stuck with the results of whatever you decide. It's a small island." He disguised his impatience. Hell in a wheelbarrow, Lee was a native, and anyone who had lived here his entire life shouldn't have to be reminded of the obvious. Then again, Overmyer hadn't exactly ever been known for his mental wizardry. The sheriff shrugged. "Hell, man," he said, "you know as well as I do, there are damn few secrets on Flannery. Word tends to get around."

Overmyer gave Elvis a bitter look. "Yeah, and I suppose in this case it's pretty much guaranteed to."

The look Elvis returned didn't contain cocky triumph. Instead, it was filled with contempt. "Don't look at me, you scum sucker," he snarled. "Mrs. Overmyer's always been real nice to me." And people like that weren't so thick on the ground he could afford to deliberately hurt one. "She ain't gonna hear nothin' 'bout this from me."

"Well, there you go," Bragston said cheerfully. "Maybe no one down at the station will say anything either." He jerked his head at Elvis. "Let's go, son."

Elvis straightened away from the car hood and followed Bragston over to the department vehicle. He'd already climbed into the back seat when Overmyer blew out a gusty sigh of disgust and said, "Let him go."

"It's probably for the best," the sheriff agreed. "And, Lee, the kid here will pay whatever damages your insurance deductible doesn't cover."

"The hell you say." Elvis snapped to attention. The look he gave the sheriff was incredulous. "If no charges are gonna be pressed against me, why the hell should I pay a dime to this clown?"

Sheriff Bragston looked him coolly in the eye. "Because it's the right thing to do," he said, and that stopped Elvis in his tracks. No one had ever expected him to do the right thing before; usually their expectations were just the opposite.

"I don't have a job," he muttered, sulky because it was yet another sore subject. He had tried to get after-school or weekend work, but no one wanted to take a chance on hiring him. He was poor white trash.

Glaring at the sheriff as if the dearth of employment opportunities were the man's fault, he held out his hands for Bragston to remove the cuffs, but the sheriff simply slammed the car door, sealing him inside.

"Hey!"

"You've got a job," Bragston said, climbing into the driver's seat and firing up the ignition. "Starting as of now, you're working for me." He twisted around to pin Elvis in place with the sternness of his gaze. "And if you think this is charity work I'm offering here, kid, then think again, 'cause it ain't. I expect an hour's work for an hour's pay, and if you can't hack it, boy, your narrow butt's out the door and I'll get someone who can."

John Bragston was as good as his word and he became a major influence in Elvis' life. Gruff and blunt-spoken, he was nevertheless the first adult male to give Elvis attention that was exacting and yet positive. When school report cards were handed out shortly after Elvis started working at the police station, the sheriff demanded to see his and having done so said Elvis could do a helluva lot better.

Elvis did.

He wanted to know Elvis' plans for the future. "So what are you gonna do when you graduate?" he asked at the end of Elvis' junior year.

Elvis shrugged. "Blow this burg."

"And do what?"

"Huh?"

"Dammit, son, think ahead a little," Bragston advised impatiently. "It's not enough simply to say you're gonna blow the island. You've got to have some sort of plan. Where you gonna go once you hit the mainland, boy? How you going to make a living?" He fixed him with a fierce eye. "You just going to take off for Seattle or another big city a little further away with — what? — a couple hundred dollars in your pocket? I can guarantee that'll have you peddling your ass for the rent money in about two weeks' time."

"So, maybe I'll be a cop, like you," Elvis retorted, watching the older man carefully to see if he'd laugh in his face.

Bragston merely nodded. "You'd make a good one," he said matter-of-factly. "But to get anywhere in law enforcement these days you need college. And to afford that, you might have to stay on the island for a few extra years."

Elvis did. He commuted off-island four years, and when he graduated Sam Mackey and John Bragston were the only ones there to see him. His mother said she'd come, but she didn't arrive until after the ceremony was over.

He then followed through on his oft-stated threat to leave Port Flannery behind. Securing a job with the Seattle Police department, he worked his way slowly up the ranks until a car bomb meant for a witness he was protecting put an abrupt end to his career.

Well, perhaps that wasn't strictly true. After completing nearly a year of physical therapy he could have gone back to the SPD at a desk job. Instead he opted to return to the island of his birth.

When the chips were down, he supposed, it was still the only place he'd ever really considered home.

Four

An outboard motor rumbled to life out in the bay and the faint scent of gasoline drifted in to shore to mix pleasantly with the salty aroma of the waves lapping the rocky beach. Pebbles rattled gently with the tide's retreat, a sound that was momentarily drowned beneath the raucous, echoing cry of a seagull circling overhead. Gracie, her pockets bulging with the morning's finds, squatted on the beach to examine yet another potential treasure. The gull's noisy cry and its white-winged glide across an overcast sky caught her attention, and she looked up. Tracking the bird's progress as it circled and soared, she watched with such interest and enthusiasm in her expression that Emma's heart contracted. She squatted down next to her daughter.

She was enjoying Gracie's enthrallment with the delicate pink inner whorls of a broken shell when Clare hallooed them from a short distance down the beach. Gracie immediately abandoned her position, bobbing to her feet and racing to meet her newest acquaintance. Emma rose to her feet more slowly.

"Hi, Miss-us Mackey! Lookit I found." Gracie started pulling rocks and shells from her pockets, thrusting them forward with both hands.

"Hi, Clare," Emma added her greetings as she came forward. "Are you out in search of a little fresh air, too?"

Clare shook her head. "Actually, I was changing the store window when I saw you two head down to the beach, and I thought if you were still here when I took my break I'd come say hello." She handed Gracie a little yellow plastic sand pail and shovel. "This is for you, sweetheart," she said with a soft, wistful smile. "No child should be without a sand bucket if she lives near the shore."

Gracie's handful of treasures hit the plastic bottom with a hollow rattle. "A lellow one!" Her smile lit up the afternoon. "Look, Mommy, hoos bwought me a lellow bucket for my shells and my wocks." She immediately began transferring the remaining contents of her pockets into the sand pail.

Emma bent down to properly admire it. Once done, she prompted, "It was very kind of Mrs. Mackey to bring you a present, Gracie. What do you have to say?"

"Thank you! *S'il vous plaît.*" Gracie gave Clare a huge smile, then immediately forgot both women as she plopped down to stir the contents of the bucket with the tiny shovel.

Clare watched her for several moments before she lifted her gaze to Emma's. "I was sorry to hear you're leaving Thursday," she said quietly.

Emma blinked. "My goodness, *chère,* you heard about that already? Why, Ruby just asked me this mornin' if I'd be needin' the room for another week."

"Yeah, I know. Jenny Suzuki heard you tell Ruby you wouldn't, and she mentioned it to me when she came into the store."

"Now, which one is she?" Emma wanted to know. "Is she the one with that darlin' little baby?"

"Yes, Niko. She was disappointed to hear you were leaving, too, because she was going to ask you to tune up her car for her like you did for Ruby."

"She wants a tune-up?" Emma straightened. "Uh, we could maybe stay on an extra week." She rolled her shoulders and admitted sheepishly, "The truth is, I could use the extra money." She glanced at Gracie. "On the other hand, maybe it's not such a great idea. If you hadn't come around and diverted *ma petite fille's* attention last time,

I'd probably be workin' on Ruby's car yet."

"I could do it again, if you want. I'd really like to, Emma."

"But . . . what about your job?"

"I work part-time." Clare shrugged. "And it's a family-owned business. I can take off a couple of hours if the need arises, and I really would enjoy doing it." She hesitated and then added, "Gracie reminds me of . . . someone." Distractedly pushing her hair back, she met Emma's eyes. "My son, actually," she confessed. "It just feels good to be around her."

"Why, I didn't know you had a child." Emma's eyes lit up with enthusiasm. Until this very moment she hadn't realized how much she'd missed talking with other young mothers these past few weeks. "What's his name? How old is he?"

Then she wished she had trod more carefully, for Clare's face was now pale and her eyes were filled with a deep sadness.

But her voice was even and quiet when she said, "His name was Evan Michael, Emma. And he was six years old last year when he died."

Sam walked into the kitchen and found Clare talking on the phone. Quietly, he poured himself a cup of coffee and leaned against the counter slowly sipping it while he watched her profile. He hadn't seen this kind of animation in her expression in a very long time. Not since Evan's death.

"Okay," she was saying, "so here's the schedule as it currently stands. Jenny is going to drop the car off at Ruby's at ten o'clock Friday morning. I never work Fridays so I don't have to do anything special to get the time off. How does that work into your time frame?" She listened a moment and then laughed at whatever the person on the other end of the line was saying. "Don't be silly, Emma; I enjoy doing it. Uh huh. Yeah, okay. I'll see you then. 'Bye now." A tiny smile ghosting her lips, she replaced the receiver and turned, starting visibly when she saw Sam. He pushed away from the counter.

"Hey," he said, his eyes tracking her face feature by feature. God, he hated seeing her vivacity drain away that way. Hated it that he didn't know how to reach her these days. That he hadn't *known* how for thirteen long months. Thirteen months, twenty-seven days and — he consulted his watch — six and a half hours, to be precise. "I heard you say Emma. Was that Emma Sands?"

"Yes," Clare replied. Her chin elevated slightly as if anticipating an argument.

"She's tuning up Jenny Suzuki's car on Friday, and I'm going to keep an eye on her little girl for her while she does. Her daughter's name is Gracie."

"Yeah, I know." Sam watched her carefully. Elvis had told him she'd done that once before when the Sands woman had tuned up Ruby Kelly's car. Gracie Sands was the first child he'd known Clare to show an interest in since Evan's death. Up until now she'd tended to shy away from other people's children, and the God's honest truth was he found her interest promising and was marginally heartened. Maybe there was hope after all that he'd someday get his old Clare back again. "I saw her at Bill's Garage the first day they were in town," he said. "She's a cute little girl."

"She reminds me of Evan, Sam," Clare said. "There's something about her."

God! It was the first time since Evan's death that she'd willingly spoken their son's name to him. He ached for every single thing he had once taken for granted — the instinctive understanding they'd once shared, the unquestioning closeness. Taking a chance, he walked up to his wife and wrapped her in his arms for the first time in months.

Clare stiffened and Sam's arms dropped

away. She immediately wished them back, but he'd already moved away. In any case she probably wouldn't have reached out for him even if he'd remained standing right in front of her. She'd lost the old self-confidence that used to allow her to grab what she wanted, and she sure as hell no longer knew how to ask for it. She did, however, stay in the kitchen with him. She also attempted to share something of herself with him, and that was an effort she hadn't bothered to make in . . . oh, a very long time.

"I handled all the arrangements between Emma and Jenny," she informed him. She hesitated, and then confessed, "And I purposely set everything up for Friday morning because I knew that way Emma would have to stay another week." She still couldn't believe she'd done that. And yet . . . "Maybe I'll ask her to do my car next Friday. That would keep her here for still another week." Biting her bottom lip, she gazed into Sam's face, looking for a reaction.

One corner of his mouth went up around the cigarette he'd just lighted. "You can have her do mine the Friday after." Then he smiled.

She wanted to throw herself into his arms. This was the Sam she'd married. The don't-tell-me-who-I-can-be-friends-with-I'm-gonna-do-what-matters-to-me-not-what's-important-to-this-town-Sam. She'd fallen in love with him when she was fifteen years old and he was eighteen. She'd watched him run around town with Elvis Donnelly, thumbing his nose at all the small-town strictures — but ever-so-politely and always with that big, beautiful smile — and she'd thought, *This is the guy for me. I'm gonna marry this boy.*

And she had. He'd been everything to her, too, for over ten years. She didn't know how things had gotten so out of control.

Sam opened the window over the sink and flicked his cigarette butt out into the yard. He looked at her over his shoulder. "So, what's the story?" he asked. "Clare, do you wanna keep Emma in town for herself, or because of Gracie?" Pulling the window closed, he turned and hiked himself up onto the counter. Ankles crossed, bare feet swinging, he sat observing her through level eyes.

"I suppose it's a little of both," she admitted. "There's something about that little girl that's so . . . healing. But there's something about Emma, too. She's a fighter and she speaks her mind. Yet, she's warm and friendly — I mean, my God, Sam, she even calls Elvis *cher!*" She still marveled over that little piece of gutsiness. Most of the people in this town called him Sheriff if they couldn't avoid addressing him entirely.

Sam laughed. "Yeah, I know. I don't think he knows quite what to make of her."

"I told her about Evan this afternoon," Clare told him. "I wanted to do it myself before she heard about him from someone else. And, you know what, Sam? She just reached out and rubbed my arm and said, 'Ah, *chérie,* I am so sorry. I can only imagine how you must feel.' " Hugging herself, she stared up at her husband. "I didn't get that poor-Clare-we'd-better-walk-on-eggshells-around-her look, or the 'There, there, I know just how you feel' speech, or the burst of whispers after I've walked away. I mean, I'm an adult, I *know* not everybody acts like that. But sometimes it feels like it. She's so refreshing, Sam. I like it that she doesn't know everything there is to know about me. I like it that she hasn't already heard my entire life history through the ever-efficient, ever-biased grapevine."

She arose and crossed to the stove to pour herself some coffee. Holding the mug in both hands, she turned to face her silent husband. "Most of the time I really love Port Flannery, and I do realize that small towns like this have a lot of positive things to say for themselves," she said. "But the lack of privacy is a drawback, Sam. It's a definite drawback."

The lack of privacy on this island is a pain in the ass. Elvis dwelled on the thought more than once as he went about his business. It seemed to him that everybody and his brother had heard about Emma Sands and just had to know more. What did they think he was, her personal chamber of commerce?

In the morning he pulled Evert Dowdy over for speeding. Evert sat in his pickup truck working a plug of chewing tobacco between his cheek and gum while Elvis wrote up the ticket.

"Goddam cops," he grumbled. "Why don'tcha spend your time arrestin' real criminals? Go bust a couple a dopeheads. Wouldn't that make a nice change of pace from costin' law-abidin' citizens their hard-earned wages?"

Elvis refused to respond, but he did raise his head to pin the older man in place with a level look. Evert shifted uncomfortably. Deciding a change of subject would perhaps be prudent, he said in a slightly friendlier tone, "Heard tell there's a new woman in town name of Sands."

"Uh-huh." Elvis handed the ticket book

through the window. "Sign here, sir."

Evert signed but didn't immediately pass the book back out. "So's it true what I heard, that she's some kinda ace mechanic?"

"Yeah. She knows her stuff all right."

"And she backed ol' Bill down over a piece of carbon on the piston?"

"Yep."

"If that don't beat all." Evert let fly with a stream of tobacco juice, expertly aimed out the window for the most distance with the least amount of fuss. He handed back the ticket book. "So," he demanded. "Ya reckon she's a dyke?"

Elvis snorted. Tearing out Dowdy's copy of the ticket, he passed it to the man. "You haven't met Mrs. Sands yet, I take it."

"Nah."

"Trust me. A lesbian she's not."

"Humph." Evert worked his chaw. "I guess I did hear she's got herself a kid."

In the afternoon Elvis knocked on the door of a neatly tended but run-down house out in his old neck of the woods. The woman who answered his summons was probably in her mid forties. She looked older.

"Afternoon, ma'am," he said. "I'm

Sheriff Donnelly. You're Mrs. Steadman, aren't you?"

"Oh, dear God." Color drained from her face and she grasped the doorframe with white knuckled hands. "Is it one of my boys?"

"No, ma'am, it's okay," he hastily assured her. "As far as I know your kids are just fine." Watching her sag against the doorframe, Elvis added contritely, "I'm sorry, Mrs. Steadman, it wasn't my intention to frighten you." Relieved to see the color return to her cheeks, he gently informed her, "I'm here about the trash I found tossed over a bank. Off Emerson Road out by the old Bailey place."

The look she directed at him suggested he'd lost his wits. "What on earth has that got to do with me?"

Elvis handed her the old issue of *Good Housekeeping* he'd found among the garbage. "I found this smack-dab in the middle of it, ma'am."

She pulled her gaze away from the scar on his cheek and looked down at the magazine in her hand. On the front cover, faded but clearly marked, was an address label bearing her name. "What on earth . . . ?" Then she snapped upright. "*Damn* those boys!" She looked up at him. "Sheriff, I swear," she earnestly tried to assure him, "I gave my sons a ten-dollar bill yesterday to take a truck-load of stuff to the *dump.*"

"An old bed frame, newspapers, Styrofoam, some furnace filters?"

Her lips grew tighter with each new item he listed. "I'll kill 'em! I will hang those two up by their thumbs and skin them alive."

"They're teenagers, ma'am. If this is the worst thing you ever have the law come knocking on your door for, you've done a pretty good job. Have them clean up the mess first thing Saturday morning. Then send them to me. I'll put 'em to work picking up litter around town for the rest of the afternoon."

"Yes . . . okay; I'll do that." She noticed he had real pretty eyes. "Thanks, Sheriff. I know you could have slapped me with a fine or something, and I'm tellin' ya, I honest to God don't know where I would have found the money to pay it."

Yeah, he remembered those times very well. Elvis nodded politely and turned to go.

"Uh . . . Sheriff?"

He turned back. "Ma'am?"

"Is that new lady still in town? That Emma Sands?"

"Yes, she is."

"Is her little girl as adorable as they say?"

A crooked smile tugged at Elvis' lips. "Yeah, she's a cutie."

"Where are they from?"

"New Orleans, I think."

Mrs. Steadman stepped out into the yard, closer to him. "Is it true she really calls everyone that French word — that sher-ree?"

"Pretty much."

"And does she actually know how to work on cars?"

"Yep. She gave Ruby Kelly's car a tune-up. When I left the boarding house this morning she was doing Jenny Suzuki's."

"My." Mrs. Steadman couldn't have looked more enthralled if he'd said Emma Sands performed brain surgery. "Imagine that." After looking at him consideringly for a moment, she said, "Wait here."

She disappeared into the house, but was back within moments to extend a piece of paper to Elvis. He looked down and saw it contained her name and phone number. "Will you give this to her and ask her to give me a call?" she asked shyly. "There's something the matter with my Chevy that maybe she can fix."

What was he, her messenger boy? Elvis almost shoved the paper back into her hands, but then stopped himself. Just an hour ago she probably would have crossed the street to avoid having to talk to him at all. He shrugged and pocketed the slip of paper. "Yeah, sure."

"And tell her I could watch her little girl while she looks at it. It'd be fun having a female to fuss over for a change."

That evening he stopped by his mother's house. He was barely through the back door before she, too, started in on the subject of Emma Sands.

She poured him a cup of coffee in an Elvis Presley mug and sat down across the table from him. "So tell me about the new woman," she demanded, sliding the plate of Oreos closer to him. "This Emma Sands. Is she really the walking wet dream I keep hearing about?"

Elvis looked at his mother. Good God. Here he was, thirty-two years old and just as conflicted in his feelings toward Nadine as he'd been as a teenager. Why couldn't she be like other people's mothers? "She's . . . pretty," he replied cautiously.

"And? *And?*"

"And built, okay?" He looked down at his mug and grimaced with distaste. "Good God, Mom, if I have to drink out of a damn Elvis Presley cup, couldn't you at least give me one of the ones where he's not a fat slob and a lousy dresser?"

She was easily diverted as he'd known she would be. Snapping upright, she ordered, "Don't you insult the King, Elvis Aaron!" Neither, however, was she stupid. "And don't try to change the subject. What is it about this woman that's got all the guys drooling?"

"Streaky blond hair. Big brown eyes. Really great tits." Then he scowled. "All *what* guys?"

Nadine's eyebrows rose. "Relax, baby," she advised, reaching across the table to stroke her son's large hand. "It's just some of the older gents; no one for you to worry about."

Elvis' big shoulders shifted. "Who says I'm worried? And what older gents?"

"Bill Harris. Rick Magoody."

"Goddammit, Mom!" His mug slammed down on the tabletop, sloshing coffee. Those particular "gents" were two of her old clients. "Have you been turnin' tricks again?"

"Oh, certainly," she retorted sarcastically. "And suffer the embarrassment of being arrested by my own son? Spare me." Her eyes, the same brilliant blue as her son's, met his bitterly. "You made it abundantly clear, the day you were elected sheriff, that I was no longer in business."

"So what're you doing discussin' Emma Sands with the likes of Bill Harris and Rick Magoody?"

"I *am* still allowed a social life, I trust? Paying my bills doesn't give you leave to take away my rights to that, too, does it?"

Elvis slid his good hand off the table and onto his chair, sitting on it to keep from reaching for her throat. God, she made him *crazy* sometimes. "No, ma'am," he said through his teeth, "that was never my intention when I turned over my life savings to you."

And because that was exactly what he'd done, she relented. The truth was, there was no retirement plan in her line of work and she was going to turn fifty in a couple of months, which was a little long in the tooth for turning tricks. Elvis had presented her with a large cashier's check the same day he'd put her out of business, and he'd never once thrown it up to her in order to control her movements. It was just . . . he could be so damn rigid sometimes. And she hated knowing that he was ashamed of her. She understood it, but she hated it.

She nevertheless softened her attitude. "I simply had dinner with them, okay? Bill took me off-island Tuesday night, and last night Rick took me out to The Razorback."

"Yeah, okay, I'm sorry," he apologized. "I jumped to conclusions." He looked away uncomfortably. The black velvet Elvis painting hanging on the wall down the hallway reminded him of a subject he'd meant to raise. "So, when are you leaving for Graceland?"

Nadine's mouth formed a little moue. "Well, I really wanted to be there on the sixteenth of August. Such a sad, sad day."

God, give him strength. The anniversary of Elvis Presley's death. She'd have the damn flag flying at half mast on that day, something she never bothered to do for presidents or veterans or Martin Luther King. "But . . . ?" he questioned in resignation.

"But the vacation calendar was already booked up for that date at MarySue's workplace," Nadine retorted. "So our pilgrimage will have to be a little earlier. We've got a flight out on the fourth of July."

"MarySue must get a couple of extra days off because of the holiday, huh?" Nadine's best friend worked the afternoon shift down at the Anchor.

"Yeah, so we might as well get an early start." Nadine pushed back from the table and bussed their cups to the sink. Glancing at Elvis over her shoulder, she added wryly, "Call me silly, but I have this niggling feeling that my presence won't be sorely missed at the annual parade."

"Oh, I don't know, Mom." The corner of Elvis' mouth quirked up. "Who the hell is everyone going to talk about if you're not there?"

Ruby and Emma were talking about Elvis.

When he'd walked into the café a moment ago the two women had both looked up and fallen silent, momentarily forsaking the conversation they'd been holding at a table in the corner. They watched him as he stood by the cash register waiting for Bonnie to pour his coffee-to-go. His expression contained its usual austerity as he looked down at the shiny chrome napkin holder on the Formica counter, staring at it with the sort of unfocused intensity that people give objects when they're concentrating on inward thoughts.

Emma found her gaze traveling over him from the top of his thick black hair to the scuffed toes of his cowboy boots. "Have you ever in your life seen a body nicer than that one?" she demanded in a low voice, allowing herself to double check the long length of his back from the immense shoulders that stretched his khaki shirt to the narrow waist and the tight little butt hugged by the worn denim of his jeans. She fanned herself. "I'm tellin' ya, *chère,* there's just somethin' about that man that makes my toes curl."

"Elvis?" Ruby looked at her in surprise. "You think he's *sexy?*"

"Oh, my yes. Don't you?"

"No." Ruby tried to study him objectively but couldn't get past the scar or the prosthesis. "I think he's . . . well, okay, maybe not creepy exactly, but — I don't know — intimidating, I guess."

"What — his size, the scar, the hook — what?"

"Yes." Ruby nodded. "Exactly." She watched him the same way someone else might observe a snake poised to strike, half fascinated, half repelled.

Emma had noticed the same attitude in other islanders. "The way everybody treats that poor man like Leonard the Leper Boy," she said, "it's something of a wonder to me that y'all could bring yourselves to elect him sheriff."

"I don't see where one thing has to do with the other," Ruby retorted, shrugging a pink-uniformed shoulder. "He was some hotshot big-city detective, and Sheriff Bragston trusted him. In my book that qualifies him for the position. On the other hand, his mama practiced the world's oldest profession until *he* himself put a stop to it; I can still remember the days when he used to fight at the drop of a hat; and he's scary looking. I want him to keep my town safe. I don't want to socialize with him."

"But that's so unfair, Ruby." Emma was genuinely puzzled. "He's not responsible for his *maman's* career choices, and he's obviously outgrown the need to settle a situation with his fists. Certainly you don't hold him accountable for the explosion that maimed him, do you?"

Ruby considered her for several silent moments. "It probably is unfair," she finally conceded, "but it's the way I feel, Emma. Partly, I suppose, it's fear. Things don't change rapidly here. Not the way we think; not the way we view things."

"*Oui,* it's a small town; I think I understand what you're sayin'. Except . . . fear, Ruby?"

Both women watched Elvis accept the steaming cardboard cup from Bonnie and dig change out of his front pocket. He said something in a low voice as he extended the money, took a sip of his coffee, and then walked out of the diner. Ruby turned back to Emma.

"Port Flannery isn't a comfortable place to have a different point of view in," she said. "There are certain accepted . . . convictions here. But even if I had any desire to fly in the face of public opinion, Emma, Elvis himself probably wouldn't allow it."

"Oh, come on, now," Emma protested.

"No. I mean it. He has that damn-your-eyes attitude that makes you doubt he'd even trouble himself to meet you halfway."

Emma's wavy hair slid against her cheeks as she shook her head. "Isn't that funny, *chère?* I don't get that impression at all. He seems lonely to me. And he's so gentle with Gra—" She broke off. "Where *is* Gracie?" Her eyes darted around the café, panic rising instantaneously when she didn't immediately spot her baby.

"She's got herself a little fort over there under number seven." Ruby gestured toward the table closest to the kitchen door and Emma sagged back in her seat. Gracie was sitting cross-legged on the floor beneath a table, over which someone — presumably Bonnie — had haphazardly thrown a cook's apron, forming a little private space; and she was quietly singing to herself while she removed rocks and shells from the ever-present sand pail and arranged them around her in patterns on the floor.

"I should probably clear her out of there and straighten that table before your lunch crowd starts arrivin'."

"Oh, don't worry about it, hon. The rush isn't gonna get underway for a good half an hour yet, and that table's always the last to get filled anyway." Ruby got up and wandered to the windows overlooking the square. She pulled back a crisp navy-checked curtain and stared out at something across the common.

Finally she turned away and came back to the table. "You know, Elvis did have the ability at one time to start a lot of engines to humming," she said in a thoughtful voice as she resumed her seat. Chewing the skin around her pinky fingernail, her eyes met Emma's. "I'd forgotten all about that."

"What do you mean?"

"Well, I forgot how handsome he was as a kid. Back when he was in high school." She shrugged. "I mean, I was already married and pregnant with Billy 'n' everything, but this town is *small,* and he was always a reliable source of entertainment. Fact is, with the face he had back then and that build and being so *bad* and all . . . well, let's face it, Emma, that's a combination that's damn near irresistible to your average high-school girl. I bet most of 'em dreamed nightly of dropping their bloomers for that boy, and a high percentage of 'em probably would have, too, at the first encouraging word from him."

Emma grinned. "I'll bet he encouraged like mad." *And good for you, kid,* she thought, recalling the isolation that was imposed on him as an adult. *I hope you got to screw your brains out.*

"No, that's the funny thing. I think it was a rare event when he took anyone up on her offer."

"A high-school boy who willingly passes up the opportunity for sex?" Emma scoffed. "Get outta here."

"He was loaded with pride, even then," Ruby said. "That damn-your-eyes attitude I was talking about?" Her shoulders bunched and fell. "I think the so-called good girls were willing enough to have him roll 'em around under the covers. I imagine what they weren't willing was for him to come knocking at the door and tell daddy he was there to pick up Father's little Princess or Kitten or whoever-the-hell for that night's date."

"And so . . . he denied himself?" Emma shivered. "Man. If he had that kind of control as a *teenager,* can you imagine what he'd be like in bed now?"

"Emma!"

"Well, I'm sorry, Ruby, but as I said, there's just somethin' about that man!"

"To each her own, I guess." Ruby shook her head. "Personally, I just don't see it."

Five

She should burn these damn tapes. Emma hit the eject button on the VCR, pulled the tape out, and put it back with the others in the bag on the shelf. Night after night, compulsive as any alcoholic presented with a full bottle, she found herself viewing the cursed things, and it wasn't healthy.

She *knew* it wasn't healthy. Yet, she couldn't seem to prevent the compulsion that drove her to watch them over and over and *over* again. She kept thinking if only she viewed them often enough, carefully enough, if only she could dissect them frame by frame if necessary, she would finally understand how she had failed to see that a man she had considered to be all that was gentle and good was in actuality a monster of depravity.

Then she could forgive herself for her blind and unquestioning faith in such a man.

Dear God, what a coil.

She could feel the walls closing in on her and looked around wildly. She desperately needed to breathe some fresh air. Going to the window she threw it open, and bracing her hands on the wide sill leaned out and inhaled, dragging the evening air deep into her lungs.

It wasn't enough. *Bon Dieu,* it simply wasn't enough. She had to get out of here, if only for a few minutes. Except — she glanced over at Gracie who slept, with her knees tucked under her and her bottom thrust up, in the middle of the bed — she couldn't leave her daughter unattended.

Minutes later she was knocking on the door of room G across the hall and down a couple from her own. When Elvis opened it and looked down at her inquiringly, she immediately reached out and grasped his bare forearm in both hands.

"Elvis, I'm jumpin' out of my skin," she told him with breathless earnestness, "and I think only you can help me out here."

He felt her nails digging into his skin, looked down and saw her — all flushed skin, imploring eyes, mussed hair, and gorgeous breasts rising and falling in agitation beneath a sapphire ballet top — and went very still beneath her hands.

"I know it's a giant imposition," she rushed to say before he could turn her down flat. "We don't really know each other that well. But, *cher,* the walls are closing in around me and I have *got* to get out for a while. Gracie's sound asleep, though, and I can't leave her unattended. . . ."

Well what'd you think she was gonna say, man, he wondered in self-derision. *Elvis, I'm hornier than a bitch in heat and only you have exactly the right equipment to scratch my itch? Jesus, Donnelly, get a clue before you embarrass yourself.* He extracted his arm from her grasp. "You want me to baby-sit for you?"

"Please." She couldn't read a thing in his expression and her words almost tripped over themselves in her desire to convince him before he refused her request outright. "You don't have to actually *do* anything," she assured him earnestly. "Gracie's a sound sleeper; you could read or watch TV or whatever it is you were doin' here before I interrupted. But, the thing is, she likes you, so she won't be scared if she *should* wake up to find me gone and —"

"Okay."

"— I thought of you right away because she'll be *safe* with you." She broke off. "Okay?"

"Yeah, sure, why not?" Beneath the faded black T-shirt, his wide shoulders rose in a silent shrug. "Just let me grab my book and I'm yours."

Emma snuck a quick peek around his room while he collected a hardbound book, which had been left open and turned facedown on the wide arm of an old overstuffed chair. Marking his place with a finger, he closed the book and turned back to her. "Ready," he said. "You going down to the Anchor?"

"The Anch— ? You mean the *tavern* down on the harbor? No! Oh, *non,* Elvis, I think I have given you the wrong impression, entirely." *Bon Dieu,* what sort of women did he customarily consort with, that he'd automatically assume she'd come racing over here all in a lather to ask him to watch her *bébé* for her while she went out and belted back a few emergency drinks? "It's not excitement or company I'm in need of *cher,*" she assured him, "just a bit of fresh air or open space or something. I thought I'd go sit in that little gazebo on the Green for a while."

Which is exactly what she did, he observed a few moments later as he stood to the side of her window, watching her cross the square and climb the shallow stairs to the gazebo. She sat down and his view was then limited to her lower half. He saw her pull one of her heels up onto the bench and observed her long fingers link together in a grip over her shin. She rhythmically kicked out her free foot.

Turning away, Elvis slowly wandered around the room for a moment, hand and prosthesis tucked palm-out into his rear pockets as he visually inspected the Sandses' effects spread out around the room. They were so . . . girly. . . . Alien to him and exotic, in spite of his having grown up the fatherless only child of a very feminine female. His visual inspection of little-girl stuff and the feminine trappings of a grown woman eventually brought him over to the bed, where he stood looking down at the sleeping baby. A tender smile curved the hard corners of his mouth.

God, she was such a sweet little thing. Just a tiny bump under the smooth expanse of the covers, little butt sticking up and tousled head turned to one side. As he watched, she murmured in her sleep and untucked her arms and legs from beneath her, stretching and turning onto her side. Her thumb crept into her mouth and her lips pursed to suck several times before falling slack. Sliding from her mouth seconds later, the thumb glistened damply in the dim lighting as her fingers loosely curled on the mattress next to her head. Elvis reached out to hesitantly stroke a rough-tipped finger gently over the smooth, sleep-flushed skin of a baby-round cheek. Unnecessarily, he then straightened the blanket, tugging it firmly up over her shoulder.

What had her momma meant when she'd said Gracie would be safe with him? There had seemed to be such emphasis on the word. Was there someone out there somewhere who constituted a threat to the child? Just the thought was enough to make his blood run cold.

He sat down in the ladder-back chair at the tiny table, bumped up the wattage a notch on the lamp hanging overhead, and tried to resume reading. It was a good book, and he'd been enjoying it before Emma Sands had come knocking on his door.

Now he couldn't concentrate worth a damn on the thing.

These two females, with their friendly personalities and the little one's damp kisses and the grown one's beautiful body and a mouth he'd like to *test* for kiss moisture, were starting to wreak all manner of havoc in a life he'd worked very hard to make uneventful. He'd made up his mind to return to this island of his birth, to avoid making any waves this time and to live a nice, quiet, tranquil life. And if he hadn't exactly been greeted with open arms by the people of

Port Flannery, he was at least peacefully co-existing with them. Life was pretty much the way he'd expected it to be, and that was the way he wanted it. No surprises.

So why, he wondered warily, did he have a sudden, uneasy feeling that his days of booking drunks and handing out speeding tickets were numbered?

Emma rested her chin on her updrawn knee and gazed out the open latticework of the gazebo. Officially the full moon wasn't until tomorrow night, but this evening's lunar display was in her opinion every bit as spectacular as any the calendar-sanctioned variety could produce. One really had to look hard to realize tonight's moon was perhaps the tiniest bit asymmetrical, and the meticulously kept town square was illuminated so brightly by the wash of stark white moonlight she could see a penny shining on the grass clear over by the sidewalk.

She breathed deeply of the cool, salt-laden air, exhaled it slowly, and gradually felt most of the tension, which had been making her so jumpy, seep out of her system. This was what she had needed, just a few minutes without walls binding her, without responsibilities.

She tried to think what she should do

next. If she had an ounce of intelligence, she'd pack up Gracie and their few belongings and take off for parts unknown at first light tomorrow. Keep moving; that was the ticket.

Oui. That was undoubtedly the key if she hoped to escape the detection of Grant's goons on a consistent basis. The only thing was, much as she wanted to stay a few steps ahead of the hirelings she was positive he had out searching for her, she didn't want to leave Flannery Island just yet.

And wasn't that funny? It didn't make a bit of sense, when she thought about it. She was a city girl, always had been. She liked bright lights and places that stayed open twenty-four hours a day, even if she no longer harbored any particular burning desire to personally frequent them. She didn't know sweet diddly about small towns. The closest she'd ever come to one before now was in a car, breezing through on her way elsewhere.

On the other hand, a lot had changed since she'd packed what she could, grabbed Gracie, and run. She wasn't exactly the same woman she'd been a month ago. It wasn't until she'd actually spent some time on her own, sitting up late in countless hotel rooms, worrying while her daughter slept, that she'd come to realize how directionless she'd grown these past few years. Except for her responsibility to Gracie, she'd been drifting aimlessly, casually maintaining an association with a crowd that didn't exactly typify the phrase *mature adult*.

Emma realized she was gritting her teeth again and made a conscious effort to loosen them. She inhaled and exhaled a few measured breaths. That was then, not now. She'd grown up, by God; no one could deny her that. She had taken a damn crash course in maturity. She knew her own mind better now, and that made it difficult to deny her feelings. And the fact of the matter was, she liked it here. Although she didn't always agree with the somewhat provincial viewpoints that governed small-town attitudes of people like Ruby, on a personal level she liked the woman very much. She liked Clare. These women had come to seem more real to her than most of the longtime acquaintances who had drifted in and out of her life back home. They had come to seem almost like . . . friends. And that, in all honesty, scared the socks off her. Friendship with her was almost guaranteed to be the kiss of death.

Yet the idea of having a friend again — a real friend, not some flashy here-and-gone playmate — also soothed her. She contemplated the idea for a moment. Then she thought about the work.

It had been coming in fairly steadily since she'd arrived in town, which had saved her from having to dip into the traveler's checks. The financial aspect was without question an important consideration for a woman in her situation. But even more significant was having gainful employment for the first time since Grant had more or less adopted her back when Big Eddy was sent up. Being useful had given her back a sense of purpose she hadn't even realized she'd been missing. She'd allowed Grant to assume fiscal responsibility for her for far too long. And she couldn't even blame him for it, really. It was one thing to have allowed it back when she was a minor, but after she'd graduated from Tulane she had no excuse for not having taken care of herself.

That was water under the bridge, however. The real question was did she remain or did she go? She knew what the pros were for staying. And she understood well the one big con, the chance she took if she didn't keep moving. She wasn't even going to think about her strange attraction to Sheriff Elvis Donnelly. In the final analysis that would have nothing to do with her decision anyway.

Really.

Keeping the earnest assurance firmly in the foreground of her mind, she nevertheless found herself moving quickly back toward her room. Her heart lightened with each step she took, for she had made up her mind. Her choice had in all probability been made before she'd ever begun to consciously mull over her options, but she knew now that she was staying, at least for a while, and it felt . . . liberating.

She burst into the room, smiled brilliantly, and crossed straight over to Elvis, whose head had shot up at her entrance. She grasped his cheeks in both her hands, bent down, and planted a light kiss on his lips. "*Merci beaucoup,*" she whispered, then lowered her head to give him another exuberant peck.

The next thing she knew, she was being yanked down to straddle his lap. His hook flashed with the speed of light to clip into the back belt-loop of her jeans and the rest of the prosthesis pressed her hard against him. His right fist tangled in her hair. It gripped tight and pulled — ripping her mouth away from his.

She stared at him across the short distance that separated them, feeling pushy and foolish, regretting a personality that forever seemed to allow her to do things without first thinking them through. Afraid it would start to quiver and make her look even dumber than she already felt, she sucked in her bottom lip. Elvis made a funny, rumbling sort of sound down deep in his chest and his head flashed forward. Startled, Emma's lip slid free with a little pop as her head reared back. His strong white teeth sank into her bottom lip, capturing it.

Then he just sat there for a moment, breath sawing out of his lungs to gust against her sensitive lips, blazing blue eyes heavy-lidded, arm hard behind her hips, keeping her pressed firmly forward and abruptly aware of his aroused state.

Eyes locked with hers, he scraped his teeth over the sensitized inner membrane of her captured lip and then closed his lips around it and sucked. Softly.

Firmly.

Hard.

A tiny, almost inaudible "Oh!" exploded out of Emma's lungs, and her fingers bit into the hard biceps they'd latched onto when he'd first jerked her off her feet. She scooted forward, tilting her pelvis to align the crotch of her jeans with the faded cloth of his fly where it covered the rigid length of his erection. Her heels caught in the back rungs of the chair she straddled, and she tightened her thighs.

She was a woman given to impulsiveness and such had been the case with the kiss she'd bestowed upon him a moment ago. It had been a whim, a kind of a . . . thank you. For unquestioningly agreeing to sit with Gracie. For being contained and competent. For bringing out a feeling of womanliness in her that she hadn't experienced in a very long time. Thank you's were forgotten, however, as she plastered herself against his chest. Lifting her hand to stroke her fingertips over the raised scar tissue intersecting his cheek, she rubbed her breasts against him and rocked upon his lap. There was an aching throbbing between her legs that dictated her actions. It pulsed insistently with every beat of her heart.

Then abruptly, all that heat was ripped away. The hand stroking Elvis' face was gripped by the wrist in fierce fingers and wrenched away with such force it peeled her upper torso from his chest. The hook through her belt loop yanked, sliding her hips back an inch or two. She found herself sitting upright on his knees, staring down in consternation into a thunderous expression.

"Is that your game, then?" he demanded in a raspy voice. "You're one of those?"

"Hmmm?" She blinked in confusion. "One of whose?"

He shook her, and the expression on his face was beyond definition. There was rage there, certainly. Lust. Repugnance. And . . . hurt? Oh, surely not. "You're one of those women who get off on deformities, right?" His mouth twisted bitterly. "God, I shoulda known you were too good to be true. Well, hey. Ya like the scar, baby, just wait'll ya see what I can do to you with my stump."

Emma's head snapped back as if she'd been jabbed with a cattle prod. Nose wrinkling, lips forming a perfect round *O* of distaste, she stared down at him incredulously, unable to believe he'd actually said such a thing. "That's . . . *mon Dieu,* that is so . . ."

"Accurate?" he supplied. "Dead-on exact?"

"Sick!" She struggled to climb off his lap. Without discernible effort, he held her still.

"Oh, come off it, will ya?" he demanded in low-voiced fury. "You don't have to pretend with me, okay? Christ! Let's at least have a little honesty between us."

"Oh, but *oui,* let us by all means be honest." Shifting abruptly beneath his hold, she snapped, "*Mon Dieu,* you wouldn't know what to do with honesty if it came up and bit you on the butt!" She reared away from him as far as she could, finding it hard to *believe* he'd actually said that. "Let go of me," she demanded stiffly.

He muttered something truly obscene. Then releasing his grip on her, he held his hands wide of his body in an ostentatious show of compliance. He eyed her contemptuously as she rose to her feet. "I thought you would at least be up front about this," he said with cool disdain, looking up at her as she straightened to her full height. "I gotta hand it to you though, doll, you're more subtle than most. Your little fetish isn't as overt as some I've run across." He shook his head. "The kid should have been the real tip-off, though."

Emma went very still. "The kid?" she whispered. Cold sweat trickled down her spine. *"Gracie?"*

"You got another?" he demanded scornfully. "Yes, Gracie. When she was so unaffected by my disfigurements, I should have known right then mine wasn't the first messed-up face or body she'd ever seen. You've fucked around with my kind often enough for her to be comfortable with freaks, I take it."

"You sonofabitch!" Emma swung out

wildly, slapping at his head. "You goddam, *twisted* sonofa—"

Elvis grabbed for her hands, capturing and then transferring them to his one good hand. His fingers closed around her wrists and gave them a hard jerk, yanking her back down on his knees. "Knock it the hell off," he said through his teeth. "If you think I'm gonna just sit here and let you hit me, sister, you've got another think comin'. I could throw your butt in jail for assaulting an officer — *goddam it!*"

She'd butted her head into his throat. Before he recovered from that blow, she butted him in the chin with such force his teeth clashed together with an audible click. Shit! If his tongue had been between them it would have been hamburger.

Unfortunately for Emma, his hard jawbone connecting with the top of her head also came close to knocking her out. For a second her vision went dark except for the bright explosions of color that interspersed blackness with glorious pyrotechnics. Elvis apparently wasn't taking any chances, however, for his hook tangled in her hair and roughly jerked her head back until her neck arched under the strain. Nausea swelled in her throat, tears streamed from her eyes; but her voice was low and steady as she stared him straight in the eyes.

"You can slander me till hell freezes over, Sheriff," she said through gritted teeth. "But you keep your filthy tongue off my *bébé* or I swear I'll make you rue the day you were evah born." The nausea was abating and she took a deep breath, glaring at him with cold distaste. "Gracie likes you — God only knows why," she said, furious. "It sure as hell can't be for your sunny personality, but she *likes* you. If you do anything, anything at all to hurt her, Mr. Donnelly, I will kill you."

She was eight inches shorter than he, probably weighed less than half as much, and he had her practically hog-tied. Accordingly, it should have been a ludicrous threat.

It wasn't. He believed her implicitly. Unlocking his hook, he let her hair slide free.

Looking at her, Elvis realized he'd made a huge error in judgment. She was seriously offended, not because she'd been called to account for a perversion that she'd just as soon not admit to, but because she couldn't comprehend such a thing in the first place and he'd accused her — accused her *child* — for Christ's sake, of . . .

Ah, shit. What was he supposed to say? He wasn't accustomed to being in the wrong; usually he was the one *being* wronged. Besides, there was no valid excuse he could offer. It was just . . . when he'd felt her rubbing herself all over him like the answer to his hottest fantasy and she'd reached up to stroke his scar like it was some goddam talisman . . . well, he'd gone a little nuts, is all. He'd overreacted.

In his own defense, he had run into a couple of women like that before, women who got off on scars, on amputations, the more bizarre the disfigurement the better. Encounters like that weren't something one ever forgot. The things those women had wanted him to do had left him feeling hollow and vaguely ill, and when he had thought Emma . . . "I'm sorry," he said belatedly.

And apparently inadequately. Emma stared at him, sucking on her bottom lip. God, he wished she wouldn't do that; it drove him crazy. He could sit on his hormones forever if he had to, though. What he really wanted was her esteem back. Her normally warm brown eyes were cool and distant. For the first time since he'd originally seen her in Bill's garage, there wasn't an iota of friendliness in them when she looked at him. He hadn't realized just how much he'd valued her warm approbation until it was taken away.

She couldn't even be bothered to rail at him anymore. "Let go of me," was all she said, but her tone was cool, tinged with distaste. It was as if she had simply written him off.

He released her and she rose to her feet, promptly stepping back out of his reach. Ah, man, this wasn't right; this was all screwed up. He had to try to make her understand: "Emma, listen, I'm —"

"Mommy?"

They both froze. Then, as one, they turned to face the bed.

Gracie was struggling to sit up beneath the constricting blankets. She yawned and knuckled her tangled, baby-fine blond curls away from sleep-flushed cheeks.

Emma was across the room in a flash, bending over her daughter. "Hey, angel pie," she murmured. "What are you doin' awake?"

"Heard sumpin', *Maman.*" She spotted Elvis over her mother's shoulder. "Hi, Shewiff."

"Hiya, kid."

"I'm fwee, you know," she said and gave him a sleepy smile. Without protest she allowed her mother to tuck her back down into her nest of blankets. Rolling onto her stomach, she drew her knees up beneath her, tucked in her arms, and within seconds was sound asleep again.

"Why does she keep telling me that?" Elvis asked in bewilderment, watching Emma helplessly as she marched over to the door and pointedly held it open.

"Because she just turned three last month and she's proud of it," Emma replied coolly, and then added stiffly, "thank you for watching her for me."

"Emma, I'm really sor—"

"Good night, Sheriff."

"Listen, please, I'd like to explain —"

"Good night."

Then he was somehow on the other side of the door and it was being firmly shut in his face. Shit! He stared at the sturdy old portal in dismay. How the *hell* had everything gotten so far out of his control?

Grant Woodard glanced up from his work when the intercom buzzed, eyeing the telephone with barely suppressed irritation. Thumping down his index finger to mark his place on the spreadsheets he was perusing, he jabbed the button down with a free finger. "Yes, Rosa," he said.

"I'm sorry to intrude, Mr. Woodard," she said with the same calm efficiency she bestowed upon everything she did. "But you did say you wanted to hear from Mr. Hackett the minute he called."

Grant snapped upright. "Yes, I did."

"He's on line two, sir."

"Thank you, Rosa." The words were barely out of his mouth before he cut her off by punching down and activating the second line on his phone. "What have you got for me, Hackett?" he demanded. "Have you found her yet?"

"Yeah, I think I have. I can't be a hundred percent certain until I check it out for myself, sir, but there's a small town called Port Flannery on a little island in Washington State, and I'm pretty sure that's where she is. I thought it best to check in with you first, though, boss, to see how you want it handled before I go to the island. Given the size of the town there's always the possibility she'll hear of my interest, and I don't want to spook her into running."

Grant stared at the portrait of Emma and Gracie that stood in an elaborate gold frame on the corner of his desk. "Do you think you can verify her location without alerting her?"

"Yes. It shouldn't be a problem as long as I take my time and don't make direct inquiries. But what do I do once I've located her, sir? If she's there, do you want me to bring her home?"

"No. Not yet." Grant tapped his pen impatiently against the glossy desktop. "I have to give this some careful consideration. Merely verify her location, Hackett. The minute you're sure where she is, check in with me again."

"So. I bet you're Emma Sands, huh? I'm Nadine Donnelly. Mother to our good sheriff."

Emma looked up from her steaming latte and the *Seattle Post Intelligencer* that traveled to Flannery Island on the 6:45 ferry every morning. There was a woman standing next to the table, smiling crookedly down at her. With her bright, youth-conscious clothing, bouffant, long dark hair, and flashing blue eyes, she at first glance appeared to be about forty years old. It was only upon closer inspection that one surmised she was probably closer to fifty. But a *young* fifty. The woman was either exceptionally well maintained or she must have been barely out of her adolescence when she'd had Elvis.

Elvis. Oh, God. Emma could feel her cheeks heating and she sat up straighter. She wouldn't blush. Dammit, she would not blush. It hadn't even been a real kiss, for pity's sake.

As rationalizations went, that one was

nothing short of ridiculous, and she damn near snorted aloud. *Oh, right, Missy. Like the way you rubbed yourself all over the man doesn't really count because he didn't actually* kiss *you. And what sort of a mother are you to forget yourself like that with Gracie right in the room?* She cleared her throat. "Yes, ma'am," she acknowledged. "And this is my daughter Gracie." Gracie, however, was no longer in her seat when Emma turned to present her. Emma made a face. "Well, she's around here somewhere."

"Here I am, *Maman!*" Gracie climbed out from under the table and clambered onto her chair. She plunked her sand pail down on the tabletop with a gritty rattle of shells and rocks. "Hi!" she said to her personal idea of heaven, a brand new audience. "I'm Gwacie Sands and I'm fwee years owd . . ."

"Please," Nadine interrupted her, looking at Emma, "don't ma'am me. Just call me Nadine." Then she looked at Gracie. "Sorry, doll. I didn't mean to cut you off. Mind if I sit down?" she inquired of Emma.

"Uh, please."

"So, you're three, huh?" she said cheerfully, apparently not finding it the least bit difficult to bounce her conversations between the two females as she pulled out a chair and plopped down in it. She studied Gracie. "That's old enough for an Elvis doll, I do believe."

"I yike dolls." Gracie tipped her head to one side, eyes bright and inquisitive as she regarded her brand-new acquaintance. "What's an Elbis?"

"Why Elvis Presley, hon. The King." When Gracie continued to smile and blink at her with blank incomprehension, Nadine exclaimed, "Don't tell me you've never heard of him!" The look she gave Emma was remonstrative. "This child's education has been sorely neglected."

Emma smiled crookedly and shrugged a shoulder in a gesture typically Cajun French. "*Mais oui*, what can I say?"

Nadine shook her head to hear such heretic flippancy and then turned her undivided attention to Gracie. "Elvis Presley was the King of Rock and Roll, baby," she told the toddler solemnly. "He shaped the sound of music as we know it today. But then" — she sighed — "I'm afraid he died a premature and tragic death." She looked up at Emma. "I'm leaving on the fourth of July for Memphis," she said. "My friend and me are goin' to see some of the countryside and then, of course, go to Graceland. Unfortunately it's impossible for us to be there to pay tribute at the memorial."

"The mem . . . ?" *Don't ask.* "That's too bad, Mrs. Donnelly; I'm sure it's a disappointment. But the rest of the trip sounds like it should be very, um, rewarding." Inhaling the light, distinctive scent that imbued the air around Nadine, Emma turned to Gracie. "Mrs. Donnelly is the sheriff's *maman,* angel."

"I know, I hewd." Gracie stood up on her chair and launched herself at her mother. Arms clinging in a chokehold around Emma's neck, she gave her a wet, smacking kiss on the cheek. "This is *my maman!*"

"Please, Emma," Nadine insisted, "not Mrs. Donnelly, not *ma'am.* Just Nadine."

"Mom?"

Both women looked up to see Elvis striding to their table, staring at them incredulously as if wondering what the hell Nadine was doing there talking to Emma.

Which was precisely what he *was* doing. Emma had that slightly glazed look that said clearer than billboards on the highway that his mother had been running on about Elvis Presley again. God Almighty, if it wasn't one damn thing it was —

"Oh, hi, Elvis, honey. I was just telling little Gracie here about the King. She'd never *heard* of him; can you imagine?"

Still clinging to her mother's neck with one arm, Gracie dug her heels into Emma's thighs and swung around until she was perpendicular to her mother's torso. She leaned against Emma's breasts and bounced in place a couple times. "Hi, Shewiff! Your *maman* say you the King of Wocky Woads!"

There was an instant of silence. Then Elvis broke into a huge, spontaneous grin. Plucking Gracie out of Emma's arms, he swept her up and executed a little two-step in front of the table. He was wearing worn cowboy boots and planting one underslung heel on the floor, he spun them around. Clutching at his shoulders, Gracie squealed with laughter and Elvis laughed with her.

Across the room at table five Ruby's coffeepot hung suspended in the middle of pouring refills for two housewives, the steaming stream of coffee cut off midstream as all three stared with open mouths at their local sheriff. Two farmers over at the counter lowered their forks and also gawked.

Emma felt as if she'd just been slugged in the stomach. She'd already sort of figured out that she might have overreacted last night. From things he'd said at the time, which she had thought about once she'd cooled down, she had come to realize he'd obviously had experiences in his life that were entirely beyond her realm of comprehension. And so, perhaps he had reason, or at least something of an excuse, for being so suspicious of her motives. She'd therefore already been predisposed to give him the benefit of the doubt when next she saw him. They might never be the best of friends, she'd decided, but they could at least be civil to one another.

She hadn't envisioned anything like *this,* though, and seeing him laughing and dancing with her daughter just about nailed her to her seat.

"Oh, no, Gracie honey," Nadine was saying, her fingers all aflutter, "you've got it all wrong. My Elvis is *named* for the King, honey. The *King* is Elvis Presley, not Elvis Donnelly, see? And he's the King of Rock and *Roll,* not —"

"Oh, give it a rest, Mom," Elvis said. "She's three years old, for Christ's sake. She doesn't give a rip."

Gracie beamed up at him. "I'm fwee, you know."

He smiled down at her tenderly. "Yeah, sweetheart, I do know that. You're a real big girl."

Emma watched them helplessly. Oh God, Oh God, what was she going to do? She could *not* fall in love. Her life was already too crazy as it was.

Six

"I've located her, boss."

Hackett's announcement caused Grant to set his scotch and water down on the armrest of his leather chair and sit up straight, both feet hitting the floor. "Give me the layout," he commanded. Tapping his ring in an impatient tattoo against the chunky crystal highball glass still in his grip, he listened intently to his man relate the details of Emma and Gracie's life in Port Flannery.

Except for the chime of the ring against the rim of his glass, there was an instant of silence when Hackett's recitation came to an end. The man on the other end of the line cleared his throat, and Grant said in brusque warning, "I'm thinking."

"Yes, sir."

Grant sat silently for a few more moments. Then he leaned back in his chair and reached out a foot to hook the ottoman, which he had shoved away at the other man's announcement. He took a sip of his drink then set the glass down on the end table. "All right," he said, "to begin with, this is what I have in mind." He talked at length. "What do you think?" he finally said. "Is it possible?"

"It'll depend on two factors," Hackett replied. "Let me look into them."

"You do that. Then get right back to me."

Gracie was in an agony of impatience. Clutching her little American Flag in one hand and her mother's hand in the other, she danced in place at the curb, leaning out every two seconds to look up the street. "Stawt now, *Maman?*"

"Any minute, angel pie." They could hear the high-school band tuning up somewhere around the bend and Gracie fidgeted harder. The adults around them responded to Emma's wry expression with commiserating smiles.

The sidewalks that lined the waterfront and wound their way up the hill to the square were filling rapidly. Emma hadn't realized so many people lived on Flannery Island, but it seemed that not only was the community more vastly populated than she'd imagined, the entire population was gathered today in front of Mackey's General Store right along with her and Gracie.

She'd tried to talk Gracie into watching the annual Port Flannery Fourth of July parade from their room window, as the square directly below was where it all culminated, but Gracie had seen the gathering crowd; knew she looked good in her little navy sailor dress, white lace tights, and red patent leather Mary Janes; and campaigned vigorously to join the throng. As her daughter was jostled into the street by the crowd that swelled behind them on the sidewalk, however, Emma began to question the wisdom of caving in to a three-year-old's demands.

"Oh, jeez, I'm sorry," apologized the young woman who had nudged Gracie off the curb, and along with Emma helped the toddler back up onto the sidewalk. "Somebody bumped me and I lost my balance. You're Gracie, aren't ya?" she demanded, stooping down and brushing nonexistent dust from the pleated front of Gracie's dress. She glanced up at Emma. "I'm Mary Kelly, Mrs. Sands," she said. "Ruby's daughter."

"Why, how nice to meet you, *chère!*" Emma laughed with relief and felt a bit foolish. *For pity's sake, Em, get a grip,* she warned herself. *It's a small town parade, not Vice Central.* She was allowing the events of the past six weeks to color her judgment, and that was obviously making her paranoid.

"I'm Gwacie," Gracie piped up. "I'm fwee!"

"Yeah, I've heard rumors to that effect," Mary replied. Grinning, she straightened the hem of Gracie's dress over the stiff little petticoat beneath. "What a pretty dress you have on."

"Pwetty," Gracie agreed, looking down at her apparel in satisfaction. "You yike my wed shoes?"

"She *loves* to dress up," Emma confided. "I was such a tomboy when I was a kid, it always startles me I could have given birth to someone so feminine."

Mary stared at the tall blonde in wonder. To her eyes, Emma Sands was all that was feminine. She looked like a model to her, from the sophisticated chin-length wavy bob, to the simplicity of her stark white T-shirt with its three-quarter-length sleeves pushed up to her elbows and the wide, lacy cut-work panel encircling its V-neck, to the pleated olive-drab shorts and white Keds she wore. Between her looks and that accented voice she seemed wonderfully exotic and cosmopolitan, worlds removed from dinky little Port Flannery.

"When do y'all get summer around here?" Emma wanted to know. "Back in N'Awlins it'd be swelterin' by now, but here it's so cool."

"Yeah." Mary snorted. "That's the Pacific Northwest for ya."

"Actually, I kind of like it," Emma confessed. "Being able to sleep at night with the window open is great, and it's so nice to breathe real air. Summers in the South are so sticky that from June until about the end of September it's rare to suck anything into your lungs that hasn't been conditioned to within an inch of its life."

"At least you have a summer," Mary said, but then she shrugged. "Now that the Fourth's here, though, we should be gettin' ours any day now, too."

With only a couple of discordant notes, the band struck up a rousing Sousa march and began militarily stepping up the street. Gracie squealed with excitement and craned her neck to see. Afraid she'd rush out into the street for a better view, Emma swooped down and scooped her up, settling her astride her shoulders. She held her daughter's ankles in her hands while Gracie clutched fistfuls of her hair and bobbed up and down in excitement. Feeling the narrow doweling of the little flag they'd purchased from the veteran in front of the VFW hall dig into her scalp, Emma reached up to tweak it a little higher in Gracie's grip. She felt Mary's eyes on her and grinned down at her. Giving her a friendly little bump with her hip, she said, "This is Gracie's first parade. I guess it shows, huh?"

A drum and bugle corps followed the marching band, and Gracie clapped so hard for the synchronized high-stepping girls, with their white-tasseled boots and swingy short skirts, that she dropped her flag. Mary retrieved it for her.

The drum and bugle corps was followed by the Independence Day Princess and her court, each young woman seated atop the back seat of a brand-new convertible with the name of the island Buick dealership on the door. They turned slowly from side to side, smiling Beauty Queen smiles and waving that parade-royalty hand rock, and Gracie was completely enthralled, particularly with the princess, a dimpled brunette who wore an elaborate rhinestone tiara and rode in her white satin evening gown atop a bright red car.

Then came the clowns. Emma fully expected Gracie to be as delighted by them as she'd been by everything else she'd seen that day, and she did enjoy them until one came right up to her. He only wanted to present her with a piece of candy, but he got too close. Emma wasn't sure if it was the make up, the fright wig, or what, but he ended up scaring Gracie half to death.

She screamed in terror, shrinking away from the painted face and frantically clutching her mother's hair in little fists. Emma swung her down off her shoulders and into her arms, where she held and comforted her. But her daughter refused to be consoled. She kept her face buried in Emma's throat, clinging to her neck with desperately strong little arms and continuing to sob. Finally, Emma looked over the top of her head at Mary and shrugged a shoulder. "I'm going to take her into Mackey's and get her an ice-cream cone," she said. "If you'd like to come along with us, Mary, I'll buy you one, too." Then the cacophony around them caught her attention. "*Mais* no," she exclaimed, "what am I thinkin'? You came here to see the parade, and it's probably not even half over yet."

Mary snorted. "Who cares? I've seen every parade Port Flannery's ever put on since the day I was *born.* I'll take an ice cream cone any old day." It wasn't the promise of ice cream that drew Mary; it was her fascination with this exotic off-islander and her baby. She cleared a path for them toward the storefront.

It was warm and quiet inside the store and Gracie started to relax almost immediately in Emma's arms. Her hysterical crying ceased, only an occasional shuddery little sob whispering out of her throat as she lay quietly against her mother's breasts. Pegging it a case of overexcitement, Emma rubbed her daughter's back as she strode to the back of the store where the old-fashioned soda fountain was located. There, to her surprise, she found Elvis Donnelly and Sam Mackey seated on padded red leatherette stools, drinking coffee together and talking to each other with the ease of longtime friendship.

"Well, hey," she said, sliding onto a stool herself and settling Gracie. "Y'all are friends, huh? I didn't know you two even knew each other." Given the size of the island, not to mention the brief time she'd been on it, it was probably an asinine thing to say. But . . . the local bad boy turned sheriff and the respectable store owner? It wasn't one of those natural friendships that automatically leaped to mind.

"Everybody knows everybody in this burg," Mary commented as she took the stool next to Emma's.

"That's the truth," Sam agreed. "But me and Elvis know each other especially well. We go *way* back, don't we E?"

A small smile tipped up the corners of Elvis' mouth. "We ate paste together in

Mrs. Olsen's kindergarten," he agreed.

Sam laughed. "Yeah, we did, didn't we? And he was best man at my wedding to Clare."

"Mon Dieu, you're Clare's *husband?"* Emma demanded, incredulous, and then felt like a perfect idiot the minute the question left her lips. *Oh, smooth, Emma Terese,* she berated herself, *very smooth.* She'd seen this guy around, of course; she knew he was a Mackey. It was just . . . well, she'd also seen Clare working with him, and her friend treated him more like a . . . a brother or something other than a lover. "I-I . . ." Emma swallowed dryly, wondering how to extricate her foot out of her mouth with a modicum of grace. She stroked Gracie's hair, more for her own comfort than her daughter's. Taking a deep breath, she blew it out.

"I'm sorry, *cher,*" she said to Sam. "That must have sounded incredibly rude. Don't ask me why, but I was under the impression you were Clare's brother-in-law."

"Nope. You're looking at the sole surviving Mackey male." He stood up, all easy masculine grace, and walked around behind the fountain. Her assumption was a direct hit, but his expression didn't show it. "What can I get you ladies?"

"Three cones, please. I'll take French vanilla; Mary'll have . . ." She raised a brow at Mary.

"Chocolate Ripple."

". . . Chocolate Ripple, and Gracie'll have . . . Hmmm, let me see." She looked down at Gracie's dress and then up at Sam again, cocking an eyebrow. "Got anything in navy blue?"

Gracie pulled her thumb out of her mouth. "Want stwawbewwy, *Maman,*" she murmured into Emma's chest.

"Okay, strawberry it is. Make ours a single scoop. Give Mary as many as she can handle." Mary held up two fingers.

Emma settled Gracie more comfortably, and subtly presenting the remaining customer at the fountain with a cold shoulder, swiveled her stool around to make casual conversation with Mary.

She tried to ignore the fact that she was deliberately ignoring Elvis; it felt too much like junior high school. She'd never been a particularly shy woman, but she was about as self-conscious as she could get every time she thought of how she'd rubbed herself all over him up in her room last week. Piled on top of that were memories of the way she'd felt when he'd danced Gracie around the café. She wanted to be cool and indifferent — desperately she wanted that. *This* behavior was too darned adolescent for words. Unfortunately, coolness and indifference were difficult attitudes to maintain. It was all she could do these days just to meet his gaze.

And Elvis wasn't playing the game — apparently he wasn't in the mood to be ignored. He climbed off his stool and came over to squeeze himself between her perch and the empty one next to it. Leaning an elbow on the countertop, his hips braced against the edge of the stool and his long legs stretched out, he was too big and too close for comfort as he stared down at her.

Knowing she could no longer pretend he wasn't there without looking foolish in the extreme, Emma aimed a cool social smile somewhere in the vicinity of the Coca-Cola sign over his left shoulder. "Sheriff," she acknowledged.

"Emma," he retorted, and then demanded, "what's the matter with Baby Beans?"

Emma met his eyes reluctantly. "She was frightened by a clown."

Gracie swiveled her face around and peeked up at Elvis, the first time she'd come up for air since her mother had carried her into the store. "Didn't yike him," she told the sheriff.

"No? Was he a scary guy?"

"Uh huh." Perking up, she wriggled and Emma shifted her so she sat sideways in her lap. Gracie peered up at the large man. "How come you call me Baby Beans?"

Elvis looked startled. "I don't know. There was a doll named that when I was a kid. All the girls seemed to have them. It looked like you."

" 'Kay." She accepted the explanation easily, impatient to tell him the really big news. "I getta ice cweam befo' yunch," she informed him.

His blue eyes focused on her. "Yeah? That's pretty neat."

"Pwetty neat," she agreed. "Mommy said I could."

"What the heck, life's uncertain," Emma said with a wry smile and a tiny shrug. "Eat dessert first."

Elvis watched with solemn concentration as her mouth formed the words and then slowly licked his lips. Emma couldn't tear her eyes away; she felt nailed in place by the sudden rush of heat that surged through her veins.

"Here you go, ladies," Sam said cheerfully, breaking the spell. "One Chocolate Ripple, two scoops" — he passed it over the counter to Mary — "one strawberry, one scoop —"

"How come *Mawy* gets two ice cweams and Gwacie ownny gets one?" Gracie's expression was full of indignation as she craned her head around to stare up into her mother's face.

"Because Mary won't end up wearing her second scoop on her pretty dress," Emma said calmly and then added with absolute firmness before her daughter's indignation had a chance to escalate, "Gracie will get no scoops at all if she tries to make a big deal outta this. When you're a big girl like Mary you can have two scoops, too."

Bottom lip stuck out sulkily, Gracie looked up at her mother for a long, silent moment. Finally she said, "Wanna sit with Shewiff now." It was the closest she dared to come to rebellion, knowing from past experience that her mother would follow through on her threat in a red-hot minute if she persisted. She held her arms up to Elvis.

Emma looked at Elvis' crisply ironed khaki shirt and fresh jeans. Before she could protest, however, that his uniform would not benefit from an almost certain soiling by strawberry ice cream, he'd lifted her daughter out of her lap, parked his buns more firmly on the stool he'd been leaning them against, and plunked Gracie down in his lap. He pulled a stack of napkins from the dispenser and shook one out, wrapping it around the base of the cone Sam handed him for the little girl. "Strawberry, huh?"

She looked up at him solemnly. "It's my fave-wit. You wanna lick?"

"Thanks, Gracie. I'd like one very much."

"Don't eat the big stwawbewwy, though," she cautioned him, using both hands to hold the cone up to his mouth. "Thaz mine."

Staring at Emma over her daughter's head, Elvis opened his mouth and lapped his tongue in one strong, slow motion around the cone from the base of the ice cream up to its very tip. His gaze dropped to her breasts, and his cheeks flexed as he sucked in the little swirl his tongue had created. Then his heavy lids rose again, locking his gaze back onto hers. "Good," he said in a husky voice.

Emma had to fight the sudden desire to tip her scoop of French vanilla right off her cone and into the neckline of her top to cool herself down. She took a savage bite out of the ice cream, feeling flushed all over and tight and achy in spots that hadn't received attention in more than three years. Damn him; what did he think he was playing at here? Deliberately, she swiveled around to face Mary, giving him her back.

She was wrung out by the time Gracie finally finished her cone and they were able to leave. When Elvis Donnelly did not want to be disregarded, then he just plain was *not* disregarded. It seemed as though every time Gracie asked him a question — and Gracie being Gracie, she asked a million of them — he would answer her as best he could, but would then say, "But I could be wrong, sweetheart. What do you suppose your Momma has to say about that?"

Knowing darn good and well that Gracie would immediately demand Emma's opinion and she'd be forced to turn around and deal with him once again.

She finally made her escape and, with Mary accompanying her and Gracie, went back to the boarding house. She visited with the Kellys for a few moments before excusing herself to take Gracie upstairs to clean her up — although she had to grudgingly admit that Elvis had done every bit as good a job as she would have in keeping her daughter halfway presentable. He must have gone through a good-sized stack of napkins.

They caught the tail end of the parade, watching it wind down from their room.

Then it was time for lunch. The ice cream hadn't been that long ago, but Gracie's cheeks were starting to fly red flags — a sure sign of fatigue — and Emma wanted her fed with something a little more substantial than sugar and fat before she put her down for her nap. They went downstairs and staked claim to a table before the café filled up with the post parade crowd.

Gracie wandered off as she always did once the meal was finished and Emma dawdled over a cup of coffee, thumbing through a newspaper that someone had left on the table. She visited with Ruby for several moments when the café owner brought the pot over to her table to freshen her coffee, and finally she pushed back from the table. Smiling, she looked around for her daughter. A nice long nap was certainly indicated. Then Gracie would be bearable for the fireworks this evening.

"Come on, angel pie," she said, bending to look under the table. "Time to go."

Gracie wasn't there.

She looked over to table seven, the one by the kitchen door that was always the last to be filled. Gracie wasn't there either. Her smile fading, she pushed to her feet, her eyes searching out every nook and cranny in Ruby's café.

Seven

Elvis was pecking out a report on the computer keyboard, using his right index finger and the eraser end of a pencil held clamped in his hook, when Emma burst into the sheriff's office. His first reaction when he looked up to see her bearing down on him, sans Gracie, was that she was coming to give him hell for playing games with her this morning.

He straightened, his blood running a little faster. He'd had fun messing with her earlier, a circumstance so rare these days as to seem almost alien. The brief opportunity to tease Emma at Sam's fountain had given him a feel-good rush; it had been exhilarating. Not too many occasions to participate in any sort of male-female sexual contests had presented themselves since he'd become disfigured nearly two years ago. He'd forgotten how aware of a woman you could get, how exciting it could be. One look at Emma's face, however, was enough to tell him she didn't share his excitement.

A closer look made him forget about male-female games altogether, and he surged to his feet. He was around the desk, through the open doorway, and standing in front of her before she got half-way across the room. "What?" he demanded. "What is it?"

"Gracie's gone." She stopped and looked up at him. She'd been desperately trying to hold herself together ever since she'd first realized her baby was nowhere in the café or boarding house. Telling herself to hang on, that she had to be strong, somewhere in the back of her mind had been the belief that if she could just get to Elvis he'd bring her daughter safely back to her. Seeing his solid bulk and calm expression now, tears rose in her eyes and her bottom lip lost its firmness.

Gracie was gone? Elvis felt as if someone had just slugged him in the gut. He watched Emma as she sucked her quivering lip into her mouth and brutally clamped her teeth down on it, clearly struggling for control. "She's —"

"*Missing.* Oh, God, Elvis, I've looked all over the boarding house, I tore the café apart, and I can't find her anywhere." She grabbed his forearm with both her hands, her fingers digging in just above the spot where warm flesh gave way to cool plastic. Tears spilled over her bottom lashes as she gripped him tightly. *"Please,"* she beseeched him. "You've got to find her for me."

"I will." Extricating his arm, he put his hand under her elbow to usher her over to his work station. "I will, Emma. Come on over to my desk. I'm going to need some information —"

The next thing he knew she'd torn herself away and was staring up at him in anguished betrayal, like a pup who'd expected to have its stomach scratched and had found itself brutally kicked instead. And like a wounded animal, her pain caused her to lash out blindly. "I don't need a papershuffler," she snarled, staring at him with bitter eyes. She wrapped her arms around herself in a puny attempt to stem the shakes that were beginning to make her quake from the bone on out. "Damn you, Sheriff, my *bébé* is *missing!*" On the ragged edge of hysteria, each word grew louder, shriller, as it left her mouth. "I don't have time to fill out forms and dot *i*'s and cross *t*'s; I need someone who will help me go out and *look* for her."

Jesus, such pain. "That's enough now; shhh." He tugged her trembling, resistant form into his arms, and when she would have pushed him away held her firmly. His good hand came up to stroke her hair, and he bent his head to speak with no-nonsense firmness directly into her ear. "Hush, now, Emma, stop it. We're not going to fill out forms and we aren't going to shuffle papers. I just need a little information to give me a place to start. Then I *am* going to find Gracie for you."

She stood in the circle of his arms, quivering and panting raggedly as the incipient hysteria slowly faded. A little bit at a time his strength and warmth began to penetrate the red fog engulfing her; the subtle scents of clean man and laundered cotton began to soothe. Finally, drawing a deep breath, she held it a moment, released it in a slow, shuddering sigh, and then nodded against his chest. "Okay," she said hoarsely. "*Oui.* All right." She pulled back slightly and looked up at him, eyes awash, bottom lip quivering, chin wobbly. "I'm sorry, Elvis."

"No." He brought his hand around to swipe at the tears on her face. Using his thumb to wipe them briskly from her left cheek and then whisking his finger down her right cheekbone as if he were brushing away crumbs, he looked down at her with the unsmiling directness she'd come to expect from him and said forcefully, "You haven't got a thing to apologize for, you hear me? Your little girl is missing, and you're scared to death. But we're going to find her, Em. I promise you, nobody in this office will rest until we've found her for you." *One way or another,* his professional alter ego qualified.

Her brown eyes were enormous as her gaze locked with his. She stared up at him a moment before she swallowed, nodded, and then professed in a heartfelt whisper, "Oh, *Dieu,* I love you."

Elvis' heart slammed up against the wall of his chest, even though he knew perfectly well that she was responding solely to his oath to deliver her baby, safe and sound, back into her arms. The arm that was still wrapped loosely around her waist involuntarily squeezed her, but almost immediately he was setting her loose and taking a step backward. "Come on over here and have a seat," he instructed her briskly. "I need you to tell me what the circumstances were when you first noticed Gracie missing." Escorting her over to his desk, he pulled out a chair.

"Sandy," he directed the dispatcher who had been watching the drama unfold with unabashed interest, "put in a call for Ben. Unless he's right in the middle of a shootout, tell him to drop whatever he's doing and shag his butt on back here. Call George at home, too, and tell him his day off has been canceled. Then see if you can rustle up a cup of coffee for Mrs. Sands."

"Gotcha." She set to with efficient purpose.

Elvis turned back to Emma. "Okay, tell me everything," he said briskly, so she related her routine, telling him how Gracie played in the café for a while each day after their meal was finished.

She managed to maintain a grasp on her composure when she went on to relate how on this day, when she'd expected Gracie to be in the café when she'd finished her coffee, her daughter was nowhere to be found.

"Did you look up in your room?"

"*Oui*, of course. As soon as we realized she wasn't in the café, Ruby and Bonnie pitched in to help me look. But Gracie hadn't gone into the kitchen and she hadn't gone up to our room." Emma shoved her fingers through her hair, and holding it off her face, stared across the desk at the large sheriff. "Even if she had, Elvis, she wouldn't have been able to get in. I'm not accustomed to this small-town habit of leaving doors unlatched; it's just second nature to lock them behind me." Dropping her hand back to her lap, she blew out a breath. "So we went floor to floor then, calling. And I checked out in the back lot, where I've worked on the cars. *S'il vous plaît.*" Her lip started to tremble again as she stared at him imploringly. "Can't we go out and look for her now?"

He knew she'd probably be in hysterics again if he didn't keep her occupied and moving, so he stood up, pulled his gun out of the drawer and holstered it, gathered his keys, and without thinking held out his hook to her. "Come on."

She latched onto the proffered prosthesis as if it were a lifeline and allowed him to pull her to her feet. When she showed no inclination to release him, he gently extricated himself and led her to the door. Pausing by the dispatcher's desk, he said, "Have Ben and George split the square between 'em. Instruct them to talk to as many people as possible; somebody has to have seen her. Mrs. Sands and I are going to start with the waterfront. I'll be in and out of the Suburban, Sandy, so keep trying me on the radio if you have need to reach me."

"You got it." Sandy turned to Emma, extending a steaming mug. "Here, Mrs. Sands," she said. "Take this with you. And try not to make yourself sick with worry. We're gonna find your baby."

But they didn't. Emma and Elvis scoured the beach on which Gracie had collected shells; they talked to people on the waterfront and went into every business along the harbor, up to and including the tavern that would never allow a three-year-old past its doors. Emma listened to Elvis talk to his deputies on the car radio. As she watched the digital clock on the dashboard tick inexorably forward, she grew colder and colder, hope increasingly difficult to hang onto. Where was her baby?

Oh, God, where was she?

"You might as well go on home and get yourselves ready for the fireworks," Sam Mackey said to his two employees at four o'clock. "Things are pretty dead around here, so I'm going to lock up early."

In the wake of their departure, he flipped the Open sign on the door to read Closed, twisted the lock, and turned back to the register to cash out the till.

He couldn't stop thinking about Emma Sands' face when she'd been in with Elvis earlier to inquire about her little girl. She had tried so valiantly to hold herself together, but he'd never in his life seen such public fear and naked pain. He wondered if Gracie had been found yet. Knowing only too well what it was to lose a child, there was a rawness in his gut, and he prayed she had been.

This was a quiet island; they didn't get the kind of crimes committed in the big cities —

by psychotics. Oh, sure, drugs and alcohol abounded — he sometimes thought substance abuse was more prevalent on this small island than in its urban counterparts, especially among the young, because aside from the old movie theater and the occasional dance or bingo night at the VFW hall there wasn't much organized entertainment to speak of. And where the boredom factor is high, booze and recreational drug use tend to flourish. But the crimes that occurred on Flannery Island from overindulgence in such substances tended to be vehicular in nature or acts of aggression against property and/or domestic partners. They'd had no pedophile snatch a little girl out from under her mother's nose.

Or they hadn't until now.

He knew it wasn't fair to make comparisons, yet he couldn't seem to avoid doing so during the brief drive home. Navigating the country roads by rote, he contrasted Emma's flagrant distress with the way Clare had shut down emotionally when they'd lost Evan. God, he wished Clare had worn even a *tenth* of her ragged emotions on her sleeve the way Emma Sands did, instead of burying everything she felt so deep inside of herself it had become virtually impossible to reach her. Perhaps then they could have propped each other up in their time of need and grieved together . . .

Perhaps then he could have prevented her from slipping away from him.

He'd try talking to her again tonight, he vowed as he pulled into the circular driveway and shut off the engine. He'd seen glimpses of the old Clare reemerge every now and then in the past few weeks, and it gave him hope that she was at long last coming out of her deep depression. He was determined to persist until he got her back, even if it meant digging and poking and prying. He missed his wife.

He heard the light patter of footsteps against tile as he tossed his keys in the bowl on the entryway table, and smiling, he turned to greet his wife.

The sight that greeted him caused his smile to congeal in place. His heart surged against the wall of his chest and then seemed to stop dead. When it commenced beating once again it was with a sick, irregular rhythm. Sweat beaded his forehead and upper lip. *Oh, Jesus, Clare,* he thought despairingly, *what have you done?*

"Hi, Mis-too Mackey," Gracie Sands said, looking up at him. "You know when my *maman's* gonna come pick me up?"

* * *

The radio in the department Suburban crackled. "We found her, Elvis! Tell Mrs. Sands her baby is at Sam and Clare Mackey's and she's fine."

A strangled laugh erupted out of Emma's throat. Two seconds later she burst into tears. Elvis picked up the handset and held down the send button. "Thanks, Sandy," he said into the receiver. "We're heading over there now." Hanging the handset back up, he reached across to briefly grip Emma's leg just above the knee. "You okay?"

"Um." She wrestled her emotions into submission until she had them under a measure of control and then straightened up. Twisting in her seat to face the sheriff, she scrubbed at her cheeks with the back of her wrist. "*Oui,* I'm fine. Ah, *Dieu,* Elvis, I was so scared something horrible had happened to her." Plunging both hands into her hair, she held it off her face while she stared at him with haunted eyes. "I don't think I could have handled it if she'd been hurt. Not her, too. Gracie's the only thing in my life that's worth a —" Hands dropping to her lap, she forced her eyes away. *Good Lord, missy, get a grip. He doesn't want to hear your woes.*

But it was difficult. Suddenly, uncharacteristically, she wanted nothing so much as to unburden her troubles all over Elvis Donnelly's broad shoulders.

Within moments they had emerged from a long wooded drive onto the windswept bluff that played host to the Mackey residence. Emma was out of the car almost before it came to a complete halt. She didn't notice the rich wood architecture of the house as she raced for the front door. Neither did she see, when Clare opened it, the magnificent view, which usually drew amazed comment from first-time visitors, through the expanse of sparkling glass that looked out over the Sound. "Where is she?" she demanded.

"Upstairs in Evan's old room. But, wait Emma, before you —"

She was interrupted by Emma's fierce hug. "Thank you! *Mon Dieu,* Clare, *merci beaucoup* from the bottom of my heart. You, more than any other person in the world, can probably appreciate how scared I was. Where did you find her?"

"That's what I want to talk to you —"

This time it was Sam who interrupted. "Let's all go into the living room," he suggested. "Emma, can I get you a cup of coffee?"

"No, thank you, Sam." She gave him a blindingly white smile. "My stomach's produced so much acid this afternoon I don't dare add to it. I just need a minute to get myself together before I see Gracie."

"How 'bout you, Elvis?"

If Emma hadn't caught on to the underlying tension in Clare and Sam's manner, Elvis had. "No," he said shortly and grasped Emma's elbow, marching her over to one of the couches. Seating them both, he looked up at Sam. "All right, what gives, Sam? Where was Gracie found?"

Clare's nerves jangled. No one was going to believe her. Sam didn't.

Oh, he hadn't called her a liar to her face or anything, but his tone had been too controlled, too gentle, to be anything but an attempt to keep the crazy lady from flipping out where she stood. She took a deep breath and said. "I didn't find Gracie anywhere. She was . . . uh, delivered to me."

Emma's frenetic gaiety dissolved. She felt very cold all of a sudden. "Delivered?" Aware of Sam staring at her, she spared him a puzzled glance before her full attention returned to Clare. "What does that mean, exactly? Delivered by whom?"

Clare swallowed but met Emma's eyes straight on. "You."

Emma erupted to her feet. "Are you out of your damn mind? I've been going out of my *head,* terrified to the depth of my soul that my *bébé* was hurt or maybe even *dead,* and you're sitting here saying . . . ?" She swallowed the rest of her words, swamped with an abrupt, sickening sense that she was brushing up against a mind gone off kilter.

She wondered in anguish what it was about her that drew this sort of madness into her life time and time again. Did she possess some inbred magnet for trouble? She used to believe she must be sort of a . . . a Typhoid Mary, or something, because it seemed everyone she'd ever cared deeply about ended up dying on her. Big Eddy had; Charlie had. *Then* she'd discovered that the one person she had felt it was safe to care about wasn't the man she'd thought he was at all. Now this. Had she run from everything she'd ever known, fleeing one abnormal personality only to run smack-dab into another?

"I'm not saying I saw you personally," Clare said. "Gracie just knocked at my door. But I saw your car, Emma! There's not another one like it on the whole island. And I could see that someone with your streaky blond hair was driving it." Clare hugged herself and tried not to let her protestations of innocence slip into hysterics. Already she could see it on Emma's face:

like Sam, she thought Clare was in the midst of a psychotic episode, that she'd stolen someone else's child to take the place of her dead son.

After all the strides she had made in recent weeks, it was just so damn unfair.

Then she remembered Gracie. "And Gracie *said* you wanted me to look after her. Ask her yourself." Shaking, she stared in torment at the tall woman who had begun to mean so much to her. "Emma, why are you doing this to me?"

Moving up behind her, Sam gripped her arms in his warm hands. Clare wanted badly to lean back against him, longed more than anything else in the world to accept his comfort. She was afraid, however, that it was being offered simply to stave off a case of incipient hysterics. She stood stiffly within his embrace.

"Why am *I* doing this?" Emma lunged forward, beside herself with fury and fully prepared to rip Clare Mackey's hair out by the roots. Before she could reach her objective, however, Elvis reached out and jerked her back against him, pinning her to his hard chest by the simple expedient of clamping his left arm with its prosthesis diagonally across her upper torso and his good arm around her waist.

"Let's get Gracie down here," he said with cool authority, looking across the short distance that separated the furious woman in his arms from Sam and his wife.

His own feelings about Clare were mixed, and had been since Evan's death. From the time his best friend had started dating her, Clare had accepted Elvis, simply and without fuss, as Sam's friend. Never once had she judged him the way almost everyone else on this island did, and for years he had flat-out loved her for that. Then, when he'd returned to the island after the explosion, she was one of the few women who hadn't all but puked to see his disfigurement. But — and he knew it wasn't his place to feel this way, wasn't even any of his *business* — as sorry as he'd been about the pain of her loss this past year, he'd resented her for the way she'd cut Sam out of her life when her husband had needed her following Evan's death. He'd had to stand by and watch her break his best friend's heart when Sam was already suffering unbearable heartbreak, and more than once he'd wanted to shake her silly until he made her see what she was doing to Sam.

As for this situation, he didn't know *what* to make of it.

Elvis got the two women seated while

Sam went upstairs to fetch Gracie. A few moments later they all turned toward the entryway when the sound of little feet running across the tile floor broke the tense silence. Gracie burst into the room and ran straight to her mother, flinging her sturdy little body onto Emma's lap. "Hi, *Maman!* You miss me?"

A choked laugh exploded deep in Emma's throat and she buried her face in her daughter's soft curls, breathing in the familiar, comforting scent of baby shampoo. She had to concentrate hard just to prevent herself from crushing Gracie to her chest. "Yeah, um, you could say that, *oui,*" she agreed.

"I was stawtin' to miss you, too. But Miss-us Mackey let me play with Ebben's things. He was her little boy, but he dieded."

"I know," Emma said gently, and she brushed Gracie's fine hair away from her forehead. "Did you take your nap today, angel pie?"

"Uh huh. In Ebben's bed."

Sam stared at Clare. She never talked about Evan if she could help it. Yet she'd apparently talked about him quite a bit to Gracie Sands. And as far as he knew this was the first time anyone had been invited to cross the threshold to Evan's old room since the day their son had died, let alone been invited to sleep in his bed and play with his toys. Sam sat down next to his wife and took one of her trembling hands in his.

"Gracie," Elvis said, and she looked away from her mother's face for the first time since she'd run into the room.

"Hi, Shewiff," she said. "Did you come with my Mommy to pick me up?"

"Yeah. I thought you might like a ride in the police cruiser. First, though, your momma's got a question she wants to ask you."

" 'Kay." She looked back at Emma.

"This is kind of important, *chère,*" Emma said, careful to keep her voice easy. "How did you get here this afternoon?"

Gracie opened her mouth to reply, but then closed it once again. She shifted on her mother's lap, her eyes roaming the room. Finally she glanced up at Emma's face and then away again and said, "In a caw."

"Uh huh. And who drove the car, Grace Melina?"

Gracie peeked up at Clare, and then her gaze fell back to her hands in her lap. "Miss-us Mackey," she whispered.

"No," Clare said in a strangled voice. "I didn't!"

"Why are you lying, Gracie?" Sam asked

sternly, and Gracie's lower lip started to quiver.

"All right, that's quite enough." Emma rose to her feet, her daughter held protectively in her arms. "Sheriff, will you take us home, please?"

"Dammit, I want to get to the bottom of this," Sam said before Elvis could reply.

Emma whirled to face him in a cold rage. "Oh, I think the bottom has been reached," she snapped, drawing herself up to her full height and staring him straight in the eyes. "*Mon Dieu,* if you really want to do something useful, get your wife some help." Turning on her heel, she strode from the room and from there straight out of the house, slamming the heavy entry door behind her.

Elvis joined her moments later. Unlike Emma, he wasn't satisfied that all the questions had been fully addressed. But he took one look at her closed expression and Gracie's tremulous little chin and decided they could wait for a while. It had been an extremely emotional day and discretion truly was the better part of valor sometimes. Particularly if he wanted to actually get somewhere with his inquiries. Nothing is quite so fierce and bloodthirsty as a mother mammal who perceives her young to be endangered.

It was a short, silent ride back to town. During it, Emma began to lose some of her knee-jerk, adrenaline-fed defensiveness. Something not quite right was going on. She glanced down at Gracie who was acting so uncharacteristically clingy that Emma had ended up strapping the seat belt over both of them. Her daughter was too quiet.

"Did you see all the stuff Elvis has in this big ol' car, angel pie?" she murmured into her daughter's ear. "I swear he's got more gadgets than a gourmet kitchen."

Gracie didn't so much as glance at the interior. She kept her arms locked around her mother's neck and her head buried in the hollow of Emma's throat, and this behavior aroused Emma's suspicions. Ordinarily she could count on her daughter to chat up a storm, to ask a hundred and one questions about all the law-enforcement equipment that bristled in such abundance in the Suburban. When she considered that Gracie didn't even realize she'd been missing, Emma had to wonder why she was so subdued. Could it be that her child was guilty of some major transgression?

"Pull around back," she requested quietly when they neared the town square. Clare's story was just too cock-and-bull, too . . . *lame.* Emma knew her to be an intelligent woman; so why hadn't she at least made up something that had a fighting chance of being believed? Unless perhaps *she* believed what she was saying.

It was completely beyond Emma at this point to recall whether her car had been in the parking lot earlier when she'd searched for Gracie. She imagined it *must* have been, or its absence would have been glaringly obvious. The truth was, however, she had been so beside herself with fear for her daughter's safety, conceivably she might not have noticed a Sherman tank if one had been parked in the back lot.

She didn't know exactly what it was she expected to see when Elvis pulled the Suburban into a space in the boarding house parking lot, but her car was exactly where she'd left it. With Gracie still clinging to her front like a barnacle to a rock, she climbed out of the police cruiser and walked up to her vehicle. Pulling off the protective cover she used to keep off the weather, she tried the doors, bent and peered in the windows, walked around to study the Chevrolet from all angles and finally stood back, consumed with fury all over again.

"*Dieu,* what a chump I am," she muttered in self-disgust.

"Yeah?" Elvis' voice, coming from directly behind her, made her jump. "Why is that?"

"Because I began to wonder . . ." She cut herself off, shaking her head impatiently. "But, no, I have to be realistic about this. Who would go to such elaborate lengths to steal my car? And *why*, for pity's sake? *Bon Dieu,* I can't believe I'm letting myself get sucked into this! Clearly Clare's able to effect that tremulous, why-don't-you-believe-me air of . . . of . . ." She struggled for the right words. ". . . helpless victimization because she *believes* her own delusions. It's just . . ." Emma looked at him helplessly and shrugged.

"You wanted to believe her."

"*Yes.* Damn it anyhow."

"And what about what Baby Beans here said?" he asked, looking at the back of Gracie's head, which was all he could see since she had not come up for air from the moment Emma had first climbed into the department Suburban with her. "Is this only about wanting to give Clare the benefit of the doubt, Emma, or are you picking up something as a mother that makes you doubt the veracity of what she told us?"

Emma's brown eyes flared with outrage,

but she struggled to tamp down her defensiveness. It was a legitimate question. "Elvis, I honest-to-God don't know what I think at this point, okay?" She hiked Gracie higher up in her hold and ran a hand wearily through her wavy hair. All her limbs felt leaden. "Please. Let me give this some thought," she requested. "And I really do need to talk to . . ." She tilted her chin at Gracie significantly. "Alone. The minute I know something concrete though, *cher,* I'll call you. I promise."

He studied them both for a moment, the child who was so quiescent in her mother's arms, the woman whose characteristic passion was notably subdued as she looked back at him with tired, apathetic eyes. He nodded decisively. "Yeah, all right."

All the starch left Emma's spine. "Thank you," she said. Then, fervently, "God, Elvis, *merci beaucoup* for *everything*." Unexpected tears welled up in her eyes, and she determinedly blinked them away. She reached a hand out to grip his warm forearm. "I honestly don't know how I would have gotten through this afternoon without you," she admitted tremulously.

"Just doin' my job, ma'am." Knowing a reciprocal display of emotion would probably kick the last slat out from under her shakily shored-up poise, he kept his tone deliberately light to give her a chance to pull herself back together.

Which she did with the pluck he'd come to expect from her. "Well, if that's true," she ultimately said, "then this town is luckier than it can possibly know to have such a dedicated professional at its service." She squeezed the arm beneath her hand and then stood on tiptoe to impulsively plant a brief, hard kiss on his mouth. "Thank you."

She was almost through the back door when Elvis' voice halted her. "Emma."

Stroking Gracie's back with her free hand, she turned to face him.

"If you really want to thank me," he began, and then had to bite back the raunchy suggestion that flashed through his mind. He cleared his throat. "Please," he said aloud. "Don't talk about the particulars of this afternoon until we know exactly what's going on, okay?" He saw her open her mouth and rushed on before she could utter what he feared would be a refusal. "Listen, I know everyone's going to want to know where Gracie was found, but for now could you just say the Mackeys found her and let it go at that? Please."

"All right." Emma nodded her head decisively. "For now."

"That's all I'm asking. Thank you."

She nodded again. Then she melted through the doorway and closed the door behind her.

Eight

Elvis was back out at Sam and Clare's house fifteen minutes after he'd left Emma, knocking on the door. "We need to talk," he said as soon as Clare opened it.

She stood back and held the door open, then trailed him as he strode past her into the living room. Sam walked in from the kitchen, a bottle of nonalcoholic beer in his hand. "Hey," he said neutrally. "Wanna Clausthaler?"

Elvis looked at his friend's unsmiling face. "Yeah. That'd be good."

Sam was back with one in only moments. Clare sat stiffly upright on the couch while he handed Elvis the condensation-dappled bottle. Then he took a seat on the cushions next to her.

Elvis took a pull, then lowered the bottle and regarded Clare solemnly. "I'd like to hear what you have to say about today's events," he said. "Start from when Gracie showed up, and tell me everything you can remember."

"She wasn't lying, Elvis; if that's what you're thinkin'. And she's not delusional, either." Sam's tone was flat, his expression set; and his body language suggested a preparedness to argue his wife's innocence into the night if necessary.

Clare's head swung around and she looked at him in openmouthed surprise.

"Did I suggest either of those things, Sam?" In contrast to his friend's rigid posture, the belligerent crossing of arms over his chest, Elvis sat forward with his forearms propped on his thighs, his beer bottle dangling between his spread legs.

"You're here, aren'tcha? Why aren't you at the boarding house cross-examining the brat?"

"Sam!" Clare admonished, astounded at his attack. "That's enough, now. Please. Don't call her that."

"Jesus, Sam," Elvis said in wonderment, "she's three years old. What do you suggest I do, get out the bright lights and rubber hose?"

"Works for me," Sam retorted. Then he turned to his wife. "Why are you defending her? You put her down in Evan's bed, let her play with his toys. You took care of her. And she turned around and stabbed you in the back for your trouble."

"She's just a little girl, Sammy." Clare rubbed her hand up and down his rigid arm in an attempt to soothe his agitation. "You make her sound like a conniving Lolita. She was confused, that's all."

"Or she was coached," Elvis added, and had the immediate attention of both people. "Or," he said with unsmiling equanimity, "she was telling the truth. Sit down, Sam," he ordered when his friend, fists clenched, surged to his feet. Then he turned his attention to Clare. He looked her squarely in the eyes. "To determine just what the hell did go on here today, I need all the facts. I'd like you to tell me your version of what happened."

"The doorbell rang, about one o'clock I guess it was," Clare said. She kept her eyes level and on Elvis, concentrating on presenting the facts calmly. The last thing she wanted was to come across as wild-eyed and crazy. "Gracie was on my doorstep, and she was all by herself. That surprised me, because I've never seen Emma let her get more than maybe ten or twelve feet away from her before. But there's no mistaking the Sandses' car, Elvis, and it was parked right at the top of the driveway's U, on the bluff side. It was pointed away from the house, toward the drive, and a woman with streaky blond hair like Emma's was in the driver's seat, watching the child in the rearview mirror. Gracie said her *maman* wanted to know if I could watch her for a few hours, and when I waved at Emma to indicate it was all right, she waved back and drove off."

Elvis had spent years developing radar for when people were lying, and his instincts told him Clare was telling the truth. At least she believed what she was saying.

He had a small problem with her tale, however. Emma had been in his office shortly after one o'clock that afternoon, too soon to have allowed her to get back to town, cover her car, and hightail it over to the sheriff's office — and that was even supposing *she* had told a flagrant lie, which could too easily be verified, concerning the time she'd spent searching the boarding house and café before she'd reported Gracie missing to him. So where did that leave Clare?

If she was delusional then she'd firmly believe every word she was uttering, which would explain her convincing narration. It was possible, he supposed . . . but it didn't feel right. Her descent into such behavior seemed too abrupt, and it didn't fit with what he knew of Clare. So, what did that leave except an even more unlikely scenario?

Christ.

"Did Gracie act strangely while she was here?" he asked.

"No, not really. I think at first it was an adventure for her, and she was excitable. After her nap she was a little anxious for Emma's return, but the truth is, Elvis, I don't think they've been separated very often, so I didn't think much of it. She's really a sweetie, and it doesn't take a lot to entertain her."

Sam snorted and Clare turned to him in exasperation. "For heaven's sake, Sam!" she declared. "I appreciate your defense — believe me, I do — but the way you're acting you'd think that little girl was some Machiavellian schemer plotting my downfall."

"Humph," was all he said, which was a nonanswer at best, but Clare knew him well enough to realize it meant that was *exactly* what he thought and he wasn't going to change his mind, but neither would he argue with her about it any further. *Damn!* He could be so incredibly stubborn sometimes.

Incongruously, the thought cheered her up.

The doorbell rang and Clare rose. "I'll get it," she said, grateful for the opportunity to have a second's reprieve from the almost palpable intensity in her living room.

Elvis watched his friend with interest while she went to answer the door. He'd never seen Sam so adamantly opposed to someone so unthreatening as Gracie Sands. He wondered what the story was. There had to be more to it than thinking a child who wasn't even out of babyhood had lied.

They could hear the swish of the front door opening, and then both men sat bolt upright upon hearing Emma Sands say firmly, "Gracie has something she'd like to say to you, Clare. Don't you Gracie?"

Then Gracie spoke, her voice tremulous and full of tears, without its usual happy strength. "I'm sowwy, Miss-us Mackey."

There was a pause, followed by Emma's stern command, "And? Just sayin' you're sorry is not enough, Grace Melina. Go on and tell her the rest."

"I toad a lie," the little girl whispered.

Emma had hoped to take Gracie straight to their room without encountering anyone when Elvis had dropped them off, but they'd been spotted going into the back hallway of the boarding house and before she knew it a crowd had surrounded them.

"You found her! Oh, praise be! Where was she?"

Voices asking essentially the same questions overlapped each other. If Emma had been one hundred percent certain she was in possession of all the facts regarding this bizarre and trying day, she might have indulged in a satisfying little fit of self-righteous character assassination. For about ten seconds she was tempted to malign Clare Mackey anyway. It wasn't merely her promise to Elvis that held her back. It was the knowledge there were simply too many unanswered questions.

The press of bodies and the loud voices vying for answers caused Gracie to burrow her head in the crook between Emma's neck and shoulder, and to tighten her hold around her mother's neck. Emma hugged her closer and stroked her daughter's hair. "It's been an emotional day," she said softly, glancing at each person briefly before addressing herself to Ruby. "Please. It's just too complicated to go into right now. Suffice it to say that Gracie is all right."

"And thank God for that," Ruby murmured as she patted the back of Gracie's head. She transferred the contact to Emma's cheek in a fleeting caress. Then her hand dropped to her side and her voice turned brisk. "All right, people, come on now, let's give these girls some air. We'll get all the juicy details later. Bonnie, move back, hon; Bud, get outta the way. Let 'em through."

"Thanks, Ruby." Emma gave her a grateful smile. Then her glance swiftly encompassed everyone. "*Merci* to all of you. I know y'all were concerned for us, and I appreciate it." She slipped through the opening Ruby had forged and escaped up the stairs.

Even in the familiar surroundings of their room, Gracie stuck close to her, and the misgivings that had plagued Emma in the car came surging back to the forefront. When she was nearly tripped up for the third time by little arms thrown around her legs, she picked Gracie up and sat down in a chair with the child on her lap. "Did anyone do anything to hurt you this afternoon?" she queried her softly, pushing her daughter's soft blond curls off her forehead.

Gracie shook her head.

"Remember how we talked about bad touches? Did anyone touch you today in any place where they shouldn't have?"

"No."

The breath left Emma's lungs and she sagged where she sat. *Oh, thank God.* She could deal with just about anything else. "Are you hungry, honey?"

Big brown eyes gazed up into hers. "A yittle bit."

"Well, I'll tell you what. Why don't we drive out to the Dairy Freeze and get a hamburger?" It was Gracie's favorite island eatery in lieu of the woeful lack of a McDonald's. By eating there they'd escape the dinner crowd in the café and avoid a lot of well-meaning but impossible-to-answer questions.

Ten minutes later they had cleaned up and snuck down the back stairway. Out in the parking lot, Emma pulled off the Chevy's cover, folded it haphazardly, and threw it in the trunk. She unlocked the passenger door and held it open while Gracie climbed up onto the bench seat and then into her toddler's safety seat. Then she closed the door and walked around to the driver's side. Sliding in, she stuck the keys in the ignition, tossed her purse on the seat, and reached over to hook her daughter's seat belt. It was then that something, which had been tickling her consciousness since the first rush of air had left the car, finally sank in. Midway through the buckle-up procedure her hand slowed and then ultimately stilled.

There was a lingering scent in the air, a perfumelike aroma that clung to the upholstery and teased at Emma's senses. She thought she discerned something familiar about it, something she should recognize, as if it were a scent she had recently smelled. She couldn't for the life of her pin it down, but one thing she did know for certain, it was most definitely not her own scent. She looked at Gracie and saw her shooting guilty glances at her, at the interior of the car, out the windshield.

Emma's hands dropped to her lap and she turned to face her daughter squarely. "All right, Grace Melina," she said in her best I-mean-business tone. "I want to know what the heck has been going on around here today, and I want to know it *now!*"

Clare looked down at the unhappy little girl standing on her threshold and then at the child's mother. Stepping back, she held the door open wider. "Come in," she said. Sweet relief began to rush through her veins.

"I'd like to add my apologies to Gracie's," Emma said as they stepped into the foyer. "I should have . . ." Her voice trailed into silence. What? What should she have done? She refused to be a hypocrite. Given the circumstances and the information she'd been given at the time, if she had it to do all over again she would most likely end up making the same mistake. Shrugging, she reiterated with what she knew was wretched inadequacy, "I'm sorry, Clare."

And she was, sincerely. But when it came right down to it, she now had a much, much larger problem on her hands.

Gracie shrank back against her mother's legs, and Emma looked past Clare to see Sam and Elvis walk into the foyer. Clare, following Gracie's stricken glance, looked over her own shoulder, and with a smile turned to face the men. "Gracie and Emma came back to set the record straight," she told them. "Gracie said she didn't tell the whole truth earlier."

Sam glared at the child trying to hide behind her mother's legs. "Somebody oughtta blister your butt for you, little girl," he snapped.

Gracie's already shaky composure dissolved entirely. She was accustomed to people liking her, not snarling and glaring at her as if they'd like nothing better than to turn her over their knees. Now she was in trouble all over the place and this had turned out to be one rotten day altogether. She dissolved into tears.

"Mommy awweady blistooed it!" she sobbed. She didn't understand; what had she done that was so wrong? Well, okay, she shouldn't have done the thing that *Maman* was always warning her against; but the lady hadn't really been a *stranger,* and she had only said what she'd been *told* to say, after all. . . .

"Samuel," Clare remonstrated with gentle disapproval, but Elvis' voice overrode hers.

"Jesus, Sam, why don't you go yank the wings off a couple of butterflies while you're at it," he said in disgust and stooped down in his swift and graceful way to pluck Gracie away from Emma's legs and up onto his prosthesis. As he surged to his feet, her little arms wrapped around his strong neck and she clung, her back moving visibly from the force of her sobs. "Hush, baby," he crooned, cupping his big hand around the back of her head and pressing her face into his neck while he glared at his friend. "It's okay now. Shhh, shhh, shhh, sweetheart. You're okay."

Emma felt a rush of warmth at his quick defense of her daughter, but she couldn't give herself time to savor it. Steeling herself, she turned her attention to Sam, eyeing him coolly. "Perhaps you'd be interested in hearin' *why* she said what she did, Mistah Mackey," she said neutrally. She truly tried not to let his attitude toward Gracie make her resentful, but it was difficult; she tended to get protective and defensive where her daughter was concerned. Oh, she didn't defend her blindly; she knew her *bébé* had wreaked a lot of havoc today. She also knew that the real responsibility didn't lie with Gracie.

Sam felt the condemnation of the three adults in the foyer, saw the misery that manifested itself in a tiny girl's pitiful sobs, and was torn between defensiveness and shame.

Shame won. Oh, hell. He was making Gracie the scapegoat for his own guilt. He never should have believed, upon first hearing Clare's story that she had lost all perspective and gone out and kidnapped Emma's daughter. It tore him up that only when he'd heard how she had shared bits of Evan with the child had he begun to question his immediate assumption of her guilt. Ramming his fingers through his hair, he looked helplessly at Gracie's shaking back, then transferred his gaze to her mother. "Yeah, I would," he admitted.

Emma took a deep breath and let it out. Very well, then. This was when matters might get a little dicey. "Gracie, tell everyone who took you for a ride in *Maman's* car today."

Gracie's tears had been abating under the calming comfort of Elvis' warm arms and soothing voice. She gulped the remainder back and sighed a deep, shuddering sigh. "Don't wanna, *Maman*."

"I know you don't, angel pie, but you have to all the same. You did something bad to Clare today when you lied about her driving you to her house, and she deserves to know why you said what you did. Now tell everybody who brought you here."

Gracie was afraid to look up into the face of the man who was holding her. "Shewiff Elbis' *maman,*" she said.

"What?" Elvis nearly dropped her. His eyes flashing around to lock his gaze on Emma's, he protested, "That's not possible. My mom was on a flight —"

"Ah, boy, here we go again," Sam muttered in disgust. "Does this kid even *know* how to tell the truth?"

Emma's control snapped. "Shut up, Sam," she snarled. Then she clamped a lid on her temper, pulling her composure together by sheer force of will. "Come here, *bébé,*" she said softly to Gracie, lifting her out of Elvis' slackened hold. Plunking her on her hip, she looked at Clare, who of the three adults was the only one not regarding her and Gracie with some degree of skepticism or outright disbelief. "Do you think we could go sit down a minute?" she asked.

"This is kind of a long story, and I'm exhausted."

"Yes, of course. Come on into the living room." By this point Clare wasn't finding anything too fantastical to believe. She was just happy they knew she wasn't going crazy.

Emma collapsed on the couch and turned Gracie on her lap so the child faced the room. She wrapped her arms around her daughter. Then, dividing her glance coolly between the two men, she said, "I would imagine there are steps that can be taken to check on Gracie's story. For instance, couldn't the airline be queried to see if Nadine was actually on her flight?" With a gentle finger beneath her daughter's chin, Emma tipped Gracie's face up and around until their eyes met. "I want you to tell the sheriff and Mr. and Mrs. Mackey everything that happened this afternoon, *chérie*. And I'll thank you," she said, leveling a look at Sam, "to reserve your snide comments until she's finished." Turning to Elvis, she demanded, "Do you believe *I* was involved in Gracie's disappearance today?"

"No," he promptly replied, and Emma relaxed muscles she hadn't even realized she was clenching. "No, I don't," he reiterated. "According to the timetable Clare gave me, that wouldn't have been possible."

Emma faced Sam again. "Then you might want to consider this. Somehow my daughter ended up at your house this afternoon. One way or another, while I was running around town, scared to the very pit of my soul that she'd been harmed or killed, this was her ultimate destination. And she didn't get here by herself."

Sam rolled his shoulders. "Yeah, okay; you're right. I'm sorry."

Emma looked down at Gracie. Gently disengaging her daughter's thumb from her mouth, she said, "Tell them what you told me, *chérie.*"

"Do I haffa?"

"Yes, *ma petite ange*, you do."

Gracie took a deep breath and let it out in a gusty sigh. "Miss-us Don'lee did this to me at the westawant," she said, and concentrating on getting it just right demonstrated by holding down three fingers with her thumb and crooking the remaining index finger at them in a beckoning manner. Relaxing her concentration, she looked up to see the sheriff and Mrs. Mackey looking at her with interest. Even Mr. Mackey didn't look so angry anymore. Gracie perked up, as there was nothing she enjoyed quite so much as a captive audience. "She sayed

Mommy want me to help hoo play a twick." She gave them an innocent smile. "I yike twicks."

"I like tricks, too," Elvis said. "But before we get to that, where were you in the café?"

"Undoo the table."

"And where was my mother when she beckoned to you?" His *mother.* Elvis felt ill. There had to be some mistake here.

"Outside the doe. In that hall."

Elvis took that to mean the hallway that led to the rooms upstairs and the parking lot out back. "What kind of trick did she want you to play, Gracie?"

"We pwetended she was *Maman.* She dwove *Maman's* caw and putted on hair yike my Mommy's 'n' evweething. It was funny." She smiled in remembrance, and then recalled, too, the song with the comical words that the lady had sung when they were driving down the road. " 'You ain't nuffin but a hound dawg,' " she said happily.

Elvis' stomach dropped. Convincing as Gracie's story was, until that moment he'd been striving to assure himself that, for whatever reason, she was making it up.

The Elvis Presley lyrics blew that fantasy straight to hell and gone.

Dammit, Mom, just what the hell are you mixed up in? Looking up, he saw that Sam was slowly straightening in his seat. They made eye contact, and Elvis saw the knowledge of Nadine's culpability reflected in Sam's gaze. But, sweet Jesus, *why?* Why the hell would she do such a thing? She had to have known that eventually she'd be found out. It didn't make a damn bit of sense.

"Why did you tell your mama that *I* brought you to my house, Gracie?" Clare inquired softly.

Gracie squirmed in Emma's lap. This was what had earned her a spanking — or at least she thought it was. It was either for lying or for talking to a stranger. "Miss-us Don'lee say I was s'posta." She checked out Clare's reaction closely. Finding that she didn't seem angry, Gracie continued more confidently, "She say when ennybody ask me, I say Miss-us Mackey dwived me. Haffa say *Miss-us Mackey,* don' foeget. It's pawta the twick."

Sam surged to his feet and Gracie flinched. Like a direct hit with a rock, it stopped him dead. She was *afraid* of him. *Jesus, Mackey, good going.* He'd been a father, for Christ's sake; he knew how impressionable little kids were, how easily manipulated. They just naturally strove to please the adults around them. But that hadn't stopped him from jumping down her throat. Damn Nadine anyhow; she had a lot to answer for.

But she was by no means the only one. He crouched in front of Gracie. Thumb creeping into her mouth, the child pressed her head back against Emma's breasts and regarded him with wary eyes.

"I said some mean things to you," he said solemnly.

"Uh huh." Plainly, she agreed.

"Do you know why?"

Gracie thought about it a minute. "*Maman* say you was angwy with me 'cause I toad a lie about Miss-us Mackey," she finally replied cautiously.

"Yeah, I was. But I see now that you were just trying to do what you were instructed to do."

Gracie removed her thumb and eyed him with a mixture of suspicion and interest. "What's that mean, instwucted?"

"Coached. Told. You answered the way Nadine — Mrs. Donnelly — told you to answer."

"Oui!" Gracie's head bobbed in emphatic agreement. Somebody finally understood! Everything had been handled quite satisfactorily as far as she was concerned, and she

tilted her head back to beam up at Emma. "Eat now, *Maman?* I'm hungwy."

Emma returned the smile and slid to the edge of the couch, preparatory to rising. "We were on our way to grab a burger," she explained, "when I smelled perfume in my car and knew someone had been in it. After I challenged Gracie over the driver's identity and realized we had falsely accused Clare, we came straight out here instead." She climbed to her feet and swung Gracie onto her hip.

It was over now. All taken care of, the loose ends neatly tied up. The knowledge left her curiously leaden.

Elvis reached out to halt her, placing a hand on her arm. "I still have a lot of unanswered questions, Emma," he said.

It was such a little thing, that touch. It wasn't as if he were kissing her or even slinging an arm around her shoulders in a companionable hug; he was simply detaining her. Considering its impact on her, however he might as well have been making love to her, and it nearly broke her heart.

For she knew what she had to do, and that meant the end of whatever potential lingered between her and Elvis. "I'm sure your questions can wait until after we've eaten, though, can't they?" she managed to say with creditable coolness. How could he argue with hunger? And by the time he expected her back, she and Gracie would have cleaned out their room and traveled miles down the road.

Clare rose to her feet. "Listen, why don't I fix us some dinner right here?" she suggested. "It won't take a moment to throw something together and I think we could all stand to have something on our stomachs."

Emma turned startled eyes on her. "Oh, no, *chère,* really," she started to protest, but Elvis didn't even look in Clare's direction when he overrode Emma to say, "good idea, Clare. Sam, why don't you give her a hand?" His words drew Emma's attention back to him; the sheer intensity of his will effortlessly kept it there.

Gracie wriggled, wanting to be let down, and Emma used her daughter's action as an excuse to free her arm from Elvis' grip. She stepped back, still aware for several long moments of a lingering warmth where his touch had been. She had to resist a childish urge to rub the spot.

"Gracie," Elvis suddenly said, still refusing to take his eyes off Emma. "Just how did my mother unlock your momma's car?

How did she turn on the ignition?"

Gracie's look suggested that was a ridiculous question. But she good-naturedly supplied an answer. "With a key, of course, silly."

Nine

Elvis looked into Gracie's shining little face for a moment. He glanced at Emma, blew out a breath, and turned his attention back to Gracie. "Go tell Clare and Sam I said they need your help fixing supper," he instructed her. Gracie didn't even hesitate; she immediately skipped off to the kitchen to do his bidding.

Emma opened her mouth to lodge a protest, but before she could utter a word, Elvis had latched onto her upper arm and was towing her into the entryway where they wouldn't be readily visible to the first person to poke a head out the kitchen door. He swung her in a half circle and pushed her without roughness up against the closet door. When he stepped forward, the sheer size of his body more or less guaranteed that she'd stay there. "Did you give her the key?" he demanded in a low voice.

Emma stared up into the vivid blue eyes boring into hers. It was a legitimate question, her mind assured her. His mother had helped herself to Emma's child, used Emma's car, and had concocted, for no discernible reason, some convoluted plot designed to lay the blame on Clare Mackey. It didn't make a lick of sense, and what made even less sense was the fact that Nadine hadn't even broken into Emma's car; she'd had a key to the darn thing. Of course he was going to ask.

Then why was it she felt so betrayed? "No," she replied with stiff sarcasm, "I did not supply your mother with a key to my car so she could kidnap my daughter."

But I bet you have a good idea who did, Elvis thought, and ground his teeth as he stared down into her closed face. Her eyes, big and brown and usually so warm and open, now were shuttered and cold as she returned his gaze. He'd sensed from the day she'd first hit town that she was running away from something, and considering the conversation he'd overheard up in the hallway that very first night, he'd suspected it had to do with her father or ex-father-in-law. But, dammit anyhow, that made about as much sense as his mother out of the blue snatching the kid for no reason he could put a name to. What the hell sort of man would arrange to have his own granddaughter kidnapped?

That he'd even entertain the question brought him up short. Sweet God Almighty, he'd been a cop his entire adult life; he knew better than most that there were people out there who held absolutely nothing sacred. Too *many* people. Elvis blew out a frustrated breath dredged from so deep in his lungs it fluttered Emma's streaky blond bangs away from her forehead. "Do you have any enemies, Emma?" he inquired.

Squeezing the doorknob at her back, she looked him in the eye. "No."

"Are you wealthy?"

An involuntary laugh escaped her. "Gawd, no."

"Then why would anyone want to kidnap Gracie? And why go to such lengths for what was basically just moving her from one location to another?"

To show me how easily it can be done, Emma immediately surmised. Her chin tilted up. "I don't have the foggiest notion," she replied aloud. "Perhaps the person you should be askin' is your *maman.*"

"Oh, I plan to. The minute she gets back to town." *Dammit to hell, Emma, you're lying.* He could feel it in his bones. And with a sudden burst of clarity, he knew what she was planning.

She planned to take off, to leave Port Flannery behind. Clearly whatever she was running from had caught up to her. Today's episode with Gracie had the feel of a power play to it. Or perhaps it had been an object lesson. Either way, Emma was getting ready to bolt for a brand new hidey-hole.

He bent forward suddenly, crowding her, his forearms flush against the closet door, his massive chest brushing her breasts. A blue-eyed gaze probed brown from mere inches away; warm breath washed over her lips when he inquired, "Just what are you mixed up in, Emma?"

Ah, damn. Damn, damn, damn. Emma had a sudden desire to cry. She coveted nothing so much as to beat her breast and just bawl to the heavens. *Mon Dieu,* what she wouldn't give to unburden herself to this man. Because she truly believed, that out of everyone she knew, Elvis Donnelly was probably the most likely to understand this kind of trouble. Probably the most likely to be willing to offer his help.

But she knew she didn't dare take a chance on him. As had been amply demonstrated today, Grant's reach was long, his retribution harsh and impossible to predict. The best thing she could do was get the hell out of this little town, which was no longer safe for Gracie, and try to find some place, somewhere, that was.

She sucked hard on her lower lip when it

displayed an undisciplined tendency to tremble, angry with herself when it took longer than it should have to get her emotions under control. "Nothing," she finally said woodenly. "I'm not mixed up in anything." Then, having learned at a young age that a good offense was always the best defense, she firmed up her chin and thrust it pugnaciously up at him. "Wouldn't it be more pertinent to ask what your *mother* is mixed up in?"

Elvis gave her a level look. "Probably. But she isn't here — which leaves me, until she gets back, with you and Gracie." He shrugged. "So, what the hell. Maybe by working at this backward I can figure out a reason why it happened at all." He considered her for a moment. "Well, I suppose I might have understated that a bit. It doesn't leave me with *only* the two of you. I've got your car, too, of course."

"What?" That snapped her to attention in a hurry, and she pushed away from the door so abruptly her breasts flattened against his upper abdomen. He was warm and hard, and she hastily shied away, plastering herself back against the door as she eyed him with sour wariness. "What do you mean, my car? What has *that* got to do with anything? My *car* didn't sweet-talk Gracie out of the café, Elvis Donnelly; that was strictly your mother's doing."

"Your car was used during the commission of a crime," he said through gritted teeth. He was sick and tired of having her toss his mother's guilt in his face when he knew there was a helluva lot more to this than met the eye. "And that, my little Cajun queen, means it has now become part of the investigative process." He didn't defend what Nadine had done, not by a long shot. But neither would he stand back and allow Emma to use his mother's culpability as a red herring to avoid telling him what this situation was really all about. And he sure wasn't about to let her come breezing into his town, disrupting its citizens and then waltzing right out again without bothering to impart so much as a *hint* as to what the hell was going on.

That standing here with her up against this door was shooting heat through his stomach and giving him a . . . Well, never mind. It didn't have a goddam thing to do with his reasons for removing her only means of leaving the island. One was frustration. The other, purely a business decision.

Emma suddenly thrust a hand through her hair, and Elvis had to jerk his head back to avoid catching an elbow to his jaw. He pushed back from the door and stared down into her indignant face. Chin elevated, shining bangs skinned off her forehead by retaining fingers, she stared back at him.

"You can't just take away my car," she objected heatedly. "How the heck am I supposed to get around?"

"It's not like I'm taking it away forever," he retorted coolly. "You'll have it back in a few days." *Or a few days after that.* Sometime, at any rate, after his mother's return from Memphis. "And I'm sure until then you can make do just fine."

"That's easy for you to say, Sheriff," she snapped. "*You've* got a car at your disposal."

"For Christ's sake, Emma, you live right in the middle of town; everything you need's within walking distance." Letting his hook slide away from the door panel and drop to his side he roughly scraped his hair off his forehead with his fingers. They stood almost chest to breast, breathing heavily as they stared at each other. The tension crackling between them was nearly palpable. "And, admit it," he demanded, "you haven't even driven the damn thing recently. It's been covered up for the past three or four days."

"Yeah, but it was right there if I *did* need it! What do you propose I do if Gracie gets a craving for a Dairy Freeze burger tomorrow, huh? And don't think I'm just spoutin' off some far-fetched hypothesis either, *cher,* because I promised her one tonight, and by staying here for dinner instead, I'm not following through on my word to her. Kids don't just forget those sorta things, y'know, so what do you suggest I do then, Donnelly, *thumb* us a ride? It's not exactly in the middle of town."

His hand and hook thumped down on the door next to her head, and he leaned over her in aggravation. "*I'll* take you to the fuckin' Dairy Freeze," he snarled. Emotion made his scar stand out in a scarlet slash across his face. "Okay? If Gracie wants a goddam burger, then I'll drive you to the goddam hamburger stand to get her one! *Jeez*-us, Em!"

Then he caught himself. Christ, this was professional. He straightened away from her and gave his uniform shirt a neatening tug, as if he could yank his cop persona as firmly into place. "Listen," he said, more moderately if not necessarily truthfully, "I'm not trying to make things inconvenient for you. I just want to find out who's responsible for snatching your daughter. I thought that was what *you* would want, too." *There. Let's see you wiggle out of that one,* he thought with a degree of smugness. "And don't tell me again it's my mother," he added hastily when he saw her opening her mouth to reply, "because I sure as hell don't believe she dreamed this up all on her own."

Emma's mouth snapped closed again. Well, that neatly boxed her in. "Of course I want you to find the person responsible," she said through her teeth. "I don't see what you expect to find in my car, though, since from all reports your mother was the only unauthorized person actually *in* it today, but, hey, when you're right, you're right. Finding the person responsible *is* the important thing." The smile she flashed him was sweetly insincere.

Her way of slipping in the knife at the same time she seemed to be agreeing with him almost made him smile. No two ways about it, she was one exciting woman. "Then I guess we don't have a problem, do we?" he said easily. He watched her straighten away from the door. "I'll need your keys."

"Right this minute? How do you propose Gracie and I get back to the boarding house?"

"Good point; someone has to transfer

your car to the station anyway, and I suppose that can't be me." This was said with an undertone of wistfulness, since he'd like nothing better than to get his hands on that car. Then his mouth tipped up wryly as he admitted, "It's kinda difficult to drive two cars at once. So, I guess that leaves us with tonight in the parking lot. I'll follow you home, get the keys, and make arrangements to have the car gone over tomorrow."

"Fine," Emma said stiffly.

"Good," Elvis said. They stared at each other in tense silence.

The kitchen door swung open and Sam stuck his head out. "Elvis! Emma!" he hollered. "Where the hell are you two? Get in here; it's time to eat!"

Emma was disconcerted to discover how quickly she'd grown accustomed to the quiet nights in Port Flannery. She found it almost unnerving to have to drive through town at a near crawl in order to dodge the throngs of people criss-crossing the main streets. All the islanders were apparently still in town for the fireworks lighting up the sky over the harbor, and Emma was relieved to wheel the Chevy into the back parking lot.

The department Suburban immediately

pulled in behind her and she shot it a dirty look as she climbed out of the driver's seat and circled the car to liberate Gracie from her safety seat. When Elvis slammed his car door and walked up behind her, she ignored him. Pretending he simply didn't exist, she reached inside the car.

Extending her arms to be picked up, Gracie, once she'd been swung aboard her mother's hip, laid her head on Emma's breast and poked her thumb in her mouth. She stared up at the sky, awaiting another burst of pyrotechnics. "Pwetty," she whispered when a shower of red obliged her by exploding in the sky and falling toward the water. Then her mouth stretched wide in a huge yawn.

Emma kissed her on the top of the head before fumbling to remove her car key from the key ring. "Why don't you make yourself useful and pop the trunk?" she suggested coolly to Elvis once she'd relinquished it to him. "I need the cover from out of there." When he moved to comply, she took a step to follow but then stopped, looking down at where the lace of her left shoe trailed on the ground beneath the sole of her right. "Damn, my shoelace is untied. Here." She thrust Gracie into Elvis' brawny arms. "Hold her for me, will you?" She stooped just as a shower of blue and yellow burst in the sky. "Oh, look at that one, Gracie."

Gracie's eyes were at half mast as she lay limply against Elvis' chest and Emma smiled up at her. "Ah, you're a sleepy girl, aren'tcha angel pie?" Starting to overbalance, she went down on one knee and grabbed at the car, her fingers sliding to the underside of the wheel well, thumb gripping the fender.

"Am not seepy," Gracie protested, forcing her eyes open in a display of faux-alertness.

"No, of course you're not, *bébé,*" Emma agreed. "*Maman* was mistaken." To Elvis she said, "Don't just stand there; grab out the cover, *oui?*"

Letting loose of the fender, she slid her hand into her shorts' pocket and then quickly retied her shoelace. She rose to her feet, slapped her hands clean, and relieved the sheriff of the cover. "Stay awake just a few seconds longer, Sweetpea," she advised Gracie. Then, slamming the trunk, she whipped the cover over the car and tugged it into place with the swift efficiency of long practice. She gave the covered hood a pat and Elvis an unsmiling, level look. "I expect the car back soon," she said, as she reached for Gracie. Packing her daughter on her hip,

Emma turned on her sneakered heel and walked away. She didn't bother to say good night.

As soon as the back door had closed upon her and Gracie, Emma slowed her steps. She reached into her pocket and pulled out the magnetic keyholder she'd retrieved from the Chevy's undercarriage. Sliding back its cover, she smiled grimly to herself. Good. It still contained the spare key.

Long after Emma, Gracie, and Elvis had left, Sam and Clare remained within the steamy warmth of their kitchen. Not much conversation passed between them, but he helped her clean away the dinner dishes and wipe down counters and appliances. He swept the floor while she started the dishwasher, and then by tacit agreement they took fresh cups of coffee back to the table and sat down.

"Want to go to town for the fireworks?" he inquired at one point.

"No." She hesitated uncertainly and then said, "Sam, about earlier . . . I, uh, I really want to thank you."

"You do?" He eyed her warily. "For what?"

"For defending me the way you did."

He snorted. "Yeah, I'm a real knight in

shining armor, all right," he agreed bitterly. Studying her in silence for several long heartbeats, he abruptly confessed, "Clare, when I first saw Gracie in our entryway here . . . I thought you had done it." Gripping the back of his neck, elbows planted on the table, he raised his eyes to meet hers. "I thought the grief of losing Evan must have finally gotten to be just too much for you and you'd snatched Gracie out from under Emma's nose to — oh, shit, I don't know — *compensate,* or something."

One corner of Clare's lips curled up. "So what made you change your mind?"

He opened his mouth to reply, but then closed it again, studying her uncertainly. "You aren't mad?"

"No. Not really. I mean, it's not exactly a big surprise, Sam. I knew the minute I told you Emma had dropped Gracie off that you thought I'd gone crazy, and I won't deny it, it hurt." She gripped her coffee cup in both hands and stared at him. "But you came through for me. When it came right down to the wire, you threw yourself into my corner and, God, you were somethin' to behold, Sam Mackey. You were like that boy I used to lust after from afar, the one who told this town that Elvis Donnelly was his friend and they could just go screw themselves if they didn't like it." She looked at him sitting across the table from her. *Kiss me, Sam; hold me,* she silently yearned. *It's been so long.*

That boy I used to lust after. He heard the echo of her words in his mind, and it was all he could do to remain in his seat. He wanted to dive across the table and bear her down onto the floor. He wanted to love her — hard, soft, anyway she wanted — until they were both too weak to move. God, it had been so long. Just that one time since Evan had died, and then it had been too much like making love to a zombie for his peace of mind. He'd hesitated to impose himself on her ever since.

He knew what he wanted to do. What he *itched* to do. But he was gun-shy. So he gripped the edge of the seat and then sat on his hands for good measure to keep them from reaching for her. But he could still talk. He told her what had made him understand that she hadn't had anything to do with Gracie Sands' kidnapping.

And for practically the first time in a year, they carried on a genuine conversation concerning their son.

Emma lowered her sleeping daughter into the safety seat, buckled her in securely, and closed the passenger door with a soft click.

She ran around the trunk and slid into the driver's seat. Coasting down the slight incline, she started up the car at the last minute and pulled out of the parking lot. They had just enough time to catch the last ferry.

It had been a near thing. Luckily, Gracie had fallen asleep immediately and without a fuss, which had probably been the deciding factor between making a clean getaway or being stopped dead in their tracks. When too much emotion packed Gracie's day it was always a tossup whether she'd simply crash without a whimper when it came time to go to bed or turn into the Child from Hell. Overexhaustion had been known to turn her into a loud, cranky, and entirely unreasonable little girl. Emma gave a sigh of relief that tonight hadn't resulted in such behavior.

As it was, Emma had propped her up in bed with a picture book while she'd swiftly gathered together their belongings. Within moments Gracie's head had begun drooping toward her sturdy little chest. She'd jerked it upright once or twice, but it hadn't taken long before she was out for the count. Emma had then twitched the book away, slid her daughter down flat on the mattress, and sprung into action.

She hadn't realized before she'd begun to pack just how at home they'd become in the past couple of weeks. Their belongings, spread out all over the room, had developed their own little niches. Gracie's books and sand pail belonged on the window sill; Emma's toiletries sprawled across the top of the highboy; her favorite fringed scarf decorated the night stand. She'd stowed their possessions away one suitcase at a time, placing each bag next to the door. Everything that hadn't fit neatly within the cases or into the few cardboard boxes she'd saved had been stacked alongside.

She hadn't dared remove the cover from the car and leave the trunk open while she made trips between room and car, so once everything was assembled by the door, she'd made several trips out to the back lot where she'd heaped all of it in the shadowy lee of the Dumpster. When everything was transported from the room, she'd whipped off the car cover and rapidly packed the car. Closing up the trunk, tossing the cover back over the car, she'd stolen up the back stairs one last time to leave a note for Ruby, make sure nothing had been left behind, and gather up her sleeping baby and purse.

So now they were almost home free. Approaching the top of the hill that led down to the ferry docks, Emma was aware of headlights coming up fast behind her. They were high and bright like those of a truck or a van that sat taller off the ground than her Chevy, but aside from being conscious of the vehicle's rapid approach, she didn't think too much about it, merely assumed that it was someone like herself in a hurry to catch the last boat off the island.

Although she was pleased in a dour sort of way to have pulled off her departure from Port Flannery in the face of Elvis' obvious belief that he had her all snugly corralled, she wasn't, in all honesty, very happy about the way she was sneaking off. It made her feel almost . . . criminal somehow . . . as if she were some lowlife rent-jumper disappearing one step ahead of the landlord. Given broader options than she'd had, she would have done it differently. Stood toe to toe with Elvis Donnelly and argued about the constitutionality of impounding her car. Walked away in broad daylight. Something.

Deliberately blinking away the stinging sensation that prickled the backs of her eyes, she told herself it was caused by the glare of that damn car coming up so fast behind her. But dammit, she could have made a life for herself here. A good life for Gracie. It was a funny thing to imagine, that, for she certainly never would have pictured herself being content in a place this size. Nevertheless, it would have been kind of nice to have stuck around; it really would.

She was nothing if not a realist, though, and she'd known the futility of that fantasy the moment she'd understood Grant was the engineer behind Gracie's disappearance this afternoon. *It was overkill,* she reflected bitterly, *to have stolen the tapes right out of her room as well.*

She squinted as the car behind her moved right up on her bumper, its headlights reflecting blindingly in both her rearview and sideview mirrors. *"Dieu,* will y'all just go *around?"* she snarled under her breath and stepped on the gas a bit to shake the car off her tail.

Damn Grant, anyhow. She had no excuse, of course, for being surprised at his thoroughness. Having observed him in business deals over the years, she had *known* he could be ruthless. But in no way had that prepared her for the kick of terror she'd experienced when she'd gone to retrieve the tapes off the closet shelf and discovered they were missing.

The car behind her roared up on her tail once again, and Emma took her foot off the gas, hoping if she slowed down enough the clown would tire of his silly game and go around her. Instead, blue lights suddenly swirled from the vehicle's roof and a single whoop of a siren sounded and then moaned off into silence. Emma's heart sank to the soles of her feet.

"*Merde!*" she whispered.

Ten

Elvis climbed out of the Suburban and slammed the door behind him. Gravel crunched beneath his boots as he covered the short distance to Emma's Chevy. Stopping by the driver's door, he waited for her to roll down the window and then shined his flashlight into the interior of the car.

Emma merely narrowed her eyes against the glare when the light passed over her face, but she smacked his hand down when it passed over Gracie's. "Get that light out of her face."

"Get out of the car, Em."

He stood back, barely allowing enough room for her to open the door and climb out, and the moment she had, he whirled her around to face the car. With a hand on the back of her neck, he bent her forward. Catching herself on the hood of the car, Emma braced her hands and locked her elbows. Elvis kicked her ankles wide of each other and stooped down to run his hand and hook around her waist and down her hips to her ankles. Then he patted down her inner legs from ankle to thigh, and briskly ran his fingers along the crotch seam of her jeans from the waist band in front to the waist band in back.

"Can't buy yourself a thrill these days, *cher?*" Emma asked through her teeth. The incongruous flicker of relief she'd experienced upon seeing his face at the car window expired without a whimper beneath a deluge of ice-cold anger.

His response was fierce and to the point. "Shut up, Emma," he advised tersely.

Her head whipped around. "I will not shut up!" she said furiously. She remained in the assumed position, but craned her neck in order to see into his face as he rose to his feet and imperturbably continued frisking her. "This isn't necessary and you damn well know it. Here!" She grabbed the fingers that were skimming the side of her breast on their trip from waist to armpit and pulled them around to cover the breast's full thrust. "You're so hard up for a feel, let's give you a taste of the real thing. I imagine your sex life's been mighty barren lately."

Elvis already felt like a betrayed husband with a runaway wife, and though he'd been hanging onto his temper for all he was worth, his grip was alarmingly tenuous. When he'd pulled into Ruby's back lot after a post-fireworks check of the town and had seen that Emma's car was missing, more than a decade's worth of professionalism had gone up in smoke. He hadn't given the matter a lot of weighty, legal consideration; he'd simply reacted instinctually, heading hell-for-leather for the ferry dock. Her mockery now was the shove that destroyed the last tiny vestige of professional detachment he'd managed to maintain.

Her breast was warm and resilient beneath his palm, and his fingers curled to keep it firmly in his grasp when he whirled her around to face him. Stepping between her spread thighs, he backed her against the Suburban, his arm wrapped around her waist, prosthesis at the small of her back as he pulled her in to him. The scar jumped in his cheek as he bent his head until their mouths were millimeters apart.

"Be damn careful what you offer," he advised, his breath hot against her lips, his eyes an electric blue as they bore into hers, "because you're right, sweetheart, my sex life has been nonexistent for a long time now, and I might just be tempted to take you up on it." His hand massaged her breast as he spoke, fingers sinking into the fullness, palm pressing and then cupping the abundant curves, fingers then tightening to pull and reshape before his palm flattened against her once again. "You've already played me like a fiddle once tonight," he said. "You wanna add whoring to your repertoire, hey, that's just fine with me. I could sure use the relief."

She gripped his wrist to pull his hand away, feeling hot and flushed. For just an instant the muscles and sinews beneath her fingers tensed, resisting the pressure she exerted; then they relaxed and he allowed his hand to be removed. To the very last instant, however, his fingers and thumb maintained an insolent contact, catching at her nipple and giving it a gentle tug as his hand was pulled away. Emma was sorely tempted to snarl a warning about keeping his hands to himself, but she sucked in her lower lip to hold back the urge. She wouldn't give him the opportunity to remind her that she had started this.

Holding his wrist, she thrust his hand away and her chin up. "I didn't offer to make your wildest dreams come true, Sheriff," she said coolly. "I merely gave you a taste of the cheap thrill you were anglin' for."

"Cheap thrill, my ass. I was doing my job."

"Oh, the hell you were!" Neither one of them realized how close they remained standing. Still gripping his arm, holding it off to their sides, Emma stood toe to toe with him. "I'm not a criminal and y'all know it! You *also* know I don't have any weapons concealed on my body, so the only possible reason you could've had for pattin' me down like that was to give yourself an opportunity to grab a feel! And just what is that supposed to mean, I played you like a fiddle?"

"Right, like you don't know." He muttered an obscenity then glared down at her. "Please. Do me the favor of not insulting my intelligence at least that much, okay?" His jaw muscles tightened at the stony stare that was her only response, and he recited tersely, "Let's see, there was the loose shoelace and Baby Beans thrust into my arms. Then — oh, and I thought this was a masterpiece — directing our attention to the fireworks and my attention to Gracie's sleepiness. But, let me guess, it must have been the save from that artful little stagger when you stooped down to tie your shoe that copped you the extra key to your car, am I right?"

Emma merely raised both eyebrows at him, and he grimaced. "I gotta hand it to you; doll, you're good. You shoulda just left your stuff behind and caught the earlier ferry, though." He indicated the two of them standing in the dark at the side of the road. "This is what happens to little girls who think they can have it all."

As if to underscore his words the ferry sounded its deep throated horn, one long and two short blasts, as it pulled away from the dock. *"No!"* Emma wailed in dismay, swinging toward the sound. She watched its retreat from the island and then swung back to Elvis. "Damn you," she said fiercely. "Damn you to hell, Donnelly. You don't know what you've done."

For the first time since he'd realized what a fool she'd made of him, Elvis' anger faded. Soberly, he studied her expression by the light of the moon and found it haunted. "Then why don't you explain it to me," he suggested gently.

Even as he watched, her expression hardened. "There's nothing to tell," she insisted stubbornly. She gave him a probing look, tilted her chin high, and added, "You may have delayed my departure for tonight, but I've done nothing to break the law and you know it. You can't hold me here indefinitely."

"Ah, now, that's where you're wrong," he disagreed with a smooth lack of aggression. "I can come up with at least enough to hold you for a week. I think that should be sufficient, don't you? By then my mother will be back, and once she is, make no mistake, I *will* get to the bottom of this."

"Why, Elvis?" she demanded desperately. "To satisfy your own morbid curiosity? Gracie and I were the victims here, not the villains. It can't be constitutional to trump up charges to detain me."

She was right, and for the first time in his law-enforcement career he really didn't give a damn that he might be bending a law to suit his own purpose. With or without her permission, he was going to discover what was threatening her. Shrugging, he looked her squarely in the eyes. "So sue me."

It shocked him right down to his bootheels when she started to cry.

He'd expected her to snap and snarl. He fully intended to get his own way in the long run, of course, but he'd anticipated an exhilarating verbal skirmish or two before she caved in. Instead she broke down in tears and regarded him with huge brown eyes full of abject misery. "Who'll take care of Gracie?" she sobbed. "Who will keep her safe?"

"Huh?"

"If I'm in jail, who's gonna take care of my *bébé?* She'll be scared, Elvis. We've never been separated before."

"You're not going to be in jail," he said blankly.

"But you said —"

"I said I could hold you. Jesus, Em, I meant on the island here, not in a jail cell. What do you take me for?" He shook his head rapidly. "No, never mind; I'd rather you didn't answer that." He felt like a worm. *For my next trick, folks, watch me pull the wings off a dragonfly.*

Emma rubbed her eyes. *Dieu*, she was so *tired* all of a sudden. She looked up at Elvis apathetically. "Can I go home now?" she asked with uncharacteristic meekness.

"Yeah." He studied her in concern. "You gonna be okay to drive?"

She nodded.

"Okay, then. Drive carefully, huh? I'll be right behind you."

He'd meant it as a reassurance but could only wince when she muttered, "Of course you will."

It wasn't until she reached their room, with Gracie weighty in sleep against her chest and Elvis carrying the suitcase she thought she recalled having packed their toiletries in, that Emma remembered she had sealed the room key into the envelope that contained the note she'd written for Ruby. It wouldn't have been a problem except she'd automatically locked the door behind her. Head bowing, her forehead hit the door panel with a small thunk. *"Merde."*

She could have sworn then she felt something cool and metallic touch her exposed nape, but if so it was a touch so brief and light she couldn't be absolutely positive she wasn't imagining it. "What?" Elvis inquired in that polite but remote way he so often used. "What is it?"

Wearily she told him. There was a hesitation, a rustle as he transferred the bag from his hand to his hook; then his hand, warm and rough-skinned, slid beneath her elbow. "Come with me." He led her across the hall and down a couple of doors. Digging his keys out of his Levi's pocket, he opened the door. He stood back to allow her to precede him into the room, then followed her in and turned on the floor lamp.

"You and Gracie can have the bed," he offered impersonally. "I'll sleep on the floor."

She was too tired for polite protestations. *"Merci,"* she said and eased Gracie off her shoulder and onto the bed under hastily flipped-back covers. Watching her daughter turn onto her stomach and draw her knees up under her stomach, Emma unzipped the suitcase Elvis had set on the chair and withdrew a white satin nightgown and her toothbrush and toothpaste. Looking at the slinkiness of the night apparel in her hand, she glanced warily at Elvis' back. He was standing at the window, forearms braced on the casings, contemplating either the darkened harbor or the distant lights of the mainland. She rummaged through the conglomeration of items she'd stuffed into the luggage during her rushed packing and pulled out her old leather jacket. "I'll be right back," she said. Elvis didn't turn around.

Her suitcase was on the floor, and he was sitting in the chair with his long legs sprawled out in front of him when she returned. He spared her one brief glance, then reached up to turn off the lamp. Grateful for his consideration, Emma dropped her jacket on the floor and climbed under the blankets with her daughter.

She had noticed the pallet he'd made on the floor by the window, but as far as she could tell he didn't stir from his place in the chair. At least not during the several long moments that she remained awake.

The bed bounced and dipped beneath

her. Little fingers pried up her right eyelid. "Mommy, Mommy, you awake? It's all sunshiny out and you 'n' me seeped in Shewiff Elbis' bed!"

"Gracie!" Elvis' voice was a low rumbling command. The bed dipped further as he planted his knee on the mattress, and then it leveled out again and Emma's gritty eyelid fell closed as he stood up, taking Gracie with him. "You let your momma sleep," he said sternly.

"But I haffa go potty."

"I'll take you to the bathroom. Just let me make myself a cup of coffee and grab a shirt."

"I haffa go *now!*"

"Okay, okay, keep your shirt on. We're outta here."

"Don't gots a shoot," Emma heard Gracie say as the door closed behind them. "These aw my jammies."

Emma opened her eyes and pushed up on one elbow. Yawning, she squinted against the brilliant light pouring through the window. So they did get sunshine in this part of the world after all, huh? She had begun to wonder.

She climbed out of bed and pulled on her leather jacket. Having heard the word "coffee," and spotting an electric coffeemaker on the bookshelf across the room, she was drawn to it as naturally as a nursing infant to its mother's breast. There was a gallon-sized bottle of distilled water on the floor and in the small, college dorm-sized refrigerator she found a half pound of Starbucks ground Sulawesi. Emma measured out the coffee and poured water into the reservoir, popping down the on switch. Within moments it began bubbling and hissing, and the aroma of fresh-brewed coffee filled the room.

She was rummaging through her suitcase for something to wear when the door opened. Damn. She had hoped for a few more moments of privacy. But on looking up to see Gracie race into the room, she had to smile as she always did at her daughter's irrepressible enthusiasm. Elvis followed more slowly in Gracie's wake and Emma's smile faltered, all the moisture leaving her mouth. His only attire consisted of a ragged pair of cut-off sweatpants, riding low on his hips, and the leather straps that secured his prosthesis to his arm.

Gracie launched herself at her mother. "*Maman,* you up!"

Emma lifted her into her arms, cuddling her and accepting her sloppy good-morning kiss, kissing her in return, but Emma's eyes never left Elvis, seemingly glued on him. Dressed, he was a huge man. Nearly naked, with those shoulders, those thighs and calves, *Dieu,* that *chest,* with its fan of jet hair thinning out to arrow down the rigid muscles of his stomach and disappear under the low-slung waistband of his sweats, he was enormous. And so — God, so, so . . .

She shook her head helplessly. *So.*

"Mornin'," he rumbled. He headed for the closet and pulled a long-sleeved denim shirt off a hanger. "Ah, I see you made coffee," he said. "Thanks. I'm not good for much before my first cup." When she failed to respond and simply stared at him, he added uncertainly, "It sure smells great."

"Yeah." She shook herself free of the spell. "I, um, I'm just going to go get dressed." She set Gracie down with a little pat on the rear and edged toward the door, grateful when he shrugged on the shirt. Even if he didn't bother to button it up, it nevertheless covered most of him. Maybe luck would be on her side for once and he'd be all buttoned down in his uniform by the time she got back.

"I saw Shewiff Elbis' penis, Mommy," Gracie announced brightly. "It's weally big, like that hoesie's we sawed that time, you bemember?"

Shock stopped Emma in her tracks. Agonized betrayal in her eyes, she whipped her head around to stare at Elvis, her mouth forming the word *"No."* Even as she watched, a dull red climbed up his strong throat and spread across his face. His scar twitched. Shaking his head, he stammered, "Emma, it's not . . . I had to take a . . . Jesus, don't *look* at me like that; it's not what it must sound like. I swear to you."

Gracie's voice overrode his. "It's way biggoo than Gwandpapa's."

Emma stilled. Everything inside her went cold. Ah, *Dieu,* no. Please, *please,* no. She turned very slowly toward her daughter. "When did you see Grandpapa's penis, Grace Melina?" she asked in a carefully neutral voice.

"Dunno." Gracie shrugged. "Seen it a couple a times."

Emma licked her dry lips. "And what, um, was he doin' when you saw it, *chérie?*"

Gracie gave her a brilliant smile. "Same thing as Elbis, silly. Goin' potty." Something struck her funny then, and a giggly laugh tickled her throat and burst free. "But Gwandpapa didn't go as long, Mommy. Shewiff Elbis, he wented and wented fo-*ev*oo!"

The sound that escaped Emma's throat

then was a high-pitched little whimper of relief. A choked gurgle of laughter that was too close to hysteria for comfort. Tears filled her eyes, and hugging herself, she whirled to face the window.

"Let's get you dressed, Gracie," Elvis suggested in his quiet, authoritative way. "You wanna come over here and show me what sort of stuff you like to wear?"

" 'Kay." She skipped over to the open suitcase. "I wanna wear shoats today."

"Shorts, huh? Yeah, all right; I guess summer's finally arrived. What do you think of these yellow ones?"

"Pwetty!" She scrambled through the suitcase. "And this is my T-shoot goes with it — see the lellow flowers? Haffa have panties, too. And socks." She dug some more. "I yike these wuffled ones."

"Yeah, I like those, too. Okay, that looks like the list. Come on over here." He spread her choices out on the end of the bed and patted the mattress where he wanted her to climb up. "Now keep in mind that I'm not very good at this, kid, so you're probably gonna have to help me. What do you call this big purple guy on your pajamas?"

"That's Bawney."

"Yeah? Well, let's get rid of him; whataya say?"

He was sweating by the time they were finished. Gracie could be helpful, but unfortunately it was a helpfulness that tended to last for only seconds. Then something would catch her eye and she'd try to roll, walk, or wander toward it, even if they were right in the midst of donning one of the various items needed to attire her. He wiped his forearm across his forehead when he finally straightened. Gracie scampered off the bed.

"Here," said a soft voice behind him. He turned to see Emma in her bare feet, wearing a satin nightie and the heavy unzipped leather jacket she had donned. She was extending a cup of coffee. An involuntary smile tried to tug up the corner of his mouth. She probably thought the jacket was a real effective cover-up. And it was, as far as not revealing her body went. But mostly the contrast of bulky, scuffed leather only served to stress the femininity of the slippery nightwear beneath it. And the body beneath that.

He took the cup. "Thanks."

"Thank *you,*" she said. "For . . ." She tipped her head toward Gracie, who had climbed up onto the wide window sill and was kneeling with her nose pressed to the glass as she checked out the harbor view from Elvis' side of the building.

"Man." Shaking his head, he gave Emma one of his rare smiles. "My respect for motherhood just shot up a hundredfold. Who woulda thought dressing one little kid could be so much work?"

Emma gave him a look. "Yeah. Especially when you don't make her pitch in and help."

"What do you mean?"

"You're a pushover, Donnelly. At least where my *petite ange* is concerned. Gracie knows how to dress herself. You have to ride herd to keep her at it, and she requires help with buttons and zippers occasionally, but what she needs more than anything is strict supervision. You let her ride roughshod all over you."

He stared at her openmouthed for a moment, then killed off his coffee with a few deep swallows. "Well, shit," he finally said.

"Yeah." Emma's mouth tilted up in a faint, ironic smile. "Welcome to the wonderful world of parenting."

"Emma . . ." He shifted in discomfort. "Look, I'm sorry about letting Gracie see my coc— er, that is, my uh . . ." Oh, man, he couldn't believe he was blushing. "Penis." He coughed. "I guess I didn't think it through. I had my morning hard . . . ahh . . .

I just had to go, you know? And after the ease with which she got taken away yesterday, I didn't think leaving her standing out in the hall while I, uh, took a leak was a good idea."

He was so patently uncomfortable that Emma couldn't help but take pity on him. "It's okay, Elvis," she said gently. "I didn't really believe —"

Try as he did to repress it, his expression nevertheless practically screamed bullshit, and she confessed, "Well, okay, for just a minute I *did* believe, I suppose; but not your basic way-down-deep-inside *believe* believe . . . not really. Ah, *Dieu,*" she sighed, shoving her fingers through her sleep-rumpled hair and hunching a shoulder. She peered up at him. "I'm mangling this. What I'm trying to say is, peeing in front of her isn't a crime. Most little girls Gracie's age probably go in and out of the bathroom all the *time* when their daddies are in there. But that's the thing, *cher;* that's why it's all such a big deal to her. *Her* daddy died before she was born, and she hasn't been exposed to very many men. Frankly, I didn't think she'd been exposed to *any* — not in the sense of seeing their private parts up close and personal. I know she tends to get a little fixated on male equipment when she does catch a glimpse, which is why she's still talkin' about a stallion's penis we once saw when we were picnicking."

Elvis looked down at her thoughtfully. "Yeah, that explains Gracie, all right. And it's decent of you to let me off the hook."

Emma almost smiled. Yes, it *was* fairly decent; she was rather amazed at herself. Remarkably, after all the fuss she'd gone through trying to get them out of town last night, it actually felt *safe* to be with Elvis in his room this morning. Safe for her, and more importantly, safe for Gracie. No one would ever think to come looking for them in the sheriff's room. And if someone should do so, she had faith that he would keep them from harm — at least for this one morning while they had the added protection of being under his roof.

Elvis wasn't like most people; he didn't simply accept matters at face value. He dug for deeper reasons. And that was good, that was necessary in a situation like hers. Look at his rationale for not shoving Gracie out into the hallway to wait while he used the facilities. He had obviously been thinking like a cop.

Which, she discovered in the next heartbeat, could be a detriment as well as an advantage.

"What I don't understand," he was saying, his eyes on her as he slowly rolled his shirtsleeves up over first one forearm then the other, "is why *you* automatically assumed the worst. You thought I had exposed myself to her." The expression in his blue eyes pinned her in place. "We both know you did, and what I'd like to know is . . . why is that, Em? Is it because someone *has* flashed her? Or" — he blanched at the thought — "oh, Jesus, not *assaulted* her?" Not that. *Please,* not that. He wasn't sure he could be responsible for keeping his hands off such a person!

"N-No!" she stammered. "Of course not."

Elvis recognized the ring of truth and relief washed through him. He nevertheless knew he was on the right track and pressed on relentlessly. "But you were afraid if you stuck around New Orleans someone might try to, am I right?"

"Don't be ridiculous." She stood up straight and tall, chin thrust up at him.

"I don't think I'm being ridiculous. Who was it?"

She gave him a blank stare.

"Who was it, Em?" He leaned down close and suggested quietly, "Gracie's grandfather, perhaps?"

"Oh, Gawd."

"Tell me, Emma."

Her chin jacked up yet a few notches higher, and even as he watched, her expression locked up tight. She stood in front of him as if someone had rammed an iron rod up her spine, a mulish slant to her normally soft mouth.

Curling his fingers around the zipper placket of her jacket, he pulled her a little nearer. Slowly he slid his hand up and down the leather, feeling it slide along the tunnel formed by his loose grip. Feeling the satin of her nightgown brush against the backs of his fingers. He bent his head until their noses were a mere inch away. *"Tell me,"* he commanded intensely.

Her posture wilted. Bottom lip trembling, she sucked it into her mouth and bit down hard while her brown eyes evaluated him. A moment later, the reddened lip slid free of the white teeth gripping it. "Yes," she whispered. "All right. I'll tell you." Her chin came up then. "But, Elvis, you've gotta promise me something in return. If I tell you, you've got to promise to let me and Gracie go then."

Eleven

Gracie saved him from having to promise anything. Unseen by either of them she had climbed down off the window sill and came trotting across the room. She threw her arms around his leg and hung there, craning her head way back to look up at him. "You gonna kiss my mommy?"

Elvis pulled his eyes away from Emma and looked down at her daughter, wondering where that had come from. "I hadn't intended to," he replied honestly. *But it sounds like a plan.*

"You standin' weally close yike you was gonna." She considered him for a minute, then unloosed his leg and stepped back. "Gim*me* a kiss."

"Gracie," Emma started to reprimand her, but Elvis waved that away. He let go of her jacket and squatted down. Gracie immediately clambered up onto his knee and threw her arms around his neck. She planted a damp but enthusiastic kiss on his mouth. Then she pulled back and unhooked an arm to yank up her little flowered T-shirt. "Wanna wazzbewwy, too." She laughed herself silly when he blew a satisfyingly rude noise, long and loud, on her stomach. Then she jumped off his knee.

"Give *Maman* a kiss now," she demanded and commenced to dance a little wildly in place. "Kiss Mommy, kiss Mommy!"

"Grace Melina, that's enough," Emma said sternly. "You're becomin' somewhat obnoxious." She grimaced ruefully at Elvis as he rose to his feet. "I'm sorry," she said. "She's a little wound up." Turning to her daughter she held her hand out. "Come help *Maman* pick out somethin' to wear, *chérie.* You and Elvis are all dolled up — it's time I got dressed, too."

Gracie was instantly diverted. "Wear shoats," she demanded as she skipped along at her mother's side. Stopping at the open suitcase, she threw her arms around her mother's legs and rubbed her face against the satin nightgown as she looked up at her. "Yike me, Mommy; 'kay?"

"Shorts it is," Emma agreed. "If there are any in here, that is. Oh, yes, here's a pair."

"I'll go down and get the spare key to your room," Elvis offered. "You wanna go with me, Gracie girl? Then your momma can take her shower."

"Okey dokey." She left Emma's side in a red-hot minute and trotted over to his.

Elvis looked past her at Emma. "Take all the time you need," he instructed. "We'll unload the car."

"No; that won't be necessary," Emma swiftly assured him. "Remember your prom—"

"Right," he interrupted before she could suddenly recall that he hadn't actually promised a thing. "I'll leave the bags where they are. We'll come up with another way to kill twenty minutes, won't we, kid? And don't worry." Looking at Emma, he indicated Gracie with a slight tilt of his jaw. "I'm not gonna let her out of my sight."

"Listen, this is really very nice of you. But isn't it goin' to interfere with your work?"

"Nope. Day off." He gave her a lopsided little quirk of his lips and shrugged. "Even small-town sheriffs get one occasionally."

"In that case . . . and if you're sure it's not an imposition" — Emma had been gathering together her toiletries and a change of clothing and she met him at the door — "thank you, Elvis."

"No problem. Oh, and Gracie?"

"Yes, Shewiff?"

"This is for you, sweetheart." With those words, his left arm suddenly snaked around Emma's waist and yanked her to him, bending her backward theatrically. Emma's stack of clothes and toiletries clattered to the floor. Plunging his right hand into her silky hair, Elvis kissed her thoroughly while Gracie squirmed and giggled with delight.

Emma grabbed for the button plackets of his open shirt and just tried her best to hang on as sensations exploded inside of her like so many special effects in a Steven Spielberg movie. It was a joke . . . in a dim corner of her mind she knew that. She wasn't about to make a fool of herself by kissing him back as if she were dying for it.

At least that was the plan, fuzzy-minded and nebulous as it was. Elvis must have had a different one. He didn't raise his head until his shirt was a wrinkled mass from her gripping fingers. Until her mouth was swollen and stung from kissing him back.

As if she'd been dying for it.

It was almost two hours later before the three of them walked away from town to a deserted stretch of beach. Elvis, who had developed an ironclad professional patience years ago, was ready to chew nails.

There was an aspect of arrogance built into most police work, an expectation of instant compliance that law enforcers became accustomed to receiving. If there were questions to be asked, a cop had the authority to demand immediate answers. Elvis wasn't in the habit of dealing with situations that included little girls whose needs had to be met before he could do his job.

Kissing Emma was clearly not the smartest thing he could have done this morning. It would have been okay if he'd just kept it brief and simple the way he'd originally intended. But no, he'd had to get all caught up in it. He'd tasted her mouth under his, so cool and controlled, and had thought, *Oh no, doll, you can do much better than this.* Gracie's giggles had faded into the background, blood had roared in his ears, and he'd lost himself in the pursuit of a response. Then when he'd *gotten* one . . .

Damn. He shook himself. No sense in dwelling on that now. Except to say that by the time he'd dragged himself away, instead of finding a pleased little girl, he noted that Gracie's giggles had disappeared and she stood staring up at him with huge uncertain eyes, her thumb tucked into her mouth.

What a dumb shit he was. Between them, he and Emma had generated enough electricity to make the body hair of anyone within a hundred-yard radius stand on end. Unquestionably Gracie had felt the vibrations, and too young to know what they were, had been made uneasy by the intensity of it all. He didn't even have to shut his eyes to see the look on her face when he'd finally released Emma and straightened up.

Gracie studied her mother. "He hoot you?" she asked around her thumb.

Emma dropped to a crouch and pulled Gracie into her arms for a quick hug. "Ah, no, *bébé.*" Over her head she shot Elvis a dirty look, but was smiling gently when she moved Gracie away to hold her at arm's length. "Elvis was just playin' with *Maman.* He wanted to make you laugh."

Gracie glanced at Elvis dubiously, then looked back at her mother. "We go to our own woom now?" she suggested hopefully.

"We can't, angel pie." Emma tenderly finger-combed Gracie's curls away from her face. "I accidentally locked us out of it last night. Remember? You and Elvis are goin' down to get the spare key from Miss Ruby while I take my shower."

Gracie burrowed back into her mother's warmth, head pressed into Emma's breasts. "Don't wanna, Mommy."

Emma bared her teeth at Elvis, giving him a fierce look that said, You made this mess — do something! Elvis squatted down in front of her, laying his hand with careful tenderness on Gracie's back. It covered nearly half of it.

"Hey, Gracie girl," he murmured. "I'm sorry if I scared you. I guess I just got a little carried away." His eyelids lifted and his gaze pinned Emma's. Caught in the erratic energy of that on-again-off-again sexual intensity he projected like a neon tube on the fritz, she stared back, unable to look away, and licked her lips.

"You don't kiss my mommy no more," Gracie demanded indignantly into her mother's breasts.

Can't promise you that, kid. "How 'bout I kiss you instead," he suggested and leaned forward to press a kiss against her neck where it joined her shoulders. Gracie hunched her shoulder up to her ear, repudiating the caress.

"Hmm." He thought about it a second, then leaned around and blew a little "pfftt" on the other side of her neck. "Tha's not a kiss," she mumbled. "Tha's a wazzbewwy."

"Well . . . yeah," he agreed. "But if I *really* kiss you it'll just make you laugh."

"Huh uh."

"Yes it will."

"Huh uh!"

"Bet it does." He rocked back on his heels. "Tell you what. If I'm right — if I can make you laugh — I gotta buy you . . ." He raised an eyebrow at Emma.

"A box of sidewalk chalk," she supplied.

"Right. A box of chalk. But if I'm *wrong* . . ." His voice trailed off and he gazed away, looking off into space, apparently forgetting he was in the middle of a conversation.

Gracie stood it for almost fifteen seconds. Then her thumb came out of her mouth and she raised her head slightly from Emma's cleavage. "What?" she demanded.

"Well, if I'm wrong and my kisses don't make you laugh, then I guess I gotta buy you a car."

She blew out an impatient breath at his monumental ignorance. "Can't *dwive* a caw."

"Oh. Well, then I guess I'll have to buy you a . . ." He let it trail off again.

"Twike," Gracie supplied.

"Yeah, I'll have to buy you a trike. So, whataya say? Should I give it a try?"

" 'Kay."

Elvis bent his head and pecked kisses at the contour of her neck. For several moments she remained steadfast to her desire to stay unaffected, but then she started to wriggle. He puckered up and really put his heart into it, planting noisy kisses onto her neck with abandon. A snort escaped her. Then she danced in place, muffling her giggles against Emma's breasts when he went to work on her soft little nape.

Fingers tugged at his hair, and he raised his head. He found himself staring into Emma's brown eyes. Enough, she mouthed.

He immediately rocked back on his heels. "Told ya," he said to the child while staring at the mother. "I guess that means I owe you a box of sidewalk chalk, huh?"

Gracie turned around to face him. "A *big* box," she negotiated. "With *yots* of colors."

He rose to his feet and extended his prosthesis to her. "A big box," he agreed. "Whataya say we go down to Mackey's and see what they've got?" His breath stayed dammed up in his chest until she reached out to link her fingers through the hook.

It was one obstacle tackled, but by no means the last one.

He was accustomed to most folks on the island giving him a wide berth; that was a fact of life he'd enured himself to years ago. But when he walked into the café with Gracie on his shoulders he was promptly surrounded by every diner, waitress, and cook in the place. Evidently her disappearance yesterday had generated a great deal of concern.

Elvis would have been a whole lot happier without the attention. He had no desire to explain his mother's involvement in yesterday's situation to all these islanders, at least not before he'd a chance to talk to her about it. If Emma decided to press charges against Nadine, then his mother was going to be plain out of luck, but until that happened he'd prefer her participation didn't become fodder for the rumormongers. She was only marginally tolerated by some factions on the island as it was.

It worked out to his benefit that the sudden press of strangers made Gracie shy. She unknowingly provided him with a grace period by remaining silent, one little hand clutching nervously at his hair. He couldn't see her face, but he'd bet his last dollar she was sucking on her thumb and staring at everybody with those big brown eyes of hers.

"Give the kid a little room, folks," he suggested genially enough, but the authority in his voice was enough to back people up a pace. "I know your sentiments are generous ones and that you've been concerned for her safety, but I think all this attention is making Miss Sands a little nervous." To Ruby he said, "Mrs. Sands locked herself out of her room. She sent me down to fetch the spare key."

The expression on Ruby's face openly marveled that Elvis Donnelly would fetch and tote at any woman's whim, but she didn't argue about it; she simply went to her office to get him the key. And that, in the final analysis, was all he cared about; he was basically a bottom-line kind of man. He just wanted to get them out of there before Gracie regained her friendly tendency to chatter indiscriminately. He lived in fear of her telling all and sundry that her mother had slept in Sheriff Elvis' bed last night, or, God, even worse, that *she* had seen his penis. Jesus. That was *all* it would take to ruin her mother's reputation on Flannery Island.

Emma was well regarded here. There were quite a few, in fact, who practically treated her like a lifelong islander, which, he knew better than most, was nothing short of exceptional. Damned exceptional. People who had lived here fifteen *years* were still considered newcomers. And some lifelong residents, like himself, would always be considered outsiders.

Her popularity could change in the blink of an eye, however; few knew the vagaries of this closeminded little village better than he.

Just let it be known that not only Emma, but her little angel of a daughter as well, had slept in his bed last night and they'd probably be stoning her in the streets, accusing her of God knows what perversions.

He managed to collect the key a few moments later and escape, slipping unseen with Gracie through the back door. It was one more obstacle down. But he was giving up counting them. It seemed he just solved one problem and another cropped up to take its place.

"I'm hungwy." Gracie regained her voice only moments after they had slipped out. Elvis held onto her legs and jogged down the alleyway. She tugged on his hair. "Elbis? I'm hungwy."

"Yeah, I heard you. You're going to have to hang on though, Beans, until we get back to the boarding house." She was going to have to hang on longer than that, because he wasn't taking her back in the café, but what the hell, that would be Emma's problem.

"But I want my bweakfast, Shewiff."

"You want to eat your breakfast with your momma, dont'cha?"

"Oui."

"Well then?"

She heaved a heartfelt sigh. "I shoo am hungwy."

He bought her a Twinkie to tide her over when he purchased the box of sidewalk chalk. Sticky fingers gripped his hair occasionally on the walk back to the rooming house, and he didn't even want to think about the probable evidence that was on her face. Emma was no doubt going to have his hide for loading her up with preservatives before breakfast.

His plan was to take the Sands females to breakfast somewhere — preferably The Razorback on the other side of the island, where they wouldn't be interrupted. Maybe *then* he could finally get the damn story from Emma. How was he supposed to plan his next move when he didn't even know what the hell was going on?

She agreed to the breakfast. "But if you think I'm gonna sit there and discuss this in front of my *bébé, cher,* then you aren't as smart as I gave you credit for." She lowered her voice. "This has to do with hidden cameras and depravity and the man she thinks is her *grandfather,* for pity's sake. She'd never understand all that."

Christ. Like he was supposed to be patient after being teased with that?

But of course she was right. It wasn't exactly something you could discuss in front of a little girl barely three years old. And he didn't even bother to suggest that they find a sitter for Gracie. After yesterday, Emma wasn't likely to let the kid out of her sight, and he could hardly blame her.

So they collected an old blanket off Elvis' shelf and Gracie's yellow sand pail and shovel, added to these the new box of chalk, and set off at Emma's suggestion for the grocery store to collect food for a picnic breakfast. Then they hiked down the beach away from town.

Emma got out the food while Elvis spread the blanket over a smooth patch of sand they'd found in the lee of a huge beached log. Gracie was enchanted with the idea of a picnic and squatted next to the blanket watching as each item appeared.

"Come over here." Emma held a hand out to her, and Gracie scrambled to comply. But instead of being handed something to eat as she'd expected, her mother started slathering lotion all over her exposed skin. *"Maman!"* she protested.

"Sorry, *chérie*. But we've got to get this sunblock on you before we do anything else."

"We could dwink the little owange juices foost." She was totally enamored of the individual-sized containers.

"No. We cannot. There!" Emma blew a

little raspberry on the side of Gracie's neck and let her up, wiping the excess lotion onto her own thighs. "All done. You can dig in now."

After breakfast Emma picked the box of colored chalk out of the sand bucket and, with Gracie at her heels, walked around the area. Every time she came across a large rock she drew the outline of a design on it. Finally, when Gracie was all but dancing with impatience, she handed her the box.

"Color in the pictures, angel pie."

"I'll make 'em weally pwetty!"

"I know you will. Here's your bucket, *chérie.* Better take it along in case you come across a shell or a rock you can't live without." She ran her fingers through her daughter's blond curls. "I'll be over on the blanket talking with Sheriff Elvis if you need me, okay?"

" 'Kay." Gracie picked a fat stick of hot-pink chalk out of the box, and tongue poking out of the side of her mouth, started filling in the flower her mother had drawn.

Emma sat silently on the blanket, knees drawn up to her chest, just watching her daughter for several moments. She could feel Elvis' impatience mounting. When he shifted suddenly she knew without a word being spoken that he was about to start throwing his authority around.

"I decided after Charlie died that I wasn't ever again going to get close to anyone," she said abruptly. "Grace Melina being the exception, naturally." She didn't turn her head to look at him, but divided her attention instead between her daughter, who was decorating a rock with slashes of color and gleefully disregarding the outlines her mother had drawn and the view just beyond her of giant boughs of evergreens framing sun-dappled water.

"Charlie was your husband, right?"

She nodded, hugging her knees closer to her chest. "The people I love have a nasty habit of dying suddenly," she said without emotion. "Charlie was twenty-five. We'd only been married eleven months, and one morning he was this happy-go-lucky guy and that afternoon he was" — she shook her head in disbelief — "dead."

"How was he dead, Em? Was he the victim of a crime?"

"No." She shook her head. For a moment she didn't elaborate; she simply stared out at the water. Then without looking at him, she said in a low voice, "He drowned. He'd gone fishin' — I didn't go along because I was hugely pregnant, and, well, anyhow . . . he didn't come back." She could remember as if it were yesterday the police knocking on their door that evening to inform her of the accident. They'd confirmed the worst of the myriad fears that had sent her pacing from window to window for hours, watching for his return after he had failed to come home.

She lapsed into another silence. Finally she said, "I thought it was me, you know — for years I believed that . . . that I was cursed or something. First Big Eddy. Then my friend Mary Louise at Tulane. Then Charlie. You can't imagine how carefully I watched over Grace when she was an infant. I was convinced that something awful was going to happen to her — SIDS, that she'd choke, *something*." She turned her head and finally looked at him, resting her cheek against her updrawn kneecap. "But I'm *not* cursed," she said fiercely. "I'm the . . . obsession . . . of a man I thought of as my surrogate father. Grant Woodard."

"He's not your real father?"

"No. Oh, praise God, no. At least I have *that* much to give thanks for, *cher*." She observed his bafflement and said, "Perhaps I had better explain."

For the next several minutes she chronicled the events that originally led to her meeting Grant Woodard, the way Woodard had befriended her and her brother. "When

Big Eddy was busted and he knew he was goin' to be sent up, he went to Grant and asked him to take care of me." She laughed bitterly as she met Elvis' eyes. "We thought we were so lucky that someone was willing to take me in. Someone who wasn't one of Eddy's car-thuggin' buddies. *Bon Dieu, lucky.*" She practically spat the word and shook her head at their naiveté. *"Merde."*

"What does that mean, Em?"

"Huh? What does what mean?"

"*Merde.* What does it mean?"

She looked him in the eye. "Shit."

"Ah." A corner of his mouth kicked up. "Sounds a lot more elegant said in French, doesn't it? Anyhow" — he waved it away — "go on. I didn't mean to interrupt." He studied her profile for a moment as she went back to watching Gracie squat in front of a boulder and happily smear it with color. "So you think Woodard might have had something to do with your brother's arrest?"

"Oui," she confirmed flatly. "And there's no 'might have' about it, *cher,* I flat-out believe he's responsible for Eddy being arrested, period. I think he also arranged to have my brother killed a few days before he was supposed to have been released from prison." She turned her head to look at him. "I think he's responsible for the hit-and-run

that killed my friend Mary Louise back when we were in college and for Charlie's drowning." Her eyes didn't waver, neither did they blink. "I'm sure that as a policeman this must sound pretty paranoid." She uttered a weary laugh. "Heck, *cher*, if anyone had suggested such a thing to me before this spring, *I* would have said they were crazy. For years, after Big Eddy was sent to prison and before I had Gracie, Grant Woodard was the closest thing to a family I had." Raking her hair off her forehead, she eyed him steadily. "But I don't doubt it for an instant. I've tried to convince myself I must be wrong, Elvis — I really have — but I don't believe it. Not anymore. And if I'd had any doubts before, yesterday would have quelled them."

"You think he was behind Gracie's kidnapping?"

"Do *you* think your mother came up with that scheme all on her own?"

No. He loved his mom, but he had never been blind to her shortcomings. She wouldn't in a million years have had the imagination to conceive of such a convoluted, daring plot.

He gave a succinct nod to concede the point. "What you're suggesting takes both money and connections. Does Woodard have the wherewithal and the power to do all these things?"

"And then some," she said without hesitation. "As an adult I never thought much about how he earned a living — I suppose because on some level I didn't want to examine it too closely. But I'll tell you somethin', *cher.* As a kid, nobody had to tell me that while a portion of his business undoubtedly is legitimate, the primary purpose of that portion is to serve as a front for an even larger part that is not. Those two guys I told you about, the ones who picked me up in the Silver Cloud the day I heisted it? They were goons, Elvis. He has *always* surrounded himself with goons. A legitimate businessman has no need to do that."

"Well then, I guess the big question that remains, Emma, is, why did he go to the lengths that he did?" His eyes locked onto hers. "Wouldn't you agree?"

Twelve

Emma took a deep breath and let it out in a gusty sigh. "*Oui,* I suppose it is. It's just that it's" — she waved her hand — "kind of difficult to talk about, you know?"

Elvis sat with his heels dug into the soft sand beneath the blanket and his rangy legs drawn up, wrists resting on his kneecaps, his right hand dangling loosely and the hook sticking out in rigid contrast. He watched her in silence, allowing her time to gather her thoughts.

"Okay." Abruptly shaking back her hair, she blew out a deep breath and told him how she had come across the tapes that day in Grant's library. "They dated from the day I stole his car, Elvis, and they continued right up until about three weeks before the day I viewed them. They were taken on a camera I never even knew *existed,* let alone authorized the use of."

"What sort of tapes are we talking about?"

"You name it, he managed to capture it on film." God. She really didn't want to talk about this. But she unfortunately didn't have a lot of choice. "Of the seven tapes I took, I figure they were taken on cameras that were either high up in the walls or somewhere in the ceilings. They were set in my living room, my kitchen, my bedroom — *everywhere,* and either the cameras were motion activated or the tapes were spliced to cut out all the dead time when no one was there. If it was the latter" — she shuddered — "that means not only Grant saw them but whoever did the splicing saw them, too, because Grant's not the type to do the grunt work when he can have someone else do it for him."

"What kind of shots are we talking about here, Em?" Elvis demanded. "Nudies?" The idea gave him the same bottled-rage sensation he used to get when his mother locked him out so she could turn a trick.

"*Oui,* some of them. Most of them, though, could just as easily be mistaken by the average viewer for your run-of-the-mill home video. I mean, he's got me talking, cooking, reading, watching TV, even using the bathroom! *Dieu!*" She swiped at her arms as if brushing away insects. "Do you have any idea how crawly it makes me feel to know I didn't have one private moment in that house? That sick sonofabitch even has one of me and Charlie starring in our own little porno flick. At least that's the way it feels now. How many times has he viewed that tape, Elvis?" she wondered in a low, tortured tone. "Oh, God, did he *masturbate* to it?"

She hugged her knees tighter and met his eyes again. "Questions like that have haunted me ever since I laid eyes on the first tape. But that's not the worst of it, *cher*. I mean, let's face it, I haven't had the most sheltered of upbringings; I've knocked around a bit. When it comes right down to the wire I can usually take care of myself perfectly well. Had this concerned only me, then I might have stuck around to confront Grant about it."

Elvis snapped upright. "You mean . . . ?"

"Oh, *oui*. I told you they were in chronological order? Well, the most recent one was in a brand-new location. It was taken in Gracie's room."

Ruby stopped by Emma's table and studied her critically. "You've been looking a little peaky lately," she commented, giving the barely touched fruit and muffin plate in front of Emma a censorious look as she refilled her coffee cup. She straightened up and stood with her free hand on her hip, watching until the younger woman broke off a tiny piece of muffin and popped it into her mouth. Ruby gave a nod of approval and then stated unequivocally, "What you need is a nice night out to take your mind off your troubles."

"What I *need,*" Emma replied sourly, raising her voice slightly to project to where Elvis stood at the counter having his coffee cup filled, "is a sheriff who keeps his promises."

Elvis' shoulders stiffened. Saying something low to Bonnie, he turned and strode across the room, stopping in front of Emma's table. Ignoring the few interested patrons, he planted his hook and the knuckles of his right hand on the tabletop and leaned on them heavily, bending over until they were eyeball to eyeball. "I never promised that you could leave," he said flatly. "Not once did I do that. And I'm getting damned sick and tired of hearing you call me a liar all over town."

"Ly-oo, ly-oo, pants on fy-oo," Gracie's voice floated up from under the table and Elvis' eyes flared wrathfully, more intensely blue than usual with the wild burn of emotions that scudded across their surface. Like lasers, they focused on Emma with an intensity that pinned her to her seat. He looked furious. More than that, he looked betrayed.

Well, Mon Dieu, she thought in disgust, *as if I were the one who broke faith with* him. *The man sure as hell doesn't lack nerve.*

And yet . . .

"That's enough, Grace Melina," she said sternly, bending sideways to peer at her daughter who was lying on her stomach on the floor beneath the table, using her sidewalk chalk to decorate the backside of a paper placemat. "Neither Sheriff Elvis nor I were talking to you." Straightening, she returned her attention to Elvis. "And as for you, Sheriff, *oui,* it is true you did not promise me in so many words that my *bébé* and I could leave once I told you about . . ." Her voice dropped off as she glanced significantly at the tabletop that blocked Gracie from view but not from hearing. "You know." Her volume then returned to normal as she leveled a look at him. "But you certainly understood that I *thought* we had a bargain. And you did *nothing* to enlighten me to the contrary."

"What am I — a damn mind reader?" he demanded coolly, but it was hard to put any real feeling into denying the charge when in fact that was exactly how he'd played it. "Look, why don't we move this conversation over there," he suggested, jerking his head in the direction of the hallway. He didn't mind fighting with her; as usual it made him feel all revved up and alive. But he hated having her fight with him within earshot of the kid.

"That won't be necessary," she retorted dismissively. "This conversation is at an end as far as I'm concerned."

Gracie scooted out from under the table and climbed up onto her chair. She slapped her artwork down on a clean spot on the table. "Look!" she commanded to the table at large.

"Oh, that's pretty, *chérie,*" Emma said.

"Interesting use of color," agreed Ruby, who had seated herself at the table to enjoy the latest installment of the Elvis and Emma Show. Rocking her chair back on two legs, she reached for a clean cup from a neighboring table and settled back to pour herself some coffee.

"Nice work, Beans," Elvis offered. He studied it from three different angles but decided against asking her what it was supposed to represent.

Gracie stepped onto Emma's thighs and hooked an arm around her neck. She walked the fingers of her free hand up and down her mother's upper chest and shoulder as she swayed gently back and forth. "How come you wanna go fwom Pote Flannewy,

Maman? I yike it here."

Ruby and Elvis looked at Emma speculatively, wondering how she would get out of this one. They both knew she didn't like to tell her daughter lies. They also knew that in this case she could hardly tell her the absolute truth. Not, at least, without a long, involved explanation which the child would probably not understand, concerning as it did the man Gracie considered to be her grandfather.

Emma was caught unprepared, and she stared at her daughter in dismay. "Because it doesn't have a McDonald's," she said off the top of her head.

Gracie looked thoughtful. "Tha's twue," she said, and for a moment Elvis feared that the lack of the golden arches was all it would take to turn the tables. Damn. He'd have to fight both of them, then, and God knew he didn't want to do that. Then Gracie brightened. "But it has a Daiwy Fweeze," she said.

"So I guess what you're sayin' is that you think we should stick around for a couple more days then, huh?" Emma asked, and Gracie nodded enthusiastically. Then she lost interest and jumped down from Emma's lap. Begging a new placemat and retrieving her box of chalk, she trotted over to table seven and sprawled out on the floor beneath it to execute a new work of art.

Elvis pushed back from the table. "Well, I gotta get to work," he said. Raising his voice he called, "Bonnie! Can you warm that coffee up for me?" and walked away, stopping at the counter to pick up his order.

Ruby watched him go and turned back in time to see Emma doing the same. "Why are you so hard-nosed with the man?"

The wistfulness faded from Emma's eyes. "Because he deliberately led me to believe something he had no intention of following through on," she retorted. "In essence, he lied."

"He didn't lie," Ruby contradicted her, "he omitted." She gave a careless shrug. "And, really, even if he had lied, big deal. You plan on running for the rest of your life, Emma? Trust me, hon, you'll be safer staying right here where Donnelly can take care of you."

It didn't surprise Emma to realize that the entire island apparently knew about her troubles. The exact specifics might not be general knowledge, but everyone seemed to grasp the basic concept — that she was being pursued by a powerful relative who threatened her child, and that Elvis Donnelly was preventing her from fleeing the island.

Emma gave the waitress a narrow-eyed look. "Since when have you become an Elvis Donnelly cheerleader?" she demanded sarcastically. "There's somethin' drastically wrong with this picture, Ruby. If I didn't know better I'd say the Pod People substituted you for the real Ruby Kelly. They've probably got her wrapped up in a chrysalis and stashed under a bed somewhere."

Ruby shrugged. "Hey, he's an excellent sheriff — I've *always* said that. Besides, he's . . . different . . . since you came to town. More real somehow. And you can't deny he's crazy about that kid of yours. If anyone can keep her safe, it's Donnelly."

"I don't believe this," Emma muttered, shaking her head.

"Yeah, well, it kind of surprises me too," Ruby agreed. "But there you have it. I just don't think your leaving is such a great idea, okay? If you ask me —"

"Which I haven't."

"— your urge to run is based more on instinct than intellect. I don't think you've really thought this through, Emma." Ruby picked up the abandoned coffee pot and tested its side for warmth. Finding it still reasonably hot, she freshened both their cups. "Say, for the sake of argument, that by leaving the island you *do* shake this guy who's watching you. Then what, Emma? Sooner or later he's bound to catch up with you again, and what if it's in some town where you don't know a soul? Who you gonna turn to? At least here you've got people who'll look out for you. And having the law on your side is a definite plus — anywhere else you're going to have to talk a strange cop in a strange town into believing your story before he'll even consider taking any action. And just how long *can* you run, anyhow? Gracie should be playing with kids her own age, but where you gonna stop long enough to enroll her in a preschool? Where —"

"Okay, okay; *cher;* I get the picture." Emma buried her head in her hands. "*Dieu.* This is such a mess." Hands, rising, fingers still linked, to the top of her head, she peered up at the older woman. "Ruby, do you think for just an itsy-bitsy little nanosecond we could talk about somethin' else?"

"Sure, no problem. Here, eat your fruit." Ruby pushed the plate back in front of Emma. "As for a new subject, how about this? Let's you 'n' me go to the Anchor tomorrow night, chug a few beers, do a little dancin'. Like I was saying earlier, hon, I think what you really need is a nice night out."

* * *

"Emma." Elvis' deep voice was the last one she expected to hear. "I want to talk to you for a minute."

She gave a long-suffering sigh, raised her upper body out from under the hood of Mavis Blackerton's Ford, and wiped her hands on a rag. "What now, Sheriff?"

Almost immediately she regretted her tone of voice. Having put a great deal of consideration into Ruby's earlier conversation, she had privately decided that any future encounters with Elvis should be handled in a less confrontational manner than the past few had been. Without agreeing with Ruby's assessment one hundred percent, Emma was willing to concede that maybe — just maybe — there was a little bit of value in what Ruby had said. Waving an erasing hand, she said, "Let me begin again," in quiet apology for her snippiness. Peeling off her surgical gloves, she faced the large sheriff. "What is it that I can do for you, Elvis?"

For his part Elvis manfully suppressed the urge to offer her a truly hot and nasty suggestion. Even in dressing him down, that low, Southern drawl of hers got to him, and to his disgust, he had found her antagonism the past few days downright arousing. "I, uh . . ." He cleared his throat. "We gotta talk about those tapes. I know they're personal, Em, but I'd like to see them."

"You can't, they're gone." For the first time she was glad of it. She went hot all over merely at the *thought* of Elvis seeing some of the material that had been caught on those videos. *Dieu,* part of that stuff involved moments in her life so private . . .

He snapped upright from his indolent lounging against the car fender. "They're *what!?*"

"Gone. I *told* you that, Elvis. Oh, no, I guess I didn't, did I?" She shrugged defensively. "Well, I was going to . . . but then you went and announced that unilateral decision you'd made to keep me 'n' Gracie from leaving your oh-so-hospitable island, and I guess I forgot about it."

"You forgot? Christ, Emma, how the hell does someone *forget* something like — ?" He shook his head. "No. Never mind; let's not get into that." He let out the deep breath he'd just drawn. Then through clenched teeth he commanded, "Tell me what happened to them."

"When I got back from the Mackeys' the other night — the fourth? — I discovered them gone. They were on the closet shelf before the parade, but when I went to check on them they were no longer there." She raised her head and gave him a level look. "Which means one of Grant's flunkies got into my room to recover them for him. Does this sort of give you an idea of why I no longer feel particularly safe here?"

"Had the lock been forced?"

"No."

"And nothing else had been taken?"

"No. It was an object lesson, Elvis," she said in exasperation. "Grant wanted me to know that when it comes to playing games with him, I can't win. So I packed up and ran." All right, she was already packing to run when she'd discovered the tapes missing, but it was a minor detail — and one she knew would play better with Elvis than the other way around. "Don't you see, Elvis —"

"Forget it — you're not leaving," he interrupted. God, he could read her like a book. "Your chances of keeping both you *and* the kid safe are a lot greater if you stay here where there are people who are willing and able to lend a hand if you need one. Dammit, Em!" He raked his hair back in frustration. "I wish I could make you see that running away isn't the way to handle —"

"Okay," she interrupted him wearily.

"Huh?"

"I said *okay*. I won't fight you on this anymore; me and Gracie, we'll stay." She met his eyes, and her own — normally such a clear, deep brown — were cloudy with uncertainty. "God help us all, though, Elvis, if you and Ruby turn out to be wrong about this. If anything happens to my *bébé* I will never forgive you."

"You've never forgiven me for not saving Evan, have you?" Sam asked out of the blue one evening.

Clare looked up in shock. They had been sitting in the living room, companionably she'd thought, she reading, he staring out the window at the view while he listened to Clint Black sing that the lights were on but nobody was home. It caught her flatfooted, to be suddenly hit with this.

"That's not true," she said in distress. "I *know* there was nothing you could have done to prevent him from dying!" She could still hear him yelling at Evan to stay away from the edge of the cliff, to get *back*. She could still see him running flat-out to intercept their son before Evan could reach the unfenced edge; could hear his howl of rage and despair as the undermined ground gave way beneath Evan's slight weight; could picture his futile dive for the body that tumbled out of sight over the edge.

"Intellectually, maybe," Sam said. He tore his gaze away from the view and turned to face her, his eyes moody. He hadn't intended to have this conversation. But they'd been sitting there for the past hour like two distant relatives, amiable enough but basically apart, and it had just sort of burst out of him. It was a subject that had haunted him for over a year. "Emotionally though . . ." He let it trail off and shrugged. "It's doubtful you've accepted it emotionally."

"That's bullshit, Sam. Complete and utter bullshit."

"Is it? Then why the hell did you lock me out?" He looked at her fiercely. "Huh? Why did you turn away from me during the one time I needed you most? During the one time when I needed you to need *me?*"

"God, Sammy, why not ask a blind woman to describe the nuances and shades of a Monet painting?" She pulled her knee up on the couch cushion as she swiveled to face him. "How am I supposed to explain what I don't even understand myself?" she demanded. Nevertheless, she made the attempt.

"It hurt to be touched by anyone, Sam. God" — her fist clenched on her thigh — "it hurt so bad. When Evan died it was like someone had skinned me alive. They left me breathing, but every single inch of me was one big exposed nerve ending that screamed in agony at the slightest contact. I couldn't live with that kind of torment, so I grew a shell. A nice, thick, foam-rubber outer covering that cushioned the pain and layered it with numbness."

She reached out a hesitant hand to brush a lock of hair from his forehead. "But I never meant to add to *your* grief," she said in a low voice. "I simply didn't consider your suffering; I was too busy staying attuned to my own. It was selfish, Sam, selfish, plain and simple, and I'm sorry." More than anything she longed to be pulled into his arms and held by him, but he made no move to reach for her and she felt she had forfeited any rights to make demands on him in this marriage. Girding herself to make the first move anyway, she was just straightening in her seat to offer a hug when he surged to his feet.

Sam shook a cigarette out of the pack on the coffee table and struck a match. Lighting up, he paced restlessly to the fireplace and tossed the spent match into the grate. "Are you as tired of these four walls as I am?" he demanded, coming back to stare down at her where she still sat looking up at him from the couch. He had to get them moving before he did something that she was clearly not ready for. "Let's go honky-tonkin'," he demanded. At least at the Anchor he'd have a legitimate excuse to hold her in his arms.

Clare stared up at him. Cigarette clamped between his teeth and blue smoke curling up from its tip to screen his narrowed eyes, she couldn't tell what he was thinking as he returned her look. But she liked the idea of going dancing with him. *Anything* to bring a little physical contact back into this marriage. She rose to her feet.

"That sounds like fun. Let me just go get changed."

"Fun," Emma muttered to herself. "*Fun.* I don't even know what that word *means* anymore." She lifted up Gracie to let her press the doorbell. Setting her back on her feet, she barely straightened before the door opened. "I don't know about this, Ruby," she said uncertainly to the woman standing before her. "I'm not sure this is such a hot idea."

"It's a great idea." Ruby ushered Emma and Gracie into her house and closed the door behind them. "It's exactly what the doctor ordered — for both of you." She turned to Gracie. "Hiya, kiddo."

"Hi, Miss Wuby! I gots my jammies."

"Good girl. Why don't you put your bag down over there on the couch, honey. Mary's been looking forward to having a pajama party with you ever since I mentioned it, haven't you, hon?" she inquired of her daughter, who had walked into the living room.

"You betcha. Hi, Emma. You look really pretty. Hiya, squirt." Mary squatted down in front of Gracie. "We're going to make a pizza tonight, and I rented us a couple a Disney flicks to watch. Or I've still got my old doll collection, if you wanna play with those." She looked up at Emma. "You just go on out and have a good time with my mom. I'll take real good care of the squirt here."

"Oh, *chère,* I don't know . . ."

Ruby made a disgusted noise deep in her throat and snagged Emma's arm. She dragged her into the kitchen and swung her around until Emma was up against the counter. "Now, stop that," she commanded. "Here. Have a beer. Try to lighten up." Stepping back, she looked Emma over assessingly and nodded with approval. "At least you paid attention when I suggested what to wear. You look great."

Emma looked down on her burnt-orange tank top, short, swingy, African-print gray-green, black and khaki skirt, and the twisted fabric and metallic belt that separated them. Ruby had insisted the other day that it was time she had some fun. "You and me are going to have us a girls' night out at the Anchor," she had said. "And in honor of this momentous occasion it's only right that you should break out the serious hardware. Wear a tank top and some short-shorts or something. Leave your bra at home. You've got a figure that most of us would kill for. I can't figure out why you never try to get at least a *little* extra mileage out of it."

Well, the bra remained firmly in place, but it was a demicup model constructed of antique gold lace, and Emma had decided what the hell about the rest of it. It was kind of fun to dress trashy and put on a little extra makeup for a change. It had been forever since she'd done anything like this, and she'd enjoyed herself immensely when she was getting ready. But the closer it got to actually leaving Gracie for an evening . . . "Ruby, I'm worried."

"I know you are, hon, but have a little faith in me, won'tcha? It's going to be fine."

"It was just five days ago that Gracie was

snatched out from under my nose. What if — ?"

"What if's not gonna happen," Ruby assured her firmly. "Mary and I were careful about this. I didn't tell a soul that you and I were going out tonight, and Mary didn't even tell Sue Anne Baker about Gracie spending the night with her. Now that, hon, is not a trivial sacrifice. Sue Anne is her very best friend in the whole wide world, and those two tell each other everything."

"What about your son?"

"Denny? He's visiting a friend in Seattle for the weekend; we didn't see the point in mentioning it to him. Now, logistically, did you drive the route I told you to?"

"Yes."

"And there was nobody behind you?"

"No."

"Well, there you go then, hon. You drive on back to the boarding house now, and I'll come pick you up in about ten minutes. Even if you're still being watched and we're seen together at the Anchor by your watcher, that's not going to lead him to Gracie. Mary gave me her word that if they go outside at all tonight, it will only be in the back yard, and see for yourself." She opened the kitchen door. "It's completely enclosed by that privacy fence." Closing the door again, she turned the deadbolt key. "And see here? She'll also keep the doors locked at all times." Picking up the phone receiver she pointed out the functions she'd keyed into it. "This button is direct-dial to the sheriff's office. This one's to the Anchor. Trust me, Emma." She reached out to tenderly rearrange a wave of streaky blond hair at Emma's temple. "It's going to be all right, and the truth is, honey, you need this. Gracie needs this."

So it was that Emma found herself walking with Ruby through the front door of the Anchor a short while later. The tavern wasn't a citified fern bar for the upwardly mobile; it was an old-fashioned honky-tonk with a parking lot full of pickup trucks, dim lighting, loud conversation, and good western music that provided both background noise and accompaniment for the dancers on the establishment's two small dance floors. Cigarette smoke picked up the colors of the neon beer signs over the bar and hung in a blue haze between the pool table and the green-shaded hanging light suspended above it. This wasn't the place to order a champagne cocktail.

People greeted Ruby by name, men pulled their shoulders back and sucked their stomachs in as Emma walked by, and

Emma's mood elevated like a rocket. This *was* fun. She'd forgotten how exhilarating a little uncomplicated appreciation could be.

Ruby was right, she had needed this. There had been too many emotions packed into too short a time, and the responsibility to find a way clear of the mess she was in had been solely hers. Tomorrow the problems would still be there and the responsibility would once again be hers, but for tonight she was going to allow herself an evening away from them . . . and from the ever-demanding accountability of motherhood. She could use a few hours of oblivion and the pursuit of a little relaxation wasn't such a bad objective.

She was invited to dance before she and Ruby even found a table, and at Ruby's urging, she accepted. When she got back from an energetic two-step to Kim Hill's "Janie's Gone Fishin' " she found Ruby seated with Clare and Sam Mackey at a table next to the smaller dance floor where the line dancers held forth. She greeted everyone, thanked her partner for the dance — for a heavyset man with a beer belly and barrel chest he'd been amazingly light on his feet — and took a seat.

Brooks and Dunn launched into "Ride 'Em High, Ride 'Em Low," and a new man materialized to ask Emma for a dance. Laughing good-naturedly, she fended him off with a "You have gotta let me get myself situated first, *cher,*" and turning to the waitress who had appeared requested a Jax.

"Huh?"

"A bottle of Jax, *s'il vous plaît?*"

"It's a brand of long-neck that's popular in the South, Marion," Sam interjected. "Just bring us another pitcher, hey?" Turning to Emma he said, "Jax hasn't made it this far north. You're going to have to make do with a local brew."

"Whatever," she agreed with a cheerful shrug.

Clare leaned over the table. "Love your skirt, Emma," she said, raising her voice to be heard over the music. "Are the panties built in?"

"*Oui.* This is my dancin' skirt."

"Let's hope it doesn't start a riot," Sam muttered. Every guy in the joint had probably noticed the tight little panties with the high-cut legs when Gus Moser had twirled her around.

"What's that, *cher?*" She leaned closer, cocking an ear. "I'm afraid I couldn't hear you."

"Never mind. It was nothing important."

Emma studied him for a moment and

then shrugged. "I don't suppose your music ever runs to zydeco, does it?"

"Afraid not," he said dryly.

"A little accordion maybe?" she asked hopefully. Sometimes she grew homesick for the Cajun sounds she'd grown up with.

"Nope. Just your everyday country western."

"Ah, well. The dancin's pretty much the same, in any case."

And dance she did, all night long. She waltzed with weathered farmers; she two-stepped with insurance salesmen, accountants, and machinists. A handsome young dentist claimed her for a West Coast Swing to Tanya Tucker's "It's a Little Too Late" and she joined Ruby and Clare in a line dance, doing the tush push to "Mona Lisa." A fine sheen of perspiration glowed on her skin by the time she begged off a dance and collapsed in her seat, picking up her beer and gulping it down before rolling the condensation-dewed side of the glass against her forehead.

The chair next to her scraped back and a large body dropped into it. Emma took a deep breath, then slowly let it out. Turning in her seat, polite smile in place, she was determined to beg an extra five minutes to catch her breath before starting another round of dancing.

But it wasn't a new partner, come to demand a dance. It was Elvis Donnelly. He nodded his thanks to the waitress who had set down a clean glass in front of him and reached across the table for the pitcher. Pouring himself a beer, he took a sip, wiped the foam from his upper lip with the back of his prosthesis, and leaned back in his chair to give Emma a thorough once-over. "Heard you were the belle of the ball tonight, Em," he said, seemingly without any apparent opinion on the subject one way or the other. "Thought I'd better come check it out for myself."

Thirteen

He had seduction on his mind. When Sam had called to let him know that Emma was inciting lustful thoughts in a tavern full of the susceptible and suggested that perhaps he might care to join them after work, Elvis had nearly blown a gasket waiting for his shift to end. His patience had run out with twenty minutes still on the clock, and instructing his deputy to take over, he'd raced home, changed his clothes, and shaved, gritting his teeth at the extra time it took to take care around his scar and worrying the whole time that she'd hit it off with some good-looking Saturday-night cowboy before he could get there. If that happened he didn't know what the hell he would do.

He considered her *his.*

Jesus, it was a feeling so strong, if he were a dog he'd be pissing circles around her to mark her as his territory and warn off the other hounds. And he could just imagine how well *that* sort of macho possessive bullshit would go over with Emma. She was a strong and independent woman; it was doubtful she considered herself anybody's property but her own. Nevertheless, he took heart in knowing this much. She wasn't entirely indifferent to him.

Accustomed as he was to going into Seattle whenever he could no longer fight the need for sex, he'd grown into the habit of discounting the idea of ever having it with anyone here on the island. It had therefore taken quite a while for it to dawn on him that Emma hadn't exactly beat him off with a stick that night up in her room. That she had, in fact, gone a little crazy over nothing more than a little suck on her bottom lip. The truth was she'd been primed and ready . . . until he'd gone and wrecked his own chances of getting lucky by leveling rash accusations at her.

There was a combustible attraction between them that they couldn't quite bury. Hell, look at that kiss they'd shared, the one that had so upset little Beans. Neither of them had intended it to get out of hand — it just had. So if she was looking for someone to flirt and dance with tonight . . .

"So, tell me," he demanded, "where'd you stash the kid tonight?"

She leaned close to eliminate the need to yell. It was highly unlikely that anyone in a position to overhear would have the slightest interest in her answer, but where

Gracie's safety was concerned she wasn't taking even the minutest chance. "Mary Kelly's got her," she said beneath the music, the clacking balls on the pool table, the rowdy conversations going on all around them. Scooting closer still, she talked directly into his ear, recounting how Ruby had planned this evening right down to the last detail. He draped his arm over the back of her chair while he listened.

When she pulled back their faces were only inches apart. They stared into each other's eyes for a moment, and then Elvis moved his mouth to her ear. "So Gracie's spending the entire night with her?" His breath, blowing warm across the whorls, scented with toothpaste when it drifted as far as her nose, caused goosebumps to crop up along her entire left side. She nodded, looking up at him.

"It's good for you to have a night out," he approved in a low, husky voice. Suzy Bogguss started to sing "You Shouldn't Say That to a Stranger," and his fingers lifted off the back of her chair and brushed down her bare arm. "You want to dance?"

"Oui." They rose to their feet.

The song was a slow, torchy one, and Elvis pulled her into his arms the minute they reached the dance floor. Slipping his right arm around her waist, he offered up his prosthesis and Emma slid her fingers through the hook, folding them around the clip to maintain a grasp. He then brought it in close to his chest and holding her carefully, started to move. Within moments he had them buried in the middle of the dance floor and was holding her with less caution and more intent. Lifting up his hook, carrying her fingers to his mouth, he kissed her two middle knuckles and then rubbed the backs of all four fingers against his smooth-shaven cheek. He bent his head until his lips were next to her ear. "Let go," he instructed in a low, rough voice and demonstrated his intent by giving the prosthesis a tiny wiggle. "I want to feel both your arms around my neck."

She let go and wrapped both arms around his neck. Her breasts flattened slightly against his chest as his left arm slid around her and pulled her in close to his body. Bending the arm, he aligned his elbow at her waist and his prosthesis rode the shallow groove of her spine, pressing against it firmly to keep her close. His right fingers slid over her hip below her waist and splayed out.

Tightening her arms in reaction, Emma buried her nose in the little notch at the base of his throat and inhaled. He smelled so good. Normally he smelled of soap and water, of fabric softener and starch. Tonight was no exception, the aromas that she'd grown accustomed to associating with him were ever present. But added to them was a touch of aftershave or cologne, something subtle that was there one moment and gone the next. She rose up on her toes and burrowed her face into the warm skin where his neck curved into his shoulder, seeking out the elusive scent. But it was drifting up from the triangular hollow at the base of his throat where she'd first smelled it, and she parted her lips and pressed a small kiss against the spot. The fan of chest hair that began just below that site tickled her mouth.

Elvis sucked in a breath. Jesus! Just who the hell was doing the seducing here? He lowered his mouth to her ear. "I want to take you back to my room," he said hoarsely.

"Mmmm." Her arms tightened and her breasts shifted in a subtle sideways rub against his chest.

He scrunched his chin into his neck, trying to see her face. "What does that mean, mmmm? Would you go?"

She raised her head, tilting it back slightly to look into his eyes. Her hair waved softly back from her face, and she smiled dreamily. *"Mais oui,"* she replied in a low, husky voice. But yes.

"Damn," he breathed. She squeaked at the sudden convulsive clench of his arms around her, and he forced himself to relax his grip. "Sorry," he apologized. "You okay, Em? Can you breathe?"

She took a tentative breath and, when her ribs held, nodded.

"Listen," he said urgently, "what do you say we get the hell outta —"

Suzy's last notes trailed into silence at that moment, and two men instantly materialized beside them, all but elbowing each other in unsubtle attempts to be the first to ask Emma for the next dance. Elvis' immediate impulse was to fend them off, to snap and snarl like a rabid dog, until they retreated with their tails between their legs. Instead, he forced himself to take a step back and leave the field free. Given the way the folks in this town felt about him, it would be much better for Emma if he handled this with a modicum of discretion.

"Elvis?" she said uncertainly as the crowd began to jostle them apart. She reached for his hand, but although their fingers made contact they slowly slid apart as the crowd leaving the dance floor moved them in separate directions.

"Thanks for the dance," he said politely. His voice was cool, courteous. His eyes were anything but. "I hope you'll save me another."

"Well, yes, sure. But what about . . . ?" She watched him in confusion as he turned and shouldered his way back to the table. *Dammit, Elvis, is that it? Thanks for the dance?* Absent-mindedly she took up her position in the two-step with her new partner, moving automatically when the music began. Well . . . *merde. Merde, merde, merde!* What in the name of Glory had happened to "What do you say we get out of here"?

On the other hand, it was entirely possible he was displaying more sense than she was. The people she cared about had a distressing habit of dying on her. It certainly wouldn't do, for instance, to let Grant's minions know that she was developing deeper feelings for Elvis Donnelly than she had thus far exhibited for anyone else in town. The only possible outcome she could see from that would be placing Elvis' life in jeopardy.

Yes, surely discretion was the solution. *If* that was what turning his back on her and walking away had been all about.

And not that he had simply changed his mind.

* * *

Sam refilled a glass and passed it to Elvis the minute he dropped into the seat next to his. Scraping his own chair nearer to his friend's, he stubbed out his cigarette, shoved aside the overflowing ashtray in front of him, and said sarcastically, "I thought at the very least we'd get to see a little blood flow. Damn, E, when did you turn into such a pussy?"

Elvis tore his eyes away from the skirt that swirled up around Emma's waist and then flared out again before finally swinging back into place around her thighs. He transferred his scowl to his best friend. "What the hell are you talking about, Mackey?"

"I'm talking about that sad display out there on the dance floor, man. Jesus, Elvis, I thought you'd be crackin' some heads together, but you just let those two yahoos horn right in on your woman."

Elvis shrugged, raising the glass to his lips, his eyes narrowed as they once again tracked Emma's progress around the floor. "So let 'em have a thrill," he said to Sam without removing his gaze from the floor. "Trust me, it's gonna be a momentary one. When the Anchor shuts down tonight, she's going home with *me*." Pulling his gaze off the floor, he looked at his friend and then added seriously, "But I'd just as soon the entire town doesn't know and speculate about it, Sam. No sense in wrecking her standing in the community if we don't have to." He looked back at the dance floor in time to see Emma whirled around again. She should never have been let out of her room wearing that skirt. It was too damn incendiary.

When the music changed, Emma went from one partner's arms into another man's. Sam and Clare got up to dance, and just to be polite Elvis turned to Ruby and asked if she would care to dance. He was caught by surprise when she took him up on his offer.

"Which floor?" he inquired as he escorted her from the table. "Line?" He tipped his chin toward the tiny floor where line dancing was held. "Or two-step or swing?" He gave her a quick, assessing glance. She'd pick line.

"Let's see." Ruby gnawed her lip for a second as she considered the logistics. Line dancing would be simpler, of course, for there was no touching. And yet . . . "Two-step, I think."

Again he was surprised, but his expression didn't change. He hadn't given away his feelings on any subject he didn't intend to give them away on since he was seventeen years old. "Good enough. I caution you, though, that we'll have to wing it on any spins instigated off my left hand." It was fair warning, for which he received in return a grin so spontaneous he found himself smiling back at her in sheer reaction.

"What the hell," she said cheerfully, raising her voice to be heard over the music. "I've seen you move, Sheriff, and at least I know you're light on your feet. Better we fumble a couple spins than my tootsies get trampled." She shrugged good-naturedly as she explained, "Standing on my feet all day every day, I tend to get a tad protective of them."

Ruby had never actually seen him dance before; the few times they'd been in the Anchor at the same time he'd simply sat on the sidelines and watched. As far as she knew, he had never once asked anyone to dance, not needing to be told, most likely, that most of the women in town would turn him down flat. She did, however, see him daily in the café and around town. And more than once she had noted his natural grace.

Besides, she'd seen him with Emma. When the two of them had first walked onto the dance floor, he'd handled her as gingerly as if she were made of the finest, most easily shattered china. Ruby found herself completely at ease with him, much to her own surprise, and not even a little apprehensive at the idea of touching that metal hook. Hell, even the scar on his face didn't make him seem so threatening tonight.

She recognized that her attitude regarding this man had changed quite a bit since Emma Sands had come to town.

They danced together with surprising smoothness, and Elvis didn't hesitate to ask her a second time later in the evening. He also danced once with Clare. The entire time he was on the dance floor, however, and while sitting at the table between dances, drinking beer and exchanging rude comments with Sam, he kept track of Emma's movements. When at the end of a song he saw her disappear down the dim hallway that led to the restrooms, he pushed back from the table.

Emma dried off her hands, used the edge of her little finger to smooth away a smear of eyeliner, fluffed up her hair with her fingers, and stood back to survey the results. Not bad; the ravages caused by the whirlwind of dances were mostly invisible, thank God. These Western men were an energetic bunch. Girding herself, she exited the ladies' room — and walked straight into Elvis Donnelly's chest.

"Hey," he growled. Sparing a quick glance up and down the hall, he clamped a hand around her wrist, maneuvered them into an old cloak room that in the summertime was never used, and backed her up against the wall. Then he bent his head and kissed her.

It was hot and urgent, all bold, ravenous suction and aggressive, probing tongue. When he finally lifted his mouth, Emma was gripping his waist with both hands, and mutually stunned, they stared into each other's eyes for a few moments, surrounded by a pocket of silence that was broken only by the sounds of their ragged breathing. Emma licked her lips. "I thought you'd changed your mind," she said hoarsely.

"Why the hell would you think that?" He bent his head to nuzzle her ear, pressed his open mouth against the side of her throat.

She gave him a little shove. "Why *wouldn't* I think that, you big bozo? You said you wanted to take me to your room, but then you just walked away. *Mon Dieu,* you haven't even bothered to dance with me since then."

"Oh." He thought about his actions from

her point of view. "Don't be angry with me, Em. I guess I was too damn subtle for my own good." His eyes closed briefly at the feel of her breasts flattening beneath his chest and he pressed a little harder, rubbing against her once like an overgrown cat looking to be stroked. Then he pushed back slightly with the forearms he'd braced against the wall on either side of her head. He looked down at her. "My intentions were good. I was protecting your reputation."

"You were? Why, what an amazing coincidence, *cher,*" she said, and one corner of her mouth tilted up in a wry smile as she gazed up at him. "When I didn't chase after you, screamin' 'Breach of Promise,' I was protectin' yours, too."

He stilled, dropping the tendril of hair he'd hooked around his forefinger and begun to fiddle with. "Yeah, right," he agreed stiffly, an edge of sarcasm coloring his voice as he slowly straightened. "A fella's only got his good name after all." And his wasn't worth shit in this town.

"I wasn't mocking you, Elvis, if that's what you think," she said quietly. "Anyone who gets too close to me tends not to have to worry overmuch about collectin' their social security benefits. If Grant's goon is still hangin' around I would very much like to avoid constructin' a big ol' neon arrow that points straight at you." She touched gentle fingertips to his jaw. "That's all I meant, *cher*."

"Oh. Sorry." He was surprised and discomforted by his own sensitivity on the subject. Generally, he couldn't give a rip what Flannery Island had to say about him. With Emma, though, everything seemed to take on new and crucial overtones.

Huh. Impatiently, he shouldered the thought — and all the ramifications that arose from it — aside. "Listen," he said instead, "when last call comes, what do you say I offer to walk you home? It's the neighborly thing to do, after all."

The corners of her mouth ticked up. "Being a good neighbor is such an important quality," she agreed solemnly.

"Oh, yes, ma'am, *very* important. We put a great deal of stock in that kinda thing here in Port Flannery." He gave her a lopsided smile. "So how did you and Ruby get here, anyway? Did you walk down from the boarding house?"

"She drove us," she said; then her head dropped back against the wall when he went back to kissing her neck. Her hips were beginning to make little instinctual bumps and grinds before he finally pushed back with palpable reluctance. "Damn," he breathed out. Shoving his fingers through his hair, he stared down at her. "You'd better go back to the table, Emma. I'll follow in a few minutes."

"Promise that you'll dance with me one more time before last call," she demanded. She smoothed her hair and tucked in her tank top.

"Yeah, sure. We better make it one of the fast numbers though. Otherwise I might not be able to walk off the dance floor."

Emma grinned and patted his cheek. "Why, Elvis Donnelly, you little ol' sweet talker, you. I bet you say that to all the women, just to make 'em feel allurin'."

Elvis snorted. He watched her walk away.

Then he went into the men's room and bought out the condom machine.

The early morning air was cool, wafting off the harbor with a faint scent of sea salt, and the town was dark and quiet when the door of the tavern closed behind them a short while later. Emma and Elvis stood in the parking lot with Ruby, Sam, and Clare, saying good nights that became protracted every time someone introduced something they swore would just take a second and that ultimately reminded one of the others of something that must be said. Though they were exceedingly careful to keep a distance between them and not allow so much as their fingertips to brush, the tension that arced between Emma and Elvis was nearly an audible crackle by the time Ruby and the Mackeys finally climbed into their respective cars and drove off. Then, unsmiling and authoritative as if he were conducting her off to jail, Elvis put a hand beneath Emma's elbow and escorted her from the tavern's lot to the sidewalk, politely ushering her out of the path of departing pickup trucks and American-made cars.

The last set of headlights had flashed past them by the time they walked past Mackey's General Store. Glancing down the deserted street, Elvis yanked Emma into the shadows cast by the side of the building, and she had but a scant instant to register the quiet lap of water against pilings before he kissed her. By the time he raised his head, the back of her skirt was rucked up around her waist, his hand was underneath it alternately squeezing and stroking a rounded cheek, and the back of Emma's knee was hooked up over his hip, her arms clamped tightly around his neck.

"Jesus," he said hoarsely, sliding her leg

away and taking a step back. "Making it home at this rate could turn out to be something of a trick."

"As my *bébé* would say, I yike twicks," she assured him.

Elvis gave her an ironic smile that involved only the right corner of his mouth. "Keep in mind that you said that, doll," he advised her dryly. "Because the next trick might involve getting nailed by a horny sheriff on a public street."

"Oh. Good point." She took a giant step away from him. "So, how fast can you walk, anyhow?"

They managed to make it through the front door of his room. Then for the third time that evening Emma found herself whirled around and pinned between Elvis' massive body and a hard surface, this time the wall next to the door. Hook thumping down next to her right cheek, his fingers tangling in the hair behind her left ear, he kissed her with voracious need. His tongue penetrated and withdrew from her mouth in a rhythm so insistently carnal, she ignited like a Molotov cocktail with an extremely short fuse.

Emma's thought processes weren't involved when she wedged her hands between their bodies and fumbled to unbutton his shirt; she was running strictly on instinct. Accomplishing her task, she worked the tails out of his waistband and ripped her own tank top free of her skirt, jerking it up to bunch beneath her armpits. She reached behind her and unhooked her bra, yanking that up, too. Then she arched her back, thrusting her bare breasts against his bared chest. A breathy sound of satisfaction rose in her throat.

Elvis ripped his mouth free. "Ah, Jesus, Em," he said hoarsely, and rubbed his chest rhythmically against her, feeling her breasts rub and glide across hair-roughened muscle and skin. He reached behind her and fumbled for the zipper to her skirt. Usually agile with his hook, it felt like a millennium before he accessed the series of movements necessary to get her out of the combination skirt and pantie set. But finally it dropped down around her ankles, and as she kicked free of it he scooped his prosthesis beneath her buttocks and raised her up.

Emma spread her legs, prepared to wrap them around his waist, but then she said, "No, wait — *wait,* Elvis," as she reached between them to wrestle with his fly. He raised her up a little higher just as she succeeded in lowering the zipper, bringing her breasts up to face level.

"Oh, God, these are beautiful," he said gruffly. "I knew they would be, Emma, but I didn't know they'd be this gorgeous." His tongue came out to moisten his lower lip as he stared at her breasts.

They were a young man's fantasy, something out of a girlie magazine. Soft-skinned and pale in the dim light, they were firm and high and full, capped with pert beige nipples.

Emma laughed deep in her throat. "Enjoy 'em while you can, *cher,*" she advised. "If I ever have another baby they'll probably be down around my waist."

"Did you use 'em to breast-feed Beans?" His eyes didn't leave the lush curves.

"Um hmm."

"Yeah?"

"*Oui.*"

"Oh, man, I would have liked to have seen that." Lowering his head, he nudged aside the gold lace bra that tangled above the thrust of her breasts and opened his mouth around one of her erect nipples. Electric blue eyes flashing up to lock in intent gaze on her face, he gave the nipple an experimental suck.

"Oh!" she breathed, staring down at him, watching his eyes watch hers, seeing his cheeks flex, feeling her nipple distend and then the heat, like a renegade live wire, streak from it to vaginal muscles deep between her legs. Those, in turn, clenched with a force almost painful. He sucked again and her head thumped back against the wall. *"Mon Dieu!"*

Back braced on the wall, knees wide and the soles of her feet flat against his hips, she used them to slide his pants and shorts down. She reached between them to grasp his penis in one hand when it sprang free of the constricting clothing. It was long and thick, a hot, rigid length that pulsed beneath soft, veined flesh as she stroked it with her fist.

Emma's nipple left Elvis' mouth with a pop as his head reared back, and he swore a blue streak. Then, "Oh, God. Oh, Jesus, Em. Put your legs around my waist," he commanded, groping down around his knees for his pants. He fumbled a condom out of a pocket and brought it up to his mouth, catching one edge between his teeth and ripping it open. "Help me. Please . . . Jesus. Oh, God; oh, there, Emma. *There* . . . *thank* you." And protected, he braced her back against the wall, hooked his right hand beneath her left thigh and the base of his prosthesis beneath her right thigh and pulled them wide. Her hand guided his erection and he pushed into her firmly, steadily, until he was buried deep. Breathing hard, he dropped his head to her neck.

"Hold still a minute, Emma," he begged. She brought her arms up to wrap around his neck and locked her legs tighter around his hips. "Jeez-us God!" He sucked air into his lungs, fighting for control. "Hold still, hold still, *please.* Jesus, Em, please. You feel so good."

Gritting her teeth, Emma did as he requested: she held herself perfectly still. He was big and hard inside her, and she throbbed like crazy along every inch that stretched to accommodate him, but she held still, sucking furiously at her lower lip to keep from crying out against the strain it imposed.

Elvis saw her lip disappear in a flash of white teeth and contracted his hips, nearly withdrawing, then thrust back in again, one time, hard and fast. "God, it makes me crazy when you do that," he said, and leaned forward to take her lip for himself. Sucking at it, gnawing on it, he rotated his hips, and then began to pump steadily.

Emma whimpered. Friction built with the continued firm and rhythmic oscillations of his hips, and each new thrust elicited a fresh little cry from her. Elvis pulled his mouth away, a groan rumbling up from his chest. He stared at her from beneath heavy eyelids.

"Oh, God, yes, that's it; I want to hear you," he demanded hoarsely. He began to slam into her and neither one noticed when a nearby picture bounced off its hook and slid down the wall. "Let me hear you moan, Em. I want to hear you *scream*."

Her moans grew higher in pitch. She tightened her thighs around him, gripping him like a vise, her crossed heels banging into the small of his back. Tension coiled tighter and tighter deep inside of her.

"Oh, Elvis," she whispered raggedly. "Oh, Elvis, oh, Elvis, *oh . . . !*" She broke into a torrent of French. Her arms constricted around his neck, her fingernails dug crescents in the solid muscles of his shoulders, and her head lolled back against the wall as if suddenly too heavy for her slender neck to bear upright. Interior feminine muscles suddenly compressing, she climaxed in hard, fast contractions around him. Her voice degenerated into a long, drawn-out, soft-voiced wail.

Elvis' breath exploded out of his lungs and he snapped his hips back and then slammed them forward one last time, scraping her back against the wall with the jerk of his grip against her thighs and the uncontrolled power of his thrust. *"Emma!"* He came explosively, emitting a deep, guttural groan with each hot pulsation. When the last throb finally died away, his head dropped forward and his forehead hit the wall with an audible thunk. He gathered Emma into a crushing hug.

"Damn," he said when the breath had finally quit blasting out of his lungs as if from an overworked bellows. "I'm sorry, Emma." He raised up his head to look at her. "I'm sorry; damn, I don't believe this. I usually manage a little more in the way of foreplay than 'Brace yourself.' "

Emma laughed and tightened her grip around his neck. "I feel so good, Elvis," she said. "Ah, *cher,* I don't *remember* the last time I felt this good."

"God, you're a generous woman," he murmured, bowing his head to press kisses into the curve of her neck and along her shoulders. Securing his grasp on the undersides of her thighs, he stepped back from the wall, prepared to carry her, still joined to him, to the bed several steps across the room.

That was when he discovered the pants he'd forgotten he still wore were down around his ankles, hobbling him.

"Oh, man, this is too pitiful for words," he muttered, taking shuffling steps toward the bed. "My damn *boots* are still on." He dove the last few feet, carrying her down onto the mattress beneath him but immediately pushing up onto his forearms and rolling to one side to spare her his weight. Tenderly he brushed the hair out of her eyes.

"I really wanted to do this right," he said. "My aim was to sweep you off your feet — something along the lines of Rhett carrying Scarlett up the staircase." The left corner of his mouth curled up. "Instead I came up with Abbott and Costello." Removing the condom, he leaned over, plucked a tissue from the box on the nightstand and deftly wrapped it around the spent protection. He tossed the bundle into the wastebasket beside the bed, then rolled back to face her.

"Yes, and it's a fine mess you've gotten us into this time, Stanley," Emma said pedantically. Then she let out a deep, rich, belly laugh. "You're too much," she gasped when the laughter finally subsided. Wriggling out from under him, she tipped him over onto his back and scrambled down to the end of the bed, where she presented him with an unobstructed view of her backside as she straddled his shins. Grasping one boot heel in her hands and then the other, she pulled them free. They hit the floor with muffled thumps, and she looked at him over her shoulder. Sprawled out on his back, his elbows wedged under him to prop him up, he returned her gaze.

Emma shook her head ruefully. "I love this," she said with a tiny smile. "You give me lovemakin' better than any I've ever known, and then you apologize because it wasn't on a bed of rose petals. Well, I'll tell you what." She climbed to her feet and faced him, reaching to pull her tank top over her head. The little shake she gave her shoulders sent her bra straps sliding down her arms, and the gold undergarment floated to the floor, leaving her gloriously naked. "Kick off those pants, sugah," she said, and when he complied, she climbed back on the bed and knee-walked over to him. Daintily, she settled herself astride his thighs. "What about your doohickey, *cher?*" she inquired, indicating his prosthesis. "Wouldn't you be more comfortable if you took it off?"

Elvis froze, but then reached for the leather straps that held it in place. After removing the prosthesis, he waited for her to comment on the naked stump.

But she didn't give it more than a cursory

glance, let alone take the time to say anything. Instead, she smiled gently and scooted lower, bending to brush the blunt-cut ends of her hair back and forth over his upper thighs, his lower abdomen, his groin. Elvis' penis, which had been curled in soft satiation on his thigh, rapidly straightened to stand at attention. Emma collapsed on her stomach between his sprawled thighs and reached out to wrap her fingers around his erection. She gave it one delicate little lick and then looked up at him.

"As you said, *cher,* I'm a generous woman." She met the gas-flame glow of his blue eyes, her brown ones holding traces of wicked humor although her expression didn't show a hint of a smile. "So, I'm goin' to give you one more chance. I don't want to hear any more excuses afterward either, Donnelly. You'd better get it right this time."

Fourteen

"Well, I've certainly learned my lesson, *cher,*" Emma muttered drowsily the following morning when she was awakened out of a sound sleep by the scratch of Elvis' beard against the vulnerable skin of her nape as he kissed her neck. "Honest. That was the *last* time I issue you a challenge."

There was no question that he took his dares seriously — how many times had it been last night, anyway? She'd lost count, but every time he had piously claimed he was just trying to get it right, and *damn,* he was sorry, ma'am, but he was such a slow learner.

Not that she had a complaint, mind you; it had been . . . it had been so . . .

Dieu. Words failed her.

Still . . .

With regret, she shoved away his encroaching hand, moved her hips away from the erection prodding her rear. "I'm sore, Elvis. I don't think I can. . . ."

"Shhh," he crooned and slithered down beneath the covers, mouth and fingers staying in contact with some portion of her anatomy the entire way. The covers rustled furiously for a moment, and she was rolled onto her back. Feeling his mouth press gently against her inner thigh, she kicked back the blanket to see what he was up to. He'd shouldered her knees apart to crawl between them, and was in the midst of pressing another kiss into the opposite thigh when she uncovered him.

His hand settled on her stomach, fingers spread, his thumb a mere fraction of an inch from the luxurious little triangle of golden brown hair, and he looked up at her, his electric blue eyes aglow. "This time's just for you, Em," he promised.

Ah, *Dieu,* she was in trouble. She was in big, big trouble.

How was she *not* supposed to fall in love with this man?

And yet to do so could very well prove fatal — to him. Being the object of her love had been the death of too many people in her life already.

It didn't take long to discover, however, that when it came to convincing Elvis a public association with her could be hazardous to his health, she might as well save her breath. He declined to be protected, and she really didn't know why that came as a surprise to her. The man had a will of steel and was stubborn as a goat. The way he refused to let her do anything to alleviate the pain of his unattended arousal probably should have been her first clue.

"I'll be *okay,*" he insisted for the third time as he intercepted her reaching hand and firmly returned it to the mattress by her side.

"You're hurtin' and you don't have to be." She didn't understand this refusal to let her relieve an obvious ache. He'd left her so replete she felt nearly boneless, and the man was buck naked, for heaven's sake; it wasn't as if she couldn't *see* how accomplishing that had affected him. "So I'm a little uncomfortable," she said with a shrug. "Big deal. There are other ways of takin' care of you." Her voice dropped several octaves. "Let me kiss it better, *cher.*"

He groaned, so tempted. But he didn't take her up on her offer. It had to do with the twist he'd gotten in his gut when he'd heard her say she was sore. It had to do with the instant determination her words had produced, a resolve to deny himself as an atonement for going overboard last night.

He rolled resolutely to his feet. "No," he said firmly, standing at the side of the bed and staring down at her. Sexual frustration burned in the depths of his blue eyes. But it battled for supremacy with the satisfaction he got when he took in her satiated sprawl across the sheets. "Next time, though, we're doing this in your room. We wrecked my bed."

"Um, about that, *cher;* about the next time . . ." She sat up, reaching for the sheet and wrapping it around her. Tucking the ends in between her breasts, she bit her bottom lip as she looked up at him.

Elvis had reached to pick up his prosthesis, but stilled at the uncertainty in her voice. "Don't even think this was a one-night stand," he warned her. His expression was grim as he strapped on the hook. When the task was complete, he raised his eyes to pin her in place.

Emma shifted. "Don't look at me like that, Elvis," she said. "This isn't exactly the way I'd choose to handle matters, but there are some very real obstacles we have to take into consideration."

Something dark and disappointed stirred in the depths of his eyes. Then it was gone as quickly as it had appeared, glossed over by a patina of indifference. "Yeah, I know," he agreed neutrally. "Having it widely known that you're my lover, for instance. That can be the kiss of death to any reputation in this town." He reached for his pants, thinking with dark humor that being rejected had at least caused his raging hard-on to subside.

Emma almost let it pass. Good enough, if that was what he wanted to think. Let him assume whatever the hell he wanted; instinctively, she understood it would cut through all the arguments, that his stiff-necked pride, which refused to acknowledge his fellow islanders' low opinion of him, would never allow him to ask better of her. To *demand* better, as anyone else might. Elvis would simply accept it as perfectly natural that she didn't want the hassle of being associated with him, and she would be spared a fight.

It was for the best.

It was safest for him.

And damn him for a pig-headed pain in the posterior, she couldn't do it.

"Screw my reputation," she snapped, kicking the trailing sheet out of her way as she climbed to her feet. It was the disillusionment she had glimpsed in his eyes that got to her in the end. For just an instant he *had* expected better of her, and it had cost him something to think she was just like all the other small minds in this little town. "You big jerk, you don't know me at *all* if you believe that."

"Oh, yeah?" That he cared so much infuriated him and he bent his head to scowl down at her. “Then just what the hell are all these ‘big obstacles’ you’re nattering on about?”

She snapped erect. “I don’t *natter,* Donnelly; I speak clearly and concisely. And my primary goal here is to keep Gracie safe and *you* from being picked off like a duck in a shootin’ gallery.”

“Picked off . . . ?” He stared at her in amazement. “Me? You’re worried about me?”

“Yes, I’m worried about you! People I lo— um, people who get close to me *die,* Elvis! It’s a fact of my life.”

How about that? She was worried about him. For a minute, he didn’t know how to respond. No one had ever worried about him much, except maybe for Sam during those angry teenage years and right after the explosion when he was mad at the world and depressed. Come to think of it, though, she had said something like this last night. He’d been so busy at that moment dodging his own need for her approval, it had passed him by. Huh. He’d be damned. She was worried about him.

It embarrassed him in a way. And it was kind of insulting, wasn’t it, that she didn’t think he could take care of himself? Hell, he'd been doing it all his life.

Mostly, though, it felt good. Damn. It felt real good. Emma cared enough about him to worry.

"So, big deal, we'll be discreet," he said. "That's probably a good idea anyhow, 'cause like I was saying before, having it known that you're my lover won't do a thing for your reputation. And before you start an argument about that, too," he forged on when he saw her open her mouth to respond, "*I* worry about it even if you don't."

"Well, it's a moronic thing to worry over. We've got *real* problems, Elvis, without wastin' our time on picayune stuff like that. I have a three-year-old daughter."

He looked at her as if she'd lost her mind. "*Gracie's* a problem?"

"Gracie is the love of my life." Emma stared up at him. "But discretion isn't exactly a word in her vocabulary, *cher.* Now, Grant's goon has already amply demonstrated that he can get into my room, so there is no way on God's green earth that I will leave her unattended while I slip down the hall to roll around in the sheets with you."

"Sure, I can understand that. So I'll come to your room after she's gone to sleep for the night."

"That sounds real dandy . . . in theory. Trouble is, if you sleep in my room, Gracie's goin' to know it. I mean, we can probably prevent her from catchin' us in the actual act. I'm not quite sure *how* we'll do that, *cher*, given she and I share a bed and — face it — the room itself is not that big, but we could give it our best shot, for sure. What I don't think we can do is prevent her from knowin' you are spendin' time in my bed." Emma grabbed at her slipping percale toga. "And what Grace Melina knows, Elvis, so knows the world."

Elvis looked down at her for a moment. Then one of his massive shoulders inched up in a dismissive shrug. "So what?"

"What do you mean, so what? Haven't you listened to a word I've said?"

"Yeah, I've listened, and I *thought* you said you don't give a rip if the people in this town know you're sleeping with me. Are you changing your mind now that it actually comes right down to it?"

"Arrgh!" The sheet slithered to the floor when she raised both fists to thunk him one in the chest. "You are dumb as a brick! Watch my lips, Donnelly. I . . . don't . . . *care* . . . what they think. You got that?"

"So what's the prob—"

"How long do you imagine it will take any

spy of Grant's to catch on to the fact that you mean something to me?" she demanded. "Huh? And how much longer after that before some sort of 'accident' is arranged?" Her voice grew very quiet. "Then just like everyone else in this world I've ever cared about, you'll be dead."

"No," Elvis said firmly. "That's not going to happen." He bent and picked up the sheet, shaking it out and very gently settling it around her back. Gripping the folds in his fist and hook, he drew her forward until they stood breast to chest. "This is not New Orleans, Emma. This is a very small town where it's difficult for a stranger to walk undetected down the street minding his own *business,* let alone skulk around in the shadows arranging accidents. Trust me on this one: it's just plain easier to perpetrate an act of violence in a big city. It's more impersonal. There are crowds to blend into, there's heavy traffic that can be utilized for one's own purpose."

"That doesn't mean it can't be done in a small town."

True. If one is determined enough, anything can be arranged anywhere. "No, I suppose not. But damned if I'm going to structure my life around the possibility. I'm a trained law-enforcement officer. Not some redneck small-town sheriff who dabbles in the law in order to feel powerful but a fully educated, fully trained cop. You might not believe this, but I'm extremely good at my job. I'm a professional."

"And that makes you bulletproof?"

"No, baby, that makes me a less likely target. Think about it. You yourself have told me Woodard doesn't resort to sniper tactics; his method of operation is to arrange 'accidents' that catch his victims by surprise. Well, that's a helluva lot easier to do to the average, unsuspecting citizen than it is to do to a cop. We're a suspicious lot by nature. And we're alert to the atmosphere and activities around us. Not to mention that most criminals are hesitant to start something with us, because they know it's bound to bring them more grief than they can handle." He looked down at her. "Resign yourself. You opened the door, sweetheart, and I'm not letting you close it now. One way or another, I'm going to be in your life and Gracie girl's."

He bent his head and gave her a quick, hard kiss. Then he set her back at arm's length. "You'd better get dressed and go get Beans."

"I'm not finished, *cher* . . ."

"Yeah, well, sorry, Em. If you still want to

argue we're gonna have to postpone it until later. I've got work to do."

Elvis was at his mother's house within thirty minutes of her arrival. As he had told Emma, Flannery Island was a place where everyone was apprised of everyone else's business, and when he was in need of specific information he could generally lay his hands on it fairly quickly. He'd put the word out that he wanted to know the instant his mother was sighted on the island. It took not quite twelve minutes from the time she drove off the ferry until the information reached him.

The back screen door creaked open when he let himself in and then slapped shut behind him with the smack of wood hitting wood. "Mom," he called. "You in here?"

"Elvis?" Her voice came from the bedroom, and it went high with surprise on the first vowel of his name. He heard the tap of her heels against the hallway floor and turned to observe her as she appeared in the kitchen doorway. One look at her expression and a faintly held hope, which he'd recognized as ludicrous but which he'd nevertheless safeguarded in a hidden corner of his heart, died an unsung death.

"How nice to see you," Nadine said in a

strained voice. She came forward to peck a kiss on his jaw. "Um, you want a cup of coffee? It will only take me a minute to make a pot. I'm afraid that's all I can offer you; I just got home half an hour ago." She looked at her son, so big and stern, regarding her without a speck of warmth or affection in his intensely blue eyes, and began to speak even more rapidly. "Memphis is a *steambath* this time of year, of course, but, oh! Graceland was —"

"You're under arrest for the kidnapping of Gracie Sands, Mom," Elvis said, interrupting her. He shoved away from the counter he'd been leaning against and stepped forward. "You have the right to remain —"

"What?" Stunned, she blinked up at him.

"— silent." He pulled out his handcuffs and turned her away from him, reaching out to gently pull her arms behind her back. "If you give up this right, anything you say can and will be used against you in a court of —"

"Elvis! Are you crazy?"

"Are, *you*, Mom?" He whirled her back. His professionally stern demeanor had vanished, leaving fury and betrayal in its wake.

Nadine couldn't bear to face him; she had to turn away. She knew that expression; it brought back memories of the way he used to look at her when she'd locked him out of the house back when he was a teenager and he'd known it was because she'd been turning a trick. It brought back the debilitating guilt.

"Kidnapping is a fucking *federal offense!*" he snarled. Handcuffs dangling from his hook, he gripped her upper arm with his good hand and gave her a shake. "What the hell did you think you were doing?"

"I'm sure I don't know what you're talking about," she replied without conviction.

His face abruptly regained its professional mask, all expression wiped clean. "Fine," he agreed coolly. "In that case you have the right to an attorney. If you cannot afford one, one will be provided. . . ." He turned her around again as he recited the Miranda warning and slipped a handcuff over her right wrist. It clicked into place.

OhmyGod, ohmyGod, he was serious. "It was a joke!" she said frantically, craning to see him over her shoulder. "For God's sake, Elvis, it was just a joke!"

Once again she was whirled back, this time with such force the cuff not attached to her wrist swung around on its short chain to smack her on the thigh. "A *joke?*" he thundered. "I was with the mother all that day,

Nadine. She didn't seem to think it was so goddamn funny that her baby had vanished into thin air. She was fuckin' *frantic.*" He stared down at her in disbelief. "A joke, my ass! Christ, I don't *believe* you. Emma *cried,* Mom. She cried, and she shook, and her hands were so damn cold you woulda thought it was the middle of goddamn *December.*"

Nadine's knuckles mashed her lips against her teeth. A moan escaped anyway.

"The Mackeys weren't thrilled either," he continued relentlessly. "There's no accounting for some people's sense of humor, of course, but they just didn't seem to find it amusing to have Clare accused of snatching a toddler out of the café to replace her dead son. It made her appear to be some sort of *psycho.* I don't believe she enjoyed that, and I *know* she didn't like being called a liar."

He watched without satisfaction as the color leached out of his mother's face. "Oh, and little Gracie?" he said. "I don't think she caught the humor in having her butt blistered. That was her punishment for telling a lie — Well, that and being terrorized and called a bunch of names by Sam." Elvis shrugged. "Maybe you can explain to her that it was just a joke. Oh, but that's right. I don't think she wants to be your friend anymore. Far as she's concerned, Nadine, you ain't nuthin' but a hound dawg."

"Oh, Gawd, Elvis, I didn't plan for it to get so out of . . ."

"*You* didn't plan this, period. How much were you paid?"

"What? Paid? Elvis, honey," she insisted weakly, "you've got it all wrong."

"How much, Nadine? If you think you're going to convince me you planned this all by yourself, you can save your breath. You're not that smart."

"Why, Elvis Aaron! What a thing for a son to say about his moth—" She swallowed the rest of her words when he abruptly bent down and thrust his face next to hers.

"Don't screw with me, Nadine," he said softly, spacing his words with forced patience. "If you were the least bit intelligent, you'd comprehend just how much trouble you're in. You want to claim credit for the entire scam? Fine. Then you, and you alone, will go down for it. This wasn't a prank, Mother. Get that through your head. It was a carefully thought-out, particularly vicious act of psychological warfare aimed at Emma Sands. Believe me, there is not one goddamn thing about it that's the least bit amusing." He pulled his head back a fraction, just enough for Nadine to see the flinty resolve in his eyes. "I'm going to ask you one last time. How much were you paid?"

"Twenty-five hundred dollars," she said sulkily. "And first-class tickets on a later flight to Memphis for both MarySue and me." She resented the way Elvis was treating her. Simultaneously, on a deeper level, she was horrified by the consequences of her actions that day. She had never *dreamed* —

She looked her son in the eyes and told him truthfully, "It seemed a harmless enough way to make that much money."

Jesus, Elvis marveled, *it's a damn wonder I have any values at all.* "Sit down, Mom," he said wearily. "You and I have got a lot of talking to do."

He didn't get back to the island until nine o'clock that night. At ten he knocked on Emma's door.

She opened it cautiously, chain in place. "Elvis," she whispered sternly, "whether you agreed with me or not, I told you this morning that —"

"Look at this," he commanded, and slid a drawing through the crack in the door. "I just got back from Seattle PD, where I took my mother to work with a police artist. This is a composite drawing of the man who convinced her to arrange that little party on the Fourth of July."

The door closed in his face. He heard the rattle and slide of the chain, and a moment later Emma was holding the door open for him. "Come on in," she said. Stepping back, she stared down at the drawing in her hand, studying it for a moment before she looked back up at him. "His name is Hackett," she said. "He's one of Grant's men."

"Good. That gives us a place to start." He sat down at the tiny table in the corner and as she, too, took a chair, he informed her, "I've got about forty copies of this. I'm going to distribute them all over the island."

"Where could you possibly disburse them that would make any difference?"

"Oh, lots of places, Em. To all ferry personnel, for starters. The only way on and off this island is by ferry — or private boat, but that would limit his mobility once he got here. Odds are, access to a car for getting around the island is more important than the anonymity of coming and going by private boat." He watched her absorb the information for a moment, and then continued, "If the guy's on the island for more than a few hours running, he's bound to want to eat. So I'll pass his picture out to restaurants, delis, grocery stores, and fast-food joints. His car will need gas, which he may or may not be purchasing here, so I'll distribute them to the attendants at the two gas stations on the island." He shrugged. "As I said, it's a place to start. At the very least, it should give us an idea whether or not he's still hanging around."

Emma looked over at the tiny hump that Gracie made under the covers. She stared at her daughter intently a moment and then looked back at Elvis. "Thank you," she said quietly. "It helps to know something is being done."

"It's not necessary to thank me, Emma. I'm just doing my job. And believe me," he added grimly, "it will be my pleasure to ultimately put this clown away."

He looked her over, hesitated, and then said, "About my mother . . ."

Emma's expression stiffened, but Elvis plowed on, "She asked me to tell you she's sorry." He explained the circumstances and then added, "She really isn't a malicious woman, Em. She just doesn't think things through. She saw an opportunity to make some money on something that was presented to her as a practical joke and didn't stop to consider the consequences."

Emma nodded with reluctant acceptance, and Elvis exhaled a little breath of relief. "I know you've been wondering how Nadine got into your car," he said. "She told me she was supplied with a key."

"Dieu." Long fingers spearing into her hair, Emma ground the heels of her palms into her eye sockets. Lowering her hands to the tabletop, she raised her eyes to look at Elvis. "Grant's like some damn spider, isn't he? Sitting in his web spinning out his stinkin' little intrigues." She smiled bitterly. "Come into my parlor, you poor unsuspectin' sap."

"Yeah, well let him enjoy himself, Em, because he's not going to get away with it for very much longer." Gracie stirred and Elvis watched her until she settled into deep sleep again. Then, turning his attention back to Emma, he made an impatient sweeping movement with his hook. "Look, forget about Woodard," he commanded. "I didn't come here and bring all of this up just to make you feel lousy. I wanted to let you know we're taking steps to put an end to this bullshit. How are *you* feeling?" he inquired in a low voice, and the eyes that looked into hers were no longer the objective eyes of a cop; they were suddenly very personal.

Reaching across the tiny table, he stroked his fingers down the back of her hand. "You still sore?"

"No, I feel pretty good," she replied. "Instead of usin' the shower I took a long, hot soak in the tub this mornin'. It helped a lot."

"Ah, man, Emma, I'm sorry," he said with sincere contrition. "It never should have come down to that. I should have used a little more consideration last night."

Emma's gaze snapped up to meet his. "Are you beatin' yourself up over a little residual *soreness,* Elvis? Sugah, that's pointless," she assured him honestly. "You didn't do anything I didn't want you to do. I mean you *do* realize I always had the option to say no, don't you?"

She thought about her words for a second and then smiled wryly. "No. Wait. On second thought, maybe you should assume full responsibility. Not that what I said about having options isn't true, of course, but now that you mention it I hardly ever exercise those options and that is your fault. You're always gettin' me so excited, I seem to have a hard time denyin' you anything."

"Oh, yeah? You just a girl who can't say no?" He brought her wrist up to his mouth, kissing it and then pressing open-mouthed kisses in an ever-farther-ranging march up her arm. The slight but persistent pressure he exerted on the forearm he held firmly in his grasp pulled her up onto her feet, around the table, and onto his lap. "Does that mean," he asked huskily, pressing kisses on her throat in an erratic path, "that if I promised to be very, very quiet, and rearrange just the bare minimum of clothing, you'd have a hard time saying no to me now?" His fingers slid up her bare thigh beneath the loose leg of her shorts. Halting at the lacy elastic border of her panties, they brushed back and forth, back and forth. "I have something hard for you."

"Oh, you are so bad, Sheriff." She sucked in a sharp breath when his forefinger suddenly breached the flimsy barrier.

"Uh huh. Bad. That's me." Moving his finger in gentle circles, he looked into her slumbrous eyes. "So . . . have me arrested, why don'tcha?"

"Oh, I would, I would," she assured him fervently, eyes closing and legs sliding a little farther apart. "Except, wouldn't you just know it, there's never a cop around when you need one." Then, reluctantly, she pushed his hand away. "Not here, Elvis."

He followed her gaze to Gracie. "Right," he agreed. He took a deep breath, blew it out, and gave her a lopsided smile. "So, what's your opinion of sex in hallways?"

Hackett started looking for a public phone to use the minute he drove off the ferry. He pulled over with a slam of his brakes at the first booth he saw. Cradling the receiver between ear and shoulder, he held his phone card up where he could see it and punched in the necessary series of access and phone numbers. Then he waited while the phone on the other end rang.

The line was picked up. "Grant Woodard's office."

"Rosa, this is Hackett. Is he in?"

"Yes, he is, sir; won't you please hold a moment? Mr. Woodard is currently on another line, but you shouldn't have to wait very long. He's instructed me that your calls are to be put through immediately." The line went dead as she placed him on hold. While he waited, Hackett returned the phone card to his wallet and the wallet to his hip pocket. Fastidiously, he picked a thread off his summer slacks and snapped out a pristine handkerchief to flick dust from the toes of his expensive Italian loafers.

The connection was reopened. This time it was Woodard's voice that spoke. "What news, Hackett?"

"I'm afraid I've been made, boss."

Grant swore briefly, but then said, "Well, we knew going in it would be a possibility. What happened?"

"I stopped at an oyster bar they've got at the yacht club to get some lunch. It's away from town; I figured it was fairly anonymous. But I saw the counter kid checking my face against a drawing. I got the hell outta there and off the island before that Hell's Angel sheriff could track me down." He admired his reflection for a moment in the smoky storefront window across the sidewalk and then added, "His whore mama musta been the one to supply the description. I know I can't go back there myself, but you want I should get one of the boys out here to whack her?"

On his end of the line, Grant briefly closed his eyes. God preserve him from hired help who tried to think for themselves. "No, that won't be necessary," he said, no hint of what he felt coloring his voice. "I always knew Gracie would eventually cave in and tell her mother the truth, so having Nadine Donnelly's part in the scam exposed was pretty much a foregone conclusion. What surprises me is that Emma talked to the cops, I expected she'd simply take off for a newer clime." He was quiet for a moment. Then he said, "Well, that's neither here nor there. Catch the next flight back, Hackett. I've got to put some thought into where I want to go from here."

Fifteen

Sam pushed in the car lighter and reached in the visor for his pack of Camels. He shook one out, tapping the filter restlessly against the steering wheel as he waited for the element to heat up. He and Clare were on their way home after closing down the store, and ever since they'd instituted the in-store no-smoking policy this was one of his more anxiously awaited smokes of the day. The lighter popped out and he brought the glowing tip to his cigarette. Inhaling deeply, he slowly let the smoke escape through his mouth and nostrils.

Clare stabbed the power button on her door handle and with a hum her window lowered. "Dammit, Sam, when are you going to give up that disgusting habit?" she demanded irritably. "I can't tell you how sick I am of breathing in your secondhand smoke." She flapped a hand at him and wrinkled her nose. "Not to mention how fed up I am with the stench."

The hand holding the cigarette stilled halfway between the steering wheel and his mouth, and Sam took his eyes off the road long enough to look at his wife. Mouth set at a mulish angle, she was glaring back at him. A big knot that he'd been carrying around with him for what seemed like forever began to dissolve.

This was the Clare he knew, his old Clare. She'd started giving him a hard time about what she'd termed his "nasty, foul, nicotine habit" on the day they'd met and hadn't let up for nine years. When Evan was alive she'd even had him trained to do his smoking outside where it wouldn't infringe on the air their son breathed. After Evan's death, she didn't seem to care what he did. The only reason he'd brought his habit back inside the house was to see if he could get a rise out of her.

Until today she hadn't even seemed to notice.

He'd made a promise — to himself, to God — and he reached for the pack in the visor. Shaking another cigarette out, he flipped his lighted smoke out the window and handed Clare the pack. "You want me to quit?" he asked.

"You know damn well I do, Samuel Mackey. I've only been after you to do it for the past ten years."

"Yeah? Well, today's your lucky day, honey. See this?" He held up the cigarette he'd extracted. "You're looking at Sam Mackey's last cigarette. Toss the rest of 'em out."

The pack went sailing out the window.

Sam felt only the slightest twinge of panic as he glanced in his rearview mirror and saw the pack bounce along the shoulder of the highway. He'd sworn more times than he could recall that if she would only care enough to demand one more time that he quit, he'd give the cigarettes up once and for all. He'd begun to despair that the demand would ever come. Pulling out the lighter, he put the coil to his last official cigarette.

After dinner, he tracked her down to their bedroom, where she was putting away laundry. Closing the door behind him, he began to unbutton his shirt.

Clare went very still. Watching him uncover his chest, his shoulders, and arms, and then drop the shirt to the floor as he reached for the button on his waistband, she swallowed dryly. "What do you think you're doing, Sam?" she demanded. And swore inwardly to hear her voice come out breathy and anxious instead of coolly inquiring as she'd intended.

"I don't smoke anymore," he informed her quietly, swiftly stripping down to the skin. "It's after dinner. I've brushed my teeth. I've gone through three toothpicks. I don't like gum." Straightening up from working his jeans over his heels, he faced her, naked as the day he was born and aroused to impressive proportions. "I need something to put in my mouth," he said in a low, hungry voice, coming to stand in front of her. Fingers reaching for the buttons on her blouse, he leaned down to scrape his teeth over her lower lip. He chewed on it. He sucked at it. Then he pulled his head back far enough to look into her eyes. "And, honey, since this was *your* idea, I guess that means you're elected to supply me with what I need."

The stack of jockey shorts that she'd clutched to her chest at his entrance slid soundlessly to the floor. "Oh, Sammy," she breathed out, reaching with eager hands for his naked flanks. "I thought you'd *never* ask again."

Elvis strolled into work at a few minutes before eight. Stopping at Sandy's desk, he picked up his messages. He set his coffee down on her desk to shuffle through them, and seeing nothing that needed his immediate attention, met Ben's eyes as his deputy looked up. "Anything new this morning?" he inquired.

"Got Harve Hensen locked up," Ben replied, jerking his chin in the direction of the door that led to the two cells in back.

"Harve? For what?" Elvis quirked an eyebrow. "D & D?"

"He wasn't drunk, but he sure as hell got disorderly." Ben smiled wryly. "He beat the shit out of Mike Chance early this mornin'."

"Oh, man. He finally caught on to Chance's car being parked in front of his house, huh?" Mike Chance drove the island's only taxi, and for the past several months had been boldly parking it right in front of Harve Hensen's house while he was inside carrying on an affair with Harve's wife, Kathy.

"Well . . . kinda. He overheard someone snickering about it over at Ruby's this morning and drove back home to see for himself. I think he fully expected to prove the gossips wrong. But sure enough, there was Mike's car, parked — Jesus, Elvis, get this — in Harve's *driveway* this time, and he walked in and caught 'em right in the act." Ben blew out a breath and shook his head. "Chance is over at the clinic being patched back together, and Harve is in back cooling his jets, courtesy of the good ol' state of Washington."

"Is Chance planning on pressing

charges?" Harve Hensen was big and sort of dumb. But despite the fact that he wasn't the smartest man on the island, he was considered easygoing and was widely liked because of a genuinely sweet nature. Like all men, however, his good nature had its limitations. Seeing his wife in bed with another man had obviously exceeded them.

Elvis could empathize with the way Harve must be feeling, and he hated the idea of having to throw the book at him. His job, however, was to uphold the law; so if Mike Chance wanted to press charges of assault and battery, he'd have no choice but to act on his wishes.

"Nah, I don't think so." Ben shrugged. "I could be wrong, but that wasn't the feel I got for the situation."

Sandy came in then, and the story was retold. "Ah, that Kathy is a fool," was her assessment. "Harve is such a sweet guy — not to mention a steady provider. I hope he tosses her out on her faithless little butt." Ben wasn't sure he agreed, and the two began arguing the merits back and forth. Elvis left them to it, retreating to his desk to clear up some of the ever-present paperwork.

It was just after ten when he heard Sandy say, "Well, hi, Mrs. Sands! How nice to see you again. And *this* must be . . ."

His head came up with a snap. Emma was half turned away from him as she closed the entryway door. Gracie was straining forward against her mother's hand.

"Gwacie," she supplied before Sandy could complete the sentence. "I'm fwee, you know." She quivered like a needle at magnetic north in Sandy's direction, but then swung like a pendulum in her mother's grip the minute she spotted Elvis at his desk. "Hi, Shewiff Elbis!" Shaking free of Emma's hold, she raced across the room, throwing herself against Elvis' legs before he could rise from his seat. She thrust her arms out peremptorily and demanded, "Up!"

He scooped her up and plunked her on his knee. "Hiya, kid. Whatcha doin' here? You come to visit me at work?"

"Huh-uh. *Maman* say we haffa make a repote." She blinked her big brown eyes at him and then continued chattily, "We got our tyoos cutted, Elbis."

"Your tires?" he said. Looking away from her sweet and eager little face, he watched Emma as she approached more slowly. "On the Chevy, Em?" he questioned. "Somebody slashed the tires on your Chevy?"

She sank into the chair next to his desk, long fingers reaching up to rub at her furrowed brow. It didn't take a genius to deduce there was a headache in the making. "We just discovered it. Gracie and I were supposed to go to —"

"Miss-us Mackey's house," Gracie interrupted, eager to help supply some of the details of their story.

"Right. But when I pulled the cover off the car, I found the back two tires sitting on their rims."

"Flattoo 'n' pancakes."

"It's pretty clear they've been slashed, Elvis." She rubbed harder at her forehead. "Why on earth would anyone want to slash my tires?"

"You don't think it could be . . . ?" Understood but unsaid in front of Gracie was the name Grant Woodard.

"Well, it could be, I suppose. Instigating a program of harassment, you mean?" She thought about it a moment. "Sure, I suppose anything is possible. But it just doesn't feel right, Elvis."

"Not his style?"

"No. Not really." She looked at him in frustration. "But then, what do I really know of his style? I would have said he was above all *sorts* of things two months ago."

"Who you talkin' about, Mommy?"

Emma looked at Gracie sitting with such

trust on Elvis' lap while she regarded her with big brown perplexed eyes. "Just somebody who's done some bad things, angel pie." She reached her hands out to her daughter. "Come on over here and see me, sugar," she instructed, and hugged her daughter fiercely when Gracie launched herself out of Elvis' lap and into her arms. She gnawed at Gracie's neck just to hear her laugh.

Elvis stood. "Why don't we go take a look at the damage before we file the report?" He put his hand beneath Emma's elbow to assist her to her feet and waited while she settled Gracie on her hip. "It's probably a random act of vandalism, Em," he assured her. "Unfortunately, we get 'em more often than we like to admit."

Both Sandy and Ben murmured their agreement.

"It's the lack of entertainment," Sandy elaborated. "The kids around here just don't have enough to keep them occupied."

That was Tuesday. On Friday, Emma was back, by herself this time and hopping mad.

She charged into the station at a few minutes after three. Braking at Elvis' desk, she slapped both hands onto his desktop and leaned her weight on them, breathing rapidly. "I'd like to file a report," she said between her teeth. *"Again."* Then her temper, clearly on a very slim leash to begin with, slipped beyond her grasp entirely. She began to speak in rapid, fluid Cajun French, gesticulating wildly. She concluded with an emphatic, questioning *"Oui?"* and a furious thump of her fist against his desk.

Elvis looked up at her. "In English, Em."

She sank into the chair next to his desk. "They have spray-painted my car," she spit out. "*Mon Dieu,* such filthy, foul words, all over my beautiful car." Eyes narrowed and full of fury, she raised her head to look at Elvis. "It is a damn good thing my *bébé* cannot read beyond the few basic words, *oui?* Not too many cat, rat, sat, painted on the side of my Chevrolet."

Elvis came to his feet. "Someone spray-painted dirty words on your car?" he demanded with careful equanimity. God damn it to hell. He *loved* that car. Slicing the tires was one thing. That had been difficult enough to swallow — not to mention that Emma sure as hell hadn't been thrilled to find herself out of pocket the one-hundred-plus dollars it had taken to replace them. But defacing that beautiful paint job? "I want to see it."

Standing in the parking lot several minutes later, Emma endured the heat coming off the blacktop as she watched Elvis prowl around the car. He stooped here to get a closer look, stood back there for an all-over picture, and his facial cast grew tighter, showed less and less expression with each scrawled word he uncovered. Bah, he didn't fool her. That poker face wasn't a mystery to her anymore; she had learned to read him over the time she'd known him. Consequently, even though she would have sworn it was categorically impossible, his growing fury made hers decrease somewhat. "So, what is it that's makin' you the maddest, *cher?*" she finally inquired wryly. "The fact that the car's been sullied or that my reputation has?"

"When you first told me about it — I won't lie to you, Em — it was the car." Elvis rose from where he'd been squatting by the back fender and came over to look down at her. "Damn, this is such a *fine* car, and the idea that somebody wrote all over it . . . !" Turning to survey the damage, he slung his left arm over her shoulder and pulled her into his side. Absently he rubbed his hook up and down her arm. "But I don't like the tone of these words, doll," he admitted. "There appears to be more at work here than bored teenagers on a vandalizing spree."

"*Oui,* I'm none too pleased, myself. Particularly at the thought of my *petite ange* trying to sound out some of these words."

GO HOME, YOU CUNT stared her in the face from the passenger door.

"It's going to cost you a fortune, I suppose, to have the car painted."

Emma shrugged. "I'll try to get it off with paint thinner first. If that fails I could paint it myself fairly inexpensively if I only had a spot to do it in. If I can't do something soon, though, *cher,* I'm goin' to have to buy myself a can of spray paint to block out the dirtiest words. My biggest fear right now is that someone will read them aloud in front of Gracie. Damn it, Elvis!" She felt herself getting angry all over again. Looking up into his calm face, she said flatly, "You'd better find the clown who's doin' this to me. Or I'm packin' my *bébé* up and leavin' town."

"I'll find him," he promised grimly.

The only problem was . . .

By Saturday he still didn't have any leads. And Sunday night, someone threw a rock through Emma's window.

It was that long twilight hour peculiar to the Pacific Northwest. The sun had gone down, the brilliance of the sunset had slowly faded — first to a washed-out shadow of its former glory, then to muted grays — and still the sky was only gradually dissolving into darkness.

Emma looked across the room at her daughter, who was lying on her stomach on the floor coloring in a coloring book. "C'mon, angel pie; time to get your jammies on."

"Ah, *Maman.*" Gracie put her crayon down grudgingly and looked up at her mother. "Do I haffa?"

"Yes, you do. Come on, now."

"But I wanna make you a pitchoo."

Emma's fingers clenched around her daughter's pajamas. "Grace Melina, don't make me come over there to get you. It's time to get ready for bed, and that, my darling child, is the beginning and end of that. You can color me a picture tomorrow." Seeing the obstinate slant beginning to develop in Gracie's lower lip, she bit back an impatient sigh and said firmly, "Now, *ma petite ange,* you will put those crayons and your coloring book back where they belong and get your rear end over here. Pronto."

Gracie blew out a disgusted breath and muttered something that Emma hadn't the slightest doubt was unflattering to her. She flipped the coloring book closed and pushed herself up. Dragging her feet, she walked as slowly as she dared to the wide window sill where her books and art supplies were stored. Petulantly, she tossed her box of crayons and the coloring book at it.

The window exploded inward.

It happened with such abruptness and was accompanied by such horrendous noise that at first what had caused it didn't register in Emma's mind. Then she saw the rock that was still rolling across the floor. Both she and Gracie had screamed, but when Emma's cry was cut short, Gracie continued to shriek, in outrage, in terror . . . and in pain.

She stood in the midst of the broken glass, her little body rigid, her hands fisted at her sides, her eyes wide with terror; screaming at the top of her lungs. There was blood all over her daughter's face and arms, and Emma's heart slammed up against her rib cage. "Oh, God!"

She raced across the expanse separating them, praying aloud in French and in English, ignoring the crunch of glass beneath her feet, and snatched her daughter up. Gracie's arms went around her neck and clung with desperate strength. "Hoot, hoot,

hoot, Mommy," she screeched. "Hoot, hoot bad."

"I know it hurts, *bébé.*" Tears rolled down Emma's cheeks. She tried to assess the damage, but Gracie's face was beneath her chin where she couldn't see it. "Let *Maman* see, angel pie. Let Mommy see."

"Hoot, hoot, hoot, hoot, hoot!"

Their door banged open, and starting violently, Emma barely bit back another scream. Clutching her child to her chest, she whirled to face this newest danger.

Elvis was crouched in the opening, both arms extended, his hook bracing his right wrist. In his right hand was a gun. His stance swung left, then right, then back to center. When he saw nothing that posed a threat, he slowly lowered his gun hand and straightened. "Em?" he demanded over the sound of Gracie's screams. "What the hell happened in here?" Then his focus narrowed and he absorbed the blood all over Gracie. "Sweet God Almighty."

"Help her, Elvis. She's hurt and I can't tell how bad." The last of Emma's control dissolved at the sight of him. She knew he would take command of the situation and the tears she'd had at least a modicum of control over now poured down her face in an unstoppable torrent. "Please, please . . .

help her," she sobbed.

Gracie screamed her litany of pain.

Elvis crossed the room and pried the child out of Emma's arms. He cuddled her against his chest and bent his head to bring his mouth next to her ear so she could hear him over her screams. Crooning soothing sounds and words, he carried her over to the bed. "Shhh, shhhh, shhhh, shhhh, Gracie Girl. Shhh, now; hush." He laid her down on the bed, but her arms reached up to clutch at him.

"Hoot, hoot, hoot," she sobbed. "Hoot, hoot, bad."

"I know, Beans baby; I know." He forced her hands down to her sides, which caused her cries to escalate into near hysteria. She went rigid beneath his hold. "Let Elvis see, baby," he commanded firmly. He knew from experience that sympathy usually only added to the emotionalism and he forced all signs of it from his voice. "Hush. Stop that now. Let me see what I can do to make it stop hurting." His stomach clenched at the copious amounts of blood covering her face, matting her blond curls. "Be quiet now, Gracie, and let me take a look."

He looked up to tell Emma to turn up the light and saw the other boarders crowding in the doorway. "Someone call the station," he instructed crisply. "Tell George I need him over here, stat. And have them call Dr. Simms. Tell him to open up the clinic — we're bringing Gracie in. Em, bump up the light. I can't see what we're dealing with here."

A few minutes later he had determined that while one of the cuts on Gracie's head would probably need closer attention, neither it or any of the others were life threatening. George arrived and was given his instructions, and Elvis escorted the two badly shaken females out of the building. He bundled Emma into the department Suburban and handed her Gracie. Climbing in the driver's side, he started up the car, flipped on the siren, and peeled away from the curb fronting the station.

The doctor was just unlocking the clinic doors when they pulled up. He greeted Elvis and introduced himself and his wife, the clinic nurse, to Emma. Then he tried to persuade her to relinquish Gracie to their care and remain with Elvis in the waiting room.

"Not in this lifetime," Emma said flatly.

"Look, Mrs. Sands . . ."

"I am not leaving my *bébé* and that is final," Emma snarled. "Now, please, let's proceed with this, *oui?* She's scared and she's in pain. I don't know how much blood she's lost, but Elvis said no major arteries were involved."

"Bring her in."

Emma held Gracie's hand and spoke to her with sympathetic firmness while the doctor and his wife picked small shards of glass out of her arms, face, and skull, then cleaned up dozens of tiny cuts.

"It's not as bad as it looks," Dr. Simms assured them both. "Facial lacerations in particular tend to bleed a lot because the veins are so close to the surface." He pinched together the edges of a small gash on Gracie's forehead. "I'm going to put three or four stitches in this just to insure a finer scar." He smiled down at Gracie. "Can't have a pretty little girl like you with a big old scar on her face, now can we?"

"Shewiff Elbis has a scaw on him's face. Is from a 'splosion." Her eyes darted to Emma's. "Our window 'sploded, didn't it, Mommy? Did I bweak it with my cwayons?"

"No, angel pie. A rock broke it. And the explosion that scarred Sheriff Elvis was quite a bit different from the way our window broke."

"And your scar will be a lot smaller," the doctor interjected. "I promise it won't be a big old ugly one like Sheriff Donnelly's." He expunged air from a hypodermic of topical anesthetic. "This is going to sting just a little, Gracie." To his wife he ordered, "Hold her head still," and to Emma he explained, "this is to numb the area so I can stitch it up."

"Elbis is not ugly!" Gracie said indignantly. "Him's the hamsonest — Owie! Hoot, hoot, hoot, Mommy."

Emma gripped both her daughter's arms and laid the weight of her upper body over Gracie's torso to keep her from jerking. The discomfort of the injection after Gracie believed the pain to be all through threatened to shove her daughter to the edge of a full-blown case of hysteria. "Hold still, Grace Melina," Emma commanded sternly. "Hush. I know it stung, but can you still feel the hurt?"

"*Oui, Maman!* Hoot, hoot . . ."

"Gracie, can you really? Or do you just remember the pain?"

"Weally, I can. Oh!" The tension keeping her so stiff gradually relaxed. "It's bettoo now."

"You're probably going to feel a little tug," the doctor informed her and began to stitch her up. Emma related a silly story to her daughter to take her mind off what was being done to her. She kept her gaze firmly on Gracie's eyes to avoid seeing the needle pierce her child's flesh. "So," the doctor continued genially, "you think our good sheriff is handsome, do you?"

"Yes," Gracie agreed emphatically. "Hamson. You don't say him's ugly."

"Actually, I didn't. I said the *scar* was — Well, never mind. I won't say he's ugly."

"Bettoo not."

Dr. Simms tied off the last suture. "Annnd — that does it! You can sit up now. I think this calls for a sucker, Mrs. Sands, don't you? Gracie was a very brave girl."

When the door to the surgery opened, Elvis tossed aside the magazine he'd been trying to read and surged to his feet. "How is she? She okay?" He studied Gracie closely when Emma carried her out. Most of the blood had been cleaned away, and despite the three black stitches that bristled from her forehead, to his heartfelt relief she looked a hundred percent better. "Gracie girl?" He walked over to stand close, hovering over mother and child. "You okay, baby?"

"I have a suckoo, Elbis! Look!" She yanked it from her mouth and held it aloft for his admiration. "It's a wed one! And look!" She put her hand in her overalls' pocket and pulled out two more. "A gwape one and a wootbeer!" She launched herself from Emma's arms into Elvis'. Emma's arms fell leadenly to her sides.

Elvis secured his prosthesis beneath Gracie's rump and wrapped his free arm around Emma's shoulders. "Come on," he said gruffly. "I'll take you home." He turned them toward the door, but then paused when he caught sight of Dr. and Mrs. Simms watching them from the surgery doorway. "Thanks for opening up, Doc. What do we owe you?" He let loose of Emma long enough to dig for his wallet, but Dr. Simms waved him off.

"Mrs. Sands made arrangements to come in and pay her bill tomorrow," he retorted.

Elvis nodded and his arm went back around Emma. She leaned her head wearily against his shoulder. "In that case," Elvis said, "I'm gonna say good night and take these ladies home."

"Yes, good night." Farewells were murmured all around.

The moment the door clicked shut behind the threesome the doctor turned to his wife. "Well," he said with an amused smile. "I think it's safe to say the relationship between those three is a fairly serious one; wouldn't you agree?"

His wife smiled wearily. "I certainly

wouldn't want to be in the shoes of whoever hurt that little girl when Elvis Donnelly finds out," she agreed.

Elvis unlocked the door to his room and ushered Emma and Gracie inside. "Tell me what you need for the night and I'll go get it," he instructed, then locked them in when he left a few minutes later.

His deputy arose from a chair at the table when Elvis let himself into Emma's room. "How's the baby?"

"She's okay. A couple of stitches in her forehead but other than that it was mostly surface cuts." Elvis shook his head. "I haven't had a lot of experience with kids, admittedly, but even so I can't get over how fast she bounced back. Right now she's all pumped up about the suckers Doc Simms gave her."

George grinned. "Yeah, and chances are she probably won't even need more than an aspirin when the novocaine wears off."

"That's what Emma said the doctor told her. I guess you've learned that the hard way with your own kids, huh?"

"Yep. Stuff that would send an adult in search of heavy duty painkillers usually skims right past a child. It's amazing."

"Yeah, it's something, all right." Elvis allowed himself a moment to marvel before he got back down to business. "Thanks for sticking around, George," he said. "I'm putting Emma and Gracie up in my room tonight. Figured it beats the accommodations at the jail. Tomorrow I'll find them someplace safe. I really appreciate your staying here 'til I got back."

"No problem. It's bad policy to leave the room unsecured, and since I didn't have a key to lock it up . . ." George's shrug was explanation enough. "I bagged up the rock." He indicated the freezer bag on the table. "It's got a rough surface, though; I doubt we'll get much off it."

"Well, I appreciate the effort." Elvis considered his deputy. "Until tonight the stuff that's been happening to Emma has been pretty much your penny-ante, juvie-type harassment," he said. "But it's startin' to get rough, George, and I don't like that." He shrugged. "There's not much can be done about it tonight, though, I suppose. Go on back to the station. I'll just grab a few things to make their stay more comfortable before I lock up. Thanks again for waiting."

He helped Emma get Gracie ready for bed and then stood by the side of the bed and watched as the child crashed. One moment she was demanding stories and chatting wildly, the next she was sound asleep. A smile crooking his mouth, he turned back to Emma.

She was standing in the middle of the room, hugging herself and shivering as if it were twenty below.

"Hey," he murmured. He reached out and pulled her into his arms.

Emma clutched his waist, trying to absorb his heat. "I was irritated with her," she said, and her teeth began to chatter. "She was being obstinate and dragging her feet, and it was makin' me twitch like a cat on a hot tin roof." She shook harder. "Ah, *Dieu,* and then she was screamin' and screamin' and there was *blood* all over her, and —"

Elvis' arms tightened. "Shhh. It's okay, sweetheart. It's all over now, Em, and Gracie's okay."

"Why is this *happenin'* to us, Elvis? I can't believe that Grant would —" She shook her head impatiently. "But why would *anyone* want to hurt an innocent little girl? She's never done anythin' to merit this sort of abuse." She looked up at him, her brown eyes full of fear yet at the same time fierce. "She doesn't deserve this, dammit!"

Elvis brought his hand up to smooth back her hair. Lowering his head, he kissed her. Then he pulled back far enough to look into her eyes. “No, she doesn’t, doll. And I’m gonna make it my mission in life to see that nothing like this ever happens to either one of you again.”

Sixteen

Grant picked up the phone on the third ring. He identified himself crisply. "Woodard."

"Conroy here," said the voice on the other end of the line, and Grant straightened out of his indolent slouch, pointing the remote at the VCR to turn it off. Emma's image disappeared. Conroy was the man who had been sent to replace Hackett. He'd only been on Flannery Island a week.

"Well?" Grant barked when the man on the other end of the line hesitated. "What news have you got for me?"

"Something went wrong with an . . . incident last night. The baby was hurt."

"Gracie?" Grant's feet hit the floor with a thump. "Gracie was hurt?"

"Yes, sir."

Grant Woodard swore low and fluently. But his voice was controlled, lethal, when next he spoke. "I want to know exactly what happened last night, Conroy," he demanded icily. "And if you value your . . . position . . . you won't leave out a single detail."

Dawn had barely broken when Elvis let

himself out of the room. Emma and Gracie were still asleep in his bed. He had hoped to be back before they awoke, but his business took longer to conclude than he'd anticipated and he was growing a little frantic about Emma's emotional state by the time he finally got back to the boarding house. He'd grown familiar with the way her mind worked in any situation that threatened her daughter.

Parking the Suburban in the rear lot was a task accomplished with more speed than accuracy, and he took the back stairs up to their floor two risers at a time. Bursting through the door to his room, he skidded to a halt at the sight that greeted him. "Goddamn son of a bitch," he growled under his breath.

"Hi, Elbis!" Gracie abandoned the hand game she'd been playing with Mrs. Mackey and raced across the room to throw herself at Elvis' legs.

He bent down to scoop her up. Straightening to his full height, he took a minute to examine her carefully. "How you feeling today, Gracie girl?"

"I feel okeydokey. Look, Shewiff Elbis, I have spidoo legs stickin' outta my fo'head." She tilted her chin down slightly to give him a clearer view of the stitches bristling black against her pale skin. "That's what *Maman* calls 'em — spidoo legs." Big brown eyes peered up at him to assess his reaction.

"Pretty darn tricky, kid."

"Uh-huh. Pwetty dawn twicky."

"So," he said casually. "Where is your momma?"

"I dunno." Gracie shrugged. "Haffa go out fo' a while." She angled her head to blow a raspberry against the side of his strong tanned neck. Giggling, pleased with herself for catching him off guard, she wriggled to be let down and ran off the instant her feet touched the floor, her attention already diverted to the window sill where her bucket of shells resided.

Grateful for her preoccupation, Elvis crossed over to Clare, who had slowly pushed up from the floor where she'd been kneeling to play hand-clapping games with Gracie.

His eyes, when they met hers, were accusatory. "All right," he demanded in a low voice. "Where the hell is she? And don't screw around with me here, Clare. I'm in no mood."

"She's in her room."

Elvis whispered something truly foul. "Packing again, I suppose?"

"Ummm," Clare replied unhappily. "I

really couldn't say, Elvis. She didn't tell me her plans." But it didn't exactly take a card-packing member of Mensa to figure it out.

"Well, that cuts it. That just bloody cuts it. I'm putting a stop to this crap once and for all." He turned on his heel without another word and stormed from the room. Remembering Gracie at the very last moment, he just managed to catch the door with his hook to prevent it from slamming shut behind him. He pulled it closed with exaggerated care.

He didn't execute the same caution when he entered the room down the hall. The door banged against the interior wall when he barged through it.

Emma whirled from stacking Gracie's folded T-shirts in a suitcase. Her heart thumped up against the wall of her chest until she saw it was Elvis.

Then she caught a glimpse of the look in his eyes and it commenced to pound. He was clearly furious.

He strode right up to the bed, reached around her to snag the suitcase, and hurled it across the room. The clothes that didn't scatter during its flight exploded out of it as it hit the wall and tumbled to the floor. He turned back to loom over her. When his nose was practically touching hers, he demanded in a low, contemptuous voice, "Don't you ever have one friggin' response that doesn't begin and end with running away?"

Emma's chin shot up. Hand to his chest, she shoved him back a step, knowing, by the inflexible cast of the muscles beneath her fingertips, that he was humoring her by allowing himself to be moved. There was a warm breeze blowing through the hole the rock had made in the window, and the feel of it wafting feather-light against her bare arms hardened her resolve. "I don't owe you any explanations," she said with stiff coolness.

His temper heated up several degrees in response. "Why the hell don't you?" he demanded. "Because you never wanted anything from me in the first place except a little servicing? Well, that's great." He rammed his fingers through his hair, blue eyes blazing down at her. "That's just great. Exactly what *is* my position in your life, Em? Summer stud?"

"No, of course not!"

"I think it is. I think my sole appeal is availability of a big dick, in exchange for which you'll overlook my less than ideal face and body."

Her chin rose to an even more pugnacious

level. "Don't flatter yourself, Donnelly. It's not that big." *Oh, Emma, Emma, you're such a liar.*

Well, so be it. He'd goaded her into the remark by the interpretation he'd put on her need to vacate Port Flannery. It was strictly for Gracie's sake that she was leaving.

Made miserable by the necessity, defensive as a mother bear with a threatened cub, she charged into the attack. "And I can't tell you how sick I am of having this same damn conversation with you either, Elvis, over these so-called 'deformities' of yours. It reminds me of that thing Groucho Marx said about never joining a club that would have him as a member. With you, it always seems to be if I chose to make love with you, it must have been for some obscure but surely nefarious reason, and the nastier or more nefarious the reason you can imagine, the better. It couldn't be that I simply wanted you," she concluded sarcastically. "Just *you*."

She blew out an exasperated breath. "Well, believe what you want, Elvis," she said. "I'm tired of defendin' myself."

"What is it you'd have me believe then, Em?" He stared at her flushed cheeks, at her eyes, so dark and brilliant, glaring back up at him. "Am I supposed to believe I'm the love of your life?"

Yes. *Yes.* But she couldn't admit that to him. She didn't dare; it would change everything. She'd have to stop running and take a stand. She'd have to place her trust, once and for all, in someone other than herself. Bottom lip securely tucked under her front teeth, she blinked up at him.

"Yeah, that's pretty much what I thought." He stepped back. "And if I said I loved you it wouldn't mean jack shit to you, either, would it?"

Emma's heart rolled over in her chest like a trick poodle. "Are you sayin' that?"

Elvis shrugged. "Why bother? You don't believe in my abilities as a sheriff; you don't need me as a man. Hell, you can hardly wait to shake the dust of this town from your heels."

Her hand had fisted in the material of his khaki shirt as he spoke and she gave it a yank. *"Are you sayin' that?"*

"What do you care?" He glared down at her. "You're leaving as soon as you can —"

"Damn you, Elvis Donnelly, *tell me if you're sayin' that!*"

"Yes," he roared, "I'm saying that, okay? I love you." He gave a bitter bark of laughter. "Is that a hoot, or what? I hope you get a great big chuckle out of it."

"Ah, *Dieu,* Elvis. Oh, *mon Dieu.*" She broke into a spate of French. Her tone, her eyes, were packed full of emotion, but none of it seemed to be amusement at his expense.

He looked down at her warily. "English, Em. Dammit, speak English. If you're saying screw you and the horse you rode in on, I'd just as soon know about it up front."

"I love you, Elvis." Her fingers clenched in the material over his chest, and she laughed briefly. If it was edged with hysteria, she felt that was only fair. Oh, God, she was going to do it; she was going to place her faith and the safety of her daughter in Elvis Donnelly's hands, and the thought of it scared her to death. Nevertheless, she quickly got herself back under control. Releasing the fabric, slapping her palms against the unyielding wall of his chest, she looked up into his eyes. "God knows why, since most of the time you're such a stubborn, knuckleheaded —" She gave her head an impatient shake to rid it of that conversational digression and averred almost primly, "Nevertheless, I love you so much it scares the bejesus out of me."

She didn't know what sort of response she expected, exactly, but it certainly wasn't that he would take a step back from her and snap, "Bullshit."

She took a step forward. He took another step back. "What do you mean, bullsh—"

Elvis stopped dead. "I mean don't patronize me!"

"Patronize?" She was incredulous. Puzzlement clouded her eyes as she looked up at him. "Where on earth did that come from?"

"I asked you flat-out just a minute ago if I was the love of your life, and I didn't hear you jumping in to claim that I was."

"Well, no. But that was because —"

"So don't go thinking my ego's so fragile," he snapped, rolling right over her incipient explanation, "that just because I said I love you, you have to build it up by claiming to love me, too."

She smacked him in the chest. "*Mon Dieu,* you are the biggest *dumbest* clodhopper it's ever been my misfortune to meet! I shouldn't love you, Elvis Donnelly, and that's the truth! You're stubborn, and wrongheaded, and, and —" She growled in frustration, then blew out her breath and looked up at him. "But I do, okay? I love you so much. Now you can believe that or not. But let me tell you somethin', *mon ami.* On May twenty-third I had my whole world cave in on me. Everything, which up to that point I'd believed to be good and true, turned out to be so many Tinkertoys built on a foundation of lies."

She stared up at him, one hand plowing through her bangs to scrape her hair back off her forehead. Only slowly did it filter through her fingers until all the wavy strands fell back into place. Then her hand dropped to her side. "I spent too many nights worrying it to death in too many strange motel rooms, and it got to be pretty much fixed in my head that I'm the only person in this world I can count on to keep my *bébé* safe. That's a mind-set you don't just change with the snap of your fingers, *cher.* Not even if you're moon-faced in love with a great big, stubborn, overbearing —"

Elvis kissed her. His good hand clenched in her hair, and his left arm went around her waist to pull her in close to his body. Lifting his head moments later, he grinned down at her. "You gotta quit sweet-talkin' me this way, doll. You're gonna embarrass me with all these endearments."

Emma used the tips of her fingers to trace the ridges of his eyebrows and the prominent bones in his cheeks. She trailed them softly to his scar and then to his full mouth. "I love you, Elvis Donnelly," she said seriously. "Me 'n' Gracie are in a real perilous position here, and I'm tellin' you straight out, it scares me right down to the marrow of my bones to be placin' all my faith in you. But you've got it, *cher*. You do."

"And about damn time, too," he said. Then, with a smack of his palm against her butt, he set her loose. "Pack your bags, Emma."

She stared at him in confusion. "What?" Not that she hadn't heard exactly what he'd said. It was just . . . she didn't understand it.

"Pack up. I found a safe house this morning, and you, me, and Baby Beans are moving in as soon as we can gather up our stuff. No one's gonna know where to find us." He gave her another hard, swift kiss and then straightened, and turning her toward the bed, left her staring blankly at its neatly made expanse while he crossed the room, quick and graceful as a cat, to scoop up the suitcase he'd flung away earlier. Shaking it free of minute bits of broken glass, he brought it back and tossed it on the mattress in front of her. "How long will it take you to get ready?"

"We're movin'?"

"You didn't think I'd just ignore the fact that Gracie was injured here last night, did you? I'm afraid the two of you are no longer safe here."

Emma opened her mouth to speak and then closed it. Opened it once again — and once again shut it, completely speechless. Then she burst into tears.

"Heeeey." Elvis pulled her into his arms and offered awkward comfort. His good hand patted her, his jaw rubbed her hair away from her eyes, his prosthesis rubbed up and down her back. "Hey, don't cry, now. It's gonna be okay, Em, I promise you. It's not like I expect you to isolate yourself from *everybody.* Sam and Clare can know where we are, and so can Ruby, if you want. Okay? I just don't think it's a good idea for anybody else —"

Her sobs escalated.

"Oh, Em, baby, don't cry."

She clutched his shirtfront in both fists and bawled her eyes out. She honest-to-God wasn't alone anymore — only now was it fully sinking in. There had been times recently when sheer nerve alone had kept her going, but she had Elvis now to help her keep Gracie safe. *Really* had Elvis, not just as an upholder of the law but as a man who, because he loved both her and Grace Melina, had a stake in seeing that no harm came to them. The realization flooded her with such relief, her emotions had simply given way. "I love you, *cher,*" she sobbed and banged her forehead on his chest. "I love you so much."

"Yeah, I can see that you're all kinds of happy."

A little laugh sputtered out of her, and Emma reached up to take an inelegant swipe at her nose with the back of her hand. Fighting her emotions to a standstill, she peered up at him. "I am, Elvis; God, I am. Only it's just sort of like" — she dashed away tears with the sides of her fingers — "you know those things you hear about hostages? About how they stay so strong under all sorts of adverse conditions . . . and then some random kindness breaks 'em? You made arrangements to get Gracie out of here and into some place safe. It pushed all my buttons."

Elvis shook his head. "I can see I'm probably never going to understand you, Emma, even if I live to be an old, old man," he said. Reluctantly turning her loose, he stepped back and gave her face a thorough inspection, paying particular attention to her eyes. "Listen, are you going to be all right if I leave you alone here to get your stuff together? Just for a little while?"

"Yes, sure."

"Okay then. I'd better go talk to Ruby about the both of us vacating at the same time this way."

"Oh, Lord, Elvis. I didn't even think about that." A frown of concern pulled Emma's delicate eyebrows together. "We're kind of leaving her in the lurch, aren't we?"

"You and Gracie have become important to Ruby," he replied with a shrug. "She'll understand." Or so he hoped.

Ruby did. She dragged him over to table seven the moment he walked through the doorway connecting the café to the boarding house. "I heard about last night," she said in a low voice. "Is Gracie really all right?"

"Yeah. She's got three stitches in her head —"

Ruby moaned.

"— but she's fine. She's bouncing all over the place this morning. Last night's incident is what I need to talk to you about, though." He waited until he had her undivided attention. "I've gotta give up my room, Ruby, and so does Emma. I'm moving the three of us into the Rutherford place out on Higgins Road." He fixed her with a stern expression. "That information goes no further than you, though," he warned. "You, the Mackeys, Sandy, and my deputies are the only ones who are going to know Emma's new location. Now, I apologize for the short notice —"

It was a measure of her friendship with Emma, he thought, that she barely even winced at losing two rents at once. "Don't worry about that, Elvis. I'm glad you're getting them out of here. It's obviously no longer a safe spot for them."

"I'm going to find whoever was responsible for hurting Gracie," he told her. "You can take that to the bank. And when I do," he vowed in a hard voice, "I'm going to make 'em pay."

Realizing it wasn't the most professional comment to be making in public, he gathered his cop persona more firmly around him. "In any case," he said firmly, "my rent's paid up until the end of the month. I'd like to give that to you in lieu of a formal notice and ask that you don't spread it around that I'm no longer living up there. The fewer people who realize we've moved out, the better it will be for Emma and Gracie."

"I'll do whatever you think is best, Elvis. Only, the thing is . . . can I come visit them sometime?"

"You bet, whenever you want." She appeared so upset at the thought of being cut off from Emma that he reached over and patted her hand. "That's why I told you where they'll be, Ruby. Just take every precaution to see that you're not followed, hey?" Then his eyes lit up and he gave her a crooked little smile. "Not that I foresee any particular problem in that arena. Hell, the logistics of the night out you and Emma had at the Anchor showed you have a skill a lot of cops I've worked with would have envied."

Shortly thereafter, he was climbing the stairs back to his room trying to ignore the warm glow in his solar plexus that was a result of the way Ruby had turned her hand over beneath his and said, "You know something, Elvis Donnelly? You really are a very nice man," before giving his fingers a squeeze and then turning them loose. Hell, big deal. Ruby had never been one of the islanders to ostracize him, anyway. She'd always treated him with perfect civility. He'd learned young how to read the nuances, however, and he knew that neither had she particularly liked him before.

So, okay, he'd admit it. It felt . . . good . . . to know that now she apparently did.

He figured out immediately, upon entering his room, that he wasn't going to get a damn thing accomplished in any sort of a timely manner with Gracie underfoot. At the first opportunity, he pulled Clare aside.

"Can you take her down to the store for a while?" he requested. "Please, I'll try not to be too long."

"Don't worry about it," she said and gave his arm a reassuring pat. "Take your time. If it runs into the lunch hour I'll feed her some nice high-fat, low-nutritional fountain fare. You going to tell me what's going on, though, Elvis?"

"Yeah, I will, Clare, I promise. Just as soon as I have a minute to spare." For the first time all morning he looked at her closely. There was a sort of a glow about her that he hadn't seen in a long time. "You look different," he said, and tilted his head first to one side and then the other as he tried to figure out why. "You get a new haircut or something? No, wait, I know. You've lost weight, right?"

Clare just laughed and went to pry Gracie away from the rock and shell collection she was artistically arranging among the piles of books, coloring books, chalk, and crayons on the wide window sill overlooking the harbor.

Elvis was still staring down at Gracie's piles of odds and end after Clare had let the two of them out of the room. Emma must have brought an armload of Gracie's possessions over this morning so her daughter would be surrounded by familiar things. He reached out a fingertip to reposition a sand dollar. Little nester that she was, Gracie had wasted no time commandeering his window sill to set up her effects in the manner to which she was accustomed. The only problem with it, he thought with a small grin as he fetched a cardboard box and began to fill it with her stuff, was that his room faced west on the opposite side of the building and therefore got more sun. Crayons left all day on his sill at this time of year were bound to end up as one great big multicolored lump of wax.

Elvis set to work on his room. Since his desire was to keep his and the Sandses' relocation from becoming common knowledge, he didn't think it would be a stellar idea to carry everything he and Emma owned down to their respective cars in broad daylight. He packed up all of his belongings in preparation for the move, but only transported the bare essentials down to the Suburban, where he stashed them under a tarp in the back. Loping back up the stairs to Emma's room he cautioned her to do the same when he saw that she was nearly ready. Informed as to where her daughter was, he promised to return for Emma shortly, so they could pick her up. Showing himself publicly in the café, he bought a cup of coffee, left through the café's front door, and crossed the square, where he checked into work for a while to discuss strategy with his two deputies.

It was shortly after one when he and Emma walked into Mackey's General Store. They found Gracie back at the fountain, seated upon a stack of telephone books on one of the stools. Someone had tied a dishtowel around her neck to keep her outfit clean, and it was liberally spread with mustard and relish from the hot dog she was polishing off. Swallowing the last bite, she reached with both hands for her glass of milk.

Emma slid onto the stool next to her. "Hi, angel pie. Miss me?"

"Maman!" Gracie lowered her glass and, milky mustache and all, smiled dazzlingly at her mother. "Mistoo Mackey gibbed me a *hot dawg* for lunch!"

"I can see that, *bébé*. Thank you, Sam," she said softly to the man crouched nearby stocking a lower shelf. Her hand reached out to gently finger-comb her daughter's hair, disengaging soft strands that stuck to the three wiry stitches in her forehead.

Sam finished his chore and surged to his feet. Fingers pressed into his lower back, he stretched out his spine. "We were glad to help, Emma. I'm sorry Gracie was hurt last night. Fred," he said to the boy behind the counter. "Lunch rush seems to be over. Why don't you go ahead and take your own meal break now."

"Yes, I'll take over," Clare offered, coming up. She paused at Emma's side to slide an arm around her shoulders and give her a brief hug. "How you holding up?"

"I'm fine. Elvis is —" She broke off to grimace significantly in Gracie's direction. "Are you all done, angel?"

"Uh-huh."

"Well, let's get you cleaned up and then maybe you can go check out the toy section for a few minutes." Emma pulled several napkins out of the dispenser and dipped them in her daughter's water glass. Efficiently, she erased all signs of lunch from Gracie's face and hands.

Gracie bobbed in place, impatient to get down. "Can I get sumpin to take home, Mommy?"

"We'll see. You have to be a good girl and stay out of the customers' way."

"I will!"

Elvis lifted her off the stack of books and blew a raspberry against her neck before setting her down. Giggling, she trotted off. He turned back to the Mackeys and told them about the new living arrangements.

"Excellent," Clare said crisply when he

had finished explaining. "That's exactly what's needed — to place the target out of this idiot's range. And it definitely calls for a housewarming. Just me, Sam, and Ruby," she added hastily at the horrified expression on Elvis' face. "For pity's sake, E, what did you think I meant, an island-wide invitation? Give me a little credit. I'm talking about tossing a few steaks on the grill and throwing together a salad and some baked potatoes. We've even got an old barbecue grill you can have." She grinned. "Think of it as a cheapskate's housewarming present. We'll throw in a bag of charcoal, won't we, Sam?"

And somehow, without Elvis having much opportunity to say anything about it one way or another, it was arranged. He shrugged, accepting that he'd been outgunned, and pulled Sam aside.

"Where we goin', *Maman?*" Gracie strained against the shoulder strap in her car seat. She stared at the back of the department Suburban they were following along the country highway. "Where's Shewiff Elbis goin'? How come we don't wide with him? We's goin' the same way."

"You'll see when we get there, *chère.*"

"But, Mommy —"

"I can't tell you more than that, Grace Melina. It's a surprise."

Luckily, it wasn't too much longer before the Suburban's blinker went on and they turned off the highway onto a secondary road and then a short distance later turned into a private driveway. Gravel crunched beneath their tires as they passed beneath the towering evergreens that screened the property from the road. Emma pulled the Chevy in next to Elvis' vehicle on an apron of concrete in front of a detached two-car garage.

"What is this place, *Maman?*" Gracie demanded. She looked at her mother hopefully. "Is there a little girl for me to play with?"

Emma's heart clenched. "No, angel, I'm sorry. This is our new house. You, me, and Elvis are goin' to be livin' here."

Gracie's already large eyes grew enormous. "Weally?" She drummed her heels restively when her mother got out of the car, impatient with the rules that decreed she had to wait to be let out of her seat. But she didn't have long to wait; Elvis got there before her *maman* could round the car. He opened the door and unhooked her safety harness. His proffered hook was ignored as she scrambled down unassisted.

"We gonna lib here, Elbis!" she screeched and ran into the yard. "We gonna . . . Oh, lookit! Lookit! Issa *swing!*" She made a beeline for a homemade rope and plank contraption that hung from a sturdy branch of a gnarled old apple tree. Flinging herself stomach first onto the seat, she set the swing in motion. It wobbled gently back and forth.

"Well, she's a hard sell," Emma commented dryly as she stood at Elvis' side and watched her daughter.

He put an arm around her and hugged her to his side. "I just love a low-maintenance woman," he said. Then he called to Gracie to come see the house.

"It's small," he apologized as he walked them through the living room, dining room, kitchen, and bath. "And I know the furnishings aren't anything to write home about —"

"It's fine," Emma assured him. It was true the furniture owed more to durability than it did to fashion. The most it had going for it was that it could be described as inoffensively nondescript. Still . . . "With some pretty curtains on that window and the one in the kitchen, and maybe some slipcovers for the couch and chair — why, I think it could be real attractive, *cher.* And as for its size, there's certainly more space here than either of us had at the boardin' house."

"Yeah." Relieved by her upbeat attitude, he gave her a crooked smile. "That's true enough." When he'd walked through the kitchen door and seen the kind of shabbiness he'd grown up with —

He gave himself a mental shake. Well. Never mind that. It didn't matter now, because Emma saw the possibilities. And none of them, thank God, seemed to include a single painted black velvet portrait of the King.

"I like these built-in bookcases," Emma said, and smiled at Elvis over her shoulder. "How did you ever find a place that was furnished?"

"George and Brandy Sperano originally bought this place to rent to their youngest daughter. She wanted her independence, and they wanted her near by. That sort of started a tradition. This has been the first home away from home for a lot of kids on the island. You and I are probably the oldest renters the Speranos have ever had." He laughed. "Gracie girl," he said and threw open a door off the little hallway, "this is your new bedroom, sweetheart."

Gracie raced in. She dashed enthusiastically from one feature to the next. Coming back to her mother, she grabbed Emma's hand and danced in place. "Look, Mommy! Is our new bedwoom!" Transferring her big, brown-eyed gaze to Elvis, she asked innocently, "Where *you* gonna sleep, Elbis?"

Seventeen

Elvis was there to greet Sam and Clare when the car drove into the yard. He was leaning through the driver's window practically before the car stopped rolling. "I'm glad you're here," he said to Sam. "Did you bring what I asked for?"

"And hello to you, too, Clare," Clare murmured to herself. "Nice to see you. You're lookin' good."

Elvis gave her a pained smile. "Sorry. Hi. Nice to see you. And you are lookin' good." Immediately he turned back to Sam. "Well?"

"Yeah, it's in the trunk." Sam gave Elvis a perplexed look. "What the hell's going on?"

"Nothin'. Pop the trunk. This baby's gonna save my bacon." He rolled his shoulders. "I hope."

"How the hell is a trike going to save your bacon," Sam wanted to know as he popped the trunk and climbed out of the car. He exchanged a look with Clare across the roof of the vehicle and then shrugged.

"Well, maybe save my bacon is the wrong term. I'm hoping it's gonna buy me some affection," Elvis amended. "The kid hates my guts."

"Gracie?" Sam said incredulously. "Get outta here. Kid's crazy about you."

"That was before. She hates my guts now that she's discovered Emma's going to be sleeping in my room instead of hers."

"Oh, hates his guts, my fanny," Emma said a few minutes later when Clare was relating the story to her and Ruby in the kitchen. She laughed. "Gracie and I have been sharing one room or another since we lit out from home, and she threw a fit when Elvis told her I was sleeping in the bigger room with him. Instead of telling her to knock it the heck off and get over it, he tried the Progressive-Parenting-explain-all-your-reasons-in-detail approach." All three women rolled their eyes. "With a three-year-old," Emma said with an expressive snort. "*Right.* So, anyhow, she's naturally milking it for all it's worth because it's pretty neat to have an adult practically pleading for her forgiveness and understanding." She smiled and shook her head. "Gawd, he's such a pushover with her."

"I heard that," Elvis said, opening the screen door. "And I am not. Here" — he handed her a six pack of Clausthaler's — "Sam brought this."

"Thank you, Sam." Emma took the beer and put it in the fridge. "Sure you are," she said, going back to their argument. "You're gettin' all set to reward Gracie's bratty behavior with a trike, aren't you?"

"Hey, I asked Sam to bring the trike before any of this ever came up," Elvis protested virtuously. "Besides, she wasn't a brat, Em; she was upset. She's accustomed to sleeping with you."

"Oh, well then, perhaps we'd better not disappoint her," Emma said smoothly. She pulled silverware out of the drawer and plopped it into a cup, which she handed to Ruby. "Maybe I had better sleep in her room."

Every head in the kitchen swung around to catch Elvis' reaction to the suggestion.

"With that little brat?" he demanded incredulously. "The hell you say." He gave her a crooked grin. "Okay, okay, I get your point. So how am I supposed to treat her when she gets like this?"

"The same way you'd treat someone if this were a professional situation, *cher*."

"Slap her little baby butt in jail?"

"Oh, now you're bein' deliberately obtuse," she said. Handing the stack of plates to Clare, she then turned, hands on hips, to face him. "C'mon, Elvis. When I was fixin' Mrs. Steadman's car, she couldn't stop ravin' about the way you'd handled her boys when they unloaded that junk they were supposed to be haulin' to the dump. You were firm but fair. You didn't let them get away with what they'd done, but neither did you make the punishment excessive to the crime. You gotta do the same thing with Gracie, *cher.* Otherwise you're goin' to have a little monster on your hands. Hand," she amended.

Then she shrugged and gave him a crooked smile. "Hand and hook — whatever. You know what I mean."

"Okay, I'll put the trike in the garage until she straightens up."

"Good."

Just then, the screen door swung open and Gracie raced across the linoleum. "Mommy, Mommy, there's a box out there with a pitchoo of a *twike* on it!"

"Um-hmm," Emma agreed. "That belongs to Elvis."

"Weally?" Gracie swung around to face him, her eyes alight. Elvis stared back at her in an agony of indecision. "Is it a twike, Elbis? Who's it fo'? Is it fo' *me?*"

"Well, yeah, originally I got it for you, but your momma said I couldn't —" He broke off as three females separately smacked, poked, or pinched him on the closest available body part. "Uh, that is, you don't like me anymore," he said and then drew himself up to his full, imposing height, adding firmly, "so I guess I'll just have to have Sam take it back to the store."

"No! I yike you."

"You don't."

"Uh-huh!"

"I don't think so, Gracie. You've been treating me like dirt all afternoon."

Tears welled up in her eyes. "But you want my mommy to seep in *yo'* woom."

"Yeah, I do." He stooped down to scoop her up and then squatted down while he cuddled her. "I know you're going to miss her at first, but that's just the way it is, Gracie girl. Kids are supposed to have one room, and adults are supposed to have another. You were lucky to have her all to yourself for a while, but now it's time things get back to normal. And anyhow, sweetheart, she's just gonna be one door down. It's not like I'm moving her to another house. *That's* when you'd have room to complain."

She stared at him solemnly for a moment while she thought it over. Finally, she gave an uncertain nod and said, " 'Kay," in a little voice. She obviously wasn't thrilled with the idea, but she nevertheless consented.

"Okay, then," Elvis agreed and laughed, his teeth flashing whitely in his weathered face. He tightened his grip on her and surged to his full height. "Whataya say, Sam?" He looked across the small kitchen at his friend. "You wanna help Gracie girl and me get that trike out of the box?"

"Why not?" Sam agreed. "I can't smoke, so I might as well keep my hands busy doing something productive."

Elvis stopped dead in the doorway. "You quit smoking?" he said incredulously. "When the hell did this happen?"

"Hell this happen?" Gracie demanded in a little echo that was a perfect imitation right down to the last intonation, and Elvis grimaced, meeting Emma's eyes over her daughter's head.

"Sorry, Em," he said, and then turned his full attention on Gracie. "*I* can swear," he said austerely, looking down at her in disapproval. "*You* cannot. Not until you're twenty-one, kid; you got that?"

"Uh-huh."

He continued to stare at her sternly, and she ducked her head and blew a conciliatory little raspberry against his throat to get back into his good graces. He rubbed her back approvingly and looked at Clare over her head. "He quit smokin', huh?"

She blushed, and a slow grin spread across his face. That was pretty much what he thought it meant. Then he laughed out loud. And he'd asked her if she'd lost weight. "Well, congratulations, Sam," he said cheerfully, shouldering the screen door open. "This really is a reason to celebrate."

"Maman," Gracie called from her new bedroom. "I'm thoosty."

Emma rolled her eyes and climbed off Elvis' lap.

"This is going to go on all night, isn't it?" he said in resignation, watching Emma's long-legged stride carry her into the kitchen where he heard the faucet run.

" 'Fraid so." She appeared in the doorway, a half-filled glass of water in her hand. Giving him a lopsided smile, she said, "Sorry, *cher*. It's a new place and a new situation, in as much as she doesn't have me in the same room while she's acclimating to it." Emma ran her free hand through Elvis' hair as she passed behind his chair. "On the plus side, she's adaptable. She'll be fine by tomorrow."

"Maman!"

"You hold your horses, Grace Melina,"

Emma called back firmly. "I'll be there in a moment." Under her breath she added, "*Dieu,* what d'ya think this is — your great white hotel?"

Elvis shoved to his feet. Wrapping his hand around the back of her neck, he gave her a quick, hard kiss. "I should go in to work anyway. We've got a minisurveillance going on at Ruby's, and it's about time I relieved one of my men."

"You have a surveillance?" Emma's breath stilled as she stared up at him. "To catch my troublemaker?"

"Yeah." He rubbed his thumb up and down her nape. "I'm gonna enjoy slamming this guy's butt in jail, Em."

She gave him a speculative look and then smiled. "Of course. That's why you wanted the Chevy's cover, isn't it?"

"Yep. Ben's got an old beater about the same size he's been fixing up in his spare time. With your cover over it, parked in the Chevy's usual spot, it's impossible to tell it's not the same car unless you get right up under the cover. Anyone does that, he's gonna have one of us breathing down his neck."

"Well, you be careful, *cher,*" she urged him. "After the rock-throwin' episode you can't be certain what sort of person you're dealin' with here."

Elvis grinned at her. He'd never had anyone expend much energy worrying about his safety before. "I will be," he promised. Then he kissed her again and reluctantly turned her loose. "Damn. I'd better go. Don't wait up."

Emma waited until the door closed behind his back and then took the water into Gracie's room. Gracie took two tiny sips and handed the glass back to her mother, confirming Emma's suspicion that requesting it had been no more than a ruse. "How come Elbis didn't gib it to me?" she wanted to know.

"Because you asked me to bring it."

"Well, maybe he wants to wead me a stowy."

"I'm sure he'd love to, *bébé*, but he had to go back to work."

Gracie's mouth dropped open in surprise, and indignation darkened her eyes. "But he hassa kiss me good night!"

"He kissed you good night when you first went to bed, Grace Melina. And after the trip to the bathroom, too, as I recall. And, let's see, what about when you called us both in to tell us — again — all about the swing and the trike?" She looked at her daughter's scarlet cheeks and exhausted eyes, recognized the tantrum struggling to build as Gracie fought to stay awake. Sliding onto the bed next to her, Emma gathered Gracie into her arms, where she rocked her and murmured soothing words of affection. Gracie's eyes slid shut.

Then they opened, and heavy-lidded, stared up into Emma's. "Is Elbis gonna be my daddy, *Maman?*"

Emma's heart contracted. "I don't know, angel pie," she said softly. *But I hope so. Ah, Dieu, I do hope so.*

"I'd yike him to be."

"I know you would, *ange.*" Emma kissed her daughter's brow, careful of the stitches. "But it's not your decision to make. He's a grown man, Gracie. This is somethin' he has to make up his own mind about."

"Him's not ugly," Gracie murmured, and Emma knew out of fatigue Gracie was mixing and matching snatches of last night's conversation into whatever tonight's thought processes might be. Gracie's eyelids slid shut again.

"No," Emma agreed, kissing her child's eyebrow. "He's not ugly. Elvis Donnelly is a beautiful man."

The first thing Elvis saw when he pulled into the driveway at nine o'clock the following morning was Gracie riding her tricycle in circles on the apron of cement that fronted the garage. She jumped off and raced over to the Suburban to meet him. "Hi, Elbis!" she called. "I be widin' my twike!"

"Yeah, I saw that," he replied, climbing out of the vehicle and bending down to scoop her up. She threw her arms around his neck in a hug, and he closed his eyes for a moment, breathing in her little-girl smell. "Where's your momma?"

"In the gawage."

"Let's go see her." He carried her toward the open bay door, but Gracie started wriggling to be let down as soon as they reached the apron.

"Watch me," she cried as she climbed onto the trike. Peddling hell for leather, she propelled the little tricycle into the garage. "Watch me, Elbis, watch me!"

Elvis ambled along in her wake. It took a moment for his eyes to adjust to the dimness inside after the brilliant sunshine, but he soon spotted Emma crouched down next to her car, masking off the chrome. "Hey," he greeted her. "What are you up to? You gonna paint the car?"

"Yes." Emma looked up at him. "I'm afraid it's goin' to be necessary."

" 'Cuz a bad pooson wighted on it,"

Gracie interrupted, anxious to be included in the conversation. She peddled up to the passenger door. Spelling out random letters that she recognized, she turned to squint up at her mother. "What does that wooed say, *Maman?*"

"Never you mind, Grace Melina. Why don't you show Elvis how you can turn your trike around without even getting off it."

Gracie was happy to oblige, and Emma soon turned back to Elvis.

"So you're going to have to paint it, huh?" he asked her again.

"*Oui.* The paint thinner didn't work." She indicated a spot where she'd tried it. "I'm sandin' by hand until I can find someplace that'll rent me a DA sander." She studied him closely. "You look exhausted," she said. "Any luck?"

"No." He rubbed the back of his neck. "Which isn't altogether surprising. We figured the chances of him showing himself again last night were pretty slim. It was just the night before that when he injured Gracie, and he'd have to be a fool to try anything else so soon." He rolled his shoulders. "Still. It was worth a shot. George is keeping an eye on things today. I'll catch a few *Z*'s and go back tonight." He looked around him. "So, the garage is all right for the stuff you wanna do then?"

"Yes. I *love* having a place to work. Thank you." She straightened to her full height to give him a brief kiss. "Go to bed," she commanded, tilting her head back to examine his face. "You look absolutely pooped. Go on now." She gave him a small shove toward the door. "I'll try to keep Gracie out of your hair while you sleep."

A few hours later, however, when her daughter was temporarily bored with the tricycle and the swing and Emma was occupied in the garage, Gracie slipped into the front bedroom and climbed up on the bed. Elvis was sprawled out on his side, facing her. "Elbis!" she whispered loudly. "You 'wake, Elbis?"

There was no answer, just the sound of his deep breathing. Gracie patted her hand over his scarred cheek to no response. Thumbing up his eyelid only made him mumble and jerk his hook. She blew a raspberry beneath the angle of his jaw. He continued to sleep.

Finally, with a long-suffering sigh, she turned around, slid her bottom onto the spread next to his abdomen, and settled back against him. Casually, she dug her elbow into his stomach. "How come you don't wake up?" She tried the elbow gambit several more times. Getting no more response than a soft grunt and a mutter, she popped her thumb into her mouth to think about it awhile.

Some time later, Elvis slowly swam to the surface of consciousness, heavy waves of fatigue still rolling over him and threatening to pull him back under. There was a warmth against his stomach and the inside of his forearm, which he couldn't quite identify; and a singsong little voice seemed to be keeping time with the feather-light touches just above his prosthesis.

" 'Long came the *wain* and washed the spidoo out! *Up* came the *sun* and dwied up all the wain." Deep yawn. "And itsy bitsy *spi*-doo went up the spout *again*."

One corner of Elvis' mouth tipped up. It was Beans. His arm tightened around her fractionally and he started to sink back into slumber, but her voice pulled him back once again. "*Je*-sus loves me, this I know," she warbled. "*Fo'* the Bible tells me so." Deeper, longer yawn. When it trailed off she resumed, but in conversational tones this time instead of song. "My daddy's name is Elbis Don'lee," she murmured. "He has a hook and a scaw. I have a scaw, too." She snuggled in closer to Elvis, whose heartbeat was escalating and beginning to push back the black waves of fatigue, and when next she spoke he could tell it was around her thumb. "My daddy's bigoo 'n' yo' daddy."

Ah, Christ. He felt warmth spread out from his chest and his gut to his furthest extremities. His heart seemed squeezed — and the backs of his eyes burned in a way they hadn't since he was a little kid.

Damn. Ah, dammit, Gracie. Damn.

"You think we should *what?*" Emma almost dropped the plate she was handing him to dry.

"Get married." Elvis rescued the plate and set it on the counter, tossing the dishtowel on top of it. He reached out his hand then and ran it down Emma's arm, encircling her wrist with his fingers. Tugging, he pulled her a step nearer. "I think we should get married."

Emma's heart began to thump in her chest. "Where on earth did this come from? I mean, you've never mentioned —"

"It's a good idea, Em," he said insistently. "Your reputation is going to be destroyed the minute word gets out about this arrangement we've currently got goin'. Besides, Gracie needs a daddy."

"Hold it." She held up her free hand like a traffic cop. "Just hold it right there; let's back up a step here. Gracie said something to you, didn't she, *cher?*" Emma demanded suspiciously. He simply looked at her with a blank expression, but she could read the truth in his eyes. "I *knew* it! Dammit, I knew it the moment I tracked her down to our bedroom." She rammed her fingers through her hair. "I *told* that child she had to let you make up your own mind."

"She didn't actually say anything to me, Em," he hurried to explain. Rubbing his thumb up and down the faint blue veins on her inner wrist, he added insistently in the face of Emma's skeptical expression, "She didn't. She was just talking to herself when I woke up."

Emma jerked her wrist away. "Well, thank you, Elvis," she said, as reasonably as she could. "Thank you for the offer, but . . . no thank you." It was ridiculous to feel hurt, but darn it, she had kind of hoped if the day ever came when Elvis Donnelly asked her to make this relationship between them a permanent one, it would be for the usual reasons.

"Whataya mean, thanks but no thanks? Why the hell not?" He hadn't considered that she'd refuse him and was patently unprepared for it. He took a giant step forward, towering over her with his bulk and height.

It was an instinctual move, not something he gave conscious thought to. But dammit, she couldn't say no; his gut rebelled at the very idea, and he found himself crowding her even more. If he had to use a few intimidation tactics to make her see that marriage was the right move for them to make, the logical next step, then so be it. This was more than important, dammit; it was *vital.*

A second later his cognitive processes kicked in. He thought about what he was doing and started to step away. Ah, hell, who was he trying to kid anyhow? The Devil himself probably couldn't intimidate Emma Sands into doing what she didn't want to do.

Her chin shot up the instant before he followed through on his good intentions. *Oh, perfect,* she thought bitterly. This was just dandy. Never in a million years would she have expected Elvis to resort to physical coercion, yet here he was looming over her. Was this what they'd taught him in cop school? Or maybe it wasn't a police thing at all; maybe it was simply one of those testosterone-driven instinctive reactions. Macho Man Subdues the Little Woman. Well, whatever its origins, she recognized the aggressive posturing. She hadn't fallen in with his plans, so pow! Instant reversion to Dominator Dan. "I'll tell you why not," she snarled, disillusioned and incensed past discretion. Shoving him back, she wrapped her arms around herself and faced him belligerently. "Because I don't want to be wed to *'save my reputation.'* "

"That's not —"

"Don't do me any favors, okay, Donnelly? I don't need a mercy wedding, and I sure as hell don't want to be married because my *bébé* pressured some poor unsuspecting schmuck —"

"Wait a minute, wait a minute! I think we're talking at cross purposes here. Sweet God Almighty, you've got it all wrong, Em."

"Ah, *oui,* well, there's a surprise. The woman is always wrong, is she not?"

He made a frustrated noise deep in his throat and reached out for her, but it stopped him cold when she flinched and drew away. His arms dropped to his sides. How the hell had it degenerated to this?

"Dammit, Emma," he said desperately, "that's not what I meant at all." A muscle ticked in his jaw. "My God, you gotta know you've been ripping my guts to shreds since practically the first day we met." Seeing her open her mouth to, no doubt, express in her inimitable scathing style her objections to those words also, he held up his hand. "No, let me finish here. I've somehow screwed this all up, used all the wrong words, but can you honestly see me shackling myself to someone for life over *your* interpretation of my intentions?" Shaking his head in amazement, he laughed, a low rumbling expulsion of pent-up oxygen expressing ironic disbelief more than amusement. "Emma, my idea of *heaven* is being married to you, being a daddy to your kid. Hell, having her be *my* kid, too. And when I think of maybe planting another kid in here someday . . ." His fingers, warm and hard, reached out to rub her stomach. *"God."* He pulled his hand away but stared down at her, blue eyes blazing. "I can understand how you might not want to tie yourself down to *me* or to this little nowhere town. But I love you — you *know* I love you. How could you possibly think I'd want to marry you out of some sense of responsibility? I mean, come on, Em, a *mercy* wedding?" He'd been too busy defending his position at the time to get indignant, but it pissed him off in retrospect.

Heat unfurled in Emma's midsection. Her eyes grew soft. "Well, my thinkin' that might have somethin' to do with the fact that's all you bothered to mention, I suppose," she murmured. It was only a misunderstanding, thank the *bon Dieu.* She raised a hand to softly stroke his face from cheekbone to scar to rigid jaw.

But he obviously wasn't buying it. He stood in front of her stiffly, holding himself still while frustration emanated from him in waves, and she considered for a moment his history, his past relationships with the people in his life. "Then again," she said slowly, looping both arms around his neck. "Maybe I just wasn't trustin' enough."

His eyes, vividly blue, skimmed every feature on her face, and slowly, so slowly, his white teeth emerged in a smile of blinding brilliance. "Yeah?"

"Oh, *oui.* I jumped to conclusions because it hurt my feelin's to be told we should marry to save my good name or because Grace Melina couldn't keep her little oar out of the water."

"Hey, those are both good, solid reasons," Elvis insisted, sliding his arms around her and squeezing. "I don't wanna have to knock people's heads together if they badmouth you, Emma. And Beans just breaks my heart; I want to take care of her so bad. I didn't know it was possible to feel this way, Em." He lowered his forehead against hers and rolled it back and forth. Then he gave her a quick, fierce kiss and straightened up again. He grinned. "But you're absolutely right, doll; just loving each other is a better reason. Much better. Hell, it's a beaut. So, we are getting married, right?"

"Oui," she said. "You said we oughtta. I heard it; it's a verbal invitation, and I'm not lettin' you back out of it, *cher.*" Arms tightening around his neck, she smirked up at him. "And if the thought of squirmin' out of it somewhere down the road has wriggled across your mind, you can just forget it. I don't believe in divorce — at least not for myself."

Elvis whooped and tightened his prosthesis around her waist. Picking her up he whirled her around. They bumped against the table and chairs in the tiny enclosure, sending them rattling, and he stopped revolving to bury his face in the curve of her neck.

The screen door slammed behind Gracie as she came running in from outside. "What?" she squealed, little feet planted and sturdy little torso bobbing in place as she sensed the excitement. "What Mommy? What, Elbis? What so funny?"

Elvis pulled his face out of Emma's neck and grinned down at her daughter. Soon to be *his* daughter. He threw back his head and laughed, then swooped down to scoop her up. “Ah, Gracie girl,” he said, holding his woman and child. He gave them both a fierce hug. “Have we got news for you, kid.”

They'd only meant to kiss and maybe pet a little before Elvis had to leave to go back on his stakeout. But Gracie was sleeping soundly and they were pumped up with the excitement of their wedding plans. One thing led to another, and before they quite knew what was happening, Elvis' jeans were down around his ankles, Emma's shorts and panties were on the floor, her sleeveless blouse was hanging open, and she was kneeling astride him in the big overstuffed chair, gripping his broad, khaki-covered shoulders in both hands. Her head thrown back, feeling his mouth on her breasts, she strove to meet each aggressive upward thrust with a fierce downward hip movement of her own.

They collapsed into each other in the wake of shuddering, teeth-gritting climaxes, their breaths rasping loudly in the posttwilight hush of the evening.

“Dieu,” Emma panted, rolling her forehead back and forth against the curve of his neck while her arms clung to his shoulders to hold him tightly. “*Mon Dieu,* Elvis.”

His arms tightened around her. “You can

say that again." He blew out a gusty breath. "Maybe we should look into life insurance, doll. Much more of this and they'll be carting me outta here in a body bag."

She stiffened, and his arms immediately clenched around her in remorse. "Ah, shit; I'm sorry, Em," he whispered. He tangled his hook in her hair and tilted her head back until he could see into her eyes. "I'm sorry." Bringing up his free hand, he stroked his fingers down her cheek. "That was incredibly insensitive — it was my exhaustion speaking, not my brain. Nothing's gonna happen to me, baby; not like it did to Charlie. I promise you that."

"Something *could,* though." It was her worst fear. "Something so easily could if Grant finds out about you."

He simply looked at her for a moment, chewing thoughtfully on his bottom lip. "That kinda brings up something I've been thinkin' about lately," he finally said. "Emma, we can't hide in the shadows for the rest of our lives, sneaking around to keep Woodard from learning what we're up to. We've got to put some thought into what should be done if he does put in an appearance someday."

All warmth fled her expression. "For instance?" she demanded stiffly.

"For instance," he said, looking her straight in the eye, "I think you should have a talk with Gracie. Sweetheart, if you don't warn her about Grant Woodard she's going to run to the man with both her little arms wide open."

Some of the starch left Emma's backbone. "I know," she admitted unhappily. "I've thought of that, myself. But, *cher,* how do I go about doing that? How does one tell a three-year-old girl that her adored Grandpapa is, at the very least, a voyeur?"

"I don't think you have to go into detail, Em," he said gently. "Just — I don't know — tell her Grandpa did something bad and she's not to go to him if he comes around. That she's to inform you immediately if she sees him."

"You're right. I know you're right," she agreed. "It's just . . . difficult, Elvis."

"I know it is, Em. But I really think it should be done."

"*Oui.* So do I. I'll take care of it tomorrow."

And she fully meant to do so. She simply didn't count on something else coming up that would drive it out of her mind.

Eighteen

Woodard's man Conroy regarded the pay phone as if it might at any moment grow fangs to sink into his throat. Damn, fuck, shit. This was one call he'd give a hell of a lot not to have to make, and for one reckless moment he seriously considered lighting out for parts unknown. Hell, why not? Why not simply take off and just continue on until he'd put himself beyond Grant Woodard's reach?

Because he didn't know where that was.

Finally, he took a deep breath, reached for the receiver, and punched in the numbers. Much too quickly the call went through. "Woodard," Grant said crisply.

"Conroy here, sir." Conroy cleared his throat. "I, uh, seem to have lost Emma and the baby."

There was a moment of charged silence. Then deadly quiet. Finally, "What do you mean, you lost them?"

"They're no longer in their room, sir. It's been cleared out." He hesitated before adding, "The odd part is . . . no one but me seems to realize they're gone. Emma's car is still out back, and I think the folks around here believe she's still livin' upstairs."

Another silence followed, this one fraught with emotions Conroy hadn't realized were possible to sense when one person could neither see nor hear the other. He began to sweat. Christ — oh, Christ. What were his chances of getting through this assignment with his skin intact?

Finally Woodard said with frigid control, "Keep an eye on things until I get there. And, Conroy, try not to fuck it up. It's plain to me that if I want this handled correctly I'm going to have to come out there and handle it myself."

Conroy was still mopping the sweat off his brow when the phone in his hand went dead.

"Elvis?" The walkie-talkie crackled faintly, and Elvis snatched it up to his ear.

"Someone just went in through the back door of the boarding house," Ben's voice said. "Damn, Ruby could sure use a light back here — it's too dark to see who the hell it was." Then he seemed to recall himself. "The mannerisms didn't suggest a boarder going about his own business though, not unless one of your old neighbors is carrying on a clandestine affair up there."

It could always be Darren Maycomber, Elvis supposed, coming to see Pete Greyson, who was Elvis' ex-next-door neighbor. They were a gay couple who preferred life in the closet to the hassles of coming out in a conservative little town like Port Flannery. Living one door down from Pete, Elvis had figured out that relationship a long time ago, but he didn't mention it to Ben now. As far as he knew it wasn't yet public knowledge, and he didn't feel it was up to him to make it so. "I'll check it out," he said into the hand-held transmitter. "Remain in place and maintain radio silence."

"Copy that."

Elvis left the gazebo on the square and went in through the front door of the boarding house. He climbed the stairs quietly but not stealthily, since that would be more likely to attract attention. Ostensibly, he still lived here, and no one running across him would expect him to be walking on tiptoe. Pausing at the top of the stairs, he looked down the hallway.

And saw a man with his ear pressed to Emma's door.

At first the intruder appeared only to be listening, perhaps trying to ascertain if Emma was within. Then his hand went to the doorknob. When it turned under his palm, he eased the door open and, flashing a look up and down the hallway that had Elvis pulling back into the stairwell, he stepped inside. A second later a string of low-voiced obscenities polluted the air.

Elvis moved into the hall and through the door and eased it closed behind him. Reaching out, he snapped on the overhead light. "Nobody home, is there, Bill?" he inquired with deceptive calm, looking into the horrified eyes of the garage mechanic who had whirled around to face him. "Now, ain't that just a pisser, though?"

Pushing down on the transmit button to alert Ben via the walkie-talkie, Elvis added in his most authoritarian voice, "Bill Gertz, you are under arrest for property damage and for the reckless endangerment of Grace Melina Sands. Or," he qualified, shutting off the walkie-talkie and pushing away from the door, "we can skip the legalities and just move straight to the part where I beat the shit out of you. Right here, right now." Blue eyes narrowed and deadly, he gazed at the man responsible for Gracie's injury, eyeing him up and down in consideration before abruptly nodding his head. "Yes. I *much* prefer that idea."

"Are you crazy, Donnelly?" Bill Gertz demanded in horror. "You're a cop, man — you can't do that!" Jesus, he'd never dreamed of this sort of trouble when he'd first conceived the idea of harassing Emma Sands. He'd just wanted to make her go away.

"Who's going to stop me, Gertz?" Elvis wanted to know, and the mechanic found his calm, matter-of-fact manner even more terrifying than the temper he'd glimpsed a moment ago. "It's just you 'n' me here, bud. And, hey, look on the bright side," Elvis added in an almost friendly tone as he moved in on the other man. "You've got a real sporting chance this way — you can fight back without any of that resisting arrest BS to inhibit you. Hell, how hard can it be to beat me, anyway? I've only got one good hand."

"Big fuckin' deal, one good hand; you've got a *gun*." Bill backed up for every step forward Elvis took. Even without the gun, and with only one hand, the other man was big, very big, and solid muscle. Besides, Bill hadn't forgotten Elvis when he was a kid and willing to brawl at the drop of a hat.

Not to mention the look in those blazing blue eyes that belied the peacefulness of his voice.

"I'll take it off," Elvis offered obligingly.

"In fact, maybe we should slide it across the room and see who can get to it first — whataya think? Winner gets to put a bullet through the brain pan of the loser. You should like that, Bill. Y'never did like me much."

Bill started to sweat profusely. "Jesus," he whispered. "I think you're insane."

"Yeah? I think you shouldn't have hurt the baby, Gertz."

"It was an accident!" Bill stumbled over the overstuffed chair and hastily backed around it, putting it between himself and the sheriff. "I just wanted to make her old lady stop stealing my business. I didn't mean for nobody to get hurt!"

"What the hell did you think was gonna happen when you lobbed a rock into a room where a child lived?"

"I just wanted to make her mother go away!"

The door opened and Ben stepped into the room. Bill Gertz dodged around the chair and sidled over to stand next to him. Ben looked at Elvis. "Hey," he said laconically. "What's the story?"

"I was just getting ready to read Mr. Gertz here his rights," Elvis replied.

"The hell you say!" Gertz turned to Ben. "He was gonna kill me, Ben."

Ben made a rude noise. "Yeah, right."

"I'm tellin' ya! He was gonna beat the shit outta me or put a bullet through my brain pan or —"

"Uh-huh. Sure he was," Ben said soothingly. Then, "Get a grip, Bill," he advised flatly. "Elvis Donnelly is known for his professionalism. If you think you're going to use some cockamamie bullshit story like that to build yourself a defense, I'd think twice if I were you."

"He's gonna have *time* to think, aren't you, Bill?" Elvis came up behind the mechanic and wrenched Gertz's arms behind his back. "You have the right to remain silent," he said, hooking the handcuffs over the prisoner's wrists and clicking them closed. "If you give up this right, anything you say can and will be used against you in a court of law —"

"I didn't mean to hurt the kid," Bill Gertz muttered, as they led him down the stairs. "Hell, I didn't mean to hurt nobody. I just wanted to make that Frog bitch know-it-all stop stealin' my business."

"But that's crazy, *cher*," Emma said in dazed amazement when Elvis arrived home after midnight and woke her up to tell her what was going on. She blinked at him in sleepy confusion. "*Mon Dieu,* Elvis, the few cars I've tuned up couldn't have comprised a *fraction* of his business."

"Hey, you know it's crazy and I know it's crazy," Elvis agreed, removing his badge and name tag from his shirt and throwing them on the dresser top. "Bill, on the other hand, seems to have it set in his fuzzy little mind that you were cutting into his profit margin and had to be stopped before you put him out of business." He shrugged out of his shirt, looked it over to determine if it was clean enough to handle one more day's wear and then promptly forgot about it, gripping it in his good hand while he stared across the small amount of space that separated him from Emma. "I wanted to hurt him, Em," he told her. It scared him to realize how much. "Man, I had him in my sights; there was no one around to witness whatever I decided to do, and I wanted to hurt him so bad I could taste it."

Emma threw back the covers and rolled to her knees, holding out her arms to him. "But you didn't," she assured him.

Noticing the shirt in his hand, he tossed it on the floor. Then he was across the room in a flash, reaching out to haul her to him, his arms wrapping tightly around her, his head bowed to bring his face close to hers. "I might have, if Ben hadn't shown up when he did. A few more minutes and I might have."

"No," she disagreed without a second's hesitation. "You wouldn't, Elvis. You love Gracie, but being a cop, a good cop, that's probably the most important thing in your life."

"You and Beans are the most important things in my life," he said fiercely, raising his head to glare down at her.

"We are now," she said in a placating tone and stroked his cheek. Then she sighed, speared a hand through her wavy hair, and rattled something off in French. "Damn," she said plaintively, "I'm not stating this very well." Drawing and releasing a deep breath, she tried again. "I'm not tryin' to say we're not important to you, *cher*, but your feelin's for us are relatively new ones. Your feelin's for the law go way back. You've told me things, Elvis, things about that old sheriff —"

"Bragston."

"Oui," she agreed. "About your Sheriff Bragston and how he turned your life away from the direction it was headin' in, and about how bein' a policeman makes you feel." The smile she gave him was a mixture of wryness and puzzlement. "Considering my background, I still haven't figured out

how I came to fall in love with a cop."

Then she made a purely Gallic hand movement that said, But that's neither here nor there; and in fierce defense of him, declared, "The important thing to remember here is that you opened up the mike to summon Ben on that walkie-talkie thingamajig. If you'd seriously meant to harm Mr. Bill-Stinkin'-Child-Abusin'-Gertz, you never would have done that, *cher.*"

"Hey, yeah, that's true. How'd you get to be so smart?"

"Phfft." She made another of those French mannerisms. "I had Big Eddy Robescheaux, proprietor of the biggest and best chop shop in all of N'Awlins, for a teacher."

He opened his mouth, then shut it again, hesitating. Maybe he shouldn't tell her; she seemed to believe his character was so sterling. But then he admitted, "I gotta tell ya something, Em. Maybe I wasn't really going to beat the shit out of the man — I suppose you're probably right about that. But it sure felt good to terrorize him a little."

"*I'd* like to terrorize him a lot," Emma said fiercely. "And perhaps I could borrow some of your tactics and use them on your *maman,* eh?"

Elvis shifted uncomfortably. "Now, Em . . ."

Emma knew that sooner or later she was going to have to break down and forgive Nadine Donnelly for her part in Gracie's Fourth of July disappearance. She was marrying the woman's son, after all. But she wasn't in a forgiving frame of mind tonight. One miscreant at a time; that was about all she could handle.

"You'll never believe the lame defense Bill's attorney tried to introduce tonight," Elvis said in an obvious bid to change the subject. He knew Em had no reason to like Nadine, but, hell, she was his mom and he needed her to have some role in their lives, however small. "The jerk actually thought that attacking you for working without all the legal permits would get his client off the hook."

Emma pulled back. "That man injured my *bébé* and wrecked my car, and I could get in trouble for workin' on a few women's automobiles?" she demanded.

"Well, I suppose you should have some sort of business license, doll. We can look into that on Monday. But, hey, big deal," he said with a negligent shrug in the face of her indignation. "We're talking about maybe a forty-dollar annual fee. I suggested to Bill's mouthpiece that he give that defense his very best shot and told him we'd see him in court with photographs of Gracie's little banged-up forehead. I also gave him a blow-by-blow description of her taking the stand to tell the jury how it felt to have the window explode on top of her. Then I topped it off with a little verbal imagery of your slashed tires and the truly inspiring vocabulary on the side of your Chevy." He grinned at her, pleased with himself. "I don't think he's going to be pursuing that particular line of defense, Em."

"Well, I should say not." But then Emma relinquished her indignation, hugged him, and pulled back to reach for the waistband of his jeans. "Come to bed, *cher,*" she urged, unbuttoning and unzipping and then divesting him of denims and underwear. "It sounds like you've put in an extremely full evening. You must be plumb worn out."

"Hi, Miss Wuby!" Gracie yelled, running ahead of Emma into the café. "Guess what, guess what? We — Oh, look, *Maman!* Here's Miss-us Mackey, too!" She swerved from the beeline she'd been making to Ruby and dashed toward Clare's table. "Guess what!" she screeched, clambering up to stand on the chair across from her friend.

Bracing her hands on the tabletop, her little body twisting in an ecstasy of animation, she stared at Clare through eyes made dark as Hershey kisses by excitement. "Guess what, Miss-us Mackey, guess what? Me 'n' Mommy, we's gettin' mawwied!"

Conversation ceased, crockery stopped clattering, and every head in the café swiveled in Emma's direction.

"Bonjour," she said to the room at large. She estimated it had been ten years or better since she'd last blushed in public, but there was no mistaking the source of the heat that crawled up her throat and onto her cheeks. Hastily, she took a seat next to her daughter and met Clare's knowing grin with as much composure as she could muster. Ruby arrived at the table, coffee pot in hand.

"Coffee or cola?" she inquired blandly, then gave Emma a big old I'm-in-the-cat-bird-seat-and-don't-even-think-you're-getting-off-easy grin.

"Cola, cola, cola," Gracie demanded, and her rising voice and frantic little bob in place alerted Emma that she was seconds away from losing control.

"Make that milk," she contradicted smoothly and scooped her daughter off the chair to stand on her lap. Gracie's arms wrapped around her neck. "And iced tea for me, please. What do you want to eat, angel pie?" she inquired. "Would you like a tuna sandwich?"

"Uh-huh. And 'tato chips, *Maman*. The winkled kind."

"I'll have the chicken salad," Emma contributed, and congratulated herself on having smoothly gotten the two of them out of the limelight.

Much too prematurely, as it turned out. "So who are you and your momma marrying, sweetie?" Clare demanded as if she didn't know darn good and well. Even without her broad smile, and Ruby's, to clue her in, Emma would have been conscious of the suspended forks, cups of coffee, and glasses of Coke as every patron in the place awaited Gracie's answer before continuing his or her lunch.

"Shewiff Elbis Don'lee." Ecstatic, Gracie squeezed her mother's neck with her strong little arms. "Him's gonna be my *daddy!*"

Setting aside the coffee pot, Ruby sat down at the table, crossed her arms over her chest, and grinned at Emma in pure admiration. "Girl, life around you is better than the soaps," she said, "and I didn't think it got any better than that. I swear every jaw in town has been flapping all morning long over Bill Gertz's arrest — and now you give us this, too. Elvis Donnelly, my, my, my." She shook her head. "You're gonna mainstream that boy right into this town yet, aren't you?"

"Oh, *oui, mon amie.* If it's the last thing I do," Emma agreed, and her posture regained its customary erectness. Since when had she allowed achieving her heart's desire to embarrass her? Looking around, she began meeting people's stares head on. One by one, they either dropped their gazes or gave her brief nods of congratulation.

"What's mainstweam mean, Miss Wuby?"

Ruby blinked, mouth rounding in dismay as she drew an obvious blank in her search for the right words. Emma looked from her to Gracie. "There are people around here who don't like Elvis the way you and I do, sugar," she explained, reaching out to ease her daughter's floppy curls away from her forehead. "I suppose you could say mainstreaming would be you 'n' me gettin' him accepted in this town."

Gracie puffed up. "Who doesn't yike my Elbis?" she demanded indignantly, staring around at the café patrons. There were many who couldn't meet her eyes.

"Well, Bill Gertz, for one," Emma replied slyly, seeing several people, whom she knew to disdain Elvis, squirm at being linked with the man responsible for the ugly black stitches sticking out of her *bébé's* head.

Gracie looked back at her, her forehead furrowing in confusion. "Who him, *Maman?*"

"The man who owns the garage across the street. Remember, angel pie? We met him the first day we were in town?"

Gracie's nose wrinkled. "Well, him's a bad man if him doesn't yike my Elbis. And we don't yike him, either, do we, *Maman?*"

"No, I think you can safely say he's not our favorite person," Emma agreed. "But talkin' about Mr. Gertz is not the reason we came in here, is it, Grace Melina? Remember why we wanted to have lunch at Ruby's café today? And why we were goin' to look up Mrs. Clare later?"

"Uh-huh, uh-huh; I do, Mommy!" Gracie bobbed with excitement. She looked first at Ruby to her right and then across the table at Clare. "We want you to be our —" She hesitated a moment, shooting Emma a look of agony as she realized she'd forgotten the word. Her mother whispered in her ear. "*Oui,* our 'tendants!" She nearly strangled Emma in her enthusiasm. "And guess what?" she demanded at the top of her voice. "I'm gonna get a bwand new dwess and so is my *maman!* We's gonna be pwetty as pitchoos — Elbis said so."

"Well, if Elvis said so, it must be the God's gospel truth," some wit at the counter said dryly but without any real malice. He looked at the excited little girl and the radiant blond woman as he threw money on the counter to cover his bill and climbed off the stool. Then, shaking his head, he smiled wryly to himself and walked out of the café.

Clearly there was more to Donnelly than had previously met the eye.

It was a busy week for Emma. Elvis wanted the wedding as soon as possible and, regardless of the fact that she had been married before, there were certain elements of it he wanted fulfilled for her. The problem was, a rash of vandalism had broken out all over the island, and Elvis was so busy trying to track down the culprits he was rarely available to help her put the arrangements together.

On Monday Clare went with her to Seattle, and at Jessica McClintock's in the Westlake Mall downtown they found the perfect dresses for the bride, the daughter of the bride, and the two attendants. Late that afternoon Elvis took half an hour off to join

Emma in talking to Reverend Simpson at the Seaside Baptist church.

Tuesday she reminded Elvis he needed to be fitted for a tux. She arranged for champagne and a wedding cake. Then, girding her loins, she packed up Gracie and drove her primer-dotted '57 Chevy out to Nadine Donnelly's house.

Gracie's face fell when she saw who opened the door. Emma hadn't told her what their destination was, knowing perfectly well what her daughter's reaction would have been and not willing to argue the merits of her decision every step of the way. The sight of the woman who had gotten Gracie into so much trouble clearly came as an unpleasant shock. Tugging insistently on her mother's hand, the little girl looked up at her pleadingly. "Wanna go home."

"In a while, angel pie," Emma murmured and met Elvis' mother's eyes levelly. "Hello, Nadine. May we come in?"

The sight of them standing on her porch flustered Nadine every bit as much as being there disconcerted Gracie. Emma was the only one on either side of the screen door to retain her composure. "Oh!" Nadine stammered. "Yes . . . oh, y-yes, of course." She held the door open for them.

Emma took a step forward, but Gracie dug her heels in belligerently. "Wanna go home *now!*" she demanded.

"I said in a while, Grace," Emma stated quietly but firmly before transferring her gaze to Nadine. "Perhaps there's something *you'd* like to say to her," she suggested with scrupulous neutrality.

"Yes, I suppose there is, at that," Nadine agreed. "Um . . ." She cleared her throat uncomfortably and then squatted down to put herself on Gracie's level. The little girl, her arms crossed repressively over her chest, leaned away from her. "I'm, uh, really sorry about all the trouble I caused you on the Fourth of July, Gracie," Nadine said diffidently. "It was particularly wrong of me to convince you to tell your momma a lie."

"I gotted a spankin'," Gracie informed her sulkily. Clearly she still held Nadine accountable for it. "And evewybody was angwy at me."

"I'm really sorry about that, too. Truly, I am," Nadine insisted. She studied the child's unforgiving expression for a moment. "Maybe you'd like to come in and see the Elvis doll I promised you," she suggested and rose, extending a hand to the child.

Gracie was torn. The urge to keep her

grudge was tempting as candy before breakfast. But still . . . a *doll.* One didn't simply turn one's nose up at the opportunity to obtain a new doll.

"Well, I *s'pose* that'd be aw-wight," she finally conceded. She accepted the proffered hand.

As Emma followed Nadine and her daughter through the living room and down the hallway, she tried not to gawk at the sheer preponderance of Elvis Presley paraphernalia that decorated the Donnelly house. It seemed every wall or surface contained at least one piece of memorabilia. She tried to picture Elvis growing up here among all this stuff, but it was a stretch for her imagination.

The spare-bedroom-turned-den they entered was clearly the pièce de résistance. It was one large wall-to-wall shrine to the King. Gracie, her eyes huge, turned in slow circles trying to take in everything at once. "This that other Elbis man?" she asked in a little voice. "The one that's a king?"

Emma let Nadine play tour guide for a while, but once the older woman had located the Elvis doll and handed it to Gracie, thereby preoccupying her daughter, she took her future mother-in-law aside. "I'm tryin' real hard to be as easily placated as

Grace Melina," she said in a low voice as she stared into the neon blue eyes so similar to, and yet so different from Elvis'. "But it's not easy, Nadine. You put my *bébé* at risk. Nevertheless," she added firmly. "Your son and I are gettin' married a week from next Thursday, and we'd like you to be there. It's especially important to Elvis that you have some part in his life. Please. Don't disappoint him."

Later Gracie showed off her new doll to her soon-to-be daddy. "See what yo' *maman* gibbed me? It's an Elbis doll," she informed him, climbing up onto his lap the better to display all the doll's features. "It's got yo' name, but I think you's mo' hamsom."

Elvis gazed over her head at Emma. "You went to see my mom?" he asked.

"Oui," she agreed. "To invite her to the wedding."

"And is she, um, gonna come?"

"She said she'd be there."

He didn't comment. But as he rubbed his scarred cheek against the top of Gracie's head, his eyes remained locked on Emma's. And one corner of his full mouth tilted up.

On Wednesday Emma once again reminded Elvis he had to be fitted for his tux, and she pointed out in exasperation that due to his size he probably wasn't going to be the easiest man in the world to accommodate, while time was running out. She called Clare to have her remind Sam that he, too, needed to be fitted. Then she spent the better part of the day trying to track down a photographer willing to take the wedding pictures on such short notice.

Once she found one, she was free to concentrate on finding slipcovers for the couch and chair, pleated shades for the living-room windows, and a miniblind and valance for the window in the kitchen. The reception she had planned following the ceremony was a small one. It was only going to include the three of them, plus Nadine, Sam and Clare, and Ruby and her kids, but Emma nevertheless wanted the place spruced up for it. It would still look like a rental, she imagined, regardless of her efforts, but at least *she'd* feel she'd done her best to give it a more festive look.

Which reminded her: she needed flowers, both for the wedding party and for the house. And maybe a few throw pillows. She reached for the phone once again.

Thursday she went shopping for gifts for her attendants. When she got home she was surprised to find Elvis in the kitchen.

There was nothing in his attitude that she could put a finger on as he watched her make lunch for Gracie, but she thought she caught glimpses of an underlying tension. As soon as Gracie finished eating, Emma sent her out to play. She watched her daughter skip across the lawn to throw herself facedown on the swing in the corner of the yard, then turned back to face Elvis. "Something's botherin' you, *cher*. What is it?"

He blew out a deep breath. "Bill Gertz died last night."

Emma's jaw sagged. That was the last thing she'd expected him to say. "You're kidding!"

"I wish I were, baby. Jesus, his lawyer just got him released OR yesterday and now today —"

"Wait, wait, wait," Emma interrupted. She came around the table and climbed onto Elvis' lap, curling her arms around his neck. "What does that mean, OR?"

"Own recognizance — no bail. It was his first offense and not what the judge considered a capital one, regardless of how you or I might view it." He swept that consideration aside with a wave of his hook. "In any event, the lawyer got him out yesterday morning, and when he went to talk to him this morning the guy was dead." His arms wrapped around her. "Jesus, Em."

"*How* did he die? *Mon Dieu,* Elvis, he wasn't all that old, was he, maybe forty, forty-five?"

"He was forty-three. And it looks like maybe it was a heart attack or an embolism or something. They won't know for sure until after the autopsy. His body's being shipped to Seattle on the four-twenty ferry. Sweet God Almighty, Em." He rubbed the side of his face against her breast and stared up at her. "You know I came close to wringing his neck for him, but I gotta tell you, sweetheart, this thing has really knocked me for a loop. Thinking you'd like someone to drop dead is an entirely different kettle of fish from having the guy actually *do* it."

"I guess so! What an incredible shock, *cher.*"

"Yeah." He exhaled audibly. "You can say that again."

On Friday Emma took Gracie to the clinic to have her stitches removed. Everyone and their brother seemed to be in Port Flannery on that day, and each and every one of them, it appeared, was dying to talk to Emma about Bill Gertz's sudden death and how it had affected her and her little girl.

With a shake of her head and a significant look at her daughter, Emma managed to discourage first the receptionist, then the nurse, and finally the doctor as each tried to introduce the subject. That tactic didn't work nearly as well with several of the locals who stopped them out on the street on the way back to the car. Emma supposed it was human nature to want to discuss a death that sudden and unexpected, but she had never sat Gracie down to explain about the man responsible for her daughter's injuries and didn't have any burning desire to do so now. Exactly how did one tell something like that to a three-year-old anyhow? As an adult she had a difficult enough time understanding the motivations of that man.

She allowed Gracie to get a little farther away from her than she normally permitted while trying to shake off a particularly persistent gossip. Subtlety having failed her, Emma waited until Gracie was beyond earshot before ultimately lowering her voice to flat-out tell the person this was not something she wished to discuss in front of her child. Then, excusing herself, she walked away, looking around for her daughter.

And stopped dead in the middle of the sidewalk when she spotted her.

"Mommy, Mommy, lookit who's come fo' our weddin'!" Gracie called excitedly the moment she saw she had her mother's attention.

Impeccably groomed in an expensive, gray, summer-weight suit and pristine white shirt, Grant Woodard stood next to the open door of a shiny black Lincoln Continental, holding Gracie in his arms. Her little arms were around his neck in a fierce hug and her face radiated delight.

"It's Gwandpapa, *Maman!* Lookit, lookit, it's *Gwandpapa!*"

Grant's lips smiled at Emma, but his eyes were colder than an Arctic wind as they surveyed her from the crown of her head to the tips of her toes and back up again. "Get in the car, Emma," he said. The tone of voice he used was cloaked to sound like a suggestion.

Emma, however, knew an order when she was issued one.

Nineteen

Emma wasn't getting in that car with him. She crossed her arms over her breasts and regarded him through narrowed eyes. Here on the street she had some chance of keeping Gracie and herself safe. She didn't like to even contemplate what would happen to them if she blindly followed his order. "I don't think so, Grant," she said pleasantly. "Let's go get a cup of coffee at Ruby's instead. We'll talk." *We'll send someone for Elvis.*

"*Oui,* Gwandpapa, let's go to Wuby's," Gracie seconded, bobbing in his arms at the prospect of showing him off to her friends. Her little arms squeezed him tighter. "You'll *yike* hoo," she promised.

Grant, however, acted as though neither female had even spoken. Leaving the driver's door agape, he walked around the car and climbed into the passenger seat, reaching for the shoulder harness to strap Gracie in his lap. Slamming the door and pressing the lock, he leaned down to look at Emma from beneath the car's roof line and ordered, "You drive."

"But, Gwandpapa —" Gracie began to protest.

"Enough Grace," he said, and such was the authority in his voice that she subsided. But most of the shine went out of her little face.

Emma got into the driver's seat.

Oh Dieu, how had it come to this? She berated herself silently as she pulled her shoulder harness across her body and snapped it into place. How on earth had she allowed herself to grow so complacent that it had come down to this? Dammit all, Elvis had *told* her to warn Gracie about her grandfather. And she had meant to; oh, God, she had meant to. But between one thing and another, it had simply slipped her mind. And now, now . . .

And now it was a day late and a dollar short.

She started the ignition, but then turned her head to look Grant in the eye. "Where to?" she demanded with crisp neutrality.

Grant hesitated. He should say the ferry dock and get them the hell off this rock pile as quickly as possible. He didn't have the contacts here he had at his disposal in New Orleans.

But having learned of Sheriff Elvis Fucking Donnelly and the upcoming nuptials, he was feeling grim and edgy and didn't care to wait until they hit the shoreline on the other side of the Sound to demonstrate his displeasure to her.

Besides. He might be far from his own stomping grounds, but he had power; he always had power. It had been a millennium since his days as a whorehouse tootsie who catered to a select brand of deviants. That was a lifetime ago, barely remembered except when he deliberately chose to look back on it. And he only did that when he wanted to remind himself of the extent to which his omnipotence had grown since the day he had slid an icepick through the base of the madam's brain and taken over the operation of her place. And it continued to grow. His sense of invincibility was now so ingrained that he'd long since forgotten what it was like to wait for anyone's permission to do anything. What Grant Woodard wanted, Grant Woodard got. Immediately.

And no two-bit, one-handed cripple with a wrecked face and a tin badge was going to come along and change that.

He directed her out of town.

Clare walked out of the gynecologist's office in a daze. Pregnant. She was *pregnant.*

She shouldn't be surprised. God knows

she and Sam had been going at it hammer and tongs, as if to make up for lost time, ever since the day he'd quit smoking. And it wasn't as if either one of them had given so much as a second's consideration to birth control. So what right did she have to be caught so flatfooted by the news?

Maybe none. But she was stunned by the news nevertheless.

What on earth is Sam gonna say? she wondered. Oh boy, *there* was food for thought. Clare climbed into her oven-hot car and simply sat in it, the door hanging open as she stared blindly out the front windshield. She didn't even know what *she* thought about the news. She knew she still mourned Evan. Indeed, the knowledge of this new child made his loss seem much sharper somehow, and she missed him desperately. She also acknowledged a feeling of terror. What if something should happen to this baby? Dear Lord, she didn't think she'd survive it — not even with Sam's strength to lean on.

And yet . . .

Underneath it all, beneath the grief and the fear, was a kernel of pleasure so sweet she could barely contain it. She was pregnant.

Sweat trickled down her temple and

jerked her from her reverie. She pulled the door closed, started the engine, and cranked up the air conditioning. Pulling up to the parking-lot exit, she looked up and down the street. What to do, what to do. Should she drive to the store and tell Sam now? Or should she go home and prepare a special evening? Her lips curled up at the corners in a secret smile.

Daydreaming, she looked down the street and saw a silver-haired, elegantly dressed stranger holding little Gracie Sands. Her smile abruptly faded and she leaned forward. As she watched he climbed with the child into a shiny black car that was equipped with the darkly opaque windows usually found in stretch limousines. Through the open driver's door, she saw him lean sideways across the seat, his hand on Gracie's back to prevent her from tipping off his lap, and she saw Emma, stiff-legged and awkward, her usual grace totally absent, walk to the car. Emma climbed into the driver's seat. She pulled the door closed and everyone inside vanished from view behind smoky, dark-tinted windows.

Oh, sweet Jesus. Clare's hands gripped the steering wheel with a force that turned her knuckles white, and she practically felt the blood drain from her head. She took a deep, controlled breath to drive out th woozies and slowly expelled it. Took another and expelled it, too. That had to be Grant Woodard. Oh, God, oh, God. Emma had told them about him — not everything, Clare was certain, but enough for her to know that Emma's and Gracie's being in that car created a very precarious situation. If not a downright dangerous one.

Clare pulled out onto the street behind the Lincoln as it glided past her.

She had trailed the black car to the crossroads at Orchard Highway and Emery Road before she fully comprehended her mistake. Dear God, what was she doing? She should have driven straight to the sheriff's department and gotten Elvis or George or Ben — *some*one. There were only two main roads in and out of town and the sheriff or his deputies probably could have caught up with the Lincoln without very much difficulty if she had just used her head instead of blindly following her instincts. Now it was too late to turn back because, out here away from town, there were too many little back roads on which one could disappear. So she hung back in hopes of not being spotted by Emma's captor. And she cursed herself for turning her nose up when Sam had offered to install a cellular phone in her car.

* * *

"Elvis." Sandy looked up and waved him over with a flip of her hand when he walked into the station. "You have a call slip here from Danny White. He says the Lincoln he told you about yesterday bought another ticket to the island today on the twelve-twenty."

"Thanks, Sandy." Elvis took the pink slip with a delicate maneuver of his hook and studied it thoughtfully. Slapping it against his palm, he looked back at his dispatcher. "Call whoever's on duty today —"

"George —" she inserted.

"— and tell him to keep his eye peeled for it. Here's the license number." He handed back the slip. "If he spots it, Sandy, have him call in immediately. We'll decide what to do about it then."

He'd put the word out with the ferry workers that he was interested in anyone boarding the island ferry in a rental car. The ticket taker on the mainland had reported three rentals in the past two days, but the black Lincoln Continental with the dark tinted windows was the only repeat thus far. Elvis glanced at the paperwork piling up on his desk, but instead of diving in and getting started on it, he picked up the telephone and dialed home.

Beans' stitches should be history by now. He'd just check in real quick.

He listened to the phone ring and ring and finally tossed the receiver back in the cradle. His phantom hand started to itch like crazy and he rubbed the prosthesis, where it joined his amputated lower forearm, against the seam of his Levi's in a futile bid to scratch it. Hell, there was nothing unusual about the phone going unanswered. And there was certainly nothing to worry about. Nothing at all. Em was probably racing all over the island, gathering up all that last-minute stuff for the wedding.

The thought made his neck muscles tighten into knots of guilt, and he reached up to massage them, but almost immediately gave it up in favor of digging his nails into his forearm in an attempt to alleviate the madly itching missing hand. *He* should have been doing more to help; he was the one who'd insisted on a real wedding. Em had been perfectly content with the idea of a quick trip to a justice of the peace, but he wouldn't hear of it.

Then his mouth curled up in a one-sided smile. What the hell. He wasn't sorry about that. The truth was, he wanted to see her all decked out like a bride, because that's what she was going to be. His bride. Giving up on the unscratchable itch, he grinned at the thought and sat forward to attend to the paperwork.

Ten minutes later, Sandy's voice, low and urgent, cut through his concentration. "Elvis," she said, ripping off her head gear and leaping to her feet. "Your mom just called in. We've got big, big trouble."

Clare was driving past Nadine Donnelly's place when she knew she had to do something more constructive than just follow Woodard's car. Granted, she was keeping a tab on the Sandses' location, but what good was that going to do anybody if she didn't get someone out here to help them? She stomped on the brakes and threw the car in reverse, roaring back to the driveway she'd overshot.

The car was still rocking on its shocks when she jammed it into park in front of Nadine's back door. Thrusting open the driver's door, she shot up the back steps and pounded on the screen door. She could hear "Love Me Tender" playing in the living room. "Nadine!" she shouted, banging on the wood framing the screen. She cupped her hands around her eyes to peer into the dim kitchen. *"Nadine!"*

"I'm coming, I'm coming!" Nadine's exasperated voice increased in volume as she drew closer with each word. "For heaven's sake, keep your shirt on." She shoved the screen door open. "Well," she said blankly, staring at Clare. "For heaven's sake. Clare Mackey."

Clare reached out and grabbed her arm, gripping it tightly. "Call Elvis," she commanded tersely. "Right now. Tell him Grant Woodard has Emma and Gracie. *This is important, Nadine,*" she said fiercely when the older woman continued to stare at her blankly. "They're in danger. Tell him if I haven't lost them by stopping here, I'll be following them. I've got four — maybe five — flares in my trunk. I'll set them up where they turn." She squeezed the arm beneath her fingers. *"Have you got that?"*

Nadine blinked several times. "Grant Woodard," she babbled. "Emma and the baby. Flares. Turns."

"Oh, God," Clare moaned and turned the older woman loose, satisfied to see her turn immediately to the phone on the far kitchen wall. Then she wheeled around and raced back to the car. *Please God, please,* she prayed fervently. *Don't let me have lost them.*

Where are you, Clare? Ah, Dieu, where did

you disappear to? Emma let up on the gas pedal a little, furtively checking the rearview and the sideview mirrors.

She'd been aware of Clare's tail since the moment in town when Clare had first pulled out of the parking lot onto the street behind them. Emma hadn't been certain if Clare were equally cognizant of her and Gracie's presence in the Lincoln, and she'd been afraid to give too much credence to the fact that her friend was trailing them out of town. She was learning the hard way it was more painful to have one's hopes dashed than it was to simply not have any expectations.

But when, following Grant's terse instructions, they had turned off the main highway onto Emery Road, Clare, too, had turned . . . and then had let Emma know she understood things were not as they should be by hanging back in the favored tradition of some of television's finest private eyes.

Thank you, Lord, thank you. Emma sent up a silent, heartfelt prayer. *And God Bless trash TV, too.* She didn't know what good Clare's presence might ultimately do her and Gracie. But it was reassuring simply to know that they weren't out here all on their own.

Grant's behavior today was so far removed from his usual as Emma had known it that the tension in the car was an almost palpable force. Gracie, in her usual chatty style, had originally attempted several conversational gambits, but even she had ultimately fallen silent on her grandfather's lap. Now her dark, apprehensive eyes were glued to her mother's face; her thumb was tucked firmly into her mouth. Emma sent her a fleeting smile meant to reassure, and Gracie's lips, pursed around her thumb, curled up at the corners.

It broke Emma's heart at how little encouragement it took to hearten her child. And she wished to hell she hadn't done it when Gracie slowly lifted her cheek up off her grandfather's chest, tilted her head back, and raised her eyes to look into his face. Her thumb slid out of her mouth.

"Gwandpapa, I'm gon' have a new daddy," she told him, certain it would thrill him as much as it thrilled her and hoping the news would bring back the grandfather she knew instead of this scary stranger who looked like her grandpapa but didn't act like him. "His name is Elbis Don'lee and he's bigoo 'n' anything. He gibbed me a twike, Gwandpapa, and sidewalk chalk and —"

"Shut up!" Grant snarled, giving her a vicious shake.

Gracie's eyes rounded in shock, and Emma immediately lost every last vestige of her hard-held composure. "You bastard!" she screamed in outrage. Swerving the car out of its lane, she brought it to a screeching halt, half on and half off the shoulder of the road. Blindly, unthinkingly, she flew at him until her shoulder harness brought her up short, and then her hands flailed at his head. "Give her to me — *give her to me!*" she demanded hysterically. "You sick sonofabitch. You hurt her again and I'll kill you!"

The noise level inside the Lincoln became chaotic and eardrum piercing. Grant roared with rage, Gracie screamed in terror, and Emma hurled invectives in French and English as her hands made dull thwacking sounds when they connected awkwardly with his head and upraised arms.

One of those arms suddenly snapped out to backhand her across the face with enough force to rock her back in her seat. While she sat, momentarily stunned, he pressed two fingers to the top of Gracie's head, slid the palm of his other hand beneath her chin, and calmly wrenched her little head sideways to an awkward angle. "Shut the fuck up or I'll break her neck."

Emma froze. *Ah, Dieu. Dieu!* All it would

take was one little snap and her baby —

"Mommy, Mommy, Mommy, Mommy," Gracie sobbed.

"Shut her up!"

"Shhh, angel pie, it's okay," Emma murmured, striving to steady her voice into a soothing cadence, reaching out to stroke her daughter's cheek. "Shhh, shhh, shhh, now, *bébé*. You have to be quiet, sugar. For *Maman*. Okay? Okay, sugar? You have to quiet down now."

"That's more like it," Grant said with a crisp, satisfied nod, and he released Gracie's head as soon as her sobs turned to soft hiccups. She sat as stiffly upright as the seat belt would allow, her little hands stiff-arming her torso away from her grandfather, her big fear-glazed eyes staring up at him while her chest shuddered with the effort not to cry. He didn't even look at her. "Drive," he commanded Emma. "I'll tell you when I want you to turn."

She took a deep breath and blew it out. Turning to look over her shoulder, automatically checking for traffic before pulling back onto the road, she blinked as Clare's car drove past, going under the speed limit. Emma pulled out behind her.

Clare slowed down even more.

"Pass her," Grant growled after several

moments of crawling along in her wake. "Goddam country bumpkins."

Emma passed, grateful for the first time that Gracie was facing in rather than out on her grandfather's — no, Grant's — lap. That man wasn't Gracie's grandfather, and damned if she'd honor him with the title any longer. Then she pushed the thought aside. The point was, the last thing they needed was for Grace to voice her recognition of Clare as Emma accelerated into the other lane and drove past her friend's car.

Three miles down the road Grant, who had been peering intently out the window, instructed her to turn. A short distance later he had her stop, back up, and turn again, this time into a shade-darkened, badly overgrown driveway hardly wider than a track. Bushes scraped the sides of the car as she slowed it to a snail's pace and its tires dipped in and out of potholes, rocking the vehicle from side to side. They bumped along for forty feet before suddenly breaking out onto a cleared plateau. There wasn't a dwelling in sight, which apparently was what Grant had been seeking. "Good," he said, looking around in satisfaction. "This will do just fine."

Emma blinked against the sudden glare of sunlight. She continued inching along until he suddenly ordered her to stop the car about a hundred feet shy of the cliff's edge. Then she merely sat for a moment, taking deep breaths. Finally, she looked over at Grant. "Now what?"

He blinked as if he were uncertain, and that scared her almost more than his physical threats to her child had. It seemed the control he imposed over his psychotic episodes was dissolving. Was it that she was seeing him clearly for the first time because she now knew what he was capable of or had his mental capacity deteriorated since she'd run away?

"Get out of the car," he instructed. Unhooking the seatbelt, he opened the door and climbed out himself, with Gracie still held in his arms. "Hand over the keys — and don't try anything cute, Emma," he warned. "My patience is wearing thin."

That's certainly understating the facts, Emma thought bitterly.

Gracie was leaning away from Grant at a precarious angle, her outstretched arms reaching for her mother; and he allowed Emma to take her as soon as she'd relinquished the car keys to him. Gracie clamped her arms and legs around Emma and clung like a monkey, her hot little face buried in the curve of her mother's neck, her breath shuddering erratically. Emma's arms came up to clutch the child tightly in return, and she rocked her from side to side with a repetitive twist of the waist.

She knew she had to do something to diffuse the situation; it had grown too volatile too fast, and Grant's mental state seemed to her iffy at best. Taking a deep breath, she loosened her compulsive grip on Gracie and attempted to smile at Grant, hoping it didn't appear half as sickly as it felt.

"Let's start over," she suggested, thinking to herself, *Oh, ducky, Em, good luck with that one.* "I shouldn't have hit you," she admitted, and wasn't even tempted to wince at her own duplicity. She would do this man serious injury if she got half a chance; lying herself blue in the face didn't give her so much as a qualm. "But, Grant," she continued chattily, "you know how protective I am of my *bébé.* Just like you have always been so protective of me."

Then she mentally cringed. *Ah, Dieu, now you've done it, girl; you've gone too far. Dammit, Em! Couldn't you have come up with somethin' more credible than that?* She wanted to scream at her stupidity, but kept her expression carefully impassive. *He might be crazy, you fool, but he's not stupid — and he'd have to be severely lacking in any form of intel-*

ligence to fall for that horse shit.

Yet, to her immense surprise, Grant's expression softened. He reached a hand out, and she managed not to flinch when his fingertips gently brushed her cheek. She even forced another wobbly smile and noted how his face lighted up in response.

It was at that moment she fully comprehended the depth of his madness, or whatever it was that drove him to do the things she knew he'd done . . . and others she could only guess at.

She realized, too, that his current amiability could be a very tenuous and short-lived thing. She didn't have a clue as to what might set him off, and for a moment was paralyzed by the myriad possibilities. She found herself almost hyperventilating, drawing shallow, rapid breaths; and she had to consciously force herself to slow them down, draw air in deeper, and hold it longer before expelling it. Once she could draw a full breath again, she wondered what on earth one said to a sociopath.

She *had* to say something.

Grant's fingers slipped from her jaw to the top of Gracie's head and slid over the child's curls in a gentle caress, for all the world as if he hadn't just threatened her life. "Like I'm protective of her, too," he said, continuing a conversation that, contrary to what it felt like to Emma, had actually only paused a moment ago. "That's why I couldn't allow that cretin who injured her to live."

Emma barely managed to bite back a sharp cry. *"Bill?"* she croaked, and then had to swallow twice in an attempt to disperse a meager amount of moisture throughout her mouth. "You, um, did something to Bill Gertz?" He simply gazed at her, brow raised, and her voice went unnaturally high, cracking between syllables when she said, "*Eliminated* him?" Eliminated. *Bon Dieu.* What a euphemistic word.

"Of course." His tone was a verbal shrug, as if admitting to killing someone were the most natural thing in the world. "He'd harmed my Gracie, hadn't he?" he demanded. "It was mandatory that the injury be addressed."

"But, I thought . . . his heart."

Grant made a dismissive gesture. "A knock on the door, a shove against the wall, a needle in his jugular. *Voilà!* Quick air bubbles to the heart or brain." He whisked his palms together with the same casualness he might have used to dust them free of sugar grains from a *beignet.* "One less nuisance in the world."

Emma didn't bother to inquire how he had learned of Gracie's injury. Quite clearly, when Hackett had departed the island someone had taken his place. It wasn't a surprise; she'd expected as much. She stroked Gracie's hair, the touch reassuring her that her *bébé* was keeping her head down. Looking into Grant's eyes, she thought almost dispassionately, *So this is what a monster looks like.*

All of her vital organs turned to ice at realizing the predicament she faced. How could she prevent him from spilling his madness onto her child? She was going to have a fight to the death on her hands. She could feel it — had *felt* it building from the moment she'd first seen Grant holding her daughter.

How on God's green earth was she supposed to effectively fight him, though, with Gracie here? The power in this confrontation was one-sided. Her daughter's presence made Emma vulnerable, and Grant wouldn't hesitate to take advantage of that. By holding her daughter hostage. By injuring Gracie. Emma didn't fool herself into thinking otherwise; he'd already given her an ample demonstration of his willingness to use her child in any way imaginable.

Or *un*imaginable.

Oh, God, this was an impossible situation. Win or lose, even if best-case scenario came to pass — defeating Grant *and* keeping her daughter safe — what kind of mother would she be, having subjected Gracie to being a witness? Hell of a nice heritage *that* was to leave a child. Not every little girl had the opportunity to see her mother or her grandfather come to harm or — worse, but in reality more probable — to watch one of them die.

But that was the heritage about to be bestowed upon her child.

Twenty

Clare moved cautiously through the woods, her heart drumming so hard she could feel it throbbing in her fingertips. She didn't know what the hell she was doing skulking through the bushes; she should be back at the turnoff, waiting to give directions to whomever showed up first to rescue them. If she were smart, that's what she'd be doing.

Well, only in her dreams did she claim relationship to an exalted intelligence. Maybe this was dumb. No, not maybe, *most likely* it was dumb. She only knew that she couldn't bear to sit in her car and do nothing while Grant Woodard was doing God-alone-knew-what to her friend and her friend's child.

She came to the edge of the clearing sooner than she'd expected and quickly brought herself up short, squatting down out of sight behind a bush. Cautiously, she peered around it.

Facing her, not more than fifty feet away, was Emma. She was standing stiffly, holding Gracie, and her face was devoid of color as she stared at the man in front of her. His back was to Clare. The black luxury car was several feet away, its doors wide open.

His back was to her.

Slowly, Clare rose to her feet and waved her arms slowly over her head. As soon as she knew she'd caught Emma's attention, she sank back down behind the bush.

Emma tried desperately to clear her mind so she could think. Clare was here, right here; this was an advantage she must find a way to make use of. *How* could she make use of it?

She looked at the man who had been her longtime guardian, and mentally holding her breath, hoping to God this didn't unlock a set of demons she was in no way prepared to deal with, she asked softly, "Why did you take those videos of me, Grant?" She was careful to abolish any hint of censure from her voice.

He shrugged. "I like to watch." No excuses, no sly hints of psychosis. A simple statement of fact.

It stopped her dead for a moment. "Uh, watch what exactly? Other people's sexual acts?"

Yes. And no. It was not that simplistic. True, voyeurism was the only way he could function sexually. But the power of control over another person's privacy was the real addiction. He shrugged again. "If you looked at those tapes at all, you know it's nothing that tacky. How many were taken in your bedroom, Emma, an eighth of them? A quarter? You're just . . . my special girl."

"Uh-huh." The vigorous bobbing of her head made Emma feel like one of those ridiculous dogs one saw in the back windows of cars. *"Oui,"* she agreed, praying all the while she wouldn't throw up on his feet. "I am." Queasy stomach roiling uneasily, she knew Grant wouldn't find her so special if she allowed the nausea to take its natural course, so she swallowed hard, forcing it back. At all costs she needed to keep him on an even mental keel, his attention firmly on her and away from Gracie.

"And I like to keep tabs on you, reassure myself that you're doing well."

A scream was building in Emma's throat, and she gritted her teeth against it. "I didn't understand," she managed to say in a placating tone. "I'm sorry; I shouldn't have left N'Awlins the way I did. I just didn't . . . understand."

"But you do now, don't you, Emma?" Grant reached across the short distance separating them and touched her hair. "You know now that you have to come back home with me. Don't you?"

"*Oui.*"

"And things will be just like they were. You'll have your little house on the Vieux Carré and we'll share *beignets* at the Café du Monde on Sunday mornings. I'll take care of you. And you'll forget all about marrying this Donnelly character. Won't you?"

"*Oui,* Papa." She saw with satisfaction that the courtesy address had disarmed him.

Gracie's head lifted out of its niche in the contour of her mother's neck. "But Elbis Don' lee gon' be my daddy," she protested, and Emma's arms clamped around her in terrified reaction, her hand raising up to cup the back of her child's head and to press Gracie's face back into her shoulder. In warning. In a wordless attempt to caution her to say no more.

Bon Dieu, not quickly enough. Grant's attention was drawn to her daughter. Assessingly, he studied the back of Gracie's head, the possessive clasp of her little arms and legs around her mother.

Not knowing if she were opening up a whole new can of worms, wanting only to divert his attention, Emma demanded, "What about Big Eddy, Papa?"

He stared at Gracie's back for several

nerve-wracking moments longer, but then finally raised his gaze to Emma's face. His expression was noncommittal. "What about him?"

"Why did you do it? I'd been livin' with you for three years by the time he was scheduled to be released. I would have stayed with you if you had only asked me to."

"No," he contradicted flatly. "You liked him best; you would have gone with him when he got out. But you were *my* special girl, Emma Terese; I wasn't about to start sharing your affections again. And I sure as hell wasn't going to allow him to take you away. Eddy'd had his chance, and he hadn't done that good a job of keeping you safe." The look he leveled at her was rife with self-righteousness. "No, it was much better my way. He was incompetent and careless. *I,* on the other hand, could give you what you needed."

Emma had to turn away, knowing there was no way she could disguise her hatred. She gritted her teeth against the pain; her eyes squeezed shut. *Ah, Eddy,* she mourned. She'd suspected it; *bon Dieu,* she had suspected it since the moment she'd first viewed the tapes. But to have it confirmed!

She wanted to cause him pain. Oh, God, she wanted to strike and strike and strike at him until he was annihilated. Eradicated from the face of the earth.

Ruthlessly she composed her features, drove the desire from her eyes. She sidled a few steps sideways and a few feet closer to the woods. Then, her face carefully free of expression, she turned to face Grant once again.

The smile she forced felt grotesquely stiff. She opened her mouth to tell him again that she "understood," but she simply couldn't force the words past her lips one more time.

She couldn't. Her mouth reformed the sickly, unnatural little smile as panic beat at the corners of her mind, threatening to smother her ability to reason, to plan. *Think, dammit! Damn you, Emma, think!*

Allowing the smile to drop away, knowing it wouldn't fool a soul, not even a man in the grip of a delusion that permitted him to see only what he wanted to see, she groped for a way to get Gracie safely to Clare. But her mind had gone blank. She simply stared at Grant.

Ah, sweet Jesus, she had to *think.*

Elvis snapped off the siren when he turned onto Emery Road. Teeth gritted, hunched over the steering wheel, he piloted the Suburban down the country road at a breakneck speed, stomping on the brakes and sending the car into a sideways skid when he came to Clare's first flare.

Bless her. Ah, sweet, merciful God, bless her. Throwing the transmission into reverse, he roared back to the turnoff and then threw it into drive and cut the wheel sharply to the right. It nearly killed him, but he kept the speed down as he searched for the next turnoff.

He was talking into the radio, giving exact coordinates, when he pulled up behind Clare's car a few moments later. It was deserted. Swearing under his breath, he grabbed the rifle out of the rack on the cage that separated front seat from back and leaped out of the car, leaving the door hanging wide open.

It was then that he heard screams filtering through the woods.

"Why are we out here, Grant?" Emma demanded for lack of anything better to say. She slapped at a mosquito that had landed on her wrist.

"I wanted a private place where we could talk."

"Well, we've talked," she retorted, deliberately petulant. She blew her bangs off her forehead. "I've said I was sorry I misunderstood you, but enough is enough! Let's go catch the ferry now and get *off* this rockpile."

"But, *Maman,*" Gracie protested, her voice mercifully muffled in the contour of Emma's neck.

"Hush, Grace Melina!" Emma made her own voice stern, praying her daughter wouldn't choose this of all times to dig her heels in. "I'm talking to your grandpapa, not you." It almost gagged her to honor him with that title.

Gracie's head reared back. "But, *Maman,* we can't go. We haffa mawwy Elbis."

Oh, please, bébé, *please. You gotta be quiet now or we're both going to be in deep, deep, trouble.* "There's been a change of plans, angel pie," she said gently.

Grant was looking at the two of them, and he nodded his head decisively, apparently coming to a decision. "Leave her," he ordered. "Let's get going."

Emma's head went back. *"What?"*

"Leave Gracie here. I thought at one time that she, too, would be my special girl. But she has no loyalty — she's turning out to be too much trouble."

Emma was stunned by his cavalier dismissal of a child he'd once considered his pampered grandchild. "She's three years old, Grant, and you scared her half to death! Of course she's leery of you." Sweet merciful mother of God. What kind of monster proposed just walking off and leaving a child on her own in the woods near a *cliff?* His being delusional was one thing, but surely he didn't believe she would blindly fall in with this plan. *Did* he? No, it was a test of some sort. One she was about to flunk. Emma's arms tightened protectively around Gracie as she prepared to run for their lives.

"I don't care," she heard Grant replying through the red mist that fogged her reasoning processes. "Leave her here. I'm tired of her shit, and from now on, it's going to be just you and me."

Belatedly, Emma's brain kicked in. *This is it, you idiot,* she berated herself. *This is how you get Gracie into Clare's keeping.* Looking Grant straight in the eye, she nodded her head. *"Oui,"* she agreed. "You're right, of course. You and me."

"And me, Mommy; and me!"

Emma could have cheerfully slit her own throat. *Bon Dieu,* what had she been thinking? She'd been so busy looking for a way to keep Gracie safe that she'd overlooked the fact that never in a million years would her vocal little daughter realize the words being said here didn't necessarily represent the truth. Gracie took the spoken word at face value, and what she was hearing from her own mother's lips was clearly detrimental to her well-being. There was no way she was going to accept this without voicing an argument.

As if to underscore Emma's realization, panic colored Gracie's voice when she insisted, "You 'n' *me,* Mommy. Go home, now, 'kay? 'Kay, Mommy?" She nodded vigorously and her voice picked up volume, lost control. She screeched when Grant suddenly reached out for her, and she batted him away with one arm. "No! I don't yike you — go 'way!" She appealed to her mother, who had danced them out of Grant's reach. "I don't yike him, *Maman.* Wanna go home now, 'kay? Wanna go home to Elbis."

"Hush, Grace Melina," Emma murmured in her daughter's ear. "Take it easy now, *s'il vous plaît.*" She fended off Grant when he reached for her child again. "Give me a moment!" she snapped. "Can't you see she's scared?" Swinging them away, cupping Gracie's head in one hand and holding it to her lips, she whispered directly into her child's ear, "Mrs. Mackey's over there in the woods, *chère*. She's waitin' to take care of you. You go to her, now, and *Maman* will get rid of Grandpapa. I'll come get you in a minute, *bébé*. In just a minute."

But Gracie was beyond hearing, let alone understanding. She'd progressed into full-blown hysteria, screaming and sobbing and clinging, while frantically drumming her feet against her mother's thighs. Emma grimly held her clamped to her torso and did her best to immobilize the thrashing legs. She murmured soothing reassurances into Gracie's ear.

"Give her to me," Grant suddenly roared, losing all patience. He reached out to snatch the little girl from her mother's arms, but Emma twisted away. "Goddamn little snot!" he fumed. "I should have snapped her neck while I had the chance. Hand her over, Emma. I'm going to put an end to this caterwauling once and for all."

"No," Emma snarled, skipping back from him. Adrenaline rushed through her veins and her heart pumped overtime with fear for her child's safety. Oh, *Dieu,* why hadn't she foreseen this? She'd used a goddamn euphemism for Bill Gertz's murder; there must have been other words she could have used to phrase this so her child wouldn't think she was being deserted in the woods by her mother and grandfather. "Just give me a moment to settle her down."

"I've given you all the time I'm going to allow. It's time for us to go. Now *hand her over!*"

"Excuse me!" A third voice suddenly intervened with strident authority. The drama on the barren mesa froze like a children's game of Statues as Emma's and Grant's heads swung to look toward the woods. Gracie continued to sob aloud.

Clare came striding across the plateau, not halting until she was directly in front of them. "Who are you people?" she demanded. "And what is all this ruckus? I'll have you know you're trespassing on private property." She latched onto Emma's upper arm. "Come. You have to leave. I'll escort you to your car."

She had dragged Emma several steps, not toward the car but the woods, before Grant recovered from his surprise. He stopped trailing the two women. "Now see here," he began, only to be overridden by Clare.

"No, you see here," she snapped. "All you city people are the same. You think you can just waltz onto our island and make yourselves at home wherever you darn well please! Well, I don't know you from Adam, sir, and this is my property, so I'll ask you to take yourself off it or I'll call the sheriff."

Gracie's hysteria had been dwindling during this tirade. Her grip on her mother's neck loosened, and she raised her head, craning her neck to look at Clare. Knuckling her eyes, she said in bewilderment, "But, you know *me,* Miss-us Mack—"

Emma thrust her into Clare's arms. "Get her out of here," she shouted. Not waiting to watch Clare whirl and run for the woods, with the once again hysterical Gracie in her arms, she spun around and rammed her shoulder into Grant's midsection, knocking him off balance. Then, Gracie's screams ringing in her ears, she ran hell-for-leather in the opposite direction from the one Clare had taken — toward the cliff's edge.

It wasn't the most ideal spot for a showdown with a lunatic, but then she didn't have a lot of alternatives, or the luxury of time to plan. Her only conscious hope was that if Grant were presented with an option, he would choose to pursue her. All she could do was assure he wasn't granted the opportunity to seize both her *and* Gracie.

But, oh, God, what if it didn't work? The smart money would be on recapturing Gracie. After all, if he had her, he as good as had Emma, since she would do anything to prevent him from hurting her child. She risked a glance over her shoulder.

And a scream exploded from her throat when she saw him mere feet behind her.

She put on a burst of speed, cursing whatever fate had led her to choose today of all days to trade in her Keds for a pair of skimpy-strapped, leather-soled sandals. At least Grant, too, had the disadvantage of wearing city shoes, and she had, by the grace of God, stuck with her original decision to wear walking shorts. For a while that morning she'd leaned toward a skirt. A short, *tight* skirt, which would have been disastrous on this terrain.

She was younger and faster than Grant, but her feet slid on the rough surface several times, slowing her down. Then her toe caught on a half-buried rock and she stumbled. She saved herself from a fall, but it cost her dearly. Grant lunged for her, catching her arm and swinging her around just as she regained her balance.

She came around swinging, catching him with a lucky punch to the jaw. He swore viciously, but let loose of her arm as his hand flew up in a reflexive action to cup the injured area. Feet scrambling for purchase, she lurched away, head whipping from side to side to determine their position.

They were too near the cliff's edge so she

whirled to run for the woods, but Grant brought her down in a flying tackle. Blue sky and dried-out scrub grass whirled in a sickening kaleidoscope as they rolled over and over. Brush scraped at her skin; small rocks and pebbles bruised her as they wrestled on the ground. Then she was on her back, looking up into Grant's face as he straddled her hips.

She'd freely bruited the word "delusional" about in her own mind this afternoon, but she knew now, looking into the face of this man she had once loved, that she hadn't fully realized its actual meaning. "Mad" was a word she'd always used to connote anger. But it was madness in its purest form that she saw when she looked up into Grant's eyes.

The urbane man who had always surrounded himself with the trappings of civilization was gone. In his place was a feral animal, intent on harm. His clothing was rumpled and stained, his hair was in disarray; she'd never before seen him in such a state. But it was his eyes that terrified her. They were the eyes of a stranger, dead and vicious. Devoid of humanity. He wanted to ravage her, to torture and mutilate. He wanted to inflict unbearable pain.

Using her heels for purchase, Emma

scrabbled, using her hips and shoulders to push herself back a few feet. Grant knee-walked, keeping pace; then his knees abruptly tightened around her hips, preventing her from going any farther. Panicked, she reached for his eyes, clawing and scratching. His hand swung up and back and then flashed forward, giving her a vicious crack on the side of her head.

Pain exploded in her temple and sensation zinged through her extremities, a weakening that she fuzzily equated to experiences in the past when she'd hit her crazy bone. Her hands dropped like lead onto the prickly grass. Blinking back tears, she stared up at him.

And saw the blood lust in his eyes as he reached for her throat.

Elvis ran through the woods. He was close to the edge of the clearing when Gracie's screams seemed nearer, and he halted, not knowing what to expect. Distinguishing the sounds of someone clumsily thrashing in his direction through the underbrush, he swung the rifle up, stock to his shoulder, barrel braced by his hook, and closed one eye as he sighted down the barrel. Then he swore and pointed it up at the sky as Clare, carrying a struggling, screaming Gracie, stumbled into view. He loped over to intercept them.

"Oh, thank God you're here," Clare panted and allowed him to scoop Gracie out of her arms. The child continued to screech and wriggle and fight, oblivious to who held her.

Elvis knew he wouldn't get any information about Emma until he'd quieted Gracie, so he handed off the rifle to Clare, brought his fingers up, and without compunction tapped the child smartly on her cheek. Her eyes went wide in shock, and he raised her up until their eyes were on a level. "You be quiet, Grace Melina," he ordered sternly. "I've got to get your Momma away from your Grandpa before he hurts her —"

"Hoots hew," Gracie agreed on a sob.

"— and I can't do that with you screaming down the forest and carrying on this way, so just knock it off." To his satisfaction, her hysteria subsided into normal tears, and he hugged her to him, whispering, "Good girl; that's my girl." She shuddered in his arms, her little lungs heaving to pull enough breath through clogged passages, and Elvis whipped out a handkerchief, holding it while she blew her nose. Breathing freely again, she let her head drop limply onto his shoulder and her thumb sought out her mouth. He looked over her head at Clare. "What's the story?"

Clare was fighting back some hysteria of her own, but she managed to say with commendable composure, "He's got her, Elvis, and they're too close to the cliff. Too close!" As soon as she and Gracie had reached the safety of the woods, she'd stopped to determine the situation. Seeing Emma and Grant rolling on the ground within feet of the cliff's edge had resurrected in her mind every nightmarish memory of Evan's death. Seeing the edge crumble out from under her son's feet, she'd turned and blindly fled, in search of the road and rescue.

Elvis snatched back the rifle and transferred Gracie into Clare's arms once again. "Go back to the car," he instructed. "Stay with it until backup arrives, then direct them to us." Gracie started to stiffen up again, and he shifted the rifle to the crook of his arm, cupped his hand around the back of her head and pressed a kiss into her forehead next to the tiny red scar. "You be good for Clare," he instructed her sternly. "You hear me, Gracie girl? Momma and Daddy are gonna be back for you real soon." Then he turned and raced for the clearing.

It took a moment for his eyes to adjust

when he burst out of the woods onto the sun-washed plateau. His heart drummed heavily in his chest, and he dreaded what he would find, cursing the time he'd taken to settle Gracie; then he located Emma, struggling with Woodard near the cliff's edge. *Still alive,* he rejoiced as he swung up the rifle. But struggling. She was on her back, flailing with arms and legs, getting in any punch she could while scrambling to get out from under Woodard, who, facing Elvis, rose above her on his knees.

"Police, Woodard!" Elvis shouted. "Stop or I'll shoot!"

There might as well have been an invisible, soundproof shield between him and the people on the cliff. Neither Emma nor Woodard indicated, by so much as a hesitation in their actions, that they heard him. Meanwhile Emma was losing ground. Sighting down the barrel, Elvis got Grant in the crosshairs, but it wasn't a clean shot. Woodard hunched over and straightened, twisted from side to side; Emma swung at him with both arms, lifting her torso off the ground with the use of her stomach muscles. It brought her in and out of Elvis' line of fire.

He swore to himself. "Stay down, sweetheart," he pleaded under his breath.

"Dammit to hell, Em, just stay *down* for a minute."

He used to test excellent at marksmanship. But that was when he'd had two good hands and had practiced regularly at the police range. Nowadays, he practiced strictly with a handgun and didn't quite trust his ability to take his opponent out with a high-powered rifle — not while that man was struggling with his woman.

Then he saw Woodard draw back his arm and direct a vicious swipe to the side of Emma's head. She flopped like a rag doll onto her back in the dirt, and Grant sat up astride her, reaching for her throat.

Rage exploded in Elvis' chest. *"Woodard!"* he roared. Then he coldly and concisely shoved the fury aside, knowing it for what it was — counterproductive. Bragston had taught him not to let his emotions get in the way. They were always going to be there, the old sheriff had counseled; but the trick was to learn to function through them. It had been a difficult lesson to learn, but ultimately Elvis had mastered it because Bragston had expected him to.

He raised the rifle to his shoulder to squeeze off a shot.

Looking into Grant's face, Emma knew

she'd better do something and fast. His expression as he glared down at her was completely feral and he was obviously beyond rational thought. His hands wrapped around her throat.

Her own hands tingled with a pins-and-needles sensation, but she used one to dig desperately at a rock half submerged in the hardpan soil and wrapped the other around a bristly clump of tall grass, pulling it this way and that, trying to rock it loose. She could feel his fingers tightening around her throat, cutting off her air.

The chunk of grass suddenly ripped free, trailing clods of dirt and she flung it in Grant's face just as lights began to explode in the forefront of her rapidly darkening vision. Simultaneously, she brought her knee up in a weak but vengeful attempt to unman him.

The knee rammed his buttock instead of the intended target, but it shoved him off balance at least; and dirt from the grass got in his eyes, momentarily blinding him. He had to turn her loose to keep from tipping over onto his head in the rocky soil, and gasping and sucking in great draughts of air, she took advantage of the situation by ramming stiffened fingers into his throat. He gagged, and she gave him a mighty shove that rolled him off her.

She heard a lightninglike crack as she rolled out from under him, but didn't have time to worry about, never mind seek out, its source. Coughing, scrambling away from Woodard on her hands and feet, she struggled to become erect and run. She made it to her feet, but then Grant's hand clamped around her ankle and jerked. She went back down, the palms she'd thrust out to catch her fall skidding along the rough, scrub-grass dotted terrain. Tears sprang to her eyes, blurring her vision. Donkey-kicking back with her free foot, she got a spurt of satisfaction when she heard his grunt of pain. The fingers around her ankle loosened and she jerked it free, scrambling to her feet once again.

She only made it a few steps before his arms wrapped around her from behind, yanking her back against his chest, lifting her off her feet. All her senses were heightened, and she was aware of the wheezing rattle of his breath, of the litany of obscene words he muttered in her ear. She fought desperately to free herself, but his grip was unrelenting. Slowly she grew still, her lungs heaving as she fought to catch her breath.

He cautiously lowered her, allowing her feet to touch the ground to support some of her weight. He wasn't taking any chances, however. He kept her back arched and her balance skewed by wrapping one arm around her neck and the other around her waist. One false move and he'd jerk her off her toes again.

"I should just break your fuckin' neck here and now and save myself a lot of trouble," he rasped in her ear.

"Oui?" she goaded. "Why don't you just do it then, you sick son of a bitch?" Then her head shot up, cracking him in the mouth, as the sound of Elvis' voice came across the plateau.

"Woodard!" he shouted, and Emma located him over by Grant's car. He was moving inexorably nearer. "Let her go, Woodard," he commanded, sighting at them down a rifle barrel. "Let her go and you can walk away from this with your life."

"Stay where you are!" Grant yelled and shuffled Emma a few feet backward.

"I can't do that." Elvis nevertheless paused. Emma and Woodard were too close to the edge, and he didn't want to risk spooking the man into doing something rash. Grant looked about a nudge away from the need for a straitjacket. "Let her go, man, or I'm going to put a bullet right through your forehead. And let me tell you,

Woodard, while life in stir might not sound like a lot of fun, it's preferable to being dead."

Grant glanced quickly over his shoulder at the cliff a couple of feet behind him. Then he looked back at the sheriff, who was nearer than he'd been a moment ago. "You're wrong," he said, thinking of everything that had gone sour since that day in May. "It isn't."

And he took a giant step backward, going over the cliff.

Twenty-one

"NO!" Elvis dropped the rifle and sprinted for the cliff's edge. That one word was the last sound Grant heard as he plummeted into space, and he experienced a hot, savage rush of satisfaction at having robbed the scar-faced cripple of his heart's desire. If he was going, then so, by God, was Emma. No one betrayed Grant Woodard and lived to tell about it.

Emma's hard head snapped back and broke his nose, and her sharp elbow viciously jabbed ribs. He regretted the reflex that made him lose his grip on her.

Then he knew only terror as he plummeted silently to the rocks below.

Emma propelled herself away from Grant's body and managed to catch onto a piece of the cliff's rim. *Ah, Dieu, thank you.* Terra firma beneath her instead of a free fall through space; she would have gladly kissed it. But it was too soon to pay homage — she had only a tenuous grip on it, hardly more than her bare elbows digging desperately into the hard ground.

She thrust her arms forward, grabbed

onto clumps of the sharp-bladed, tough grass, and tried to pull herself up over the brink. Her torso hung free, her legs kicking in air.

Hand over hand she pulled herself up, digging her elbows in and using them for additional leverage until she had firm earth beneath her stomach. With every movement she made, dirt crumbled from the edge of the cliff and dropped away.

"Emma! Hold still!" She raised her eyes to see Elvis drop onto his stomach and crawl toward her. "The cliff's undercut here," he said, using his own elbows to propel himself nearer to the edge. "I know it's easier said than done, sweetheart, but don't struggle, okay? Just hang on . . . and try not to do anything that'll generate pressure against the fault."

She looked ahead of her and saw what he had seen — a ragged fissure in the ground perpendicular to her dangling body. She froze, except for her hands, which gripped with even more desperation the dried clumps of grass less than an arm's length beyond the crack. As her fingers assumed a death grip, she regretted her knowledge of physics, understanding even as she hung on that if the chunk of overhang supporting her weight were to suddenly drop away, her puny grip wasn't going to do a damn thing to prevent her from dropping onto the rocks below.

Suddenly, the undermined section of cliff did exactly that. With a soft rumble, a huge section of sod and scrub brush fell out from beneath her, and her one hundred twenty-seven pounds dropped like a sack of wet cement on the end of a string. Long blades of grass ripped through her clutching hands. Clawing frantically for an alternate grip, Emma was aware that her weight was dragging her toward oblivion faster than her hands could find purchase on protruding roots or rocks. Then there was nothing left to grab for and she was sliding into space.

To be yanked to an abrupt halt by a hard grasp on her left forearm.

She screamed as the ball joint of her shoulder was wrenched in its socket. Dangling now, she made the mistake of looking at the jagged boulders far below, and adrenaline shot through her. Her abused throat involuntarily loosed an entire series of rusty squawks, the pressure behind her eyes made them bulge as she stared down at the surf lapping at the craggy shore, and she barely controlled her legs' desperate desire to kick, to outrun danger.

"Emma!" Elvis roared. "Look at me — at

me, sweetheart! Yes, like that. Good, good girl . . . look right into my eyes." He held her panicked brown gaze. "Grab onto my hook, now," he commanded, extending it to her. She made one grab for it and missed; then he saw determination replace the panic on her face and she reached out again and this time connected. A measure of pain faded from her expression once her right arm had taken up some of the drag threatening to dislocate her left shoulder.

Elvis started inching along backward on his stomach. Dirt and pebbles and clumps of weed and grass, weakened by their activity, continued to crumble away from the cliff's edge and fall into space, but he took his time, stayed flat, kept his weight evenly distributed on the unstable ground, and little by little dragged Emma up over the verge.

The ragged edge of the cliff scraped the soft inner skin of her upper arms, flattened her breasts, dragged her blouse from her waistband and ripped it free of its buttons, abrading the tender skin from her abdomen and chest. Embedded rocks raked her thighs, her knees, her ankles.

Elvis continued to pull her on her stomach across the rocky ground long after she'd cleared the brim. Finally, they were at a distance he considered safe, and he rocked back onto his heels, knees spraddled wide, to pull Emma into his arms. The sounds of the surf, the seagulls' mocking screams, were drowned beneath the harsh, sawing gasps of their combined breathing.

"Sweet mother of God, I pray to heaven never to go through anything like that again," he panted hoarsely, his good hand roughly stroking her hair as he rocked them both back and forth, back and forth. "Oh, Christ, Emma, I was so gut-screaming scared — I thought I'd lost you." Pulling on her hair until he could see her face, he shook her once, suddenly furious. "And how the hell would I have explained that to Gracie, huh? You just tell me how the hell —"

The words clogged into a hot ball in his throat. Wrapping his big hand around the back of her head, he pushed her face into its niche in his shoulder again, and his arms tightened around her convulsively. He recommenced rocking them, whispering swear words, words of thanks. Emma clung to him mindlessly.

Finally, she pushed back and looked into his face. Her hands stroked his cheeks, his jaw; they smoothed his hair into place. "It's over," she said, and it wasn't until the words were spoken that it abruptly sank in. Her voice was all froggy and hoarse from the abuse to her vocal cords, but still, wonderment colored her tone when she repeated, "It's really all over, *cher.* He *is* dead, don't you think? I mean, he's got to be; nobody could survive that fall."

"Yeah, he's dead." Elvis would be amazed if anyone lived through a dive onto those rocks, but he wanted to be on the safe side. "I'll send for a search party to recover his body as soon as we get back to the Suburban."

"I can quit looking over my shoulder, Elvis," Emma marveled. "And finally put Gracie into a program with other kids her own age. Oh, *merde!*" she exclaimed and climbed to her feet. "Gracie!" She looked down at him, still kneeling at her feet, staring back up at her. "*Mon Dieu,* Elvis, we've got to let Gracie know everything is okay."

"When's *Maman* comin'?" Gracie asked for the twentieth time. Her head rested on Clare's breast as she sat quietly in the woman's lap, but Clare knew better than to trust in the duration of this current quiescence. Gracie's moods had been fluctuating, going from one end of the spectrum to the other at about thirty-second intervals.

Clare stroked the child's soft hair. "Soon, Grace Melina," she replied soothingly, and pressed a kiss into the child's baby-fragrant curls. "She and your daddy-to-be are gonna be here real soon." *Oh, please, God, if You're listening, don't let me be lying to this child.*

"Mommy and Elbis gon' be here weal soon," Gracie agreed. She tipped her head back in order to see into Clare's face. "When, you think?"

"Soon."

The other department Suburban pulled up behind them then, and Clare turned off the engine she'd been running in order to use the air conditioner. Watching Ben climb out, she glanced down at Gracie before opening the car door, wondering if the necessary explanations were going to upset her all over again. Well, there was no help for it if they did; hiking Gracie into her arms, she got out of the car and went to greet the deputy.

They met by the bumper of her car, but before two words were exchanged, Gracie had started bouncing in Clare's arms. "Mommy, Mommy, Mommy!" she screamed, straining to the right with her arms extended. Clare's head whipped around and she sagged at the knees to see Emma and Elvis emerging out of the shaded drive.

Emma broke into an awkward trot at the sound of her daughter's voice. Moments later, dirty, disheveled, scraped and bruised, she had Gracie in her arms, holding her tightly and being squeezed in return by sturdy little arms and legs. She looked at Clare and laughed, a tremulous sound that verged on tears. Freeing an arm, she wrapped it around her friend and pulled her into the embrace. "Thank you," she whispered. *"Ah, mon ami, merci beaucoup."*

"Oh *God*, Emma, I'm so grateful you're safe!" Relief, like fine wine, sang in Clare's veins. She wiped her cheeks free of the tears that kept falling. "So *grateful.*" Then the two women and the child simply stood for some moments in a three-way hug, each temporarily content not to move or speak.

Elvis observed the blissful expressions on the faces of his woman and his child and smiled to himself. Stroking Gracie's head from crown to nape, he pressed a kiss on her brow and then walked over to talk to his deputy. He needed to begin the process that would recover Grant Woodard's body and put this mess behind them once and for all.

He talked to Ben and issued orders to Sandy via the car radio for quite a while. He behaved with consummate professionalism, but he could not prevent his eyes from frequently seeking out Emma and Gracie. He'd come too damn close to losing Emma this afternoon, and he needed constant affirmation that she was all right. Discussing the events of the past twenty minutes with his deputy, he watched as Emma bent her head to whisper in Gracie's ear. Then he saw his daughter-to-be's head snap up, a smile like dawn breaking over the horizon spreading across her face. She craned around, obviously searching for him.

"Elbis, Elbis, guess what?" she squealed when she spotted him. "*Maman* says I getta stawt goin' to *sunny school!*"

"Don't get mad at me," Elvis ordered Emma as he came through the kitchen door after work on Tuesday night. "But I invited Ben and George and Sandy to the wedding." Gracie, who had run to greet him in the yard, was hanging from his neck piggyback style, and her grip, where she'd locked one small hand over the opposite wrist, was centered right on top of his Adam's apple. He paused, boosted her up his back until he could swallow freely again, and then confessed, "And . . . uh . . . their families, too." Emma turned from the stove to stare at him, and he gave her a sheepish look. "They really seemed to want to come, Em."

Emma suspected it had probably amazed the heck out of him, too. He'd spent too much time believing he was at best only tolerated on this island. "What's a few more people?" she demanded with a good-natured shrug. "Gracie invited her new best friend, too."

"Sawah!" Gracie contributed, specifying the little girl she'd met on Sunday at the Seaside Baptist Church for all the world as if she hadn't been talking about Sarah nearly nonstop for four days straight.

"Right," Emma acknowledged. "And, Elvis, you're the one who insisted on a three-tiered wedding cake, so it's not as if we won't have enough to go around. You might want to pick up another bottle of champagne and maybe a few bottles of sparkling cider for the kids, though. Oh, and reserve more chairs from the Rent-It shop."

He leaned over to kiss her neck, then reached around her and lifted the lid off the pot to see what she was cooking. Jambalaya. No wonder it smelled wonderful. "I'll go after dinner," he agreed. "Come on, kid," he said over his shoulder to Gracie, "let's go get washed up."

"Okeydokey."

Heading for the doorway with Gracie still riding his back, Elvis paused to look back at

Emma. "I promise, Em," he vowed. "I'll take care of everything first thing after we've eaten. I'm not going to leave this for you to arrange, too."

Emma laughed softly. She wasn't worried.

It was two days before their wedding, and she felt as if she'd never worry about anything ever again.

The logical part of Emma tried to tell her it wasn't possible to be free of all anxiety. One simply wasn't allowed to get through life without worries, be they large or small. But her emotional side merely shrugged. Sure, matters were bound to crop up in her life that would give her some sleepless nights. But she certainly wasn't going to waste any of her precious time sweatin' the small stuff. Not anymore.

It wasn't that long ago she'd been unable to envision a future for herself and Gracie, no matter how much effort she'd put into trying to find something workable. She hadn't been able to foresee a time for them, pure and simple, that didn't include constantly moving from one place to the next, of living their lives in the shadows. Now they had everything.

Never, never, never, get smug, she decided caustically forty-five minutes later. *Just look where it gets you.* She was now the proud owner of an additional something, a situation she hadn't foreseen and sure as heck didn't want.

She was replacing the telephone receiver just as Elvis and Gracie came through the kitchen door. "Em?" Elvis called out, and Gracie raced ahead of him into the living room, where her mother was sitting in the overstuffed chair with its new green- and white-striped slipcover.

"Dawk in here," Gracie observed and climbed up on the couch to turn on the lamp. "There!" she declared in satisfaction when a pool of light illuminated the area, including her mother's pale face. "Tha's bettoo!" She slid down the couch back, bounced on the cushion, and then climbed down and trotted off to her room.

Elvis stood in the doorway, staring at Emma's white face. "What is it?" he demanded, crossing the room to her. He scooped her out of the chair, dropped into it himself, and rearranged her on his lap. Unease crawled through his stomach. "Jesus, what's wrong? You look like you've seen a ghost."

"Do you think I'm unnatural for not feeling remorse over Grant's death?" she asked him. "I mean, it *is* kind of abnormal, isn't it? I lived with him for several years, after all, and up until a few months ago I thought he'd been so good to me. Hell, sugar, I thought I *loved* him." She clutched his shirt and stared up at him. "But in the end I hated him, and I'm not sorry he's dead, Elvis — I'm relieved."

Elvis chewed it over for a few moments. "I'd say, under the circumstances, there's nothing abnormal about it," he finally replied and his tone was businesslike, flat. "He constituted a genuine threat, sweetheart — to you and to Gracie. It's not like you're blowing off his death because he denied you some small favor after years of doting on you. There were unnatural aspects to this situation, all right, but they sure as hell weren't yours." And though she might not be consumed with remorse, neither was she as unaffected as she'd like him to believe. He had seen her startle at unexpected noises and assume a defensive position before she recollected that there was no need for it. All because of the violent turn Grant Woodard's unnatural affections had taken.

She pressed her cheek against his shoulder and said softly, "He left me everything he owned."

"What?" Elvis tipped down his chin in

order to see Emma's face.

"That was his lawyer on the phone just now. He read the will this mornin', and except for a few minor bequests I was Grant's sole beneficiary." She shuddered. "Oh, *God,* Elvis. It never even occurred to me. What am I goin' to do, *cher?* I don't want his filthy money."

Elvis propped his chin on the top of her head and tucked her in a little closer on his lap. He thought about it for a few moments. "Has anything occurred to you that you'd like to do with it?"

"No. My mind is just one great big blank. This whole thing just sorta hit me on my blind side, Elvis."

"But we're agreed that you don't want to keep any of it, am I right?"

"Absolutely. I thought for about thirty seconds of putting some in a college fund for Gracie, but the idea made my blood run cold. He would have discarded her like an old Kleenex, *cher.* We'll save our *own* education fund, thank you very much." She felt his nod against the crown of her head.

"What kind of money are we talking about anyway, Emma?" he inquired, and then whistled long and low when she told him. They sat quietly for a few more moments, the only sounds to disturb the stillness those of the refrigerator's motor as it kicked in and Gracie's occasional thumping in her bedroom.

"You know," Elvis finally said, "it occurs to me that there must be hundreds of ways you could put this money to good use." Feeling her stiffen slightly, he gave her a comforting squeeze. "Not for your own personal gain, doll. I'm talking about ways of spreading the money around so it would benefit a lot of people — and be kind of fun to disburse."

Emma pulled herself up to sit on the arm of the overstuffed chair. She pressed the arches of her feet into Elvis' hard thigh, wrapped her arms around her shins, and studied his face. "Give me a for instance."

"Well, hell, right here on the island we've got a food bank that's always in need of cash," he said. "And we could seriously use a community center that stayed open late." He smiled crookedly. "Okay, the truth is, we could use any kind of community center. If we gave the island kids something to do Friday and Saturday nights they probably wouldn't spend so much time racing at breakneck speeds up and down country roads, knocking back half-racks of beer and snortin' their allowances up their noses."

She considered him with interest. "The

Edward Robescheaux Community Center," she said slowly, savoring the sound. Her eyes came alight at the idea. "Oh! Big Eddy would've liked that."

"Hell, yeah. And with the kind of money you're talking about, you could afford to buy the land, build the building, and pay staffing costs for the next thirty years."

"Or buy it, build it, and deed it over to the community with the stipulation that they make the center self-sufficient within, say, five years."

"Yeah. Better, yet. The point is, Em, there's always a lot of needy causes out there, and you can have fun with 'em if you take your time deciding who gets what. What you *don't* have to do is resolve everything right this minute."

She rocked his thigh with her feet. "You're so smart."

"Hell, yeah," he agreed smugly. "Smart enough to get you to marry me."

Emma made a rude noise. "*That* was a no-brainer, Donnelly." They grinned at each other, and then she sobered. "What about Gracie, *cher?*" she asked. "You think she's as well adjusted as she appears?"

"Yes." Elvis tugged her back down onto his lap, looked her in the eye, and stated uncategorically, "I do."

"I don't want to see her on some talk show twenty years down the road with a caption on her chest that reads Early Trauma Ignored by Mother."

Elvis snorted. "Em, she had *one* nightmare. And it seems to me you talked her through that one pretty easily."

"I didn't tell her the complete truth, though."

"Hell, no, and a damn good thing, too, if you ask me. A three-year-old's not gonna understand a grandfather who takes a walk off a cliff and tries to take her momma along with him. All she knows is a man who used to dote on her suddenly turned up and started scaring the shit out of her. You told her that her grandpapa did some bad things, and he's gone away forever. You promised he's never going to come back to be mean to her again. You did good, doll. Give it a rest."

"*Oui;* I suppose." Then, more firmly, "No, I *know* you're right." Cupping his cheeks in her hands, she pulled his head down to touch foreheads. "I'll tell her the whole story when she's old enough to understand." She sighed, content to simply appreciate for a moment the warmth of his skin beneath her palms, the cool thickness of his hair between her fingers.

Then she said, "It's sure nice to have someone to share these problems with. It's a luxury I've never had before. Heck," she confessed, "I'd given up believing in happily-ever-after, period."

He made a funny sound in his throat. "Yeah, me, too." He'd never believed in it in the first place.

"But, you know, *cher* —"

"When it comes to you, me, and Beans," he interrupted.

"— I think it just may be possible, after all," she concluded.

"Damn straight," he agreed.

"Oui." She looped her arms over his shoulders, rolled her forehead back and forth against his, and smiled. She loved this man. His strength, his honesty, his good sense.

"Damn straight."

About the Author

Susan Andersen lives in Emerald City with her husband, Steve, their college age son Christopher, and a cat named Styx. The inhabitants of her little piece of the world are weird and wonderful, and she credits the attempt to stay one step ahead of them with keeping her young.

Susan very much enjoys hearing from her readers. If you would like to write her, please send your letters to P. O. Box 4788, Seattle, WA 98104. Those desiring a reply please enclose a self-addressed stamped envelope and she will respond as quickly as possible.

The employees of Thorndike Press hope you have enjoyed this Large Print book. All our Thorndike and Wheeler Large Print titles are designed for easy reading, and all our books are made to last. Other Thorndike Press Large Print books are available at your library, through selected bookstores, or directly from us.

For information about titles, please call:

(800) 223-1244

or visit our Web site at:

www.gale.com/thorndike
www.gale.com/wheeler

To share your comments, please write:

Publisher
Thorndike Press
295 Kennedy Memorial Drive
Waterville, ME 04901

OAK RIDGE PUBLIC LIBRARY
Civic Center
Oak Ridge, TN 37830

#3-10 6/15
1/12

#2/09

JUL 1 9 2005 #1/09